THE KEEPER OF THE BEES

THE KEEPER OF THE BEES

BY

Gene Stratton-Porter

KALPAZ

ISBN: 978-93-5128-996-8(PB)

First Published in1925
Indian Reprint in 2017

Published by

Kalpaz Publications
C-30, Satyawati Nagar,
Delhi – 110052
E-mail: kalpaz@hotmail.com
Website: kalpazpublications.com
Ph.: +91-9212142040

CONTENTS

The Keeper of the Bees

CHAPTER I

HIS OWN MAN

"JAMES LEWIS MACFARLANE."

The bearer of this name swung his feet to the floor and sat up suddenly, cupping his big hands over his knees to steady himself. For the past hour, between periods of half-conscious drowsiness, he had been hearing the verdict that men in authority were pronouncing upon men over whose destinies they held control; but it had not appealed to him that his own case might come under consideration.

That morning he had sat for an hour in the sunshine in front of the huge hospital where our country is trying to restore men who had been abroad to take their part in the war. Of late he had been realizing that in his fight for health he was waging a losing battle. He had not been able to combat the shrapnel wound in his left breast with the same success with which he had fought the enemy. So he had resolved to test his strength. He had got up and started down the road to learn precisely how far his legs would carry him. He had forgotten to reckon on the fact that going down a mountain is much easier than climbing one; so he had gone on until his knees began to waver and he found his strength exhausted. He had rested awhile and then turned back, but the upward trip had been slow business, painful work—work that set a cold perspiration running and a gnawing fire burning in his left breast, while the bandages over his shoulders and around his body had become things of torment. The hot sun of California had beaten down on him until he was panting for breath. He was forced repeatedly to stop and to seek a resting-place on any projecting stone or dry embankment of the mountain-side. His tired eyes were wearied with the panorama of brilliant colour that lay stretched everywhere around him—the green of the live oak, the bright holly berries and the pinkish-white urns of the manzanita, the purplish velvet of the pitcher sage, the clotted blue-lavender cobwebs of the thistle sage. The only things he did see were the frequent heads of Indian Warrior, and he saw them because they were like wounds on the earth, as red as real blood, as red as the blood that had soaked many a battlefield, dripped in many a hospital, that he saw every day on the dressings that were removed from his side.

He had seen so much blood that anything that reminded him of it was nauseating, so he turned from the gorgeous flower eagerly painting the mountain-side, and looked up to the blue of the sky. But looking toward the sky only more clearly defined the rough path he must follow. There came to his mind a passage that he had heard his father read from his pulpit on Sabbath mornings with the burr of Scotch that a generation of our country had not eliminated: "I will lift mine eyes to the hills from whence cometh my help."

He was lifting his eyes to the hills, but no help came. He wondered whether this was because he was obeying the dictates of other men, or whether it was because he had forgotten God. In his childhood his father and mother had taught him to pray and to believe that his prayers would be answered. When he had gone out to serve his country, for some inexplicable reason he had stopped praying and concentrated all his forces on fighting. There were atrocities that had been committed against men of his race and blood in the beginning of the war that drove all men of Scottish ancestry and sympathies a trifle wild.

He had reached the war period one of the gentlest of men. But he had embarked in the venture, that other men of our country of different ancestry felt was freeing the world from tyranny, with outrage in his breast, a feeling that was shared by all men of the race and country of his people. Things had happened to one certain band of Scots that no man having a drop of Scottish blood in his veins ever could or wanted to forget. Under the stress of this feeling, the lad whose mother had always lovingly referred to him as "my Jamie" forgot her teachings and her God, and went out to see how much personal vengeance he could wreak upon the men who had wounded the heart of all Scotland deeper than the exigencies of ordinary warfare need wound the heart of a nation.

He had gone for vengeance and he had revenged himself thoroughly on many an enemy; then the hour had come when a rugged sliver of filth-encrusted iron had entered his breast and poisoned his blood. After weeks on the border-land he had dragged back to his feet, and now he carried with him two wounds that would not heal, one in his heart that the world could not see, and one on his breast over which doctors and nurses vainly laboured.

When it was definitely settled that he could not go back to service he was sent home. There another wound was added to the already deep ones that were torturing him. During the three years of his absence the frail little mother, eaten with fear and anxiety for her only son, had made her crossing, and his father, always dependent upon her, had not long survived. The small property had been sold to pay for their resting-places, and nothing remained in all this world that belonged to him—neither relative nor fireside. Even his friends had scattered, and there was nothing for him but to remain a ward of the Government until such time as he was pronounced able to begin life again for himself.

In recognition of valiant service, indicated by a couple of medals and a Service Bar pinned over the wound he carried, he had been sent to California, where it was hoped that the brilliant sunshine, the fruits, and the clean salt air, the eternal summer of a beneficent land, would work the healing that the physicians had been unable to bring about. He had been given the benefit of the best place there was to send men in his condition. The mountain resort, Arrowhead Springs—high on a mountain covered with the foliage of every tree, bush, and vine native to such a location, where the air was perfumed with flowers and full of bird song—the Government had taken and had made into a great hospital; and the reason for the location was that at this point Nature brought to the surface a stream of boiling-hot water, water so hot that it was not possible to thrust the hand into it, water that boiled from some cavern below where the unquenched fires that are always burning in the heart of the earth flamed their reddest and the streams came up with the tang of sulphur and many chemicals, and with unvarying heat year after year. The springs were piped through the hospital, where all their medicinal properties were turned upon the men who, like Jamie Macfarlane, must be healed of stubborn wounds before they could return home to take up a man's work in the affairs of our land.

As he struggled up the mountain that morning the perspiration streaked his cheeks. While his knees wavered and his white hands clutched at any tree or shrub that offered support, James MacFarlane was thinking. He was thinking fast and thinking deeply. He was wondering, since one year at these boiling mineral springs had done him no good whatever, whether another year would accomplish what the first had failed in doing. He was wondering if he were not weaker, less of a man, than he had been a year ago. He was wondering how long the Government was going to keep him at these springs when their water did him no good. He knew of the bitter denunciations that were being made all over the country of those in charge of caring for our returned soldiers. He knew of the red tape, the graft, and the slowness involved in reaching the boys with the treatment that they needed and which should have been accorded them with all the speed that was used in starting them on their perilous venture. He knew there was bitterness in the heart of almost every wounded man on this point. There was poignant bitterness in his own heart. So many weeks had been wasted. So many months had passed before decision had been made as to what was to be done, and how it was to be done, and where it was to be done. So much had been taken for granted and so little efficiently accomplished after peace had been declared.

In his enforced moments of rest, he kept lifting his eyes to the sky. He could not look at the sky without his thoughts climbing very high, and sometimes that morning they almost skirted the foot of the throne. He realized that he would have given anything in this world if he could have gone home and knelt at the knees of his mother, laid his head on her lap, and tried the one thing that he had not yet tried—just the plain, old-fashioned thing of asking God for the help he had not been able to secure from man.

And so at last he had reached the palms and roses, the loquats and oranges, and the grape-covered slopes where cultivation had begun to provide food for those who lived on the mountain-top. He looked at the bloom-laden orchards almost with distaste. He was so tired. The air was sickeningly sweet with the penetrant and enduring perfume. He thought with impatience that he would be glad if his eyes might rest upon some spot where a blood-red flare would not strike them to bitter memory, for persistently around the rocks of the mountain-side, close to the spots of cultivation in which each tree was rooted, there blazed the flame of the Indian Warrior. So he had at last dragged up the driveway and up the front steps, where he had done a thing that was not customary.

All the grounds and the side verandas were for the men, but disabled soldiers were not supposed to drape themselves over the reed davenports near the big entrance doors. There happened to be a davenport standing under a broad window at one side of the entrance that offered him the first solution of a resting-place. He glanced at several motor-cars he did not recognize as he climbed the steps; then he headed straight for the lounge and stretched himself on it, where for a time he lay unconscious of what was going on around him.

As he became rested, voices on the inside of the window at first were only voices, and then, as his heart quieted and the burning in his side eased and his tired limbs relaxed, he realized that name after name was being read from a list and each name represented a man whose case was being discussed and what was eventually to become of him was being decided upon. But he had not realized as they went down the J's and the K's and the L's that M was coming soon. He had been in the hospital so long; he was so accustomed to his room, to his nurses, to the routine, and the men he knew, that the place was home, the only home on earth he had. Everyone had been kind. He had no fault to find with the doctors or the nurses. They had done their best, and he had done his best; but the truth remained that he was no better, that lately doubts had arisen as to whether he were even as well as he had been when he came. And then, with all the suddenness of an unexpected blow, clear on his ears came his own name, in that cold, impersonal tone of business men transacting an affair of business with an eye single to the welfare of the greatest good to the greatest number. He did not recall ever having heard his name spoken in precisely such tones before. It made him feel as if he were not a man, but merely an object. And then he realized that the matter under discussion was the disposal of that particular object. He heard his place of enlistment, his war service, his awards, a description of his wounds, recited in such a monotonous tone that he realized it was being droned from a book, and then a brisker voice inquired:

"How long has MacFarlane been here?"

The answer came: "A little more than a year."

Then the question: "Have the springs done him any good? Is he better?"

Then the answer: "Not so well. His wound is stubborn, and in spite of all we can do it refuses to heal."

The sweat of Jamie's exertion had dried up on his body, but it broke out again with the next question:

"Is he tubercular?"

And the answer was: "No. Not yet. But he is in a

condition where at any minute tuberculosis might develop. There never was more fertile ground for it."

Jamie MacFarlane sat gripping his knees and licking his dry lips and waiting to hear the verdict. It came in a few words.

"Send him to Camp Kearney."

For a minute the red of the Indian Warrior flamed before the eyes of the listening man until he could see only red. For a minute hot anger seared his body in scorching protest. He had heard them say that he was not tubercular, but that he was fine breeding-ground for the dread disease. Now they were planning to send him into a place where every man either had the plague, or was so near it that he had been sent to take the risk of contracting it, as was proposed in his case. It was not fair! It was not just! He had enlisted early and eagerly. He was not a drafted man. He had fought to the limit of his power. He had taken whatever came uncomplainingly. The medals he wore attested his daring. He would march into that room and he would tell those doctors what he thought of them and their callous decision.

He tried to rise and found that he was too weak to stand on his feet, and then he heard the doctor who had read off the names voicing a protest in his behalf: "I can hardly feel that it is fair to send a man of MacFarlane's achievements and in his fertile condition to what is admittedly a place for the tubercular."

The other voice answered: "If a year here has left him not so well as he was, why hope that another year will do more than keep him in the place of a physically better man who might come in and make a recovery if he had MacFarlane's chance?"

At the cold justice of that statement Jamie MacFarlane sank on the lounge and lay back on the pillow, and of how long he lay there he kept no count. He only knew that the voices were going on inside the window and that men were being judged, that hopeless cases were being sent to what appealed to him as a hopeless place, while those who had a chance were being given the greatest opportunity to recover. And that was fair; that was just. But being of Scottish extraction, having been born with a fight in his veins and an eternal and steadfast love of the mountains and the stars and the sky and the sea and his fellow men, he decided that he would no longer be any man's man or the man of any government. He was alone and derelict. He would be his own man. If he must die, why die in Camp Kearney, where the greatest plague that ravages humanity gnawed in the breast of every doomed man? Without time for mature deliberation, without any preparation whatever, James Lewis MacFarlane reached up and gripped the window-sill with one hand, with the other laid hold of an arm of the couch, and brought himself to a standing posture. He retraced his steps down to the roadway, and there he turned to the right, which faced him toward the north, and with slow, careful steps, he began his Great Adventure.

CHAPTER II

THE GREAT ADVENTURE

Now a great adventure may be killing white hippopotami in Africa to one man and commanding his own soul for an hour to another. To Jamie MacFarlane, after years of steadily taking orders from superior officers, there was something exhilarating in assuming an erect position and for the first time deciding for himself whether he would seek his fortune toward the north or the south. Why he decided on going north he had not the slightest notion, but it was probably because the road led down in that direction, and he had found mountain-climbing more than he could endure. So he started north and on a down grade. He went very slowly; he kept looking at the sky, the trees, and it seemed to him that the blooming orange orchards he passed and the lemons and the loquats were less heavy in their perfume, the air grew more bracing. He began to wonder if he could ever reach the sea, if he could have a strong tang of salt in the air, if it might not be bracing. He picked up a stick beside the road and used it as a cane upon which to lean. After a while he came to a cross-road and there he paused intently to examine each of the three directions, any of which he might travel if he chose. Truly he was having a heady adventure!

As he stood there a car approached from the east, and noticing Jamie's uniform, his emaciated face and hands, the driver stopped, as all drivers stopped in those days, only Jamie, confined in hospitals, did not know it, and asked him if he would like a ride. The car was turning north, so Jamie said that he would very much like to ride. That is how it happened that the wheels of a motor-car carried him so far from the region of the hospital that when he was really missed and nurses were sent out to seek him, one hundred miles away and still speeding northward, Jamie was making fine progress on his big adventure.

He liked the road that led to the north. He liked it so well that when finally the driver told him he was turning west at the next cross-road, where he had business in a big city, Jamie decided that a man in a uniform who might be sought by Government officials had better remain in the country, and so he climbed from the car and slowly plodded north.

In an enforced rest, he began to realize that night was coming and that he was hungry. He had not a cent in his pockets, and to lie on the ground in the chill of a California night would probably kill him very speedily. Then he realized that quite likely death was the Great Adventure he was seeking; that in taking his fate in his own hands and walking out of the hospital and away from the provisions that were made for him by his Government, he had known that he would exhaust himself speedily to such a point that his troubles would be ended in the quickest way. He spent a few minutes wondering whether his troubles would be ended or only just begun, because the Scots have a way of teaching hell, and fire, and brimstone; and having been to the world's latest war, Jamie MacFarlane knew more about hell than any Scottish minister who ever had described it from a pulpit, and having carried an open wound in his breast for nearly two years, there was no one who could tell him much about fire, and the brimstone at the springs had not worked.

So he went on through the evening shadows until he could go no longer; then he sat down on a nice, big, warm boulder beside the road, crossed his feet, and waited to see what would happen. The very thing that he might have known would happen, had he been living among a world of well men, did happen. Another car came along, and the owner, noting his pallor and his uniform, and having a vacant seat, stopped, and again he was asked if he would care to ride.

"Slick!" said Jamie to himself. "Maybe this isn't going to be so bad after all."

He looked at the car, which was loaded to the running-boards with camping paraphernalia. He could see rolls of bedding; he could scent food. The man had a friendly face, the girl on the seat beside him was young and pretty. The woman with whom he was invited to occupy the back seat was of motherly appearance. Her round face was strong and attractive, and, under the spell of it, Jamie was guilty of evasion. He said he had just left a hospital where he had been for a year. He gave the impression that the doctors had discharged him. He did not say that he had discharged himself, that he was a fugitive. He did say that he was looking for work and that he would be mighty glad to ride with them until he reached a location where something promising offered for men newly mustered from the service and weak from illness.

The driver said that he was William Brunson from Iowa; that he and his wife and daughter had been touring California in their car during the winter, but now they were going to the north part of the state to visit friends until it came time to head for home, as they must reach Albion in time to put in the crops.

And Jamie, fearing that in starting his Great Adventure he might get into the papers, neglected to say what his name was, but he did say that he would be wonderfully glad to ride with them as far as they were going in his direction.

He was glad to ride, but he was not half so glad to ride as he was when the car stopped and in the mouth of a canyon near the road a camp was made. He hoped no one saw that he staggered or how short his breath came as he tried to help in unloading the car. He had to be careful because the one big thing for which he was thankful beyond words had happened. He had only looked towards the hills. He had only *thought* about asking the Lord to help. He wondered vaguely if there might be a possibility that God had been looking in his direction at that instant, if He had seen his need, if He had sent these kind, hearty people who were offering supper, a bed-roll for the night, and a lift on his journey for the morrow. That was that much. And so he put up the very best bluff that he could at being a whole man and a sound man while he gathered wood for a night fire, and prospected for a place to spread the beds and find comfort. He had a feeling that he did not quite deserve the thing that was happening to him. He had been wondering if he would be forced to crawl away among the bushes like a whipped dog and in the chill of the night find a certain but painful release. This was not exactly as he had expected things to happen. He was going to have a supper of hot food and a blanket. In deference to his white face and shaking hands, he had been offered a choice location close to the camp fire, so there was no reason why to-morrow should find him any worse for the experience.

Ann Brunson was a jolly soul. She was everybody's friend. She persisted in calling Jamie "You Mr. Soldierman", and when she saw how very white and uncertain on his feet he was, she mercifully gave him a seat and set him to peeling potatoes, while she left her daughter and her husband to do the rougher work of completing the camp.

As he had made his way down the driveway from the hospital to the road, it had occurred to Jamie MacFarlane that for a man in his condition to walk out of the only shelter on earth to which he was entitled without a penny in his pockets was a Great Adventure. As he sat peeling potatoes for Ann Brunson while her daughter and her husband showed him all the tricks that could be concealed in and around the body of a five-passenger car—the neat little cupboard on the running-board for dishes and food, the tiny refrigerator, the two-plate gasoline stove for boiling the coffee and cooking the meat and potatoes, the possibility of getting many things into an amazingly small compass—he thought that his adventure was going to be homelike and common and that the country was full of kindly people who had not forgotten their soldier boys. There was a bare chance that he might find some light work that he could do, that something might happen which would at least be better than permanent retirement to the City of the White Plague. So he tried to be very careful and peel the potatoes thin and handle them as he had been taught by his thrifty mother when he helped her in a kitchen of childhood. As he worked it did not appeal to him that there might be an adventure each minute drawing nearer. He had taken the precaution to place himself behind the car so that any passer-by might not see him, and after supper was finished and the beds made up, he had lifted a pair of eyes trained to scouting and had seen a flickery light, far above but slowly descending, so he had said that he would take a short stroll.

He had left the Brunsons and slowly and quietly had made his way back through the canyon among thickets of holly and live oak, looking for a spot where he might rest for even a short time and watch that uncanny light, be alone and try to plan for the morrow. One thing he felt imperative to his flight, and that was as speedily as possible to get rid of his uniform. If the officials really missed him from the hospital, if they sent out a general call, his uniform would be the thing which would quickly identify him. Every man in uniform would be scrutinized; there would be radios, telephones, newspapers against him. He must think what he could do and how he could do it.

So he went up the canyon until he left the light and the voices of the camp behind him, and when he found he was tired he sat down in the white moonlight and looked up for the light and it was gone. Foolish of him to be uneasy. Someone had lost the trail and had now found it. He did not realize that the rock upon which he sat so blended with the overhanging branches of a live oak that he was invisible. He did not realize it until, one breath of soft breeze sweeping down the mountain at his back, he found himself face to face with plenty of adventure and of sufficient size to satisfy him. He did not realize how long he had sat figuring on what he could possibly do. What aroused him was a Something coming down the canyon on his right, and as he looked steadily in that direction, he saw the figure of a large man emerge from the bushes and begin carefully making his way, with as little sound as possible, straight toward him.

As the man cleared the shadows and stepped into full moonlight, Jamie could see that he was tall, bareheaded, in his shirt-sleeves, wearing boots and breeches. There was a heavy belt filled with cartridges around his waist, and when he turned to look over the path that he had traversed and to listen, Jamie MacFarlane could see the big gun on the right hip convenient to the man's hand. So his breath came very softly, and as stilly as in No Man's Land he wormed farther back among the overhanging branches.

The reason a great adventure is an adventure is because the things that happen are so very simple and so very natural. Why it is great is merely because one has not expected it, not because it could not very well have been expected had one's wits been working. A formidable man with a big gun headed down the canyon toward Jamie, he reflected, *might* constitute something of an adventure. The might grew to large possibilities when the ears of Jamie, who had done quite a bit of scouting and much work on his stomach between firing lines, realized that down the mountain to the left of him there was coming a Something else that was alive, Something that was slipping, that was using the utmost caution, and yet slowly and surely was coming his way.

The adventure loomed large enough to suit Jamie's wildest ideas of adventure when a second man, not quite so large as the first but still formidable, a darker figure since he wore a coat and hat, who carried an ugly revolver in his right hand, slowly parted the bushes and stepped into the canyon slightly to the left.

Then Jamie sat in open-mouthed wonder while these two men met because of the signal light he had seen, and the big man told the other that he had been down to the road to see what the smoke and the fire meant; that there was a party of tourists, a mere mouse of a man—they could risk his being unarmed, while either of them could handle him with one hand. The turnout looked as if undoubtedly a few hundred dollars could be depended on somewhere about the man, or one or the other of the women, or the car.

The second man had straightened up and asked slowly: "One man and two women. Are the janes young and likely-looking?"

All the blood in James MacFarlane had rushed to his head, and then back to his hands and feet, where fighting blood is most at home. He was no longer a sick soldier dependent on the mercy of a passing stranger. His stomach was fortified with the potatoes and the meat and the coffee and the bread that smiling Ann Brunson had shared with him. He had drunk the water that laughing little Susan had brought to him, and bathed his tired face in it. He had no doubt but money to pay the expenses of the journey was in the pockets of one of the party. They had earned it by hard work on a farm. They had gone pleasuring as was their right, and so far they had had a pleasant time, but if they were to be robbed of their money, if William Brunson were to be beaten to insensibility or killed, if the women who had befriended Jamie were to be left to the mercy of these two in the canyon before him, then there was something very worth while in the world remaining for him to do, or at least to give what life he had left in attempting to do.

So, like snake over the stones, he drew himself together and felt with a long arm for a big piece of loose rock, and when the precise moment arrived at which the big man drew near to the smaller one to hear what description he would give of the women of the camp, softly, under the cover of the oak branch, at one and the same time, Jamie MacFarlane did two things. With his right hand he reached for the revolver in the holster on the back of the big man ; with his left he smashed the jagged rock squarely into the face of the man who was slavering over the description of a sweet young girl. When the big man wheeled he found his own revolver in his own face, and there was nothing to do but to back away with his hands in the air as he was ordered, while Jamie MacFarlane, even taller and more massive of frame, slid down from the rock and extricated the weapon from the fingers of the bleeding and half-senseless bandit. With the two guns in his possession, Jamie put sufficient distance between himself and the men for safety.

Then he said to the bigger one : "Throw me your cartridge belt and your shoes and trousers." In reference to the smaller man he said : "Peel off his coat and throw it to me, also his hat." When he had these garments in his possession, he backed still farther away, and then he laid one of the guns very conveniently and, with the other shifting from his right hand to his left, he managed to shed the uniform of the soldier of the United States. He got out of the boots and the breeches and the coat, saving nothing but his identification tag and valour medal, and he put on the things that he had accumulated.

Then he kicked together in a bundle the things he was leaving, and, with both guns and the belt in his possession he backed his way down the canyon until he had put sufficient distance between himself and the two bandits so that he dared to turn and make his way as speedily as possible back to camp.

In the darkness made by the shadow of a branch, he awakened

William Brunson as quietly as possible and explained his change of wardrobe, and he thrust into the hand of his host one of the guns that he carried. In the fear that there would be accomplices who might follow with the bandits, camp was broken hastily, everything piled into the car, and speedily many miles were placed between themselves and the men who preyed without discrimination upon the purses and the happiness of others.

When the car moved away with its load, Jamie MacFarlane leaned back and rested his head against the supports of the car top and laughed weakly.

"After all," he said to the Brunsons, "Army training is not so bad. If I had never been a soldier, I doubt seriously if I could have made myself invisible or if at one and the same time I could have taken the gun of one man and smashed the face of another. And as for collecting their wardrobe, I understand that our Government does not desire soldiers who have been discharged to use their uniforms for any great length of time, so it is well to get rid of mine the first day I become a plain American citizen."

Exactly what William Brunson and his wife and daughter might have thought of this in the safety of an Iowa farm, where time for thinking occurs frequently, is one thing. What they thought of it as they fled down a California road with two guns in the car, two irate bandits behind them who might possibly overtake them in a speedier car at any minute, and possibly a third bandit with them, was a different proposition entirely. Susy Brunson sat on the front seat and held the revolver that had been given her father convenient to his reach. Mrs. Brunson sat on the back seat with her eyes round and a heart full of consternation. William Brunson stepped on the accelerator and turned at every cross-road he encountered. He did not in the least care where he went. All he wanted was to lose proximity to where he had been. He had a feeling that the lights of any small town that California proffered would look very good to him at that minute.

As for Jamie MacFarlane, he had enjoyed his supper; he had clothes that would not identify him as the man who was missing from the Arrowhead Hospital; he knew where he hoped to get his breakfast, he considered himself lost to the world of hospitals, and if he could achieve this adventure during his first day of freedom, there was every hope that he might be able at least to hold his own on the morrow. And so, through utter exhaustion, his head began slowly to sink down and over. Mrs. Brunson, dubious about the clothes, studied him as intently as she could by the night light. He looked exactly like any decent American of Scottish extraction, debilitated by illness. Finally she whispered to her daughter,

"Susy, can't you dig out a pillow for this poor boy? You can see he has been awfully sick and he is plum tired out."

Susy managed to get the pillow from the end of a roll on the running-board, and Mrs. Brunson laid it on her shoulder and against the back end of the car and pulled Jamie's head over on it, while Susy knelt on the front seat and, with tears of thankfulness still wet on her young face, tucked a blanket over the shoulders of Jamie MacFarlane as she said, "I tell you, Ma, from what he said to Pa, we have had a pretty close call, and I believe we'd better ship the car and get on the train, and go north by the quickest, safest route."

But Mother Brunson, being made of sterner stuff, replied: "Oh, I guess not. We will just keep closer to the towns when night comes. We will stop this sleeping beside the road. We'll keep the gun your Pa's got and get some cartridges for it at the first stop. I think we can make it all right and finish our trip."

CHAPTER III

THE BEE MASTER

"MA, do you think we've shook 'em ?" inquired William Brunson over his shoulder in the cold, still hours between three and four the next morning.

"Got any idea how many miles we've come ?" asked his wife, and William said he had not. He had forgotten to look at the speedometer when they stopped to make camp, but he was certain that he had turned a hundred corners and taken every cross-road he saw, and the small town they were entering appeared as if there might be some place in it where they could find a clean bed and have a few-hours of rest. As they drove down the main street they saw the open door and the lights of an hotel, and so they decided that they would have beds and a good rest, and then they would have baths and breakfasts, and after that they would hold a counsel and decide what they would do.

When it came to leaving the car, they found their guest of the road sleeping so heavily it seemed a pity to awaken him, so they locked the car, threw an extra blanket over him and left him to the luxury of the entire back seat. That was how it happened that when the life of the town began to stir on the streets that morning, James MacFarlane awoke with a bewildered sense of being lost. He had no idea what had happened to the Brunsons or where he was, but he speedily learned that, by reading signs on the streets around him, and he figured that nothing could have happened to the Brunsons in a town of several thousand population ; so his first thought concerned breakfast. He had hoped the night before that he would be with the Brunsons, probably at the location on which they were camped before making a start for the day. Now, evidently, their plans had changed. They would probably come from the hotel before which the car was standing, refreshed with sleep, baths, and food. He reflected that he had enjoyed refreshing sleep, he could postpone the bath, but there was an insistent demand in the pit of his stomach for food. He was in no mood to be particularly choice. He was so ravenously hungry that he felt he could have eaten almost anything, and tantalizingly there arose from restaurants, from the hotel building, from cafés and corner stands around him, the odours of ripe fruits. Later the aroma of coffee and cooked foods assailed his nostrils, so he began to figure on how he could materialize breakfast.

It occurred to him that he would step from the car and stretch his legs on the sidewalk and see if he could shake himself into slightly better circulation. He found himself sniffing ham and fried potatoes and toast and coffee and bacon and waffles somewhere in the immediate neighbourhood; merely from force of habit, because he knew there was not a penny in his pockets, he ran his hands into the region where the pockets of a male are usually located and stood in stupefied bewilderment, because he brought the hand back to the light and in it there was quite an assortment of nickels and dimes, a quarter or two, and a fifty-cent piece. His mouth fell open slowly and his eyes widened, and, without in the least knowing why he did it, he looked above the line of the buildings over the range of the mountains in the distance and on across the cloudless deep blue of the California sky and said, very politely: "I thank Thee, Lord."

He could not have told how long it had been since he had reverently said, "I thank Thee, Lord." He had been figuring that in the few years past he had not experienced very much for which to thank the Lord, at least not since a fire had been eating in his breast and weakness had assailed his limbs and shaken his big, capable hands. He did not stop to reflect either that the Lord might not have had much to do with the fact that he was wearing another man's trousers, but, after all, Jamie felt that he needed the trousers; he needed them exceedingly, and he had given his own, which were much better-looking and infinitely cleaner, in exchange for the ones he had acquired, the looking down upon which filled his fastidious soul with repulsion. He reflected that if he had been in a position to see the trousers he might have risked one more day wearing his uniform.

Having no idea when the Brunsons might return to their car, and being increasingly hungry since there was money in his fingers and he need not delude himself with the idea that he was not hungry, he squared his shoulders and looked around to see if his particularly sensitive nostrils could detect from which of the surrounding places where food was being cooked exactly the most delicious odours were emanating. That recalled him to the change he held in his palm. He spread his right hand in line of vision and with the forefinger of the left slowly pushed the coins around. He was so rejoiced over his findings that he could have shouted like a small boy. The half and the quarters made a dollar; the nickels and the dimes and a few pennies for good measure totalled eighty-seven cents.

He reflected that by judicious ordering, by making it mostly coffee with a little toast and bacon to add backbone, he would not be utterly at the mercy of the world for another day at least. Since he had thanked the Lord merely for the feel of small change in his hands, it occurred to Jamie, even in his hunger and his desire to keep near the car, that he might ride further if possible, that it would be a good thing once more to pay tribute. So again he looked to the sky, and this time, with a burr that might have descended to him from the tongue of a grandfather on either side of his house, he said, right out loud there on the sidewalk of the California town: "It's unco gude o' You, Lord." And when his ears heard him talking like a Scot they telegraphed the strange proceeding to his brain, and Jamie, who a few minutes before had felt decidedly aggrieved, laughed aloud and, turning, started down the street toward the most insistent odour of bacon and coffee that he could detect.

It was while he was sitting on a high stool with his feet on a railing before a counter that the clothing he had adopted drew closely around him and he became aware that he was wearing a hip pocket that contained something that from the feel of it might have been several things; but at first shot Jamie decided that he would guess a bill book. Then it occurred to him that it might be a good thing, since one pocket had yielded a living for a day at least, to go through all of them. And so he began on the outside breast pocket of the coat, in which he found a couple of cheap cigars. In the other pockets there were some bits of string and several buttons and a filthy handkerchief, the big revolver and a handful of cartridges. Then he tried the inside pockets and found a couple of letters, which he decided to attend to later. Then he ran his hand in his left trousers pocket and brought it away empty. And then, to finish the job, he reached around to the hip pocket and brought out the bill book. It really happened to be a bill book, and it really happened to have several bills in it, and instantly Scotch caution asserted itself in Jamie's mind. He had heard considerable about bandits and light-fingered gentlemen and taking your neighbour's property without his knowledge or consent. On the mere knowledge that there were two or three bills that might be of reasonable denominations, he slipped the book shut and slid it back in his pocket, and then he leaned his elbows on the counter and thought deep and fast.

He was not a thief. He never had been. But he was on a great adventure. It was becoming greater every minute. He reflected that if his little mother, up close to the throne, had been looking down at him and praying with all her might for his safety and his success in his undertaking, and if the Lord had been bending her way and listening with loving, indulging ears, Jamie thought he could not have got along much better so far. Only half a day, only a night, and through the blessing of a motor-car—two motor-cars, to be exact—he was more than two hundred miles from where he had started, and since those two hundred miles led to the north and the west, he must be considerably nearer to the sea. Precisely why all his being had begun clamouring for the sea the minute he had got to his feet and made his start, Jamie did not know. He had not taken time to analyse himself or to try to find out why he wanted water, worlds of water, clean, jade-green and sky-blue and indigo-blue water, salty water, and foam, great swaths of snowy foam. He wanted to see waves, big waves, piling up high on a beach, and then he was obsessed with the ridiculous feeling, probably because he missed his morning bath, that he wanted to get in that water. Then he wanted to lie on the sand and bake in the sun and sleep endlessly and go back to the sea-water again. Possibly it was not boiling water from an interior spring that was needed to fit his peculiar conditions. Maybe it was cold water, salt water, sea-water that would turn the trick.

He was thinking so intently of the bare possibility that the sea might do something for him that the springs had not done that he almost forgot the odours of food around him. He could afford to forget, since he would not be forced to abstain. He was going to have a cup of coffee, with thick, rich cream in it, and crispy toast and real bacon in only a minute. About the money in his pocket—he did not know precisely what the man to whom the breeches he was wearing belonged owed society in general, but he had an idea from the enterprise in which he had found him engaged, from his talk and familiarity with the situation, that this man might owe a fairly heavy debt. Jamie had the feeling that, since he had captured two guns and defeated the brutes, the two of them, in what he had heard them saying aloud in clear English that they intended to inflict upon a man who evidently was a very decent man and who, through long years of economy and hard work, had amply earned the vacation he was taking, he was entitled to the contents of their pockets. As for the fresh young girl and her equally wholesome and interesting mother, a wave of nausea swept Jamie's whole being and, regardless of who might be looking, he pulled the bill book from his hip pocket and opened it wide and emptied it, and found in his amazed fingers exactly forty-nine dollars, even, in ones, fives, and tens. This time he was really stunned, and the ceiling of the restaurant was so uninviting that, if he did glance upward, even involuntarily, he forgot his thanks. He made a wild and desperate resolve on the instant: when he had eaten the food he had ordered, he was going to have a bath, he was going to have clean, fresh underclothing, he was going to have trousers and a coat that fitted and would not fill him with repulsion, and he was going to have a hat in which he might appear at least as attractive as it was possible for him to look.

He gave the ethics of the case very slight consideration. He had frustrated the attack on the camp; he had got away from two men with their artillery. He had been of sufficient benefit to William Brunson and his wife and daughter so that they should be willing for him to have forty-nine dollars as his reward, and from the depth of his soul and the ceaseless grind of the wound in his left breast he felt that the Lord would absolve him for buying clothes that were new and clean. What was it the doctor had said? That he was the best breeding ground imaginable for germs? One glance at the legs of the trousers he was wearing made him feel like the original factory in which germs had been invented. So he stuck his long arms as far out of the coat sleeves as he could and pushed the side lapels as far back as they would go and gulped coffee so hot it almost scalded him and ate bacon that really was crisp and toast that was properly browned. He paid his bill and, carrying the wealth of a mint on his person, went back to the sidewalk and looked for the Brunson car.

It was standing where he had left it, so he went over and walked past the hotel office. He could see no sign of any of the Brunsons, so he went to the clerk and asked to see the register. When he found what he was looking for, he told the clerk to tell his friends, if they came down before he returned, that he had gone to get a shave and some fresh clothing. Some way he got a decided feeling of uplift from the fact that he would not have to tell William Brunson and his wife and daughter that he was whipped and sore, a broken hulk of a man with not a penny in his pockets and fleeing from a Government with whose regulations he was not even familiar, so slight was his own prospect of release. Such a thing as walking from the care of the Government without any notion as to where he was going or what would happen to him had never occurred to him, even among far-reaching possibilities, and, now that he was doing the thing, he had to admit that he did not know whether he was a deserter or not. Certainly he could not be a deserter, because the war had been over for so many long months. Of course, there was some formality that probably had been gone through with to keep him on record and in care of the Government. There was the barest possibility that a day might come in which he would want to ask for the official history pertaining to the decorations he carried.

He left the hotel with instructions from the clerk as to where the best outfitting store of the town could be found, bought himself the clothing he needed to make him clean and comfortable. Sparingly, of the cheapest things he could find that would possibly serve his needs, he bought what he felt he required, and then he went into a barber's shop, and when his hair was cut and he was freshly shaved, he paid for a bath, and this he followed up by a change into his new clothes. When before a mirror in the bathroom he tried on his new hat, he reflected that if he had red blood in his veins and a hundred pounds of beefsteak on his bones, he might not be such a bad-looking man. Tall he would always be, and big-boned like his Scottish ancestors; his lean hands were tapering, his features were finely cut, and his deep blue-grey eyes at least looked as if they might be honest eyes, kind eyes, interesting eyes.

So Jamie went back to the hotel carrying a neatly wrapped bundle which contained another man's coat and yet another man's trousers. He meant to drop it by the wayside somewhere along his journey, merely in case some man as sorely pressed as he had been might find it and it might fill a need, even as his needs had been served.

When William Brunson walked into the office, Jamie, fortified by neat grey trousers and a coat that really fitted him and a shirt that was clean and fresh, arose smilingly, holding out a hand, but instead of recognition he received a cold stare. He had to remove his hat and work his Scottish burr before William Brunson would accept him as his passenger of the previous day; while the wonder with which he had gone to sleep as to whether he was leaving his car in the possession of a third bandit for ever vanished from his mind. There had not been even the ghost of a bandit for ten generations in the ancestry of the man before him. On that William Brunson would have taken oath. As he stood holding Jamie's hand, he looked at him laughingly and said: "Well, I'll be darned! I didn't know you, and, if I stand away from you, I bet Ma and Susy won't either!"

Jamie laughed in return. "I made that lightning change in the dark last night," he said. "Moonlight is a mighty deceptive thing. I only wanted to shed the uniform of Uncle Sam pronto, so I took the first chance that offered, but when I woke up this morning and found that my clothes were better fitted to walk than I was, I decided that I'd see how quick I could change them."

"Come on to breakfast," said William Brunson.

"Thank you, I've had my breakfast," said Jamie MacFarlane. "If you are going to be good enough to let me ride with you so long as you are going north and west, that will be fine."

"There's isn't any question about how long you may ride with the Brunsons," said the husband and father of the Brunson family. "You may ride just as long as you darn please. It doesn't make any difference to me if it is all the way to Iowa!"

So Jamie picked up a morning paper and read until Mrs. Brunson and Susy came into the office, and they really did not know him, so he had to work the burr on them before they would believe that he was their passenger of the previous night. Both of them quite agreed with the judgment of the husband and father. They did not care how long this man rode with them and he did not care either. So they went a considerable distance that day, with dinner by the wayside and the night at a small hotel, and then Jamie felt that the time had come when he must turn west. He could journey by easy stages. He had enough change in his pockets to carry him through food and lodging for several days, he figured, and so, throughout the long, sunny day, plodding along, he made his way west. Then he found he had gone too far north, so he laid his course west by south.

He had no desire to go where cold would rack his aching bones. He wanted to stay where the sunshine was uninterrupted and penetrant. He went slowly and sat awhile frequently, and at noon rest, when he felt that it was almost time to be thinking about lunch, in the mottled sunshine of a live oak, with his arm on a stone for a pillow, he fell sound asleep, and when a passing drove of cattle finally awakened him he rose, picked up the stick he had been carrying, and stretched himself for his journey. As he did so he missed something. He had to think a minute to recall what it could be. It struck him that his trousers were not setting exactly as they had when he fell asleep, and running his hands around his body he encountered an empty hip pocket, and then an empty coat pocket—the gun, too.

Almost sick with shock and disappointment, Jamie sat back on the rock and looked around him. Lying on the ground a few yards up the mountain-side he could see the bill book he had appropriated. There was no use in exerting himself even to climb to it. It lay spread open, rifled, of course, and so he was once more about where he had started. Enough remained of the nickels and dimes in his breeches to carry him through that day and perhaps breakfast for the morning, but the bed which he needed almost more than food had gone as mysteriously as it had come.

Jamie looked more nearly Scot than he did American as he sat on the stone, dourly frowning. Exactly why he had not put that bill book in his breast pocket and buttoned his coat he could not imagine. He had found it in the hip pocket, it fitted there, and he had put it back mechanically. If he had been using his brains, he reflected, he would have practised caution. He reflected, also, that there must be something in the fact that a large part of the world had lost its ancient sense of honour. There had been no question of honour between the bandits who meant to prey on the Brunsons. They had talked as if anything the Brunsons had might belong legitimately to them. Jamie recalled the fact that he had not been troubled by any particular qualms about taking what he had found in the bandit's trousers. He spent a minute on the subject and still remained firm in his convictions that he had acquired a right to it, and that was why he was feeling so particularly sore that he had not taken better care of it. When a bed meant the question of whether he lived slightly longer or died very speedily, and probably very painfully, why had he been so careless with that which meant necessitites and fresh bandages that he would soon be needing?

After a while Jamie arose to his feet and laid out his course still west by south. The honest hunger that had been in the pit of his stomach an hour before was replaced by a flat nausea, and he had not gone far when he found a cold perspiration beginning to break out in his palms, at his temples, on his body. He did not even look up at the sky to decide whether he would voice an appeal or not. He deliberately walked in all the sunshine he could find because, from a taste of night out of doors, he thought he would need all the stored warmth he could accumulate.

At his last resting-place he took all the change from his pocket and carefully divided it. He might reach a town where for fifty cents at some cheapest of lodgings he could hire a bed. What remained would have to be equally divided between supper and breakfast. After that he was at the mercy of the world again, and at that minute he was feeling that the world might very possibly be quite as much against him as it was for him. The one consolation upon which he could rest was that if a call had been sent out from the hospital and descriptions of him had been posted, thanks to the bandit, he was so changed that no one would feel that he was the man who answered the descriptions that would be given. So Jamie followed his programme until after breakfast the next morning, and then, with only a few cents left, still headed west by south, he stumbled on. He realized that he was almost at the limit of endurance. Persistent walking had tired his feet and legs until they were beginning to swell so that his shoes were feeling too small. The sun had beaten on his unaccustomed head until he was dizzy. His eyes were so tired that he could have cried for the relief of dark glasses, and the price he might have paid for them at that time yesterday was lacking when he needed it so badly to-day.

Of the greater part of that day Jamie had no very clear memory remaining. The most he knew was that he had alternated walking as long as he could with dropping at any place he could sit or lie when he could go no farther. Just where he got into a road that led him into a canyon he did not know. He had been pushing on so nearly insensible to everything around him that he had not realized that the road had narrowed to a bridle path and the bridle path had narrowed to a footpath, and the footpath had begun to wind around the base of one side of a mountain that in the general upheaval of things had been split asunder from top to bottom. He had rounded a curve and faced the panorama before him suddenly, and at one and the same time he realized two things. He was hearing singing water. He was hearing water that was rushing and falling and spilling and laughing and doing all the heartening things that water knows how to do when it is left to follow a rocky bed down a canyon.

Jamie stood still and looked to the right and left and at his feet. On the right he saw walls opening up that began at ordinary range and climbed higher and higher until hundreds and then thousands of feet had been attained. These walls had stood through so many ages that the crevices and irregularities were filled with live oak and holly and sage, with yucca and frosty, blue-green cotyledon. Ferns were hanging down near places where the high walls seeped water. On the left the same panorama of exquisite beauty spread before him, and at his feet lay a well-defined, smoothly worn path, a path that he could see had been beaten by the feet of countless foot passengers, and here and there his eyes, even though over-tired, could detect the hoof-print of a horse: a range-rider, he thought probable.

The water at his feet seemed clean. It had to be cool. It was falling over rocks. It was leaping small precipices. It was dropping down before grottoes, fern-lined, of delicate beauty, and trim little ouzels were darting through the spray, very likely to nesting places that lay protected by falling water.

Jamie promptly sat down in the sunniest place on the warmest rock he could find and studied the situation, and after he had rested awhile he got down and drank from his cupped hands. Then he dusted off his new clothing, which was getting rather rough usage, and took up his stick and followed the footpath. It was not so difficult to follow, because it was downhill all the way, and before he had gone any great distance he began hearing voices. Then he realized that a place of such exquisite beauty would attract people, that probably campers or picnickers might be enjoying themselves beside the water that ran so impetuously that never before had he seen water travel in such haste. Jamie reflected that there was a possibility that he had done the wrong thing in discarding his uniform. From the frequency with which he had been offered rides when he wore it, from the utter indifference with which cars had whizzed past him hundreds of times that day, even when he had stood very close and raised his hand to ask for passage, he figured out that a man in uniform would be given assistance. A man in civilian clothes might be loaded with revolvers and have a mind full of evil intentions. The day seemed to be past when any traveller having a vacant seat would have despised himself if he had failed to offer anyone journeying on foot the privilege of riding.

There was no question of riding now. Right foot forward, then the left, and then the right again, and oh, but they were swollen stiff, and oh, but they ached! Just when Jamie decided that he would take off his shoes and stockings and bathe his feet in the cold water to see if he could not reduce the aching and the swelling, he came face to face with a freshly painted big notice which stated that the range before him supplied Clifton, no doubt a town near by, that a ranger rode the canyon to protect it, and that anyone who in any way polluted the water would be promptly arrested. So Jamie smiled dourly and looked down at his aching feet and realized that he had better leave his shoes where they were, since if he ever removed them there was a large possibility that he could not induce his feet to return to their capacity.

At any rate, his direction was right. Each step he forced himself to take was carrying him west and south. At first, tired though he was, he had not been able to ignore the beauty of the canyon through which he travelled. Within reach of his hand Hunter's rock-leek was blooming. There were ferns and mosses; there were red larkspur and lavender, blue and yellow lupin, and the red of pentstemon and many yellows, and one little pool filled with the pearl-white of blooming lizard's-tail with its rank foliage, its attractive flowers. None of these Jamie knew, for none had been included in his study of botany in the East.

On and on Jamie went down the canyon. How slowly he went he did not himself realize, but by and by he began to see people. Then he knew that he had been right when he thought he heard voices. There were places where smoke ascended, and suddenly and joyfully Jamie felt his problem for the remainder of that day solved. All he had to do was to wait until the picnickers left the canyon and then he would search where they had been and gather up the dry wood of dead branches and twigs that they had collected or that had fallen, and in one of the places where they had been cooking he would make a fire so big and warm that he could spend the night in comfort. So he sat down and waited until the sound of the canyon had been reduced to bird notes and falling water, running water, laughing water, singing water. Then he began picking up everything big enough to burn, and in the crook of his left arm he stacked it as he went along, until he had as big a load as he could carry. Presently he found a cavern of stone in a side wall of the stream where people had been cooking, and far back in the ashes over which water had been poured he found a few living coals. So he scraped the wet ashes away and drew the coals to the front and petted them with tiny twigs and dried grasses, and by and by he coaxed a feeble flame, and this he fed until, as the sun went down and the air grew chill, he had heat with which to comfort his aching body.

Then, on one of his excursions after wood, he crossed the stream and made his way down the right-hand bank close to the foot of the mighty wall leaning over and frowning above him. There he came to a small open plateau of stone, and what he saw made him laugh aloud. The picnickers who had spent a happy day there had let the remains of their lunch. They had set it out on the rocks for the birds and the squirrels; and the squirrels had not yet found it and the birds had long since gone to rest. There were several slices of bread-and-butter. There was a cold tongue sandwich; there was a hard-boiled egg and the half of a dill pickle, not to mention crumbled pieces of cheese.

So the soldier of the Government, now a soldier of adventure indeed, sat down on the big rock, still warm from the heat of the day, and ate all the supper he wanted of very excellent food. When he arose to go the father in him said: "Leave what remains for the wee folks as you found it." And the mother in him said: "Take with you every crumb that remains against the morrow. The wild things know how to fend for themselves. You are sick and you are almost at the limit of endurance, and you will need, oh, so badly, the slice of bread for your breakfast in the morning."

Jamie thought that over. He had not cared particularly if he took the bandit's breeches. He had not cared enough to keep him from using the contents of the bill book. He had filled his stomach to repletion with what had been left for the wild folks, and none of the wild folks had preyed upon him or refused him anything. It might be that in all the greenery climbing and trailing from and festooning the walls that shut him in there was food better to the liking of the wild than what had been left for them. But there was a streak of something in Jamie, the same streak that had carried him to the woods and the forests, that had sent him uncounted miles along the banks of the trout brooks of his boyhood, a streak of decency and cleanliness in his soul, and that streak now said to him: "Take your chances as the wee folk take theirs."

So Jamie got back on his knees and crumbled the bread and broke the crusts. Whimsically he laid one last piece of crust on his tongue, and then he went on hunting wood. When he felt that he had enough accumulated, he built his fire and, warm and as comfortable as need be, he curled up before it, and with his arm for a pillow and a stone for its support, he fell asleep in a very few minutes. He never felt the tiny lizards that ran over his feet; he never saw the trade rat that sat on its haunches and surveyed him with questioning eyes to see whether there was anything about him that it would like to exchange for the half of a pearl button that it carried in its left cheek. The hardness of his bed awoke him in the night before the fire was gone, and so he piled on the remainder of the wood and turned his cold side toward the flame and the warm one down and went back to sleep again.

When morning came he washed his face and hands by wetting his handkerchief in the stream, and after that he wet his handkerchief several times and wrung the water over the coals he had left, scattering them widely and obliterating every trace of fire that could possibly spread. Then, with feet still aching in the shoes he had not dared to remove, he started on down the canyon.

About ten o'clock that morning he met the Ranger. The Ranger of this particular canyon was not so lonely as were the range riders of the mountains, but for all that he was friendly. He stopped to talk a minute, and as he casually glanced at Jamie he saw the attenuation of the figure, he saw the whiteness of his hands, he saw how the skin of his face settled on the lean bones, and being young and full of life and having in his veins quite a drop of the milk of human kindness, he said to Jamie: "My mother tells me that if I keep to the saddle too much I will develop gout in my feet. What do you say to taking the horse for the next few miles and letting me exercise?"

Jamie said if that would be any accommodation to the Ranger he would be glad to ride for him, but he had not figured on what the gait of a horse would do to his left breast. Fit himself to the saddle as easily as he could, riding was torture he could not endure for long, and so, after a mile or two, he was forced to walk again. But he was thankful for the offer, and dimly he was beginning to formulate in his mind the feeling that the world is made up of good people and bad people, of selfish people and thoughtful people, of cruel people and kind people, and it was merely a case of luck as to which kind you met when you went on a great adventure.

From the Ranger on, Jamie's adventure stretched lagging miles of torture, still west by south, until nearly three o'clock that afternoon. Nobody had left a lunch box and there had been no place where the few pennies he carried would buy food. He had left the canyon and followed a road that had widened until it would accommodate horses and vehicles, here and there a car—not a greatly travelled road; not a busy, well-kept road; a road that became increasingly more difficult to Jamie to follow because his feet had endured almost all that human feet can endure when they are attached to a sick man who is gamely driving himself to the ultimate limit.

Near four o'clock the hunger that had been in abeyance since the night before began again to torment him. He was exhausted to the point at which he found himself taking two or three sidewise steps to keep from lifting his feet even a slight degree higher to step over a small irregularity in the road. He was beginning to realize than there was slight chance of shelter for the night. There was equally small chance of food. So far his adventure had yielded its bright spots, its thrills, its pains. At that minute, between the scorching in his breast and the burning in his shoes and the general ache all over his tortured body, he could not see much of it. He began to wonder if he could make his way back to the hospital and whether they would take him in, and then he thought of the White Plague which they said had not as yet attacked him, and so he shut his lips very tightly and stood swaying on his feet as he peered like a half-drunken man down the road before him, trying to decide whether the wheel track on the right seemed the least bit smoother than the wheel track on the left. When he had decided that the one on the right was the one for him to travel he reeled widely and started forward, and furtively his eyes began to search the road on either side for the spot where ultimately collapse would come. He wondered, if he stumbled and fell and could not rise, if he lay unconscious in the middle of the road, whether anyone would find him and what they would do with him if they did.

It was from searching the sides of the road that Jamie missed the point where there was a turn until he found his feet following it, and then he looked ahead and his eyes widened and his breath came in a light gasp. Down the road, only a few rods on the right, he could see a small house, and of all the houses that he had ever dreamed about and thought that he would like particularly to own and to live in, that house appealed to him as the most inviting.

It stood close to the road. A white picket fence ran along the front of it. A neat white gate shut it from the highway. Its painted face was soft and attractive. New England was obvious all over it. Flowering vines were climbing up its corners and over the tiny front veranda. Outside the gate he could see a circle of crushed shells, and he thought the walk that led to the front door might be made of shells. It seemed to lie very close to the road and there was not much ground on either side of it. All that there was seemed to be filled with the very flowers that Jamie had helped take care of in his mother's New England garden. He could see hollyhocks, as high as the eaves of the house, and in many colours; to the left and to the right he could sense the gay hues of nasturtiums and zinnias and marigolds, and his sensitive nostrils could pick up the tang of heliotrope and mignonette and forget-me-not and violets; but above everything else he had the impression of a cloud of blue, sweet, restful blue.

Jamie rocked on his feet and stared at the house yearningly. His vision carried beyond it, and he saw that on the other side of the line fence there was another dooryard and another house, and then houses began gathering in a friendly way on either side of the road, and leading away as far as he could see here and there were other houses, other signs of life. At that instant there came softly to his ears the slow, steady wash of what might possibly have been a low tide of the sea.

In his exhaustion, his senses numbed with pain, he had travelled most of the afternoon, a plodding, half-conscious thing, but now, touched by the nearness of humanity, touched by the beauty of somebody's home, excited with the prospect that by some possibility he might find shelter and food, his sluggish blood surged up, his head lifted, his dull eyes brightened slightly, and his keen nostrils turned to the west and sniffed inquiringly. Then said Jamie, right out loud, right from the depths of nowhere:

> " If my old nose don't tell no lies,
> 'Pears like I smell . . .

what ought to be the Per-cific Ocean!"

He had not the faintest notion either why he called it the *Per*-cific Ocean. He probably did it because he was so desperately tired that if he did not manage a chuckle about something, there was every probability that he was going to tumble down in the road and lie still without giving his new clothes the slightest consideration, or any other thing in all the world.

At that minute the screen door that led from the veranda into the secret of the beautiful house, whose whole exterior was one delicate luring invitation, opened, and there came through a man, a tall man, a slender man, an aristocrat from head to toe, lean, and with long silken white hair flowing back from his forehead and a soft, short beard of silver-white wavy silk coming down on his breast, a man with long slender nose, big deep-set eyes, and white lips. He reeled as he came across the veranda, and both his hands clutched his left side and he kept on wavering to the right and the left until he reached the gate. Then he took his hands from his side and clung to the gate. He leaned over it and hung on to it and he looked up and down the road, and there he spied Jamie. He lifted one of his hands and beckoned.

Jamie stood there staring at him, and then slowly and deliberately, slapping one swollen foot and then the other on the hard road, he took a few steps in the man's direction. He stopped again to stare at him, to note the fine lines of the anguished old face, the immaculate apparel, the stricken attitude of the frame hanging across the gate. So, with all the strength that he could muster, Jamie took a few more steps and came within speaking distance, and on his dazed and incredulous ears there fell the strangled cry, "Help! For God's sake, lad, help me!"

One minute before Jamie would not have believed that he could help anybody or anything. He had been figuring that he had reached the end of his endurance, that if he did not have help himself in a very few minutes he would be past the place where he would ever need it. There was something about the whiteness of the fine old head, something about the breadth of the shoulders and the leanness of the frame that reminded Jamie of his father, and possibly because he was reminded of his father, Jamie lifted his eyes above the wonderful white house, above the lace of the trees surrounding it, above its sheltering vines, away up to the blue, and far down in his heart he gave an imperative order. "Now you've *got* to help me, Lord! You must help me now!"

Then he clenched his fists very tightly at his sides and covered the three steps more to the gate. He found the combination by which it opened, and he put his arm around the old figure leaning on it, and in a dry, breathless voice he heard himself saying: "Why, of course, I'll help you!" and he had not the faintest notion whether he could manage three steps farther himself or not.

But he did accomplish the three steps farther, he pulled the screen door open, he headed the stricken man he was trying to support toward a big davenport and let him down on it, easing him back against the pillows that he punched up hastily. Then on his knees, grasping the side of the couch, he spoke again in his voice of dry breathlessness: "What must I do?"

Instinctively both hands of the stricken man had sought the region of his heart. Jamie's thoughts, as his mind cleared at another man's extremity, was: "He's got it mighty near where I have." And so he repeated again: "What must I do?"

The answer came: "The telephone. You must call my doctor. You must get me to a hospital."

Pushing against the couch, Jamie rose to his feet and looked around him. Then he saw a telephone on the wall and a small table before it and an open telephone book, so he sat down on the chair and drew a deep breath or two. Then he asked over his shoulder: "Can you give me the number?"

After a paroxysm of pain that brought sweat to the white dome above the white brows sheltering the big eyes that were pools of darkness, there came the answer: "You will find the number and the name on the list beside the 'phone. Doctor Grayson."

Jamie hunted down the line and found the name and number, and then he put in the call, and while he waited for it he again asked over his shoulder: "Whom shall I say?"

The gasping reply was: "The Bee Master."

So presently Jamie found himself insisting that Doctor

Grayson come to the telephone personally, and when he had the assurance that Doctor Grayson was speaking, he found himself mustering strength to say: "The Bee-Master has been stricken with a very bad heart attack. He wants you to come and to bring an ambulance. He wants to be taken to the hospital immediately."

The answer had been: "All right. I can reach him inside of an hour."

Then Jamie had cried into the telephone: "Instructions! Give me instructions! What shall I do for him?"

The answer was: "Aromatic spirits of ammonia. Bathe his face and hands. Give him a few drops. Keep him nearly upright. I will cut the time as much as I can."

So Jamie went back to the davenport, and as he laid hands on the strcken man he whispered: "Now, help, Lord!" and from somewhere he drew strength to pull the Bee Master more nearly to a sitting posture and to pile the pillows higher behind him. Then he began looking around to see from what direction he might conjure aromatic spirits of ammonia. The doctor had spoken of it as if the remedy might be somewhere near and its use customary. When he could not see anything that suggested a bottle, he ventured a question, and a wave of the hand directed him to an adjoining room where, on a table beside a bed, there stood a bottle labelled "Aromatic spirits". So Jamie brought it, and then he stumbled to the back of the house and in a hasty survey of the kitchen in which he found himself he caught up a towel. For one brief instant he glanced from the back door, and that back door led to a porch and on over a few level feet, and then a walk started in a slope none too gentle that seemed to lead down, and down, and down, and with a quick look Jamie exulted softly: "My God, I've reached the sea!"

He caught up the towel and hurried back to soak an end of it from the bottle, and surreptitiously as he thrust it toward the sick man he carried it past his own face and inhaled to the depths of his lungs. He kept very near as he managed bathing the hands and face, and from the ammonia he drew enough strength to stand and return to the kitchen. Then he took the liberty of prising the paper lid from the bottle of milk he had seen at the back door, and slowly, with deliberation, he gulped half its contents. That so put heart into him that he was able to find a suitcase on the top of a closet in a bedroom; he was able to open a chest and transfer to the case certain papers, and to relock the chest and give the key into the possession of the stricken man. Then he found an overcoat and slippers and other small articles he was instructed to collect, and when everything was ready he sat with the ammonia-saturated towel to await the ambulance. Then he heard himself being asked to remain in the house, to take care of the bees until it was ascertained how ill their keeper was, and when he would be able to return to his work.

"I don't know the first thing about bees," protested Jamie. "I can't take care of them. Can't you direct me to someone who can see to your property in an intelligent way?"

"There is nothing to do," said the Bee Master. "Keep the water pans filled. My next-door neighbour brings my food. You can sleep in my bed. You look tired and sick yourself. I am not afraid to trust a man having your touch, your face, your voice. Promise me that you will take my place until my return."

So Jamie reached in his pocket and held out the decorations for valour before the eyes of the stricken man. He said that he had recently been discharged, that he had no home at present, that he would be glad to remain in such a friendly house and do what he could, but that he must have instructions, full instructions, as to what he must do for the bees.

The Bee Master smiled a rare and illuminating smile and sank back on the pillows as if he were content, and then he said: "Any day the little Scout may walk in, my side partner, and you can ask anything you want to know and you'll get an intelligent answer. Margaret Cameron next door can tell you a good deal, and she is a rare cook. Tell her what you like and help yourself to my clothes and bed."

Then he shut his eyes and dropped over the edge into unconsciousness.

A few minutes later the ambulance came and the frame of an old man having a face suitable for a model for the most exquisite likeness of any patriarch of old was started on its way to a hospital. In only a minute with the doctor who had come for him, Jamie secured the hospital address, and the promise of a telephone call after an examination had been made. He had liked Doctor Grayson, had liked the touch with which he laid his hands on the fine old wreck on the davenport, liked the sympathetic way in which he bent over the stricken figure, liked every tone of the voice in which the explanation of the case had been given.

"The Bee Master has been putting off his evil day to the limit. He must go to the hospital. He must remain for an operation he has been fighting for a year or two. I hope you can arrange to settle here, if you are the man he has selected, for several months at least."

Jamie lifted a shaking hand to dry lips and iterated and reiterated: "But I don't know a thing about bees! I don't know a *damn'* thing about bees!"

After the ambulance had driven away, he staggered back into the house and straight through to the kitchen, where he finished what remained of the milk, and that so heartened him that he stepped through the back door and looked down the side of a small mountain where all the world seemed alive and aglow with flowers upon flowers of the same old-fashioned kinds that bloomed around the front; and on either hand, down the outer line of a wide stretch that must have covered at least two acres, there were literally hundreds of domed white hives toward which heavily laden bees were winging in a low humming. Then he could see a stretch of sands that looked like silver, and then he could both see and hear the rhythmical sweep of the Pacific at low tide.

He stood there until he could stand no longer; then he closed and latched the door and went back to the davenport. He dropped on it, worked off his shoes, pulled his coat from his shoulders, and drew an Indian blanket over his chest, slid the pillows lower, and then unconsciousness overtook him as it had overtaken the Bee Master a short time before.

CHAPTER IV

IN THE GARDEN OF THE BEES

It was afternoon of the following day before James MacFarlane awoke, and he did not regain consciousness feeling either refreshed or invigorated. On trying to assume a sitting posture he discovered that he was sore through and through, that every bone in his body ached with an ache that was nearly intolerable, and when he set his feet on the floor and examined them carefully and then looked at his shoes, he realized that the shoes were not going to contain the feet for some time to come.

Remembering the Bee Master's offer of clothing and his bed, he hobbled through the house until he found the bedroom, and he uttered a thankful exclamation when he stumbled into the bathroom adjoining. A thorough soaking in hot water with a cold shower afterward helped considerably with the ache and soreness. He borrowed of underclothing he found in a chiffonier in the bedroom to make himself comfortable, and a pair of moccasins on a shelf were the thing for his feet.

Then the scent of cooked food assailed his nostrils, and as he came into the living-room he had at the door his first vision of Margaret Cameron.

Margaret Cameron did not in the least resemble Jamie's mother, but she resembled a woman who might well have been typical of a universal mother, and exactly the right kind of a mother at that. Her face was beautiful with a severely cut beauty that always indicates an indomitable spirit. With one glance at Margaret Cameron one would have been safe in arriving at the conclusion that she would be drawn and quartered before she would renounce her religion, her country, her political opinions, or her family. She was tall; she carried no ounce of superflous flesh. Her hair was white and her eyes were blue. There was colour in her lips and cheeks. She looked wonderful to Jamie when she smiled at him.

"I had a ring from Doctor Grayson this morning," she said. "He thought you would be sleeping and he didn't want to waken you. He told me you were to take care of things here until the Bee Master comes back to us. I never was sorrier about anything than I was over being away when he was stricken. A young relative of mine needed me sorely; there was death in her family and I was forced to go to her."

"I think," said Jamie, "that I found everything the Bee Master required, and I believe there was no time lost."

There was a hint of finality in the slight gesture in which Margaret threw out her hands.

"I haven't a doubt," she said bluntly, "but the Bee Master had everything he needed. There is no one on earth who wouldn't do anything Michael Worthington wanted. The point is that he was forced to call on a stranger for help that I, as his friend of long standing, would have loved to give."

"I see," said Jamie quietly. "I am sorry you weren't here. I think you are right about anyone doing anything he asked, because here I am, and anyone less suited for what he asked of me couldn't have been found in the state. But because he asked it, I am here to try."

A dry smile crossed Margaret Cameron's face. Her eyes narrowed as they followed a line of vision that carried through the living-room, through the combination kitchen and dining-room, across the back porch and out to the unmeasured leagues of the sea beyond—the pacific sea, the peaceful ocean that smiles and lures and invites and so very seldom shows the fangs and the jaws of the monster that lies lurking in its depths.

"I understand," she said quietly. "I know why you are here, and I can see that you are not fit for work. Doctor Grayson mentioned that you looked mighty seedy. He thought you might have been one of ours, across."

Jamie ran his fingers in his pocket and produced a Service Bar and two decorations for valour and held them toward her, and Margaret Cameron came forward and took his unsteady white hand in both of hers and said: "God love you, boy! I've got the Bee Master's routine by heart myself, and, while I don't know as much about the bees as he has really been making a business of teaching the little Scout, I know enough to show you where the water pans are and how to keep them filled with the right combination of water—strange, but they like a sprinkle of salt in it—and I can go over the flowers with you and show you which need the most water and when. I think, if you rest a few days, you can make it all right, and I will cook your meals as I always have cooked the Bee Master's. Only you might as well tell me what you particularly like and how you want it. No two people have tastes alike."

"That's mighty good of you," said Jamie. "I am ready to confess that I am ravenous this minute, and whatever you have brought will be fine, I am sure.'"

So he went into the kitchen and ate the food that Margaret Cameron had provided for him. He learned how to operate the gas-stove in case he wanted a hot drink at any time. He was shown where a small ice-chest stood on the back porch in which there was daily deposited a bottle of cream and a bottle of milk, and he noticed a basket of eggs and some fruit, and then together they went over the garden and he located the different hose attachments and was given exhaustive instructions about watering the flowers.

Noticing how very unsteady he was on his feet and how terribly those members were swollen, seeing his thin white hands with the blue veins standing in ridges, Margaret Cameron drew her own conclusions. As they came up the back walls she advanced very slowly to give Jamie time to keep up with her, and when they reached the back door she asked of him : "Are you bee immune ?"

Jamie looked at her in a speculative silence for a moment, pondering that question, and then he said: "I'm not at all sure that I know what you mean by 'bee immune'."

Why, I mean," said Margaret Cameron, "that there are people in this world whom bees won't tolerate. There are people to whom it would mean certain and mighty unpleasant death to go down either side line of this garden. There are people whom a bee naturally hates, and there are others with whom they instantly make friends. One man may lift the roof of a hive and scoop up a handful of working bees. There's a man who comes to help the Bee Master sometimes who carries bees around in the crown of his hat. But that doesn't prove that they are a safe proposition for everyone."

Jamie thought that over.

"How do I go about finding out whether I am 'bee immune' ?" he asked, as he leaned against the casing facing the woman before him and noting that she was almost his own height.

"Right there," said Margaret Cameron, "is where the little Scout comes in. There isn't anything the Bee Master knows about bees that he hasn't carefully passed on to his side partner —his first assistant. I imagine you will have a visitor to-day or to-morrow. If you don't I will telephone. Take my advice and keep away from the hives until you get your instructions."

Then Margaret Cameron gathered into a basket the dishes

that Jamie had been using, crossed the side yard, and through a small gate entered her own premises.

Jamie stood and watched her going to a low white house that seemed cheerful and homelike, that appeared as if it might have required the same amount of labour and the same length of time to construct, and yet, in some way, lacked the luring charm of the home of the Bee Master.

Refreshed by the food, Jamie went out to the middle of the road and stood looking at the house and grounds. There was such a slight variation in the width of the eaves and the angle of the roof, one could scarcely have told where lay the difference between it and the other houses that stretched away down the street.

As he stood studying it, Jamie had difficulty in defining the difference to himself. Maybe it was the setting, the whitewashed paling fence, and the quaint sloping veranda. Maybe it was the particular colour of paint that preserved the wood. Maybe it was the rare vines, the odorous shrubs, the gay flowers clambering everywhere with absolutely no hint of order or precision. Anyway, there was something about the house, shaded by tall eucalyptus trees and lacy jacqueranda, with its gaudy surrounding carpet of blue-flower magic, that gave to it—Jamie could think of no other term—a welcoming face. It seemed to be a human thing and it seemed to smile the warmest kind of welcome.

Then Jamie looked beyond it to the scintillating blue of the sea and the equal blue of the sky, and then he looked higher. He stood there thinking intently, and before he realized what he was doing he had repeated a phrase in his father's tongue that he had used a few days before: "You are unco gude to me, Lord!"

Then Jamie smiled through misty eyes at the house, and he went into it, carefully noting the side seats and the delicate vines trained over the veranda. He looked at the rugs on the floors and decided that they were Persians of antiquity and price. He was unschooled in rug lore. He knew that the furniture was antique and priceless. He ran his fingers appreciatively over pieces of rosewood and mahogany that were old and shining from use and that had been designed by master craftsmen long ago across far seas.

The bookcases, ranging from floor to ceiling almost around the room, held his attention for a few moments, and then he stopped before a writing-desk, open, the quill of the Master in the small horn holder of shot, the sheets of an unfinished letter lying on the pad. With that fineness inherent in the heart of a gentleman of Scotland, Jamie picked up the sheets, lifted the pad, laid them face down on the mahogany of the writing-desk, and returned the pad to its place. The letter would lie there untouched until the return of the Bee Master.

Then Jamie's eyes wandered to the case above the writing-desk. He had been reading names prominent in literature from the beginning, but each volume in that small case seemed to be either completely concerning or in some way related to bees. At one instant Jamie's hand lifted to open one of the doors. Probably its weight roused him to the fact that he had better rest a few more days before he began on a task that might be over quickly or might be long. In detail he went through the adjoining sleeping-room, noting its neatness, the precision of its arrangement, the delicate beauty of the etchings and engravings, the rareness of the books that lay here and there, the quiet grace of the furnishings.

He went back through the kitchen and the back porch and came out into the open shine of the afternoon sun. He was thin enough and cold enough to love its warmth.

As he stood there looking down the stretch of the garden to the sea, he thought it comprised the most beautiful picture that he had ever seen. It covered two acres of the Sierra Madres where they meet the Pacific. A crude walk, fashioned from stones collected from the mountain-side, ran in steps down to the beach below. There was a pergola loaded with grapes as they are allowed to run in the gardens of the East, but lavishly among them grew wistaria and clematis, roses and vines, and vines whose names, habits, or flowering he did not know. On either hand, sometimes with abrupt juttings of big rocks, sometimes in tiny fertile plateaus, sometimes on gentle slopes, there grew every fruit tree that loves to flourish in the soil and sun of California—loquats and figs, oranges and lemons, plums and peaches, pears and nectarines, dates and grapefruit—only a tree or two of each, and between and beneath them tiny cultivated beds of vegetables.

Prominently bordering the walk half-way down the mountain-side, staked and rankly growing, Jamie's eye was caught by a blare of purple-red where stalks of tomatoes lifted huge fruits, some of them bursting with ripeness, and on either hand everywhere, bushes, shrubs, vines, and flowers, and flowers, and yet more flowers, and because Jamie recognized nearly each one of these, he knew they were the quaint, old-fashioned flowers that his mother and his grandmother had grown. There were Madonna lilies that, in the warm soil and the luring sunshine, had opened to bloom at two or three feet less height than in the cold gardens of the East. Carpeting around them were beds of cinnamon pinks, touching the fresh salt air with their spicy sweetness, mignonette and heliotrope, forget-me-nots and great blue blooms of myrtle the like of which Jamie never had seen—a whole world of flowers and fruit.

On either hand, steadily, slowly, came the low hum of millions of working bees—bees hived, not in the ugly flat houses used in numberless apiaries he had passed on his journey, but each stand in a separate spot raised above the earth on a low platform and having a round pointed roof that gave to the hives a beauty, a quaintness, an appropriateness to the location. On close examination Jamie found that each hive stood in a bed of myrtle blue as the sky. And then he saw that back of the hives the fences were a wall of the blue of plumbago, delicate sheets of it. And above, one after another, great lacy jacquerandas lifted clouds of blue to the heavens. And then he realized that, facing the hives, around and near them, there was a world of blue: blue violets, heliotrope, forget-me-nots, blue verbenas, blue lilies, larkspur, bluebells, phlox, blue verain, blue and yet more blue: Past his head and face, lured by the reds and brilliant colours around the house, darted the jewel-throated and crowned humming birds, but the bees lived in a whole world of blue. It seemed as if the blue flowers dearly loved to creep up to these white hives, to vine around them, to cling to them, to bloom above them. Alone, close to the back walk, Jamie noticed several big hives that stood by themselves where he would have to pass within the distance of a few feet when he made his first journey the length of the garden, out of the gate, and across the strip of sand to where the ocean, in a great bay, came lapping up the shore and then slid back again, gently, softly, with only a low murmur song that would be the finest thing in the world to lull a tired man to sleep.

Slowly, with wavering feet, Jamie made his way across the back end of the house. Under a jacqueranda tree on the east side he saw the most attractive bench. So he went and sat upon it at just the precise spot where the branches of the tree threw a mottled shade over his head and left his lean body stretched in the sunshine. He sat and tried to think. Because the sky was so beautiful, and the sea was so beautiful, and the garden was so painfully beautiful, there came to him the old thought he had dragged around for the past two years: How much longer? How much time had he, anyway? How soon was the sky going to lose her eternal verity and the sea to cease smiling, and flower faces and bird song and the hum of the bee and the chirp of the cricket—how soon were they to be over for him?

Because he had tried himself so sorely, because he was so desperately strained and over-tired from his journey, he was not very hopeful. Everything concerning himself looked the blackest it ever had. The bandages that he had removed for his bath bore brilliant stains, telling anew the story of angry wounds that refused to heal. So that afternoon Jamie's individual case seemed more hopeless to him than it had seemed when he had arisen in hot rebellion and walked out from the protection of his Government. But the irony of the whole thing was that, when for himself matters could scarcely have been blacker, all inadvertently he had fallen into one of the most exquisite beauty spots that the face of the world had to boast.

There are only a few places where love and artisanship build a small house with a welcoming face. There are only a few places where love and good horse sense build a garden, half of wildlings and half of quaint old-fashioned things that evolved without the help of crossing and fertilization and other makeshifts that produce growth so rampant and sizeable that it is difficult to believe that the blooms are living things. There are only a few places where the side of a mountain walks down, and slides down, and jumps down, and meanders winding, flowering ways until it reaches the white sands of a brilliantly blue sea, and it is easy to believe that such a location would naturally be the home of tiny round white houses with round roofs where millions of bees make honey to sweeten the food of a world.

It is easy to see that the hum of the bees and the scent of the flowers would draw the birds to a place like this, and across any stretch of ocean shore-line there is bound to be the wide sweep of great grey pelicans and the black-winged anhingas, and the wild ducks, the snow-white of the gulls and the scimitar-winged sea swallows, like birds of carved ivory, arching and sailing for pure love of blue sky and blue water, and to indulge the powers of flight. There are bound to be Mother Carey's chickens and little stilt-legged sandpipers and killdeers tilting along the shore, and there are sure to be little children digging in the sand, and grown folk having an hour of pleasure stretched in the sunshine, asking earth to heal their bodies and the Sun-god to heal their hearts.

As Jamie sat on the bench under the jacqueranda feeling so ill that the tears of self-pity were stinging the lids of his wide grey eyes, he vaguely wondered what it would do to him if he were to go down to the sea and soak his body in the cold salt water and let the sun drive home every medicinal property that sea-water contains. He had tried a year of hot water from the boiling bowels of the earth. How would it do to try a year of cold water from the seas of the surface and the sun of the heavens?

Jamie's lips twisted bitterly. He was probably as near heaven as he ever would be until heaven passed him by, and it might be that only a few days would end his tenure of the little white house and the mountain garden, and it would be his lot to move on until his case grew even more desperate than it was at that minute.

CHAPTER V

THE LITTLE SCOUT

THE following day, as Jamie sat on the same bench, his mind occupied with the same subject, in a wide flare between earth and sky, a slender bit of child sailed over the fence and landed expertly on the sanded walk of the garden. As the small figure righted itself, one hand caught the band of a pair of particularly dirty breeches and the other stuffed more securely therein the tail of a not overly clean shirt. Standing on one foot, the youngster removed a canvas shoe from the other, shook the sand from it, and replaced the shoe on a bare foot. The child drew a deep breath and stood still an instant with a wandering gaze roving over the garden.

In that pause Jamie took mental account of the lean, flat figure. One trouser leg was fastened at the knee. The other had lost its fastening and hung half-way down the ankle with a loose strap and a flopping buckle. The sleeves of the green khaki shirt were cut off at the elbows and one of them was ripped lengthwise to the shoulder. Hands and arms and legs as well bore the traces of climbing and rough exercise. The little face was rather flat; the nose a faint pug; the mouth wide. The eyes seemed not overly large. At that distance Jamie could not decide what colour they were. The hair might have been brown if it had not been bleached by California suns until the outer layer was a flaxen tan; where it fell apart darker streaks appeared. It was cut evenly in a circle from ear lobe to ear lobe and across the forehead in a bang. "Dutch," Jamie supposed; and as he sat watching, the child with a movement exquisitely deft and graceful began to pirouette, to dance in the sunshine.

Sometimes with arms curved above the head until the tips of the fingers touched, sometimes with the right arm extended and lifted and the left trailing behind like a flying Mercury, up and down the walk went the small figure, whirling, reaching as if snatching butterflies from the air, dancing all alone there in the mid-afternoon under the California sun. Then, tiring, a sudden change from the dance to a walk started the youngster straight toward Jamie. Half-way between lay the Madonna lily bed. Opposite it the child paused, bent forward, and peered at the lily faces, and then Jamie's eyes widened and a queer, incredulous grin crossed his face. What he was seeing was a very small person on bended knees, elbows akimbo, hands at the sides, in a half-crouching attitude, with eyes rolled heavenward, ecstatically sucking, one after another, the pistils of the Madonna lilies!

Jamie's grin widened to a chuckle when once he noticed that a pistil overflowing honey had dripped a drop on a petal, and the child supported the under side of the petal and licked away the drop with an appreciative tongue and then arose and came slouching down the walk until Jamie drew back his toes because they happened to be particularly sore and tender and he did not want them stepped on.

The youngster stopped and looked at Jamie, from the crown of his tired, sick head to the soles of his very badly swollen feet, and an expression of wonderment crossed the small face, but there was not the slightest sign of fear and there was no backward movement. Ground attained was firmly held.

"Oh, hello!" said the child.

"Hello!" said Jamie, as cordially as he could say it in a voice that had so recently been roughened with the emotion of self-pity.

"*Where's* the Bee Master?" asked the small person.

Jamie hesitated. He was near enough now to look to the depths of the eyes trained on him, and it struck him that they had more depth, more expression, more comprehension, than any pair of eyes that he had ever seen on a person of anywhere near that age. There were things lying away back in the depths of the brownish-grey eyes meeting his that awoke Jamie to caution.

"He went away for a few days and left me in charge," he answered.

"Oh! But we don't know you, objected the small person.

"But I'm here," said Jamie.

"So you are," said the small person, "and you probably wouldn't be here if the Bee Master hadn't said you might, and whatever he *says, goes*!"

With that "goes" both hands were spread out on a level with the belt line and given an emphatic downward and outward sweep that seemed to cover long distances with perfect accuracy.

"I am glad you think I'll do," said Jamie.

"I haven't had time to think anything," said the small

person. "I am no acrobat in my head. I can't think quick. If the Bee Master told you to come here and stay here, you've got to come and you've got to stay and you've got to do. That's all there is to that. I'm the Bee Master's side partner. Look me over. Kid! It ain't expensive!"

Jamie smiled, and when Jamie smiled, which was not any too frequent an occurrence, there were tiny dancing flecks of light in his eyes and a stretching of the skin over his lean face and a twitching of his lips that made an appeal that had not as yet failed in its effect. The child advanced a step and laid a hand on Jamie's arm while an impish grin overspread the small features. The inquiry was shot at him suddenly.

"Did you see the pirouette?"

Jamie nodded.

"Did I pull it off pretty well?"

"I thought you did famously," said Jamie.

"We got to do that darn stuff in school," said the small person. "It's the bunk! But when I get off where I think I'm alone, I practise it. I think I can do it better to the bee music and to the waves than any other kind. It's sure goofy! I wish you could see Fat Ole Bill pirouette! But if your school *makes* you do it, you might just as well keep everlastingly at it until you do it a little better than the other fellow."

"That's sound logic," said Jamie. "If you start out with that kind of an idea in your head and keep 'everlastingly at it', there isn't any place you can land except at the top of the heap."

"That's the way I've got it figured," said the small person casually. "And I've learned, while only just as wide and just as high as I am this minute, that I can't be Scoutmaster and Chief of the Robbers' Den and First Assistant to the Bee Master unless I hoe it down."

Jamie decided that the little figure before him was surely a boy. There was a slight drawing closer, a lowering of the voice, and the small person asked confidentially: "*When* did they take him to the hospital?"

Jamie drew back and looked inquiringly at the child.

"I didn't say anyone was taken to the hospital," he protested.

"No. You didn't," conceded the small person. "But if you had known the Bee Master as well as I've known him, in all the time we've been partners, which is ever since I've been big enough to climb the fence, you'd know that there wasn't any *place* they could take him away from this garden *except* to the hospital, and you'd know there wasn't any *way* they could take him except flat on his back."

"I suspect that's about the truth," said Jamie.

The youngster, in an instant gesture, threw out wide arms with spread fingers and nodded emphatically.

"That's just edsactly the truth, because he has needed to go for months and months and Doctor Grayson's told him to go, and coaxed him to go, and tried to make him go, and none of them could make him. He thought he'd do anything in the world for me. He *said* he would. So when I saw that he wasn't going to go and couldn't be made to go"—there was a sudden straightening of the small figure and a squaring of the shoulders—"I didn't tell him to go to the hospital. I told him to stay at home and do what he felt like," and here the youngster chuckled, " 'cause I knew darn well that was what he was goin' to do anyway, and I didn't want to spoil my record! When you got a position to hold you might as well look a little to keeping up your fences."

There was no reason that Jamie could see as to why he should not laugh, and anyway, he had done it before he knew it was coming. But it did not disconcert the small person; not a particle.

"*When* will they operate?"

The question upset Jamie. He slowly shook his head.

"I don't even know what his trouble is," he said.

"Neither do I," said the child. "I guess it's the only thing on earth that really hurt his heart that he didn't tell me about. He told me about all the things that hurt him and drove him from his home in the East, and about the little girl with gold hair that he had to give up in such a horrid way, and I've been all through the big carved mahogany chest and straightened all the papers and seen all the pictures in it. I know about how he loved Mary, and I know about the home he lost. I even know the secret that broke his heart, and I know all he can teach me about the bees."

The small person paused and dropped into a voice of absolute business impartiality.

"About bees, now. There's so much to learn that the men who write the books haven't found it all out yet, so, of course, the Bee Master couldn't teach it *all* to me. But I know all he could show me about the hives and about the bee bread and foul brood and about queens and nymphs and workers and drones and nurses. That about nurses is the sky-blue limit! You wouldn't hardly believe that a hive of bees would have nurses, now, would you?"

Thinking of recent experiences, Jamie said slowly: "Nurses are among the most wonderful things in the world, and I have heard that bees are very wonderful, so I think it's probable that they do have nurses."

"Right you are, Pat!" said the small person. "I can take you to any of these hives and open them up and show you maybe as many as forty thousand nurses taking care of the white nymphs."

And then, for the second time, Jamie faced the question: "Are you bee immune?"

And again Jamie answered: "I don't know. I've had no experience."

The small person chuckled appreciatively.

"Neither had I—until I got it. After I had stuck around from the first time I ever saw his white head and away back into his eyes until he said I might be his partner and help him with the bees, *I* hadn't had any experience, so I went back one morning, down along the east side over there, to see whether I was bee immune, and we always thought afterward that I made a mistake. My *scent* wasn't right."

Jamie bit his lip and swallowed hard because, as a matter of fact, the young person before him smelled more strongly of horse than of anything else, while dog ran a close second, and mingled with the odours of horse and dog there was a strong hint of Madonna lilies and onions. The combination played on Jamie's delicate sense of smell in a peculiar way. It was not so long since his eyes had been smarting with self-pity, yet at that particular minute he wanted to whoop. And there was no good reason at all why he should not. Without in the least understanding his mental processes, the small person proceeded gravely.

"My scent wasn't *right*. You know, a bee has got smell hollows instead of a nose. They are in two little tubes that stick out where a nose would be if it wasn't on a bee, and each one of the worker bees (which are the ones that do the business around a hive)—each one of the worker bees has got five thousand smell hollows. And a worker isn't a patchen to a male. A male's got thirty-seven thousand eight hundred smell hollows, so he'll be sure not to miss the scent of the queen when he goes out to love her up. So, if a male came near me, a fat chance I had, all gummed up with horse and dog. That was the whole trouble —my scent wasn't right. The Bee Master said it was too aggressive. I had been riding Queen and playing with Mom's dog, and when I get into a scuffle with Chum, half the time he's on top and half the time I am, and I was all smeared up with dog and horse and things like that, things a bee doesn't *like*. The Bee Master always said if he had used any judgment himself it wouldn't have happened. He always felt bad about it, but I didn't mind so much. It's a pretty good thing to know just edsactly what you are getting into; and then, if you think you can stand it, why, most likely you *can*. Anyway, I said I would go down before the hives in the east row the way the Bee Master went to fill the watering pans and to watch that there wasn't any robbing going on and to see if the queens were all happy and laying a few million eggs or so, and I went meandering along, and first thing I knew, out came a big working bee zooming right above my head, and behind it came two or three more, and they were between me and the Master, and I didn't want to cut through his flowers—he's just about as particular as anybody God ever made about flowers—and I didn't know edsactly how to get my chance to dust the home plate, 'cause I had only two eyes and each one of them had maybe six thousand on each side of its head.

"Then the Bee Master yells at me and he says: 'Zigzag!' And that was all right if he had a-said it in Spanish or French or something, but there wasn't any use in talking English before his bees, because they understood him just as well as I did! I tried hard enough to do what he told me, but whenever I'd zig, the darn bee would zig, too; and whenever I'd leap to one side and try to zag, the bee had zagged just a little bit before I had, and just naturally, workin' it that way, we interfered. Say, did a Black German ever zip you?"

Jamie's face went black for an instant, and then he looked at the eager little face in front of him and let the instant pass as he said quietly, "Not with the stinger of a bee. No. But I've had a few experiences with wasps and hornets out in the fields and woods when I was a boy. I get the general idea."

"I hardly think you do," said the small person. "I hardly think there's anything, in the stinging profession, wearing six legs, that's got quite such a sharp, long, ready-to-use stinger as a Black German bee. By gravy, they can ping you to the liver, and when about three of 'em takes you on the back of your neck and around the ears and into your arm muscles—oh, boy!"

Both hands clenched and then unclenched and were thrown outward in a wide-spreading sweep.

"When I got back to the Bee Master, I was shaking like I had a chill, and I bet enough of salt water was running down my face to make a good soup-spoonful of salt. Because the Bee Master says every bucket of water you take from the ocean is three and a half per cent salt, but I bet two bits I'm saltier 'an *that*. If I'd a-died I couldn't a-kept my salt water back. The Master said it was rotten, and he held me tight and rubbed off the stingers, 'cause that's the way you must; if you pull 'em it makes them worse. And then he turned the hose on a clayey place and mixed a cool poultice of mud and spread on the stings and he said he ought to be booted for lettin' me go 'mong the bees when I was all smelly of dogs and horses.

"So I wiped up my eyes and I said I reckoned that was the trouble. What I ought to a-done was to put on his old bee coat and rubbed some lilies on my head and some cinnamon pinks on my britches. So I went to the back porch and got his coat, and when I commenced putting it on he asked me what I was going to do. And I told him I was going to get my scent right and 'try, try again'. He just sat there looking at me, and I never saw his eyes get so big and black, and I never saw his face get whiter when the pain was hurting him the worst, and away back under his breath, so I could barely hear, he whispered, 'Before God, you wouldn't do it, little Scout?'

"And I said, 'God ain't got nothin' to do with this. It's between you and me, and I'm *going*!'

"And so I buttoned up the coat and I went down to the cinnamon pink bed and I just about rolled in it. I don't know but I treated the pinks rougher than the Master liked, but you'll understand if you ever get stung by a Black German why I was anxious to get plenty of cinnamon on. And then I smashed the sweetest lily I could find and I rubbed it all over my hair. And then I started down the east walk. I thought I'd try the Italian bees first. They're a lot decenter than the Germans. I ain't much of a whistler, but I whistled 'Highland Mary' the best I could, and I went along, soft and easy, and I ain't right sure but I carried the last lily in my hands, and keeping serene —around bees you just naturally got to keep serene; no rough stuff goes, but I wasn't oozin' certainly so's you could notice it— I stopped by the door of every last Italian and they never done a thing to me. So the Master *was* right. I took my medicine because my scent was wrong. So I rubbed up the lily a little when I headed for the Black Germans, and I went and stood in front of them and counted ten. Then I double dared 'em to come and sting me. They sort of fussed around a little and two of 'em came pretty close, but when they got the flowers strong, they went back again. Anyway, I faced 'em down. And when I went back to the Bee Master, he took me up in his arms and he said he wished to God he'd lived to see the day when his little Mary would've showed spirit like that, and he hugged me so tight he nearly cracked every bone in my body, and he gave me the first kiss I ever got off him. And I ain't had half a dozen since.

Believe you me, he's no necker! And he said that I could be his partner and help him about keeping the bees. Let me tell you, you'll get on your uppers and you'll do something worth while, you'll stir your think-tank posulutely to the bottom, before the Bee Master comes across! His coat's hanging on the back porch and there's flowers a-plenty here in the garden. Any time you want to find out how the bees feel about your soul, you can soon get it over with, includin' war tax. But, oh, boy, lemme tell you *this*! Before you go near the hives of the Black Germans, get your *scent* right!"

"But how do I get my scent right?" asked Jamie.

"Well, for one thing, I'll show you the right coat. Put that on and then go and stick your head in the cinnamon pinks and rub it all around like I did, and then take a Madonna lily and smash it and rub it all over your hands, and maybe you better go down by the water tap where there is a little spongy place and pull a handful of mint and rub that all over your britches. Whatever you do, don't *weaken*! You better whistle the right tune. Can you whistle, slow and easy, 'Highland Mary'? That's the one the bees like best. *Her* name was Mary. And if you can whistle it real soft and easy and lots of love, and lots of coaxin', and lots of lonesomeness, if you can work it up just right —you are about his height—the bees *might* not know the difference. Yes, I guess they would, too. You prodibly never heard of such eyes as bees have got. A worker after you has got six thousand eyes on each side of its head, and a male—'cause on account of the queen again, when she flies clear nearly to heaven, way above the birds and everything—a male has got thirteen thousand eyes on each side of its head. So you better believe, if one got roused up about you, he'd see that your head wasn't white. All the bees would miss the Bee Master's white head. It was always bare. And they'd miss his beard and his big, dark eyes. Ain't he wonderful?"

"Yes, I have an idea, from the few minutes I saw him and from his home and his library and his profession, yes, I've an idea that he is rather wonderful."

"He's just the only wonder of his kind," said the small person with the wide-spread downward gesture that was becoming familiar to Jamie.

Then the question came abruptly: "Was he *awful* sick?"

Jamie looked into the wide eyes of comprehension before him and thought of neither lie nor evasion.

"Yes," he said. "He was the sickest man I ever saw, and I've certainly seen some sick ones!"

"You can't tell me much about him," said the small person. "I've helped him up the back walk and to the davenport an' got the ammonia a few times when I didn't ever think I'd pull him through. I've seen him suffer until the sweat would run right down and drop off the tip of his nose, just a drop at a time, slow, and fall on his shirt front, splat, splat !—and I'll tell the world, it's pretty awful ! If he's sick like that again, maybe he'd better go on and die."

At the casual tone in which the suggestion was uttered, Jamie reeled back on the seat and stared hard at the impersonal face of the youngster before him. He had been under the impression that this child adored the Bee Master. At that minute he felt that he was facing a little pagan who did not adore anything, or even have a fair conception of what the word might mean. Yet there had been considerable conception of what the word might mean in the instructions as to how he was to whistle "Highland Mary", so Jamie, through narrowed eyes, looked steadily at the little Scout and then he said tentatively: "I thought you *liked* him."

"Liked him ?" said the little Scout. "Say, look here !"

Before Jamie's eyes was thrust a grimy right hand. Smash down like the blade of a knife came the left across the wrist. Slowly the fingers of the right hand opened and closed.

"I need *that* in my business," said the little Scout. "I couldn't ride Queen ; I couldn't be leader of the Scouts ; I couldn't paddle my canoe ; I couldn't be the Bee Master's partner without it, but if it would take that pain out of the Bee Master's side, I'd give it to him, just like *that* !"

The right hand was severed and discarded in mighty effective pantomime.

A great big lump rose up in Jamie's throat, threatening very nearly to choke him.

The small person stood on one foot and set the other on the bench, and clasped a pair of grimy hands around the bended knee and leaned towards Jamie.

"I guess you got me wrong," was the surmise that fell on his astounded ears. Then suddenly that position was relinquished and Jamie felt a small body beside him and a small head leaning precariously near the wound that made red stains on his breast, and one little abused hand lay down on one of his hands, and a small face was lifted to his, and a voice, low and mellow and exceedingly sweet of tone, said to Jamie softly: "Do you know how beautiful dying can be ?"

Perhaps that hit Jamie the hardest of all, because he had

not been contemplating death as a beautiful thing, and he had been contemplating it day and night for other men for more years than he liked to enumerate. In his own case, two was plenty. He could not speak, so he shook his head.

"Just like me," said the small person. "I didn't know anything at all about it, but Nannette did. Nannette's my big sister. She had the rottenest luck. At the lake where we went last summer, a man got drowned and next day Nannette was playing along the shore with some other kids and ran right into him just as they got him out of the water, and he had been in long a-plenty and the turtles hadn't done a thing to him. And she came home and mother said she had the hysterics, and she kept on havin' 'em in the night in her sleep till I got so I saw about what she'd seen. So not long ago, my mother's little old Aunt Beth went to heaven, and first mother said we couldn't go and say good-bye to her. She went in the night, you know, in her sleep, with her hands folded on her breast and the strangest little mysterious smile on her face. It was like she knew a beautiful secret that she'd love to tell, and she was smilin' over it while she decided whether she *would* tell or not. Dad said maybe it'd be a good thing to let us go. Maybe Nannette would see something that would make her feel better. Nannette didn't want to go, but after dad said that, mother made her. So we went after dinner when we had come home from school. Mother washed us up and put on our Sunday clothes and dad took us in the car, and right at the front door the beautiful part started.

"There was a big wreath that nearly covered the door and it began in little blue forget-me-nots and violets and heliotrope, and it ran into white hyacinths and gold hyacinths and blue ones, and there were sprays of lavender heather and white roses and pale pink roses, and at the bottom, where it was tied with lavender chiffon that hung clear to the porch door, the loveliest white lilies. I never saw anything that was so beautiful."

The small face lifted to Jamie's.

"Did you ever see anything as lovely as that?" he was asked.

Jamie shook his head.

"In the living-room, where, ever since I'd known her, Aunt Beth had sat in a wheel chair, it was just flowers everywhere. All our family sent them, and all the neighbours sent them, and her church sent them, and people we'd *never heard of* sent them, because everybody loved Aunt Beth. Mother said she was the biggest little liar in the whole world. Days when you could see she was twisty with pain, she'd look you straight in the eye and say she was better. She was always better. And she had the funniest house. You never went to it that from somewhere she couldn't pull out a cooky with candy on it, or red peppermint sticks, and she always had the best raisins. My, you never tasted such raisins as she always had! Or sometimes popcorn, or doughnuts, and the last time I had been there, the spiciest gingerbread—it smelled like the geography of India sounds!

"We went back into Aunt Beth's bedroom, and over her bed there was a lavender satin spread, and she was lying upon her pillow and her hair was soft and wavy—she had a big roll of hair and it was bright brown. She was eighty-seven and you couldn't hardly find a grey hair on her head. It was in soft, silky coils and it waved so pretty.

"And death had gone and magicked her. There wasn't a line in her face, and her throat was round, and her lips were smiley. My, she was the prettiest thing! And her dress was like it was cut from soft grey clouds, and the sleeves and down the front was all cobwebby lace, and at her wrists it tied in perky little bows.

"Nannette stood and looked at her and she kept creepin' closer to her and she looked and she looked, and then she grabbed me and she said, 'My, I thought she'd be like the man I saw!'

"And then dad and all of us found out for the first time that Nannette thought *all* the dead people everywhere looked like the man that had been in the water among the turtles and everything; and I'll tell you, we were glad then that we'd brought Nannette to see Aunt Beth! She was so pretty—Nannette wanted to untie the ribbons in her sleeves and fix 'em the way she wanted 'em, and that made me want to do something for her, and so I asked what I might do, and they said that I might put her slippers on her. They turned back the lacy spread with the lavender lining that covered her, and I got to put on her feet her little grey slippers with white fur on 'em. They were the prettiest little things! And then I fixed her skirts, her grey satin petty, and her lacy dress; and Nannette fixed her sleeves and we covered her up and kissed her good-bye, and we came away and you can't scare *us* with being dead any more!

"Nannette hasn't jumped in the night since, not once. We know now that there are several kinds of being dead. There's the kind where you've had a bad heart and you haven't told true and you've taken things that didn't belong to you, and you haven't played the game square with God, and you haven't had any respect for your Government, and, of course, you ain't goin' to look very well whether you're dead or alive if you've got things like that inside you. And then, added to that, there's accidents that might happen to anybody—lyin' in the water a long time and turtles is one thing, or bein' burned in a fire or blown up in a factory. That's your hard luck. But if you get to die at home, just to go to sleep softly in your own bed in the night, so softly that you never lift your hands off your breast, and when you see God a little sweet smile creeps over your face . . . Gee! I bet God and all the angels were tickled to pieces to see Aunt Beth when she came walkin' in all slender and straight and young in her softy cloud dress! Nannette put forget-me-nots and Parma violets and heliotrope in her hands when she got her sleeves tied right. If she still carried them when she got to heaven, all around her would be smelly with flowers. None of us *wanted* her to go. We all liked to take care of her. We all liked to take her fruits and flowers and books and papers. Every one of us saved every funny story we found to tell her, but at that we were all kind of *glad* when she went, 'cause her bones must have hurt her, and she couldn't have told true when she always said she was better, because she *had* to give up and have the doctor sometimes, bad as she hated it."

The little Scout stood up with outflung hands in a gesture of finality.

"After I've told you *that,* you can see how the Bee Master might look if God decided that he should go to sleep in the night, and there wouldn't be any more pain in his side or any more sweat drippin' off his nose. I bet all the harps and all the trumpets in heaven would go 'Zoom! Zoom!' and all the angels would come flocking if the Bee Master went through the gates! I bet God Himself would stand up when the Bee Master came up so straight and tall to salute Him, because some time, somewhere, he'd been in a war. He's got a bully uniform and he can pull off the snappiest salutes! He's been a soldier and I bet you've been a soldier, too, 'cause you look a soldier and you move like a soldier, and I think it's punk that you ain't got your uniform on. I just love uniforms!"

And then Jamie's mouth fell open and his eyes widened. A cautioning hand was thrust backward toward him. A sibilant hiss that was intended for a warning to silence struck his ears. Leaning forward, softly, a step at a time, one hand thrust outward for balance, one thrust back for caution, the little Scout crept in a crouching attitude down the walk, eyes fixed straight ahead. Leaning over to get the alignment, Jamie saw a big bumble bee clambering over the entrance petal to the horn of a trumpet flower. He saw the little Scout measure off a certain distance, crouch, and then quick, quicker almost than he could sense what was happening, a stream of saliva shot straight and hit the bee, knocking it off its moorings. The little Scout sprang into the air and uttered a whoop that would have startled an Apache on the warpath. Wildly whirling and shouting, with beating hands, the child, in a shrill, boyish voice, cried, "Hit him? By Golly! I hit him! Knocked him ping!"

Then, turning, the small figure made a rush towards Jamie and a hand gripped each of his knees.

"Say, if I bring Fat Ole Bill and the Nice Child and Angel Face, will you tell 'em? Will you say I did it? We got a bet. I'm two bits to the good. I'll lick the hide off 'em if they don't take my word, but I could put up a heap bigger swank if you'd tell 'em you saw me."

Jamie finally got his mouth arranged in a position in which it would speak recognizable English.

Then he said: "Surely! Any day you want me to, I'll meet your pals and I'll testify that fairly and squarely you hit the bee."

"I've been practising on that for a week," boasted the small person proudly. "I've been trying, and I bet a quarter that I'd do it, and two bits is some bet, lemme tell you! There's lots of things you can do with two bits!"

Jamie thought of times when he had contemplated less than two bits in an open palm during the past few days, and admitted the truth of the assertion. Talking of money evidently started a new train of thought. With inquiring eyes the youngster studied him.

"Will you go to the hospital to see the Bee Master any time soon?"

"I'm waiting for a telephone call," said Jamie. "Doctor Grayson told me that he would call and report progress, and as soon as the Master is able to see me, of course I'll go."

The little Scout dipped in a breeches pocket and brought to light a handful of numerous things, and from strings and buttons and buckles and pebbles, with the left hand, selected a dime and two nickels and held them over to Jamie.

"When you go, will you stop at the nearest lunch counter and get a hot dog and a bottle of strawberry pop for him and give 'em to him from me with a tight hug and a kiss?"

Jamie accepted the money with a sober face.

"Surely," he said enthusiastically.

"I'll give you the kiss for him right now," said the small person, and without any preliminaries Jamie had pasted fairly on his lips the hardest, hottest, sweetest little kiss of all his experience. He found his hands on the shoulders of the small person and his eyes intent on the face.

"Look here!" he said. "Are you a girl or a boy?"

The small person, with a deft twist, slipped through his fingers like shifting sand and took a step or two backward.

"If you can't *tell*, it doesn't make a darn bit of difference, does it?"

And Jamie was constrained to admit that it did not.

"I guess I'd better be goin'," said the little Scout. "I wish you'd get on the job with that hot dog im*press*ive. The Master likes 'em with the bun toasted and the boiled wienie split and fried and striped with a line of mustard and a thick slather of fried onions on and a slice of dill pickle. Can you remember that? Is that the way *you* like 'em?"

"Love o' Mike!" said Jamie, licking his lips. "I haven't had one in ages! Sure I can remember!"

"Then that's that!" said the small person. "Do you feel like you're *sure* goin' to get on the job and you're *sure* goin' to take care of things here?"

"The level best I can," said Jamie. "But I'll have to tell you as I told your partner, I don't know the first thing about bees."

"And you don't look chipper enough," said the small person, "to coast down the east side and climb up the west side of two acres of bees. You sit still and I'll go see if they are all right myself."

So Jamie sat under the jacqueranda and waited while the little Scout went down the east side, carefully inspecting every hive of bees, and returned with the report that the water pans were all right, the queens were all laying eggs, the workers were all busy, the drones were droning, like the disagreeable, mussy things they were. There was not any foul brood, and there were no robbers at work.

"Just common, honest bees," said the small person, "working hard to gather up all the honey they can find in the flower gardens where the Sierra Madres smash through the Santa Monicas right into the sea."

The small party insisted on leading Jamie into the house and showing him the library of bee books. All the volumes that could be read with profit to find out how to take care of the bees were pointed out, and then a light finger ran over volumes on a shelf by themselves with the comment: "Now *these* are the funny ones."

A small blue volume which opened of itself was selected,

and from it an amused voice read, " 'There are several kinds of bees; the best are small, round and va-ri-e-gated.' Can you beat it?" asked the youngster.

Jamie, glancing over the little Scout's shoulder, caught "Aristotle" on the title page and had perhaps his hundredth shock for the afternoon. After the volume was closed and set back on the shelf, the child turned towards him: "And Pliny says that when bees cross the Mediterranean in migration they each one get a little pebble and carry it with their feet to make them heavy enough that the wind won't blow them away!" And a laugh that was clear and silvery broke on Jamie's ears. "Ain't that the bunk? You ought to hear the Bee Master laugh when he reads Pliny on bees! And there are a lot more of them that are just as funny, but these are not funny at all. These are mostly what you need to know to get really interested."

The small finger ran across Lubbock and Swammerdam with the remark, in passing, "He has got wonderful pictures of how bees are inside," and paused on Huber. "You'll want to read Huber," the little Scout said. "He was blind, but he thought out all the experiments and made all the investigations, and a man with eyes kept the records. He's wonderful, too. His book is named *New Observations on Bees*. Pretty good for a blind man, *I'll* say. You know, being a bee master is a lot of other things beside just bees."

The explanation was offered offhand, gratuitously.

"It's being outdoors most of the time. It's flowers and what flowers bees like best. It's a case of quick eyes and a steady hand, and *I'd* say you'd got to be decent. You'd better be certain you're hitting on all your cylinders before you go around bees. The Bee Master says that bees *know*, and if anybody's a liar and a cheat and got the odours of sin and selfishness hangin' around 'em—tell it to papa! The bees know it like a shot, if you're mean; and they haven't got a bit of mercy. The minute they get a whiff of what you are, they punksher your tyre. If you know, away down deep inside you, that you ain't right, and that God wouldn't let you into heaven if you went to sleep in the night, you better throw up this job and let me hunt somebody else to look after the bees."

Jamie stood very straight. He emptied his pocket of his distinguished-service decorations and lowered them to the eyes of the small person.

"In so far as I know," he said quite seriously, "there is no reason why the bees should dislike any odours that might emanante from my exterior or even from the most secret places of my soul."

"Well, then, that's all to the good," said the small person. "You just look to me sometimes as if you wasn't sure whether you was going to stay or whether you was going on."

"I'll admit," said Jamie, "that is has been difficult for me to decide whether I'd stay or whether I'd go on, but if you will help me, I think it would be better for me at least to try what I can do."

Jamie stood still and watched the small person go down the walk toward the fence which had afforded the means of entrance. Poised on the top of it and in the act of swinging over, there came clear to his ears the admonition: "Better stick around, bo! You'll *like* it!"

CHAPTER VI

"GOOD MASTER, WHAT SHALL I DO?"

FOR an hour after the departure of the Bee Master's partner, to whom the Master had so tenderly referred as the "little Scout", James MacFarlane sat and stared at the whitewashed panel of fence over which the child had disappeared. First a whimsical smile played over his features as he recalled the straightforward humour, the businesslike attitude, the flashes of tenderness, and the ruthless acceptance of facts following one another so rapidly in the mentality of the youngster. Then he seriously pondered, for a few minutes, on whether this peculiar small person really was a boy or really was a girl. The only definite conclusion he arrived at was that sometimes *he* was a boy and sometimes *she* was a girl.

His mind travelled on to the thing that was always foremost. What was it the youngster had said about death? That there were several ways? What he had been facing for the past two years was death, and the pitiful thing about it for him was that he had never faced it so imminently nor so surely as at that minute. His aching bones reminded him of his weakness every time he moved. His swollen feet cried out whenever he bore his weight on them, and as for the burning in his left side, he had carried it around with him for so long that it was almost like an incurable heartache or a mental strain from which one never found surcease. Jamie felt reasonably sure that he could eliminate the death by water, fire, and explosion. He did not feel that any of these things were likely to happen to him. So there were the two remaining kinds of death; he must face one or the other.

That carried his mind back to the time when as a little boy he had said his prayers indiscriminately at the knees of either his mother or his father, for his father had been woman-tender with his only child. There had been a period of years when he had knelt beside his bed and repeated what he had been taught with some additions of his own. There had been still later years when he had got into bed and muttered a makeshift prayer. And then there had been another stretch of years when, in the pride of his strength and the diverse interests of the full day, he had been so sufficient in his own body and his own mentality to any need that assailed him that he not only had not prayed a prayer of asking—because he was getting along very well without asking for anything—but he had not offered a prayer of thanksgiving. And as he sat there that afternoon, looking over the blue garden that was merely a small mountain running down to the sea, studying the beauty of the flowers, the foliage and the fruit, and then looking on to the white reaches of sand and the blue of the ocean and the sky stretching away half-way round the world, he was assailed by a distinct sorrow, a feeling of regret that he had ever ceased his nightly prayer. If his arms had been strong and his brain had been sufficient, if he had not needed to ask physical help, he might have asked that his mind would be kept from the very thing that had happened, and there was always the prayer of thanksgiving. Since the mists had cleared in the beginning and the sun had shone through and coaxed the earth to foliage and fruit, and animals and man had evolved after the ordained scheme of things, there always had existed in some degree the same exquisite beauty that lay before him now. There always had been in the breast of every man born to enjoy it a heart which should have rejoiced and should have given thanks for such a heritage. There always had been lips that should have spoken up and told the Creator how wonderful was the mystery of the earth and the majesty of the sea and the beneficence of the sunshine and the healing hours of moonlit darkness. There always had been the duty his father bravely had assumed, to acknowledge his obligations, to point the way to other men less sensitive to the call of God and Nature.

Jamie fell to wondering about how he was going to make the kind of death that the little Scout had played with and kissed and rejoiced in, had thought lovely, become a reality for himself. As he remembered what the child had said, Jamie was devoutly thankful that whatever his mistakes might have been, whatever his errors, whatever sins he had committed, he had not wronged his fellow men, he had not soiled and disgraced any innocent women, he had not lied and cheated and smirched his soul in trickery and unfair business dealings. He had intended when he left college to study forestry. He had meant to be a tree man. Always he had loved the woods, the fields, the flowers; but to him a tree had been a living thing, a thing with feelings, a thing with feet in the earth and a head in the sky and widely reaching arms of beneficence that gave either shade or fruit or the pleasure of flowers for the benefit of the world. He had meant to go to the greatest doctor of trees and, under his guidance and instruction, take a thorough course in tree surgery; then he had meant to begin the great work of saving every possible tree now in existence.

He reflected that working as a bee master was not so bad. Always he could do what he might for the trees, and at the same time a world of flowers were necessary to furnish a sweet that from the dawn of history had delighted man, had been medicinal, healing. A noticeable factor in the wealth of the world was the work that the humming gauze wings swarming up and down the garden before him were carrying on. If a man were going to live; if he had the chance to remain for any length of time in a place like that; if he could learn the profession without expensive tuition, without lengthy apprenticeship, it might be a quicker way to a livelihood, and it might be as pleasant and more interesting. There was a possibility that the volumes on the shelves above the Bee Master's writing-desk might contain information that would make a living bee, capable of what seemed remarkably near to thought and preconcerted action, quite as interesting as an immovable tree, which certainly could not be imbued with mental processes even by a far stretch of the imagination.

Just when Jamie had decided that, in the event the Bee Master came home from the hospital weakened and incapacitated and approved of the manner in which he had cared for his home and watered the garden and the trees, had taken care of the bees, merely in case he should make himself useful and interesting and should be asked to stay—just when he had resolved that he would find out for himself whether the prophecy that by "sticking around" he would like it in the garden of the Bee Master—up popped the old black thought: How much time are you going to have in which to like it? How long will you, trying to do something for the Bee Master, resemble the case of the blind leading the blind? If he were not going to be sufficiently well, if he were not going to be sufficiently strong, if in a few months humming bees and chirping crickets, singing birds and running waters, the blue of the garden and the sea and sky were to be over for him, what was the use?

Down below he could see where towers and mountains of rocks had been gnawed and eaten by high tides and smashing waves. Why should not he, when the Master came home and the trust he had assumed was over, why should not he just accidentally step off one of those frowning crags and go down in an undertow that might carry him to China for all he knew?

And then in a flash vivid before him came the mental picture that the little Scout had conjured up when he had told so casually about the drowned man and the turtles—sharks it would probably be that would worry his lean carcass. The smile was rather gruesome that twisted Jamie's face when he reflected that his sharks would not find much nourishment in bone and muscle. Then he carried the thought a trifle farther and reflected that the muscle would likely be fairly tender. He might make a mouthful for something.

Then up, big and bright, before his eyes popped that childish enumeration of the kinds of death, and the description of the little old lady who had lain on the spread of lavender-satin covered with delicate lace, the beloved lady who softly and gently had gone to sleep in the night without even lifting her folded hands and who carried to her grave a look on her face that the little Scout had described as "a smiling secret". There was in this child the paganism, the frankness, the cruelty of childhood. (What was it La Fontaine had said about children? That all of them were brutally frank, brutally cruel?) Large streaks of cruelty had been discernible in the little Scout, but not so large as the streaks of generosity, of tenderness, of the love of fair dealing. Jamie could see the grimy palm in which buttons and strings and sinkers and corks and buckles were pushed around to find the coins that went to pay for a treat for the Master.

Then, too, there had been in the back of the head of the little Scout the penetration to fathom the look on the face of the sleeping woman. Jamie reflected that if he purposely went down to the crags of the Pacific and threw himself to the sharks, when he came before God and his father and mother, he could carry no smiling secret on his face. He would not have kept the faith. He would have broken the laws of God and man. He would have allowed frail women to surpass him in courage, in endurance. He shut his eyes to close out even the imagined look on his mother's face. So right there Jamie crossed off the Pacific from his scheme of release, and he registered a solemn oath in his breast that no matter what happened, no matter if he again came to the fortunes of the road, to the callous indifference that so many wayfarers encountered, no matter what, anything at all that the most imaginative could think of, he would not take the chance of facing the Creator with a craven soul. He swore by all that he ever had loved and reverenced that he would try, try with all his might in the short time that might remain to him, to master the secret that had given birth to the smile, and that whatever of good he might be able to do for the Bee Master or for anyone he encountered in the time he had left, so far as he possibly could, he would forget himself, he would put his own pa and chagrin and disappointment, his own feeling of defeat and uselessness, his own craving for love and intellectual companionship in the background, and he would see if the more than six feet of bone and muscle that contained his being could do any small service that might come his way for God and his fellow man before he went. Maybe if he could accomplish some little thing, something that would ease the ache of even one heart that ached as his was aching at that minute, just maybe that knowledge would be the secret that he might carry in his breast, that would set the stamp of an indelible smile on his face so that even a child could discern the majesty of the impulse and he would not be ashamed when the end came.

Then he arose and resolutely, though painfully, hobbled down the long stretch of the curving and irregular mountain stairway until he reached the gate. There he sat down and looked the length of the remaining steps and up and down the coast. On his left hand, not so far down, he discovered the most attractive young mountain of stone. It stood boldly, proudly, with defying arrogance, in the edge of the Pacific Ocean, and there seemed to be a way by which one might climb it at the back. Jamie imagined that somewhere on the top of it there might be a grooved space where one could sit and look to the north and the west and the south, across the measureless miles of sea face, into illimitable space of sky country, into the starry orchards of heaven. He wondered if any king had ever ruled from a throne like that, and he decided that none ever had. He decided that he would set that spot as his goal. To-day he would go no farther, because he had learned that going down a mountain is far easier than climbing it. But to-morrow he would open the gate, and he would go to the exact spot where the trumpets of the tolúache and the exquisite lavender beds of a dainty creeping flower that was sand verbena—Jamie had never heard of sand verbena, but he had very sensitive nostrils, and at that hour of the evening he could pick up an exquisite perfume, and he watched a few late bees journeying back and forth to the delicate beds of colour—just at the line where the pinkish lavender of the verbena and the gold of the beach primroses opened to the sun; he would go that far the coming day. And the following he would march right straight ahead until he attained the crest of the dauntless rock.

To reach it he must pass a long stretch of breaking waves, each of which seemed to say to him: "I dare you! I dare you to come on!" Jamie sat there and contemplated his feet and thought of their swollen and aching condition, and a great longing assailed him to thrust them into the cold salt water of the ocean. Once he half started to rise, and then the thought came to him that if he became chilled, if he took a heavy cold, if he developed a cough . . . Jamie laid his hand on his left breast and sat still. That would mean the end very speedily, and if it were a possible thing he intended to fight until the Bee Master came home and relieved him of the trust that he had assumed when he had agreed to remain with the bees. But the longing, the desire to step into the cold salt water had been awakened.

When he heard his call to supper, he started slowly, painfully, up the winding stairway. Every few steps he paused and turned to look at the lazy waves creeping up the sand and rolling back again, and he said to himself that, as sure as there was light in the sky, one of these days he would go down there and he would put at least his feet in the ocean; he would climb that mountain of rock and he would sit on a high peak as far into the night as he chose. He would watch the Pacific Ocean when the moon was threading it with a million silver pathways. Some time there might possibly be a storm. There might be waves that would lash almost to the top of that towering mountain of stone; thunders might crash and lightning might dart in forked tongues and the waves might go mad and do their worst in unchecked frenzy. Then he would make a point of being on the top of that rock, and he would watch that storm of the elements and see how nearly it resembled a storm that for a long time had been raging in his heart and in his mind. It would be something to think about, something to work for, a definite objective in view merely to reach that lofty rock crest.

He climbed a few steps farther and paused again to study the face of the sea and the towering crest that in his own mind he named the throne. It was a throne, a place for a man to captain his own soul. A man would be a monarch of all he could survey even for a short time on that crest, and it was better to be a monarch even for an hour than never to have had a kingly aspiration.

So Jamie went to the supper that Margaret Cameron had

prepared for him, and because that climb had wearied him so, because his feet were throbbing almost unendurably from the long, unaccustomed march to which he had forced them, he decided that he was not so well as he had been when he left the hospital. And right there he made a large mistake. His body might have been tried to such an extent that it was not so well, but his heart and brain had been given some exercise that was decidedly beneficial.

While he ate his supper, Margaret Cameron went through the rooms, touching a curtain here and there, wiping a speck of dust from the wonderful pieces of old furniture, searching with jealous eyes to see if the stranger were doing any damage to the property of a neighbour whom she had learned, through the years, not only to respect but to cherish with a devotion that was deep and lasting.

Presently she came from the living-room and dropped abruptly to a chair beside the table at which Jamie was eating his supper.

"You know," she said, "I've had about all I can stand to-day. I'm worried over matters of my own. I've only one child and she has always been a good girl. She did her school work well and her training course, and she hadn't any difficulty in getting a school when she wanted it, but I can't see why she was bent on going so far from home when she might have had a position here where she could have stayed with me. Maybe she was tired of the little house and the exacting old woman always scouring and cleaning, always fussing about how the young people are going to ruin. I'm not sure that I didn't drive her away, and I am sure that her Cousin Molly coaxed her away. I'm not sure that there is any sense in the idea that the present generation is going to ruin. My mother thought exactly the same thing about the girls of my day. When I wanted to go with the boy I married to a barn dance or a corn husking or on horseback to a picnic or a rally, she thought surely we were doing something that youngsters had never done before, and that perdition was yawning wide for us. Maybe it was, for all I know. Anyway, I'm unhappy about Lolly. She seemed to me to have something on her mind that she wouldn't tell me, and that isn't all.

"I am free to admit that if the Bee Master doesn't survive this operation and come back to his home and his neighbours, the rest of this world is going to be decidedly tasteless to me. We've lived here, side by side, for a good many years. I've come over and helped him fix up his place, and he's been over and helped me fix up mine, and when the young folks would go away in the evening and the time dragged, he'd come over and we'd play cribbage or checkers. I never had brains enough to play chess so it would interest him. Sometimes I'd come over here and he'd sit there by the fire and read aloud from some of those fine old books." She paused and looked at Jamie. "Are you familiar," she asked, "with Donne's *Devotions* ?"

Jamie nodded.

"They were in my father's library," he said, "but nobody even thought to save his books for me. He died while I was in the war, and mother had gone not long before, and they sold everything; not even a scrap of clothing or furniture did any of the neighbours save for me. Donne's *Devotions* went with the rest. I don't know where, and I was too sick to search, and I hadn't the money. I had to stay where the Government would care for me. But I can see what it would mean to see the Bee Master with a tinge of firelight on his fine old face and John Donne in his lean fingers."

Slowly Margaret Cameron nodded.

"Yes," she said, half breathlessly, "yes, it was a wonderful picture he made. Never in all my life have I seen even a painting of a man so physically and spiritually beautiful as the Bee Master. I hope when he comes back that you will stay until you learn the fineness of his spirit. It would be a help to you all the rest of your days only to learn how gentle and tender and fine a man like Michael Worthington can be. The papers to-day are so full of what men are that they should not be. I wish every young man in the whole world could live a year with a man like the Bee Master in order to learn his patience and his forbearance, his breadth of view, his loving outlook on life, and his fearlessness concerning the hereafter."

"Then, why," asked Jamie, "did he fight the operation so?"

A dingy flush of red crept up into Margaret Cameron's cheek.

"Well, for one thing," she said, "he came here with a broken heart. He never has talked to me in detail, but I have started over here on two occasions when he was talking to the little Scout, and I think that child knows who it was or what it was that broke his heart. I think that kiddy knows what he fled from when he came here alone with only furnishings for his library and his bedroom. There is a picture in his bedroom, probably his wife. I asked him once about her and he said that she had been dead for many years and that he had lost, too, her child, whom he adored. But there was something more than that. Death isn't insurmountable if it's accompanied by hope, and the face of the woman who hangs in the Bee Master's bedroom might very well stand for a typical portrayal of hope, of purity, of steadfast courage—almost any fine quality that any woman could have. He had lost her, he had lost her child: I feel sure he had lost his home and friends. I think he deliberately went to the end of his tether, and when he could go no farther he fell and left his case in the hands of the good Lord."

So they talked on until dusk. When the remnants of his supper were packed in the small basket and Margaret Cameron went home, she invited Jamie to come over at any time he was lonely, and she promised to help him with the morning work until she was sure that he had learned to do the watering right, because the lilies must not have enough water to rot the bulbs, and the roses must not start mildew, and the palms must be just dry enough, and the acacias just wet enough. Jamie felt, by the time she had finished enumerating the reasons as to why she should come, that there certainly was necessity for her presence when he began operations.

Then he went into the living-room and, because his blood was full of poison and circulating slowly, he scratched a match and lighted the fire that was laid on the hearth. He looked at the chair that stood beside it for a long time, a high-backed chair with wide arm-rests, a chair of invitation. Without even closing his eyes he could see the silken hair and beard and the white forehead and the beautiful eyes of the grand old man whose spirit was the master of the bees and the master of the house and the master of his soul, and something in Jamie that was part of the thing that made him what he was refused to take the Master's chair. He pushed it back to one side and selected another that he thought would fit his long frame very nearly as well. Then he opened the case above the writing-desk and picked down one of the volumes that the little Scout had pointed out to him. It fell open of its own volition at one page, and the first paragraph that Jamie's eyes rested on read: "There are two kinds of rulers among bees—if there are too many rulers they perish, for thus they become distracted. The olives and the swarms of bees multiply at the same time. They begin by making comb, in which they place their progeny. The comb is deposited with their mouths, as those say who affirm that they collect it from external sources. Wax is made from flowers. They bring the material of wax from the dropping of trees, but the honey falls from the air, principally about the rising of the stars and when the rainbow rests upon the earth."

When Jamie read that paragraph his shoulders shook

with a dry chuckle. He paused and began communing with the fire.

"Left on this job to keep the bees," he said, "what I should do is to go over there into the working library and select a volume of instructions for beginners and find out for myself about a few of those things the little Scout mentioned—how to tell a queen from a worker, a drone from a nurse. I think I'd feel mentally brilliant if I could look at a bee climbing over a rose and tell whether it was a working bee or a nurse. I wonder if the little Scout knows those things?"

Jamie looked at the fire.

"I shouldn't be surprised a particle," he said. "I can see that what I should do is to get the practical part of the bee business first and read the romance afterward, but, by my cross-bow and halberd, I swear this romance of the bees is entrancing reading!"

Jamie drew the lamp closer and threw another oak knot on the fire and slouched to comfort in the chair and read on until he found his eyes were tiring and the fire was low, and then he went to bed.

When he awoke the following morning from a long, sound sleep and managed his bath and the straps that bound the bandages on his chest over his shoulders and around his back to hold his dressings in place, he had made a distinct step forward because he was not thinking about the wound or how soon it would finish him. He was thinking about whether the little Scout would come again that day; about whether, after he finished the work he must do, he would have strength left to carry him to the lavender-and-yellow boundary of the beach; about honey that rained from heaven so very obligingly for the bees of ancient times to gather it up and fill it into cells. He was thinking about almost anything, except himself, and that was one of the best things that had happened to him in two long years.

That day, when the watering was over and he had taken a nap after lunch, he made the journey that he had contemplated and sat on the hot sands, and he was so intrigued with the evening perfume of the little lavender flowers that grew there, so charmed with the beauty of the gold, that he decided that he would hunt through the Bee Master's books and see if he could find a book on flowers that would tell him what these strange and beautiful things were. And as from the higher point of vantage he looked with longing eyes toward the clean, cold water of the sea and toward the stretch that lay between him and the throne, he decided that possibly in a week he could make it that far, because his feet were feeling much better, after the night of rest, after long application of water, and his muscles were not so stiff and his bones were not aching so intolerably.

That evening at six the telephone rang and Doctor Grayson reported that the operation was over, the Bee Master was back in his own room, and was conscious. Almost his first question had been whether there was any message for him concerning the bees, and the Doctor had told him that everything was fine, but if there was any special report that he could make for the morning dressing it might help. So Jamie reiterated the statement that everything was fine and added particulars as to the watering and inquired when he might see the Bee Master.

Doctor Grayson had replied: "He doesn't realize how precarious his condition is or how weak he is; but I should think that in a week of ten days you might come for your first visit. In the meantime, I will call you and give you a report each evening, to let you know how he is, and I would be interested in knowing how you are feeling yourself."

Jamie hesitated over that. He did not know exactly what to say. But before he had time to say anything, the Doctor continued: "There was no time when the life of the Bee Master was in jeopardy to give you any attention; but you look to me like one of our boys who was carrying a pretty serious problem somewhere in his anatomy, and I had my doubts as to whether you were equal to the job you were undertaking. Any time you would like to come in and let me look you over—get a pencil and I'll give you instructions how to reach the hospital, if you are a stranger in these parts."

So Jamie said he was a stranger, and he would very much like to have the location of the hospital, and when he came to see the Master, if the Doctor would be kind enough to keep that offer open, that would be famous.

So another day and then another went by, and each day Jamie finished watering the flowers and the fruits and mixing the drink for the bees and his inspection of the hives slightly earlier. He had followed the little Scout's advice. When he went among the bees he had donned the coat worn by the Bee Master and he had rubbed Madonna lily over his hands and hair and made himself intimately familiar with the cinnamon pink bed. There was a question in his mind, from what the child had said, as to whether the sensitive organs of the bee might detect a faint odour of the dressings he wore and resent it as unfamiliar, but nothing of the kind had happened. He had been so near the Bee Master's height and form ; he had worn the familiar coat ; he had practised frequently on "Highland Mary," and the bees paid no attention whatever to him in so far as he had given them a chance. The isolated hives of the Black Germans he kept away from. Down in the depths of his soul he had a feeling that if he got near a hive of anything that was named Black German, he would very likely muster what remaining strength he had and kick it into the middle of the Pacific regardless of what might happen by way of retaliation.

When he hung the coat on the hook on which he had found it, his fingers struck something rough and warm which on examination proved to be a bathing-suit of wool, a warm, heavy suit. Jamie took if down and fingered it eagerly and then he walked to the back porch and looked out over the blue waters of the sea. He held the bathing-suit up to his shoulders and drew it around him, and wondered whether it would cover the bandages and what would happen if the dressings were soaked with salt water.

He was afraid that would not do, so he turned back regretfully and slowly hung the woollen bathing-suit, not where it had been, but on the first hook nearest the casing of the back door, hung it right up prominently where he must see it each time he went in and out that door, and every time he saw it he stood and looked at it, and in a few days more he decided that it would not be a bad idea to put it on and go with bared feet down on the hot sands. There would be no chill about that during the heat of the day, and then he might walk where the little waves were breaking enough to wet his feet, merely to feel the joy that he imagined he would experience in having those cold, salty waves creep up and run over them. He could go back to the warm sand and dry them rapidly, and why might not a process like that stimulate circulation ? Why would not the hot sand draw the sluggish poisoned blood in his veins to his feet ? Why would not the cold salt water drive it back ? Why would not the stimulation thus gained help to throw off the poison bred by the wound in his breast ?

So, through the warm golden days, Jamie kept his trust with the Bee Master the level best he could, with the help of Margaret Cameron, and his mind had as much exercise as his body. Much sooner than he had expected he reached the foot of the throne. The climb was not bad at all and he did find, around on the side of the huge rock facing the sea, a long gash that made a wonderful seat, a seat that fitted the curves of his body, a seat that, when upholstered with the Bee Master's old working overcoat, would be wonderful to slouch in, to rest, to soak in the sun, to breathe in the salt from west of the crest.

He had not reached the point where he had definitely decided that he would fight. His mind was merely stirred with suggestions, conjectures, possibilities. If anyone had asked him, who had the right to ask, and had been given a frank answer, Jamie would have said that six months, without any doubt whatever, would be the length of his tenure. A year of the best treatment the Government could give him had left him worse. He thought about six months would see the finish. Sometimes he was considerably disquieted because the call for him to visit the hospital had not come. Each night at six o'clock he answered the telephone and heard that the Bee Master was barely holding his own. He was not yet able to converse or be bothered about business.

Each time he received one of these reports, he called the little Scout at the number that had been given him and passed the report on. Twice the little Scout had been in the garden for a short visit after school hours. Each time Jamie parted with his new friend with deeper regret. Each time he had seen some new emanation of the mentality of the youngster that had surprised, sometimes shocked, sometimes delighted him, and as for the question of sex, he was not a bit nearer the solution than he had been the first day.

After supper on the ninth day, for the second time Jamie made his way the length of the back wall, across the beach, and climbed to the throne. He was armed with a broad-brimmed old slouch hat and the old overcoat. He climbed the throne and settled in an especial seat of his own that he had managed with considerable work and more strength than he had known he could muster. He had collected some broken pieces of rock and fitted them in differently and farther to the left; then there had been an accessible seat. Wrapped in the overcoat, he dropped on the seat and faced the eternal verities of sky and sea. No land was intruding. It was the bowl of the sky closing down: the smooth wash of the sea rolling in; and away in the distance a faint red glow marked the spot where the sun threw its light on a world that was steadily turning from it.

There Jamie did some more thinking. He was having plenty of mental exercise in those days. He still thought Death, but at least he had a manlier thought of facing it. And when he thought Life, he did not think of himself, or upbraid his Government, or pity other wounded men. He thought merely of that one thing he might possibly do and what it might possibly be that would give him some justification, when he faced his Maker, for the spending of his latter days.

CHAPTER VII

THE STORM WOMAN

THE new day was one of fog and of stillness and then a cold wind that Jamie did not care to face. Just at evening, when he looked from the back veranda and down across the stretch before him, he realized that the thing he had wanted to see was going to happen. There were heat flashes across the horizon. Forked tongues of light were beginning to flicker up and there was an ominous stillness, and away up to the north and west he could see big black clouds beginning to mass and to gather.

Jamie straightened up. "A storm!" he said to himself. "The storm! By all that's good and peaceful, I'll see it from the throne if it's the last thing that I ever do!"

He looked over the garden, putting away several things that high wind might damage; he carefully closed the windows and locked the doors, and then he went into the closet on the back porch and ransacked the Bee Master's belongings for suitable clothing. He laid out the bee coat and the old overcoat, and then he found a heavy raincoat that was precisely what he wanted.

He put the bee coat on, and carrying the overcoat and the raincoat and wearing the old broad-brimmed hat, he locked the back door behind him and slowly made his way down the back walk, across the sands, and climbed the throne. Putting on the overcoat and spreading the raincoat so that he could draw it around him, he dropped into the niche he had prepared for himself and drew his covers snugly so that he would not chill. Then he sat watching the coming storm in intent eagerness.

He did not know that he was matching forces. He did not realize that for two years the storm that wracks the soul and body of a man even to destruction had been raging in his battered breast, in his heart, in his brain. He did not know that he had dimly realized the strength, the terror, the futility of it. He did not know why he wanted to see the sky reach down and the sea rise up and do their utmost. He did not know that he wanted to compare the storm that may sweep the heart of a man with the kind of storm that may sweep the world. He honestly tried to protect himself so that he would not hasten what might be in store for him. He did not want to fail, when the Bee Master had trusted him with the home and the possessions and the occupation that were all he had of his very own, and he did not know that as the storm drew nearer, as the clouds grew blacker, as the heat waves resolved themselves into definite flashes of lightning, as the night closed down black as velvet around him—he did not realize that his moral and mental forces were rising with the tide of the storm, that all the remnants of manhood left in his shaken body were gathering together for some sort of culmination, just as presently the storm would reach its height and then subside.

Without moving a muscle, almost breathlessly, he lay back in his rocky nook and wondered exactly how high the tide would rise. He had not informed himself as to whether the point of rock might be surrounded. He thought it would be an unprecedented storm that would sweep over it. At any rate, he was taking the chance. He might have asked Margaret Cameron whether that point ever was completely submerged. He was certain that it was high above any level to which man had seen the ocean lift, that it must be safe.

At the point where Jamie realized that he was having the best time he had had since the guns were booming and the rage of battle was smashing and he had been able to deliver what he considered a few effective blows, each of which he had invariably accompanied by a grinding shout, "In the name of the Forty-second Highlanders!"; just when his blood really was tingling and his spirits were answering to the smash of the waves that were flinging spray to his feet, to the roar of the thunder and the crash of the lightning; just when the fight was going good and Jamie was a Forty-second Highlander and with a sword of magic cutting off the heads of innumerable Germans with each sword-thrust of lightning, the most astounding thing happened to him that ever had happened in all the years of his existence. All around him and enveloping him there came slowly and faintly creeping a strange odour.

Jamie dropped from the sky battle to everyday realities and turned his head to the right. Delicately as when he was creeping belly-down towards the Germans in No Man's Land, hunting a lost comrade or scouting enemy locations, he sniffed the night air. The first absolute information that he felt he could rely on that his nostrils telegraphed to his brain was "sage". He took another sniff and recognized the lavender flower of the beeches:

"sand verbena", one of the most subtle and exquisite faint odours in all Nature, and then a whiff of primrose crept up. And then, just when the crack that seemed to split the heavens wide was followed by the boom of the reverberating thunder, there came to Jamie's ears a wrenching sobbing that was the most pitiful thing he ever had heard. Still as death he sat in his wrappings, his head turned, his nose and his ears alert; and by and by, sniffing and listening, he reached his conclusion: the throne that he had thought so wonderful, that he had pre-empted, that he had meant to occupy on many a night of communion in his effort to make his peace with God, was not his personal throne. He was an interloper. Someone else was familiar with the winding way that reached the eminence from the back. Someone else had a fight that needed the healing of God through Nature to help him to wage. Beside him was someone who smelled of the sage of the mountains, of the lavender and the gold flowers of the beaches, and this someone else had the voice of a woman, not the cracked voice, not the breathless voice of an old woman. God knew Jamie had heard women cry, the women of France, the women of Belgium, the women of England. He was an expert on all kinds and varieties of sobs of anguish that could be wrenched from the frame of a mother, a wife, a sister, a sweetheart.

Slowly, softly, as nearly without sound as possible, he turned to face this woman. She had found her seat where he had first sat. She probably did not know that another seat had been made, beyond the place to which she must have been accustomed, or she never could have found it in the darkness of the storm. She must have been familiar with that point through other storms, or she never would have sought it when that one was raging at its fiercest.

As Nature wore herself out and began gradually to ease in the storm she was waging, another amazing thing happened to Jamie. The raving wind that had been sweeping from the west was gradually shifting to the north and it began blowing something across his face, something that was soft, something that was silken, something that was tugging and pulling, and plastering to him with the driving spray and the beating rain. In dumbfounded bewilderment he worked a hand to the surface and softly touched his cheeks, and across them there was streaming the silken banner of a woman's hair. Jamie realized that when the woman learned that there was a man there, she probably would be so frightened that she might throw herself into the boiling sea a few feet below them. He was afraid to speak, afraid to move, and the one thing that he did not figure on was that there might be beside him a pair of nostrils sensitive as his own, and that there might very presently emanate from him an odour that would become discernable to someone else.

Just how that would have worked out Jamie never knew, because at the instant that his hand crept higher to work the blinding hair from his eyes, a long, low flash of lightning struck the breast of the ocean and for one instant lighted the rock like day. In that instant Jamie saw the white face and the big, wide eyes of a woman, eyes that he would remember while remembrance remained with him, a face that by no possibility could he ever forget. The sharp gasp of astonishment at his presence there, where anyone accustomed to the rock might well have supposed there would be no one, his quick ear told him came from a woman accustomed to self-control. She had not screamed. She had not jumped. It was merely the catching of a breath.

Jamie was in a measure prepared. He had been trying to plan something. He was not taken unawares as she was. What he had meant to say, what he had thought would be a wise thing to say, never was uttered.

What he heard himself saying was: "Don't be startled! What hurts you so? Let me help you."

Then a voice that was going to take a place in Jamie's mentality along with the eyes and the face—a deep, rich contralto voice with a touching quaver of pathos through it, a voice shaken with emotion and accented with tones native to his ears—answered him: "Why did you come here?"

Jamie replied: "Very possibly for the same reason you did."

The voice answered: "Oh!"

Jamie combed the streaming locks from his cheeks and his lips with his fingers and sat tightly holding them in his hand. And he who had gone out to compare the battle of Nature with the battle of his soul forgot all about himself as he said to the girl beside him: "Did anybody ever tell you that a trouble shared is a trouble half endured?"

Then he laughed a deep burry Scotch laugh. He threw out his right arm and felt to the north until he circled the shoulders of the woman beside him.

"You aren't half covered," he said, "and you are drenched! Creep over here in the protection of my coat. And then, because it is night, and because I know that your soul is wracked and maybe your body tortured, tell me the truth. I'm sure I can help you. There is always a way. I can think of something."

Jamie never forgot that when his arm reached across the shoulder beside him there was no shrinking, no repulsion, no hesitation. It took one more flash of lightning to show him that the woman he was trying to comfort was young. She was not beautiful, but she was luringly human. Plastered with rain, wrenched with grief, he had no right to judge her.

"I mean it," he said, taking up the thread of his thought again. "I mean it. If you will tell me, I promise to help you."

"But—but how can you help me?" said a voice, every tone of which Jamie registered as it fell on his ear.

"I don't know," said Jamie. "I don't know how I can help you, because I don't know what you need. I only know that I *can* help you, that I *will* help you if you will tell me what it is that troubles you."

In the long silence that followed, Jamie manipulated the Bee Master's raincoat to the best advantage possible and tightened the grip of his right arm. At last, above the rumbling of the subsiding storm, above the crashing of the waves below them, Jamie heard again the voice for which he was waiting.

"I can't tell you," said the woman, whose breast was still heaving, whose shoulders were still quivering. "I can't tell a stranger in the darkness, in the storm, what it is that is hurting me!"

"Oh yes, you can," said Jamie casually. "Better now than at any other time. If it is anything you aren't proud of, the darkness will cover you. If it's anything you are afraid of, you may depend on the strength there is in my right arm. If it is anything that as much of a man as I am can do for you, I want you to understand that you are my mother or my sister, or any relationship that you can think of that a man who is trying to be fairly decent wouldn't violate. I'll give you my word of honour that I will not follow you; I will not make any effort to learn who you are or where you come from. If you came here to-night intending to throw yourself into the undertow that sucks down from these rocks, you needn't be any too sure that I didn't come with the same intention. I'll admit that I've thought about it. I've got a storm of my own in my breast. I've got my wounds that are still open and bleeding. There's nothing about me that you need hesitate over. I'm just telling you that your voice is young, and your face is young, and your body is strong, and in some way there can be healing managed for young hearts that are breaking, and I *do* believe that trouble shared is trouble at least half endured. Tell me."

Jamie could almost feel the thinking process that was going

on in the mind of the woman whom he was trying to shelter and to support.

"It's a long story," said the rich voice at last, "and it's a story that's got what the world calls shame in it. And the world is right in calling what there is in it shame, because I am ashamed. I couldn't sit here in broad sunlight and let you shelter me, and look at me, and tell you. I could only tell you in such darkness and turmoil as this, and you can't possibly do any good, but there is this about it: if you came and weathered the storm and resolved that you could go on with what you call an open wound in your breast, I'll promise you that I'll not go over the rock. I'll promise you that I'll find my way back to the friends I left; that I'll go home; that I'll take up my work; that I'll do the best I can."

"That's fine," said Jamie, "as far as it goes. But it doesn't go far enough to do you any more good than the good of saving your soul alive, because we don't get life at our own volition in this world, and we have no right to give it up until the God who gave it says we have lived it. What I am offering to do is to take the burden that's crushing you off your heart. Isn't there a little bit of shelter in the arm across your shoulders? Doesn't my voice sound sincere? I haven't the least objection in the world to telling you who I am, where I come from, or where I am going when I leave this rock. I have told you that I will not follow you. If there is anything in to-night that you would blush for to-morrow, I will not intrude myself, but I do beg you to believe me when I say that I know I can help you, if you will tell me."

And that was a very bold and daring statement for Jamie, with six months to live and nothing in his pockets, to make to any woman in distress. Yet he made it in the utmost confidence, and there was something in his voice that carried conviction. Before he knew precisely what had happened to him, the thing for which he had striven occurred. The length of his frame he felt the relaxation of the taut muscles beside him. He bent to extend the shelter of the raincoat.

"That's a good girl," he said, in exactly the same tone he would have used to a six-year-old. "Now, go on and tell me what happened to you. You needn't make it a long story. You could probably tell it in ten words if you chose. What hurt you? How can it be fixed?"

Again he could sense the intense thinking.

"All right," said the voice beside him. "What I need above everything else on earth at this minute is a marriage certificate and a wedding-ring, and a name for an unborn child. My need is desperate. That's all. Now go ahead and make good your boast!"

"All right," said Jamie smoothly, instantly. "The proposition you have put me is almost the easiest thing I could manage. I've got a name and it is of no particular use to me, and I haven't much time left in which to use it. I've strength enough to manage a licence and a marriage ceremony if it's necessary. If you pledge me your word of honour that the trouble in your heart can be healed by giving you a name I am going to quit using shortly, you will grant I was right when I told you I could settle your difficulty. I've been wondering for days past what I might do that would be something fine and shining that I could lay at the feet of the Master when I go farthest west, as I am going very soon, to render my last account, and you have opened the way. I think it would be very decent, I think it would be something the Master would approve, if I left my name to a little child that is making its way toward earth and facing a heritage you wouldn't want for it."

Then suddenly Jamie felt the woman in his arms merging her form with his. He felt her hands on his breast. He felt them reaching to find his face. He felt the hot breath of her voice.

"You wouldn't!" she was panting. "Oh, you wouldn't! You wouldn't get me a marriage licence! You wouldn't stand through a ceremony with me! You wouldn't let me use your name!"

Jamie found the hand on his face and gripped it tight with his left hand. He had presence of mind to tighten his grasp around the shoulders yielding to him. He was enough of a Scotsman to command the situation.

"You are mighty right, I would!" he said. "I'm telling you true. Here, if you don't believe me. I'll convince you." And he shifted the hand he held until the finger of it could touch the bandages across his breast. "You feel that?" he asked. "You're not touching the body of a man. Those are bandages covering the body of a man, and under those bandages there's an open wound that will never heal. I am telling you true. There's no one on earth who is closely related to me. There's no one to care what I do with my name or with the few remaining months of my life. The nearest I can come to a family is a mother and a father, and they are both in heaven, and if either of them were here this minute, they would say: 'Cover the shame baby with your name, Jamie!' "

"Jamie!" said the voice beside him a little breathlessly. "There isn't a sweeter name in all the world that could be given to a little child, if it happened to be a boy. But it's too big a sacrifice! It's a thing that shouldn't be asked of any man, no matter how free, no matter how willing!"

"Well," said Jamie, "I'm telling you I am free. I'll prove it by citing to you records you can look up. I'm part of the aftermath of war. You can find my name if you look in the proper place for it. I'll tell you right here that it's James Lewis MacFarlane, and from the time I can remember my mother and father made it Jamie. I ran away from a hospital a few days ago because my case was hopeless and I wouldn't go where they wanted to send me. You know Camp Kearney? You know the village of tents that means the White Plague? I hadn't it and I wouldn't go there, so I ran away. I got as far as the apiary just below here on the mountain-side and I couldn't drag any farther. I was staggering toward the Bee Master to ask him to help me, but he beat me to it, and asked me to help *him*. I thought I couldn't, but I did. I helped him to the hospital in time for his operation. I am staying in his house, taking care of his property. I am telling you truly what my name is, where you can find me. I am telling you that you may have my name any time you want to claim it."

"To-morrow?" said the girl breathlessly. "May I claim it to-morrow?"

"Any time you say, any place," said Jamie. "Tell me where you want me to go and what you want me to do."

And then, quite before Jamie knew at all what was happening to him or what was going to happen, he felt another shift of position of the woman in his arms, and for the next second he was in her arms. Hands had found the sides of his head, and his face was turned up and a wet, cold, salty face was laid against his, cold lips were touching his cheeks and a breathless voice was saying: "Oh, you're good! You're good! I didn't know there was a man like you in the whole world! Will you meet me to-morrow at three o'clock at the Marriage Bureau in Los Angeles? Will you truly have a marriage licence made out? Will you stand beside me through a ceremony that will mean life and the lifting of a black burden?"

"I will!" said Jamie. "Don't give yourself another minute's worry. Dry your eyes and cheer up! I'll be right there as sure as God is in His heaven and there's any justice for women in all this world. And if I am not there, you can know that the red tiger has eaten through to my vitals until I cannot get there; but you needn't worry, because I shall be there. God wouldn't give me this shining chance and then snatch it away from me."

"Will you sit here, right in this spot, for a few minutes more?" asked the girl.

"I'll sit here all night if you tell me to," said Jamie calmly, and it was not so calmly either, because his heart was tearing until he was afraid it would fall out of the opening above it, and his blood was racing as blood had never raced in his veins. The girl in his arms might be cold and clammy and salt-pasted, but he was neither cold nor clammy. He got one more tight hug and one more kiss—which happened to land squarely on the tip of his nose, not the location in which he wanted it in the least—and then she was gone and he heard swift feet going down the back of the rock, and his trained ears could hear the first few footfalls across the dark beach.

He sat there and waited and looked down into the boiling surf and out over the battling sea, and by and by he calmed himself so that he could think straightly and evenly, and then he said: "Such quick action as this seems to indicate that my time is short, and if there is a big thing that I have a chance of doing in this world I've got to do it and do it quickly. So to-morrow afternoon at three o'clock I'll start on what appeals to me as the shining part of my great adventure."

CHAPTER VIII

A NEW KIND OF WEDDING

WHEN the faintest sound of footfalls had died away, Jamie settled back in his niche in the rock, drew his wrappings around him, and turned his face in the direction of the sea, the face that had been held between a pair of strong, impetuous woman's hands, the face that had been showered with wholly impersonal caresses merely as an expression of release from a thraldom of shame. He had been paid in the coin of the realm of womanhood most desired by men, therefore most frequently offered by women in extremity.

Jamie sought among his clothing and found a handkerchief. He pulled it out and carefully wiped his face. There was nothing about the clammy, salty kisses he had received that he wished to perpetuate, not even the memory of them, because the girl who gave them had not meant them for him personally. She had bestowed real kisses elsewhere. These were the first available expression of thankfulness for freedom—freedom to lift up her head, freedom to face the world, freedom to go on with her life in such a manner that the ever-ready "finger of scorn" need not be pointed at her.

Jamie grinned dourly as he scoured his face.

"I hope she doesn't think," he said to the boiling surf below, "that she fooled me any with those kisses. It's all right. She's welcome to my name. She's welcome to her ring—if she buys it herself—and her certificate. I didn't see her very well, but what I did see didn't look like a fast woman.

"I'll say *that* for her. And she didn't act as if she were used to calling on other people to shoulder many of her burdens. God knows she wasn't afraid for her body, or she wouldn't have been on this rock close to midnight in this storm: not afraid with physical fear; but I suppose it's the mental strain that gets people the worst. I suppose it's mental fear or nerve strain, or whatever you might call it, that's been eating me for the past two years. It's not that I'm afraid of death physically. God knows I've seen enough of it so that I can take my medicine as I saw thousands of boys take theirs! It's just that since I *am* alive, since I *am* breathing, since there *is* the ghost of a possibility that I might have a slim fighting chance, I hate standing still and watching myself going out by the inch. And the reason I hate the going is because I've never lived; I've never had the things that, to a man, constitute real life, and I want a taste of *life*! I know just enough about the sky and the sea and the earth to want to get on the tree job and run it down as I've always intended."

Then, for a time, long past the stipulated time, Jamie sat and watched the gradual clearing of the sky, the calming of the sea. It was not long before he could see the stars again, and some way a star always was connected in Jamie's mind with a suggestion of hope. Ever since he had read an oration by the greatest agnostic of his day in which he had said at the grave of a beloved brother, when put to the ultimate test himself: "In the night-time of despair, hope sees a star and listening love can hear the rustle of a wind," Jamie had thought that perhaps the lips of man never had uttered more beautiful words. This might have been a "night-time of despair" for a young thing that he had held in his arms for a few brief minutes. Every night for a long time had been a night of despair for him. He was sorry, sorry to the depths of his heart for the grief that racked and tore and drove frantic such a fine, strong young thing, with an odour of the woods, with the sage of the mountains and the lavender and gold flowers of the beach distilling like incense around her. That was the pity of it. How had shame happened to a woods girl? Jamie knew that while he lived there would remain in his nostrils the scent that had first assailed them, carried by the winds of the storm, and as if it had not been removed he could feel the clinging of the silky strands of hair. She must have a perfect mane. Then he wondered how it came to be unbound. Then he remembered something else—the one revealing flash that had shown him the girl most clearly. He had not thought of it at the time, but he remembered it now. That flash had disclosed bare feet and a streak of white above them.

"By Jove!" said Jamie softly to the Spirit of the Sea that was drawing up very close to him in that hour. "By Jove! She wore a nightdress and one of those eiderdown kimonos over it! I remember by the feel of her and by her bare feet. She asked a few minutes' grace before I should start. That means that she had gone to bed and was so driven she had decided that she'd bed in the sea, and she'd put on the kimono and come as she was to this point she knew how to find. She couldn't have come up those rocks as still as thought, and she couldn't have gone down them with the swiftness and ease she used if she had not known them perfectly, and a few minutes wouldn't carry her far across the sands of this soaked beach. That means that she came from somewhere very near here."

And then, as an outsider might speak to him, Jamie added: "And if you will recall what you said to her, old man, you gave her your word of honour that you wouldn't try to find her."

Then Jamie answered back and said: "But how am I going to keep that promise? How am I going to marry a girl with such a noble face, with hair of silk, and hands of such assurance; how am I going to stand up and swear that I'll love her and take care of her as long as we both shall live, and then not work for her, not wonder where she is and what is happening to her, and whether I could not do more for her than to give her my name at a pinch?"

Then Jamie, for the second time that night, thought of his Great Adventure, and he said to the sea and to the near-by personality who had commenced the conversation with him: "I'm not so sure that what I called a Great Adventure in jesting merely to hearten myself may not possibly prove to be more of an adventure than I've reckoned on."

Then the outside voice talked back to Jamie again, and it was a jeering voice that laughed at him and sneered at him. It said: "Well, Mr. Married Man, you'd better be getting home and fortify yourself with rest and sleep. You'd better press your trousers and see if the Master has got a decent scarf you can borrow. If you're going to be a bridegroom you'd better think about starting your preparations."

Jamie, detecting the sneer in the voice, defended himself. He said: "Well what would *you* have done? If you hadn't a relative on earth, if you knew you wouldn't live to see the consequences, if a woman creature, young and attractive, was ready to throw herself into the sea before you, wouldn't you save her by any means you could? Wouldn't you give her a name that couldn't hurt and that might possibly help her all the rest of her life?"

He did not hear any answer to that, and so he turned his attention to the sea again. "I'd like to know," he said dourly, "what a lot of the mothers in this world mean. If they've known enough about the awful power of sex attraction themselves to marry a man and bear a child, why, in God's world, don't they know what they are letting the young folks up against when they turn them loose in utter and untrammelled freedom on the mountains and through the canyons and on the beaches and in the parks and the dance-halls and the streets? Can't they see that, however times and customs change, the desires of the heart and the urge of the body do not change? They only grow stronger with the freedom and licence and physical contact allowed in these astounding days."

Then Jamie arose unsteadily and drew on the raincoat and, shuffling his feet before him, made his way down the steep pathway with which he had become sufficiently familiar during the few times he had climbed it to negotiate it safely. He followed his way down the beach by gyrating between the slopping of the waves and the entangling primroses. When he found he was among mats of primroses that threatened to trip him, he veered toward the water. When he splashed in the water, he veered toward the primroses, and by so doing he came at last to where the lights of the Bee Master's home threw a welcoming beam down the mountain-side. Then he felt along the back fence until he found the gate, and after that it was easy to reach the back door; and he was entirely ready for the back door by the time he opened it. He dropped on the first chair he encountered to rest awhile.

"I'm none too sure," said Jamie, "that my contract for to-morrow, or is it to-day?"—he glanced up at the clock and saw to his surprise that it was to-day—"won't be about all I can accomplish in one day." But that one word that had been jeeringly thrust at him out there on the rock, "bridegroom", persisted in his ears. It meant something to a man to be a bridegroom under any circumstances. It should mean the most wonderful thing in all the world. There should not be anything, unless it might be the love of God, that would be bigger and higher and holier in the heart of a man than to be the groom of his chosen bride, in ordinary circumstances. But there was nothing ordinary about the circumstances under which he had contracted to be a bridegroom. No, there was not. The storm of the elements, the storm in his own heart, the storm in the heart of the girl——

"Holy Moses!" said Jamie. "What a storm! Regular typhoon! Anyway, for the clearing up to-morrow I'll go to bed and I'll see whether I can sleep or not. And if I can, then I wonder how much time I am going to need, and how I am going to find the place where I've promised to be."

Then he thought of Margaret Cameron. She could tell him what car lines he must take, and once he reached the heart of the city it would not be difficult to find the proper office where the business of the county was transacted.

So Jamie lay down and shut his eyes: the velvet blackness of the night closed round him and the steady sweep of the sea breaking on the shore so very near came with rhythmic cadence. There was enough wind to sing a little. He was very tired, but he had made good his boast so far. He had told the girl that if she would tell her trouble he could help her, without a notion in his head as to how he was going to help her. By the depth of her grief he could measure the depth of her relief—relief that set her lips on his face, her hands frantically clutching him. He had saved her position before the world probably. He had offered what was of not much use to him, in the stead of the man who had been too much of a hound to make good his obligations. After all, he would have something beautiful to think about when the last hour came. Maybe the little Scout had been right about the different kinds of death. Maybe when Jamie's time came he could think of the passion of relief, of deliverance, of utter panicky joy, that had obliterated the passion of fear and humiliation in the girl he was going to try to help. Maybe he could fold his hands and go softly in his sleep, and maybe at least his face could carry the smiling secret that the little Scout had talked about, if he got a chance to enter the gates and face his mother.

The next thing Jamie knew the clock that he had set for seven was burring, and he awoke from deep sleep and went to his breakfast and the watering. He merely told Margaret Cameron that he had some business in town. No, he was not going to the hospital, because he saw the desire to go with him in her eyes. He was not going to the hospital until Doctor Grayson sent for him. He would be back in the evening in time for dinner, maybe sooner. She need not mind about his lunch.

Jamie did the most important of the things he had been doing daily outdoors, postponing as many of them as he possibly could to the coming day. Then he went in and rested awhile. Later he brushed his clothing and searched through the drawers and the closets—the Bee Master had told him to help himself to his clothing if he needed changes, in view of the manifest fact that he had taken him from the road with only the clothing on his back. Jamie thought it over and then he selected an extremely good-looking grey silk shirt and a dull blue tie. He looked at his own trousers critically. He had slept in them and given them rough usage, and he had worked in them some. They were not suitable trousers for a bridegroom. He was so near the Bee Master's height and build that a pair of grey ones he found stretched in the long drawer of a highboy were exactly right. He went on searching, and by and by he had the bed almost covered with clothing that appealed to Jamie as eminently suitable for an honest-to-goodness bridegroom.

Then he went to his bath, and when he managed the fresh dressings on his left breast, he hesitated over the antiseptics—and omitted them. He would not go to his bride even with a taint of medicinal odour about him. Since she smelled of flowers herself, he would emulate the example of the greatest beau the world has ever known by having the odour that emanated from him merely that of fresh linen, of utter cleanliness.

At heart Jamie was a gentleman. When he locked the front door and started down the walk for a short trip to the trolley line which ended a few rods away, he was as white of face and hand as his condition warranted. Otherwise he was an attractive gentleman. He carried his head at a high angle. He squared his shoulders, as much military training had required. He stepped out in the Master's best shoes and grey trousers and black coat, in his grey silken shirt and his dull blue tie, and a soft broad-brimmed black hat; he stepped out habited as it was proper that any gentleman might habit himself when he was going to be a bridegroom. He stepped very carefully that he might not accumulate dust on his shoes before he reached the trolley, and in taking this care it occurred to him to wonder where the girl he was going to marry was at that minute and what she was doing; whether she really would be at the appointed place to meet him, and what she would look like, and what she would say to him, and with what words she would leave him when she had secured from him the things that she had admitted she needed so badly—a name, a wedding certificate, and a ring.

When he reached the ring in thought, a dull red flamed up in Jamie's cheek. He was not sure that he had not gone too far. Before the Bee Master had been carried from his home he had pointed to a little drawer in his secretary in which Jamie would find money for an emergency, for milk, or ice, or whatever he needed until the Master's return. From that drawer, as a fortification for his self-respect that morning, Jamie had taken ten dollars. He was not sure that ten dollars would pay for a marriage licence. A marriage licence was a commodity he had not previously considered. He had no idea what the article cost, but he felt certain it would not be more than ten dollars. Small change for car fare, and for a sandwich for his lunch and the money for the licence. Perhaps the girl would expect to pay for it, but Jamie could not quite endure the thought of a woman paying for his marriage licence. After all, if he stood up and married the girl, it was his wedding, the only wedding he would ever have probably, and he meant to have it in appropriate and decent clothing, even if he borrowed the clothing; and he meant to pay for his wedding even if he borrowed the money. If he had not stayed there and taken care of the bees, someone would have been asked to do it who would have been paid, and when his first earnings were handed to him he could return the ten dollars. He had borrowed that amount.

But about a little thin engraved circlet of gold that looked as if it might fit a woman's finger, about a little ring that he had run across among the Bee Master's collar buttons and small belongings—— He had it. He had it in his vest pocket. It might be a souvenir; it might be something precious; it might be that there was nothing among the effects of the Bee Master more dear to him. He had not at all made up his mind as to whether he might use it or not, but at any rate he had it in his pocket. He was fortified with the clothing and the price and the ring, if he should bring himself to use it.

Then a thought appealed to him. There was a bare possibility that he could materialize his thought, and so he consulted the motorman, and after making several changes landed before the old Court House with some minutes to spare. Hurriedly he made his way to the Marriage Licence Bureau on the main floor. He told the Clerk he was expecting to be there shortly with a young lady to secure a marriage licence, and he asked about the expense, and found to his relief that he had more than enough money. Then with all the haste compatible with the state of his knees, he left the Court House and regained the street. He looked around him, up and down and across, and in that survey he located a jewellery store.

It appealed to him as modest in appearance, so he walked in and faced a clerk across a case filled with rings. He laid the money he could spare on the counter and said: "Could you furnish me with a very plain, simple ring for that amount?"

The clerk had not been accustomed to furnishing rings for that amount of money, but he was of Hebraic origin; he was shrewd; he realized that the money on the counter was all the money the man before him intended to spend. If he did not take it he would not have it. So after some hunting he found a ring that Jamie thought would be the right size. It looked fairly satisfactory, so the Hebraic gentleman had the money and

Jamie had the ring. He took the shining band of gold that he had borrowed from the Master and transferred it to the left-hand pocket of the vest he was wearing, and in the right-hand pocket, convenient to his fingers, he slipped the circlet, that at least had the merit of shining.

Then he headed back for the Court House, and as he stepped into the office he faced a woman whom he knew instantly. He knew her height; he knew her eyes; he knew without knowing exactly how or why he knew. He was a bridegroom, but the woman he was facing was not a bride. She was a widow, if any story were to be told by her clothing. From head to foot the Storm Girl was in deep mourning. A tight, small hat fitted her head and was pulled so low that he could see only a gleam of the eyes that he had been positive in the lightning's flare were either black or brown. The office lights revealed them brown—grey-brown. The baffling thing about the costume the girl wore was a veil. He would have called it a widow's veil. It was thick; it was black; a broad satin band finished the edges. The band covered the mouth and chin; the hat shaded the eyes, and a mask-like gleam of eye and a line across the cheek and nose were all Jamie was permitted to see of his prospective bride.

For a minute he experienced a sense of shock, and then he realized that in some manner death figured in the adventure he was embarking on that day. The girl was in mourning. Possibly, after all, the man whose place he was taking was a dead man who might have fulfilled his obligations if he had been granted the opportunity; but at any rate the girl had distinctly said that she must be rescued from shame. So if a dead man figured in the case, he hadn't been very much of a man, and it was shameful that he had left the marriage ceremony to any chance of disaster.

These things were tearing through Jamie's brain swift as light flashes, while Jamie himself lifted the Bee Master's hat and brought his own heels together and presented a figure that would at least have been worthy of consideration by any woman. His hasty rush after the ring that was to save his self-respect, that was to put a crowning touch of pride on his only wedding, had set his heart pumping unduly, and so his cheeks were not so white as they had been, his lips were not so blue. A flush of red had surged to his face, and he looked very much as any lean, self-respecting, well-dressed man of Scottish origin and American birth and training might be expected to appear. From force of habit, as he straightened from his bow, Jamie extended his hand, and recognized the touch of the hand that met his; and then he lined up shoulder to shoulder and said casually: "We figured time from the same watch, didn't we?"

The girl beside him merely assented. Jamie took charge of proceedings with all the self-assurance of a man who was accustomed to captaining his own affairs. Whatever the woman beside him was getting out of this, Jamie had made up his mind that he was going to get a wedding, and it was going to be his own. He took the arm of the girl beside him and piloted her to the clerk's desk. Whether she had the correct impression now or not, Jamie did not know, but he proposed that when she got through with that wedding and went her way with the ring and the certificate that were to save her self-respect, she should at least go in the belief that she had married a man. He had forgotten all about telling her that very shortly he would not be a man; he intended for the few minutes that were to come to be all man.

So he impelled her to the clerk and announced that they wanted to fill the forms necessary to procure a marriage licence. While Jamie wrote down the names of his father and mother and the date of his birth and his residence and his occupation and all the things required, beside him stood a tall, self-reliant girl, who was filling in the blank that had been given her. When these documents were filled out as the law required, to keep the Storm Girl firm in the impression that he was a man of his word, Jamie picked them up and signed first, then handed them to her for her signature. When the clerk finished his share of the proceedings and offered the long envelope to Jamie, he waved toward the girl he was marrying, and the clerk gave her the document. They were directed to the office of the Probate Judge, and it was not any time at all until the necessary papers were signed, sealed and delivered to Jamie, who, without one glance of examination, handed them to the Storm Girl. Jamie paid the fee and walked beside her to the street without knowing even the surname of the woman he had married. She might be either Smith, Jones, or Brown. It was ridiculous, but it was true that the touch of a hand, a strip of white face decorated with dark eyes, and "I, Alice Louise, take thee, James Lewis, to be my lawful and wedded husband," were all the information he had.

So he had married "Alice Louise". He was not particularly well satisfied with the name. She did not look like Alice, and she did not the least in the world resemble Louise. He had known Louises by the dozen all his life, and they always had light hair; always they had blue eyes, and they were always clinging, dependent little things. Never since he could remember had he known of a woman who could touch shoulders with a six-foot man and carry her head like an empress, who extended a hand mighty near as big as, evidently firmer than, his own, and in a voice of mellow contralto from away down in a deep chest answer to the name of Louise!

Jamie cupped his hand around the elbow of Alice Louise merely to show her that he considered himself enough of a man to take care of her in case she needed him, and he piloted her to the street, and there, standing on the sidewalk, for the first time they looked at each other. Jamie deliberately waited to hear what the lady had to say; and as he waited, with concentrated vision, he strove to pierce that crow-black costume and fix in his memory the form and all he could see of the face of the woman before him.

He had given his word that he would not seek her, and he was not any too sure that he was going to keep that word. He was not any too sure that he was not going to know who she was, and where she lived, and why she had used him to ease her heart and her conscience, to save her body from the ocean. As he waited, looking straight into the face of the girl opposite him, he saw that the muscles of the cheeks and the lips were all in a quiver and that the steady stare of the eyes looking into his was going to dissolve any minute in an uncontrollable gush of tears. Tears did the same thing to Jamie that they do to any man when an attractive woman admits she is facing something that is too much for her, that she needs his help. He had intended to force her to speak, and the first thing he knew he was no longer facing her. He had stepped beside her and was saying to her in low tones: "Steady yourself! You'll be all right in a few minutes. Are you taking the car at this corner?"

She had merely nodded in assent, and still with her elbow in his palm, Jamie piloted her through the crowds and helped her onto a street car, and the people surged between them. As he saw her enter the car and make her way to a seat he realized that "Alice Louise" and "I do" were all that he had heard her say. He had not kept his determination to force her to speak. He had felt so sorry for her, when he realized she was near a breakdown he had spared her. Anyway, he had shown her her that he was a man who could run his own affairs. He had helped her to a street car, and away from him. He could not honourably board the same car. So he stepped back, raised his hat, lifted his chin and looked at the car, on a bare chance that she might glance his way before the car started and carried her from sight.

Then Jamie put on his hat and regained the sidewalk and

said to himself in not very pleasant tones: "Well, can you beat that!"

He had not expected much, but he had expected a word or two, and not only had the words not been spoken, but the lady herself had not even turned her head to see whether he was going to take the same car or not. She had walked down the aisle, taken her seat with her back toward him, and sat immovable until she was carried from sight. It did not avail much that he might see what car she had taken or in which direction she went. She might take any car and she might leave it in a block or two in order to use the speediest opportunity to escape him. She had gone away Mrs. James Lewis MacFarlane, with the necessary credentials and the ring he had produced at the proper moment for a finger that had hesitated to receive it; now he was left standing on the sidewalk, and the best thing for him to do was to see how soon he could reach home and restore the Bee Master's wardrobe to its accustomed place. He had been a bridegroom and there was nothing to it, not even "Thank you". If he wanted to extract any romance whatever, he would have to get it from the salty kisses that had swept his face the previous night. And, being honest, he had to admit that if the rock upon which they had sat had been the means of the girl's salvation, she probably would have kissed it with as much, or possibly more, enthusiasm.

Jamie stood on the sidewalk and waited for his knees to stiffen slightly before he began searching for the car he required to carry him back to the garden of the bees. When he found it and boarded it and sank into a seat, he said to all and sundry: "Well, of all the darned weddings!" He knew that he said it, because he heard the words, but nobody else seemed to have heard them because everybody was interested in their papers and their friends and where they were going.

So Jamie went back to the house and returned the borrowed raiment and assumed his own. Then he went out in the sunshine and sat down to think things over. He had half a mind to tell Margaret Cameron that this was his wedding day and she might prepare him any kind of feast she saw fit to offer for such an occasion. A wry grin crossed his cheeks when he thought of the look that would come on her face if he told her that, and then she would speak and she would ask where his bride was; and where his bride was happened to be a secret and the business of the bride herself. He reflected that if she was where she had been at midnight the previous night she would not be so very far from him at the present minute. He was assailed by an impulse to go down and walk up and down the beach, to scan each house accessible from the shore-line to see whether in any of them there was visible a glimpse of a girl clad in the deepest kind of mourning.

How much that mourning meant Jamie could not decide. He remembered that the girl had offered to begin at the beginning and tell him the story. It had been he who had told her to use a few words, merely to state what she wanted. If she had been as full of Scottish blood as he, she could not have taken him at his words more quickly or more completely. She had stated the bald facts and he, Jamie reflected with another twisted grin, had materialized the facts. The lady had said that she needed a ring, a marriage certificate and a name; and she had stood beside him, she had allowed the ring to be put out on her finger, she had taken possession of the certificate. One thing he did recall. She had laid the document on her breast and folded both hands over it and held it there as if nothing in all the world could be more precious to her. And his name. At least she had accepted it in marriage whether she meant to use it or not.

Jamie felt something of a fool that he had not at least stretched out his hand and picked up the record the girl had written and read it. He had not been much of a man, and he had not managed his own wedding in his own way quite as he had thought that he would. It all harked back to the fact that he had given a promise, that he had said that he would not intrude himself, he would make no effort to find her. He had said that he would be content merely to offer what assistance he could, and the amount and kind of assistance that the girl required had been very clearly specified to him. He had accepted the bargain. He had gone through with it. The thing to do now was to go out on the back porch, put on the Bee Master's old bee coat, raid the lily and the cinnamon pink beds, and while his body was free from the taint of surgical dressing, go down and face the Black Germans and find out for himself whether he was bee immune for sure. It was a piece of knowledge that he wanted to have before the little Scout put in another appearance.

So Jamie donned the coat and applied the lily and wiped his head through the pinks, and slowly, deliberately, with as much assurance of step as he could assume, he made the long march down the east line, pausing before hive after hive of bees, looking at the tiny things that were coming and going so busily on humming wings, realizing that he did not know a drone from a worker, a nurse from a queen.

He resolved, as he stood before one of the hives, that when Doctor Grayson called him that evening for his daily report he would ask how soon now it would be possible for him to see the Bee Master for a very few minutes, and he would ask how long it was, probably, that he was going to remain in the hospital. Then he reflected that if he had not been called yet to see the Bee Master there was every chance that he was so weak and so ill that he might be away a matter of weeks, possibly of months. Besides, bees were very closely related to trees, and what the little Scout had pointed out to him of bee lore was so alluring that he might as well go deeper; he might as well read some of the technical books and see what they contained. It was going to be some time yet before his fate was decided, and in that time possibly there was nothing more interesting, nothing more useful that would come within his possibilities, to which he could turn his attention, than just bees.

So Jamie, doing his best on "Highland Mary", went slowly the round of the hives, and as he turned up the back walk and sighted the big hive of the Black Germans he remembered something else. He hunted for the water tap around which grew the mint. He pulled a handful of it and rubbed it over his trousers and over his sleeves and crushed it on his hands, and then, doing his best on the tune prescribed, he slowly approached the Black Germans. He planted himself in front of their first hive. He stood there as long as he pleased. He knelt down and peered into the opening. He studied them so intently that he realized that they lacked the gold of the Italians. They were of different shape. When he slowly walked away he felt that the next person who asked him if he were bee immune might safely be given an affirmative answer. He believed that the next time a bee alighted on a flower before him he would at least be able to say whether it was an Italian or a Black German.

He so disliked the name, that he told himself as he climbed the back walk that if those bees belonged to him he truly would pick up the hives of the Black Germans and carry them down and pitch them into the Pacific Ocean. He would not have anything called a Black German, not even a bee, where it was a daily reminder of what true Black Germans had done to men of his father's race and country, to men who carried the same blood in their veins. Of course it was silly to carry the loathing contempt he felt for a race of men into his feeling for a hive of bees. It was not very sensible, but Jamie reflected, as he slowly climbed the walk, eating a big red tomato that he had picked from a vine he passed, that there was not much reason to most of our likes and dislikes in this world. What we liked was so a matter of individual preference, and preference was so controlled by the manner in which one had been reared, by environment, by individual taste, that necessarily there had to be a wide range given to personal preference.

Jamie wiped his fingers and threw the core of the tomato as far as he could fling it down the mountain-side, and went into the house. On the back porch he changed to his own coat, and entered the living-room to select the particular book he intended to read, with two thoughts foremost in his mind. His tenure of the Bee Master's garden had resulted in three things: He was a bridegroom; he knew a Black German bee from an Italian; and he had found out that there was something particularly and peculiarly satisfying about a big, dead-ripe tomato. He would try that tomato stunt between meals every day. The fruit slid down his throat and landed in his stomach with a sort of cooling, refreshing effect that was better than any glass of wine he had ever taken. There was no heat about it, no forced stimulation. It did the work and felt wonderful where it was and left an urgent invitation for more.

So the bridegroom stood before the small writing-desk and, opening the case above it, ran an investigating finger over the titles of many books. Then he selected one and dropped into the chair that he had decided to use as his own, and tried to concentrate all the mentality he had upon the subject of what is necessary for the beginner who would keep bees. He found himself reading paragraph after paragraph about proper hives and comb-cases and smokers and all sorts of paraphernalia that he could find in a big case on the back porch if he opened it and knew what to look for. His eyes were reading the words and his brain was fixing with unbelievable stubbornness—which, after all, was not so unbelievable in a man of Scottish ancestry—his brain would persist in dwelling on a surprised hand that had drawn back and then advanced to be decorated with a wedding-ring, on a marriage certificate that had been held tight against a breast that looked capable and immensely attractive. Then his brain would focus on a pair of keen brown eyes bespeaking nerve strain to the limit. His brain would keep making his eyes see quivering lips and twitching cheek muscles.

The thing he had done was going to stay with him for a while. He was not going to be able to put it aside and concentrate his thought on anything, not even a thing as interesting as the little Scout had said bees were. He truly did want to get on with a real bee book. That about bee nurses. Who would train a bee to become a nurse? Were bees sick? Did they need nurses? Did they sting one another and have wounds that would not heal on their small anatomies? He must find out about that speedily, but he could not find out about it at that minute because he had a number of things that were forcing him to think about them. And these things were, after all, important. You could not alter the fact that events had put him legally in a position where he was a married man, and you could not alter the fact that an immensely attractive woman had stood beside him and put herself in a position where she was legally a married woman; and there was not any reason why he should try to get away from the fact that she would be of much more use to the world, to her family, to a nebulous little person, as she stood, even in her black dress, in enforced composure, than she would have been as a formless thing wasted by an undertow leagues away and worried to the bone by the lean hounds of the sea. To have saved the life of a woman like that was worth thinking of. He had thought last night that it might be the one worth-while thing that he could do before the end. Since he had nothing else to do, and since it would intrude, he could not very well be blamed for thinking about it. Evidently no one else was going to think about it. He *had* coveted a word. He had not received even a "Thank you". But that was all right. He did not ask or expect anything.

Right there Jamie closed the book with his finger in the place and went to open his front door. A messenger boy handed him a parcel and a letter and disappeared with such miraculous swiftness that there was no conclusion left for Jamie except that he had been told to make his delivery and also to see how speedily he could vanish.

Jamie laid down the book without looking to see what page he had been reading and slipped the letter from the band that held the small oblong box in his fingers. With the letter in one hand and the box in the other he contemplated them. He studied them. He turned them over and around, and he caught an odour emanating from the box that he knew.

Before he opened it he recognized what he would see. He was sufficiently sensitive to odours that his brain told him, even as his fingers worked to confirm the message, that when he slipped the paper and lifted the lid of the size of box that florists used for violets, he would find a big bunch of the pinkish lavender flower that grew on the sand bordering the Pacific Ocean. Now he *would* get the flower book. And when he got it, as he did later, he learned to know sand verbena by its real name, and he learned that the six-o'clock odour of this flower is perhaps as sweet a scent as can delight the nostrils of any lover of evanescent perfume. He lifted the delicate blooms and hunted through the Master's belongings until he found a little bowl of antique copper, and this he filled with water, and into the water he carefully put the flowers.

Then he took the letter and sat down in the chair and slowly and deliberately broke the seal. Again Jamie felt that he knew exactly what he was going to see. The thing that the eyes and lips had been unable to say because the effort of speech would unlock a floodgate of tears, that thing had been written. So he was not in the least surprised, but to the depths of his heart he was pleased when he raised the flap of the heavy oblong envelope and extracted an equally heavy sheet of paper that he unfolded to read:

My dear Mr. MacFarlane,

The reason I left you without saying one word, without one backward look, was from the physical necessity of keeping my lips tight shut and my eyes wide open in order that I might not attract the attention of passers-by and humiliate you by making a scene before people.

I want you to know that what you did for me has given me life, the chance to go on with my work with the same prideful assurance I always have taken in it. You have eased the heart of a woman who was slowly dying from fear and anxiety.

All my life I shall thank you for your kindness of last night, for your unparalleled act of to-day. If you are correct in your statement that you have not much time, believe this, that every night before I go to bed I shall ask God to extend to you His utmost clemency, the deepest depth and the highest height of His mercy.

It is quite impossible that I should voice adequate thanks for what you did for me, and now I find that it is equally impossible to write anything on this paper that will come any nearer expressing my sincere thanks for the obligation to you under which I find myself. With all my heart I do thank you, and I hope that God will bless you and keep you. I hope that you may be mistaken, and that there may be a long and happy life in store for you.

Half a dozen lines ahead of it, Jamie got it, and it hit him in the face like a blow. It was written there in a firm, beautifully legible hand, just such writing as Jamie had imagined the hand that he had held last night, and had seen in operation that afternoon, would write:

With undying obligations,
Alice Louise MacFarlane.

"Well, I'll be darned!" said Jamie. "Can you beat it? Is she really going to take my name? Is she really going to use it in some kind of business? Is she really going to bring a child into the world and call it 'MacFarlane'?"

Then Jamie began the process of reading the letter again, and it was not long until he could have repeated it a word at a time backward. Just why he kept getting it out and holding it in his fingers and turning it over and examining the paper and studying the script, he did not know. It was wonderful, it was right, it was all his heart could have asked. It sounded exactly like the girl who was just the height, who had the strength of body, who had the mane of silken hair, who had the keen brown eyes, who had the firm breasts, the capable hands, the mellow, luring voice, that Jamie always had imagined would be exactly what he would want when he met the woman who would be the one woman of all the world to him.

CHAPTER IX

VITAMINES AND SCOUTS

THE last thing at night Jamie again read his letter. He opened the envelope and unfolded the sheet, very carefully scrutinizing each written word. It was not in the least necessary that he should do this in order to know the contents of the letter. Some way he liked the feel of the paper in his fingers. If he had been buying stationery for the Storm Woman, who had stood shoulder to shoulder with him during an official marriage ceremony, he would have bought that kind of paper. He thought very likely that he would have been willing to stake a small wager on the fact that this particular woman would use green ink. A woman who carried about her a distinct odour of sage and of sand verbena and primroses *would* use green ink. He thought that a hand such as he had held would fashion the letters of the alphabet as they were fashioned in his letter. He thought that she would express herself clearly, tersely, and in excellent English such as had been used.

As he read it and re-read it and repeated it from memory, when he was busy with the watering or occupying his hands with something that prevented him from taking it from his pocket lest he soil it, a doubt began to spring in his mind. The doubt had not the slightest reference to the girl who had written the letter. What he was vaguely beginning to distrust was his own judgment. He could not quite couple the feel of the woman he had held in his arms, the tones of her voice, the silken length of her hair, the agony of her cold, salt-encrusted face laid against his; he could not quite couple the brow and the eyes, the wide mouth and the firm chin that the meagre lightning flames had revealed; he could not couple the quivering lips and the twitching cheeks and the tear-suppressing eyes, with dishonour. He could not quite keep on, day after day, hour after hour, thinking over and over each least detail of his latest adventure and feel that this nameless, troubled girl was wanton. The real truth was that he did not want her to have been soiled. He did not want unbridled emotion ever to have swayed her. He did not want to feel that there was anywhere in all the world a man who could sully her honour. Sometimes he tried to figure on what manner of man he was who could have brought such trouble into the life of a girl who so filled his conception of exactly what a girl should be. He kept thinking about what a wonderful companion she would make; what a journey along the trail through the canyon of hurrying water would mean with her for a comrade.

Without the slightest knowledge of what had happened to him, Jamie's thoughts had taken a new turn. When he awoke in the night and shifted his position to rest his wounded side, he answered the demands of pain and immediately fell to thinking of the Storm Girl.

It probably would not be a debatable question with doctors as to whether Jamie's journey and his subsequent experiences were the best thing for a sick man. From their books, from their teachings, from their practice, they would simply know that such an experience would kill a man in Jamie's condition, and Jamie, in the little ones and twos of the night, stretched his long frame on the Bee Master's bed, moved either leg and either arm, and twisted his spine and felt that the soreness had thoroughly gone out of him. The pain of the long march had left his feet and legs; his hands and arms seemed to have sufficient strength for one day more. Then his attention was attracted by the rhythmical sweep of the waves as they came washing up the sands below his window and rolled back to the mother of big waters again.

Jamie turned his head and listened to the song of the Pacific Ocean. He decided that there was a reason why it had been called the Pacific Ocean, the peaceful ocean. From the window beside which he lay his vision carried for miles across the moon-silvered water, water so calm that it was scarcely ruffled by the waves that kept in undulation almost as regular as breathing. Just when Jamie had decided that the Pacific Ocean had been well named he remembered the Storm Girl. That recalled to his mind the storm, and he reflected further that perhaps the ocean was like a woman, that it was the still waters that ran deep; that after many days of peace, when the storm finally came it really was a storm to make even the God of Storms look down and take notice.

The thing that a doctor never could or would have figured on about the entire circumstance was the thing that happened. Breathing in unison with the sweep of the waves, Jamie very shortly went to sleep again. His last conscious thought was not about himself. It was a commingling of lazy, sunlit waves, a feeling of being drawn somewhere by a rope of hair across his face. He went over the top into dreamland in imagination clutching a letter in one hand, and in the final drop into unconsciousness the last thought that he sensed in his brain had something to do with a bathing-suit and a gorgeous, big red tomato.

When Margaret Cameron finished dusting and entered the kitchen to gather up the dishes from which Jamie had eaten his breakfast, she found that long, lean individual sitting at the table and looking at her speculatively. There was a question in his eyes, a humorous quirk around his mouth. His fingers were drumming the table. Then he spoke.

"Margaret Cameron," he asked, "are you a lady ?"

Margaret Cameron took hold of a wooden chair-back, and leaning forward studied Jamie intently, but she answered him quietly and readily enough :

"I try to be."

"Oh, I don't mean," said Jamie, "have you got a long line of highly-bred ancestors ; are you skilled in the fine arts of society ; do you wear exquisite clothing and live a life of elegant leisure. What I want to know, to put it briefly and bluntly, is, would you faint at the sight of a drop of blood, if it happened to be human blood ?"

Margaret swung a chair round and sat down on it.

"Can't you manage your dressing ?" she asked quietly.

It was Jamie's turn to be disconcerted.

"You know," said Margaret, "when you bent over to reach the hose, and going through the garden, the bandages across your back and the straps over your shoulders show, and they look to me to be cumbersome things. I've wanted to speak to you for a week. I believe I could take some unbleached muslin and make a kind of jacket, and fold some supports across your shoulders that would hold it up exactly as well and not be half so uncomfortable."

Jamie sat silently staring at her.

At last he said : "I think what I had in my mind was this : I was going to ask you, if you could stomach it, if you would take one good look at a decoration I wear on my left breast, and then I thought I'd go to work and put a kind of schedule that I've thought out for myself into practice for, say, one month ; and then I'd ask you if you would look again and see if I'd done any good. I've got a shrapnel wound and it must have been particularly filthy shrapnel. It carried with it some sort of damnable poison that defied the best doctors at the base hospitals, and passed me on to London and then to this country and clear across the Continent. I've had a year of boiling in hot water and fussing with nurses and doctors and I'm worse than I was when I began their treatment. Just as a little secret between you and me, I'll tell you this. They were going to put me in a tuberculosis place, when they knew and admitted I didn't have tuberculosis yet, and I wouldn't stand for it. I got up and walked out, and I've come this far. From the minute I started, and for long before, when that hot, chemically-saturated boiling spring water soaked into me, I couldn't help feeling that it was fostering germs and breeding more. For six months I've wakened in the night thinking about the sea, and I'd got to the place where, when I decided to walk out, I headed for a cooler spot and for the ocean. Now I've got here and I've made up my mind that I am going to try it. I want to go over a list of food with you; I want you to cook me plain, simple, nourishing stuff, something that's got iron in it, something that will have a tendency to purify and to clean up blood saturated with poison.

"When I finish my morning rounds with the bees I am going to put on that bathing-suit at the back door; I am going down the back walk and I'm going to squeeze a tumbler level full of the juice of a couple of those big red tomatoes and drink it, and then I'm going on down to the sea and I am going in mighty close to the edge of those bandages. I'm not so sure that I am not going heels over. Then I'm coming out and I'm going to lie on the hottest sand in the hottest stretch of sun I can find, and cover the bare parts until I get toughened enough that I won't blister. I'm going to let the sun dry that salt water into my anatomy. I'm not going to rinse it off. Then I'm coming up and eat whatever you prepare for me in the kind of combinations we agree on that will go towards the making of a man. Then I'm going to take a nap. Then I'm going to get up and drink a glass of orange juice. Then I'm going to go out in the garden and see what I can do for the flowers. There are some dead leaves on the lilies that need to come off and there are some that need propping. I could clip the seed-pods from the roses that have bloomed to help keep up the succession. I can find a world of things to do. Then we will arrange a dinner that will have at least a tendency to be what you might call a gesture in the direction of making a real man out of particularly big bones and peculiarly flabby muscle. I'm going to walk down to a place on the beach that I call the throne and I am going to sit there, and thoroughly wrapped in the Master's eiderdown dressing-robe and his old working overcoat on top of it so that I cannot possibly chill, I am going to breathe fog and mist and salt water until my tongue tastes salty in my mouth. I am going to lie down there and go to sleep if I take the notion."

Margaret Cameron stretched out her hand.

"Now look here, Jamie," she said, "you're all right up to that point, but you had better cut that right out. You had better not try sleeping outdoors in fog and mist. Maybe it's all right to go and breathe it for an hour, but don't go to sleep and let your circulation run down and the fog settle over you and wet you and chill you to the bone. That's a wrong idea. Change that part of your programme, and as for the rest, I'll think hard all day, and you think hard, and this evening we'll talk it over and see if we cannot make out the menu you want to follow. You try with all your might and I'll try with all my might and we'll see what we can do, with the help of the good God and all outdoors, to put you on your feet. Now, come on, let's have a look at that sick side of yours."

So Jamie stretched himself on the bed and uncovered his breast. Margaret Cameron, bending over him, could feel the blood slowly receding from her face.

"My, but that's an angry wound!" she said at last. "The flesh looks as if it had been burned. It's almost angry enough for what we used to call 'proud flesh'. And it is deep and it's wide."

She stood staring an instant. Then she shifted her eyes to Jamie's.

"Are you good for a strenuous diet and a stiff pull?" she asked.

"If you mean have I got the courage, yes," said Jamie. "If you mean have I got the strength or have I got a chance—I don't know. All I know is that I am going in the ocean. All I know is that I am going to soak in sunshine. All I know is that I am going to be a calamity to the tomato patch. Why I want these things I don't know. But I am ravenous for all of them, and, since they are here, why shouldn't I have them?"

"Where'd you get that tomato idea?" asked Margaret Cameron.

"I ate one yesterday and it seemed to fill a long-felt want. It seemed to hit the exact spot. I had a feeling that it was cleansing and cooling. I got the idea that if I'd squeeze the juice from a couple of them and drink it at a time when my stomach is empty, it might do something for me from the *interior out* that medicines and boiling springs have not accomplished."

"It's a queer thing," said Margaret Cameron, "but there

may be something in it. There's a housekeeping magazine I take that has a health department in it that I have been reading for several years, and in the last year or two they have been stressing nothing in all the world but just the thing you have hit on. Just tomatoes. I didn't think I'd ever pay much attention to what the little Scout would call 'bunk' about vitamines and calories and the like, but the other day something funny happened to me. I went down to the city to do some shopping and to pay a visit to a niece of mine who teaches in the schools there, and she took me to lunch in a lovely big room in one of those enormous department stores. At a table right adjoining us there sat a woman whose name Molly whispered to me across the table, and I remembered that wherever English is spoken all over the world her songs are sung. She had a noble face, a kindly face, an intelligent face. I couldn't keep my eyes from the efficiency of her hands, and the beauty and individuality of her clothes. With her there was a little dumpling of a girl. You couldn't imagine anything healthier; you couldn't imagine anything prettier or more appealing. At one time when I was feasting my eyes on the child, because she reminded me so of my own girl when she was a little roly-poly thing like that, just when I was looking straight at her, with her spoon poised halfway to her mouth and her eyes very serious, she asked, 'Grandma, how many calorith ith there in thith jello?'

"And 'Grandma' threw back her head and laughed until half the diners in the room looked in her direction. Then she took off her glasses and wiped her eyes and said, 'Lord love you, child, your old Grandma wouldn't know a calory from a calumet! You'll have to ask your up-to-date mother.'

"Then the youngster laid down her spoon and announced very positively, 'I can't eat thith jello leth I know if it's got the right number of calorith!'

"And the white-haired lady answered, 'Well, my dear, I am a pretty good physical specimen myself, and I've got along all my life without knowing whether I was eating calories or vitamines or rattlesnakes. I just go ahead and eat food that is what I want and tastes right, and nothing happens to me. There won't anything happen to you if you eat what you want for one day while you are lunching with me, and to-morrow mother can tell you whatever it is that you want to know.'

"The baby thought that over and then she said cheerfully, 'All right. I'll dust eat it and thee what it doth to me! Maybe it will reduthe my hipths. Don't you think they sthick out a little too much?'

"I looked at the little person carefully. She had the brightest eyes and the finest skin. You could see away down into her cheeks. Her lips were so red and her flesh looked so firm that I thought to myself, 'Well, whatever calories and vitamines may be, they have certainly done very perfect work on you. If I were your mother, I'd keep you right straight on the path you're going.'

"I asked Molly something about it and she tells me that she broke down a little with her school work last year and she took a trip to Denver. There she heard about a doctor who cures everything that ails you with what you eat. The idea seems to be that there are certain food combinations that you can't safely mix. The point Molly brought out was that the great American breakfast, eggs and toast and bacon and coffee, is about a deadly combination. Molly said that doctor proved that the yeast of bread and the albumen of egg and the fat of bacon and what caffeine you get in coffee would kill a guinea-pig in short order. It seems that you may eat all the eggs you want cooked any conceivable way, but you must not take them in combination with the yeast of bread and the acids of meat. You may eat all the starch you please at one meal; but you must not take it in combination with the acids of meat or albumen. You must keep the bread and potatoes and starchy things confined to one meal. Then for dinner you may have any kind of meat you want; but you must take it with vegetables that are not starchy. You must cut off the bread, beans, potatoes, any starch. You must confine the desserts to fruit and jellies and leave out the pastry. It is simple; it is easy. Merely a slightly different arrangement in combinations of the same things you have been eating all your life. But Mollie says it makes all the difference in the world. She's been trying it for a year and she says her flesh is so hard and her muscles work so fine, and her brain functions better and she doesn't know she has a stomach. She thinks it's wonderful. What I am going to do is to make a point of seeing her and get her to write out the combinations, and then I am going to try them on myself and I can try them on you at the same time. And on your own hook you can try the sand and sunshine and the salt water and the sea fog and the tomato and oranges, and we'll see how we come out."

"At any rate," said Jamie, "it will be more interesting to put in time planning a fight to live than to spend months moping around figuring on how soon I am going-to die. In the meantime, if you would be so good as to fix up that arrangement you talked about for bandaging, I'd be very grateful. If I could get out of the weight of all this harness I'd almost feel as if I'd been redeemed spiritually as well as physically."

So Margaret went home to bring her sewing-basket and her measuring-tape, and Jamie sat on a chair while she took his measurement for the length and width the bandages need be, and figured on the shoulder-straps to support them. Then Jamie returned to his work.

At exactly ten o'clock he came up the back walk and selected two of the biggest, ripest tomatoes he could see on the Bee Master's vines. He carried them to the kitchen and worked the juice from them through a small round sieve he found hanging on the wall, and when he had a tumbler overflowing he lifted it and drank it with the keenest relish.

"That certainly hits the spot!" he said.

Then, being Jamie, and his early rearing being ingrained, he emptied the pulp into the sink basket and turned the faucet on the sieve, and when it was thoroughly cleaned he wiped it on a towel hanging above the sink and laid it in the sunshine of the window-sill to be quite sure that it dried thoroughly without rusting. From the hook beside the door he took down the Master's bathing-suit and, going to his room, divested himself of his clothing and stepped into the suit, and when he drew it up to button it over his shoulders he was not wearing anything by way of dressings for his wound save a pad of gauze fastened in place with such binding as he could secure from a face towel pinned with safety-pins. His bare shoulders felt wonderfully released. He was as elated as a woman with a hair-cut.

In old slippers to protect his tender feet, and with an old Indian blanket to keep his unaccustomed flesh from burning, and a handful of towels, Jamie went down the back walk, travelling slowly, out through the gate, and standing there he selected one spot where the waves of the bay stretched before him looked peculiarly clean and foamy white. Then he made his way between the mounds of gold primrose and the verbena that waited for the cool of the evening to show the loveliness of its face and to distil on the air its delicate perfume.

Gingerly Jamie set his bare feet on the wet sand. Slowly he advanced on the ocean. When the first cold waves broke over his feet he could have shouted with delight. They were not nearly so cold as he had imagined they would be. Only cold enough to give a refreshing feeling of exhilaration. A little farther out, a little farther out, he was in to his knees; then half-way to his waist; then to a point where he began to feel top-heavy, to realize that he must either swim or go back. He could not feel that swimming was exactly the thing he should undertake, so he contented himself for the beginning with walking up and down at the greatest depth he could manage and preserve his equilibrium. He could not always tell exactly how the waves were going to run, and sometimes he stumbled on an unseen rock. Once he fell headlong and felt a cold wave, half of terror, half of delight, run through his blood while a colder wave of salty water washed clear over him. He stumbled to his feet and shook back his head. He reached down and scooped up handfuls of water and rubbed it up and down his arms and over his shoulders. He swung his long arms in it and kicked out his feet, and when he found that he was panting, he walked out and, purposely, in the cleanest, bluest place he could select, thoroughly immersed himself. Then he arose and went back to his blanket. He arranged it, and the towels he had brought, in such a way as to cover his arms and legs and his head, and to leave his trunk clad with the wet suit exposed, and he stretched himself on the hot sands and let the sun of California come raying straight down until it dried the salt water in the dressing-pad and the suit into and around the wound on his breast. The amazing thing was that it did not sting nearly so badly as he had thought it would—nothing to compare with the severity of many of the different dressings that had been used until his flesh was cooked almost to the point where it would endure no further punishment.

Jamie found himself saying: "Salt. Saline solution." It struck him that he had heard of natives in uncivilized countries using salt for the healing of wounds. He remembered institutions that advertised salt baths. There must be something pretty fine about salt used medicinally. Then he remembered that the little Scout had told him that every gallon of water dipped from the Pacific Ocean contained three and one half per cent of salt.

When he had lain for an hour in the sun, Jamie got up and went to his lunch, and afterwards to twenty minutes on his feet in the garden, and then a nap. Then he drank the juice of two ripe oranges, drank it cool from the ice of the small refrigerator. It struck him, as he closed the refrigerator, that it might be a good idea to work up enough tomato juice to fill two or three glasses and consign that to the ice so that he could have it cool. So he went down to the garden and gathered the tomatoes and put that thought into action.

It was while he was in the kitchen working with the tomatoes that there came a rush of feet under the window and a blood-curdling series of yells broke on the air. Jamie dropped the tomato that he had been using extreme care not to drop, and muttered an exclamation as he recovered it, drenched it under the faucet, and laid it on a plate. Then he stepped to the back door to see what the commotion might be.

Drawn up in front of him at a particularly erect angle, and pulling off as snappy a salute as he was accustomed to seeing anywhere, stood the little Scout. Ranged along the walk there were three children concerning whose sex there could not be the slightest doubt.

The little Scout indicated the first youth in line.

"Eleven, possibly twelve," said Jamie to himself.

The introduction, accompanied by a wave of the hand and a flourish of a wooden sword, was this: "Fat Ole Bill!"

Jamie's quick eyes went to the face of the youngster. Fat Ole Bill had not the slightest objection to being "Fat Ole Bill". He grinned, did his best at a salute, and stepped aside.

The Scoutmaster waved a sword, and a boy—"Possibly ten," commented Jamie—a boy, lean, slender, with olive skin and red lips, with black hair and big liquid black eyes, a boy unusually beautiful, stepped up, trimly saluted the Scoutmaster and then Jamie. The introduction that accompanied him was, "Pa's and Ma's Nice Child."

Again Jamie's eyes searched the face of the youngster, and it was evident that the "Nice Child" did not give a darn what the Scoutmaster called him.

The sword waved for the third time as the Nice Child stepped aside and the next boy fell into line—"Possibly thirteen and maybe fourteen," was Jamie's comment—a boy taller than either of the others, with enough flesh amply to cover his bones, red hair, blue eyes, and immaculate and unusually expensive and carefully selected clothing. There was a peculiar arch to the boy's lips, a slight projection of the teeth, a flock of dancing lights shining in his eyes. The wooden sword waved a wide circle and grounded. The red-haired youngster executed a salute for the Scoutmaster so gracefully that it was a picture to see. His heels drew together, his chin lifted, his shoulders squared. The salute was wonderful. The Scoutmaster waved him on to Jamie with the introduction, "Angel Face."

For the third time Jamie looked inquiringly and discovered that Angel Face was so accustomed to the title that he probably would have been annoyed if it had not been used.

Then, with little grey points of malice in his eyes, Jamie squared his shoulders and executed a for-sure, honest-to-goodness, four years in a bleedingly bloody war salute for the youngsters, and all of them pricked up their ears and recognized the real thing when they saw it.

"Gentlemen of the Scout Company," said Jamie; "I am exceedingly gratified to be introduced to you. No doubt the Bee Master has been accustomed to welcoming you in his garden. In his absence, I extend the same welcome." He turned to Angel Face. "Would you be good enough," he said, "to give me an introduction to the Scoutmaster?"

The red-haired boy opened his eyes wide.

"The Scoutmaster knows you!" he said defiantly.

"Sure!" said Jamie. "The trouble with me is that I don't know the Scoutmaster."

At that minute a badly-battered wooden sword circled through the air.

"Attention! Scouts to order!"

The boys lined up and saluted beautifully.

"Ready!" came the order of the Master. "Tell the world the name of your Scoutmaster!"

The boys squared themselves and paused ready. The eyes of each of them were focused on the point of the sword.

"Altogether now!" said the Scoutmaster. The sword waved through the air, and in unison, at the tops of their voices, the boys began, each letter bitten off with a snap that fairly hurled it in the face of Jamie: "T-H-E, The. L-I-M-I-T, Limit—The Limit!"

They saluted and dropped back, and the Scoutmaster stepped before Jamie, sheathed the sword, straightened the right hand down the seam of the pantaloons, laid the left across the breast, and the figure swayed forward in a profound bow. Jamie knew exactly as much as he did at the beginning—slightly more, for he saw that the Scouts really were obedient and really were well-trained.

Then the Scoutmaster addressed Jamie: "The Bee Master lets us fight Indians here."

"All right," said Jamie. "Whatever he allowed goes with me."

The Scoutmaster turned to the Scouts.

"Disband!" came the sharp order. "Prepare for attack!"

Jamie looked the Scoutmaster over. He had no notion when the Dutch bob had been brushed. It was ornamented with quite a collection of the wild oats of California and a few small twigs and leaves. The face might have been clean some time that morning. It certainly was not clean then. He saw a different shirt, but equally as disreputable, and the same breeches and shoes that had been worn on the first visit. The Scoutmaster marched down the length of the walk, heading straight toward an opening in the whitewashed board fence that separated the grounds of the Bee Master from those of Margaret Cameron. Jamie watched while the right hand of the Scoutmaster went into a protruding pocket and, from a mass of things that it contained, selected a piece of red chalk. By that time Jamie had taken a seat on the bench under the jacqueranda and concentrated on the Scoutmaster. He had forgotten the Scouts. He had even forgotten to wonder why they had disappeared and where they went. With deft strokes, quick and sure, the scoutmaster was executing on the white-painted fence, with sufficient skill that the intention was recognizable, the figures of four Indians. The first was limned as leaning forward peering ahead. The second was more erect. The third faced front, and the fourth followed.

When the Scoutmaster reached the girders to which the boards of the fence were nailed, he merely lifted the chalk, made a line on the edge, and dropped back again to the boards. By the time the four figures were blocked in sufficiently to be recognized, the Scoutmaster came back to Jamie and from a breastpocket of his shirt produced a genuine police whistle, through the ring of which a leather string was knotted that passed around the neck. Lifting the whistle, the little Scout blew a shrill note, and bounding past bushes and over flowers from different directions came the Scouts. Each of them was armed with a gaudily-trimmed bow, a leather quiver on the back filled with crudely-fashioned arrows. Most of the arrows were roughly-dressed splinters of wood.

The Scoutmaster saluted.

"Scout One, my weapons!"

The imperative command was instantly answered by Angel Face. He saluted before the Scoutmaster and offered an extra bow and quiver of arrows. Gravely the arrow-pouch was slung over the shoulder and the strap fastened on the breast. Gravely the bow was taken possession of and the sword sheathed.

"Scout Two!"

Fat Ole Bill grinned the salute he could not make as he appeared round a lilac bush; his arm loaded with big, dead-ripe tomatoes.

"Scout Two, advance and do your duty!" came the command; and Fat Ole Bill waddled to the fence and set a big red tomato on the girder exactly where the heart might have been supposed to be in the anatomy of each crudely drawn Indian.

The action began suddenly—whirlwind action. The voice of the Scoutmaster was shrill with excitement.

"Attention, Scouts! The Redskins are upon us. Our homes, our children, our firesides are in danger! Keep in ambush. When you see the whites of their eyes, if you are ready, Griggsby, you may fire! Aim at the bloody red hearts of them! Fire to kill!"

The Scoutmaster darted behind a clump of Scotch broom, fitted an arrow to the string of the bow, and selected the tomato heart of the first Redskin for a personal target. Bill and the Nice Child and Angel Face chose for themselves different bushes and trees of the garden, and at the Scoutmaster's shrill cry: "Fire!" with various success in aiming, the arrows whanged against the fence.

Jamie sat watching the proceedings. He was in doubt as to what his position in the circumstances might be. The fence that had been particularly and shiningly white was most objectionably decorated in consideration of the beauty of the garden. Jamie wanted a liberal supply of those red tomatoes himself, and he had been thinking, when he gathered the ones he was preparing in the kitchen, that instead of allowing quantities of them to waste it might be possible for him to carry them to the nearest corner vegetable stand and secure for them at least enough to buy a box of blackberries or red raspberries or some other necessary food that he might want. There was a possibility that such fine fruit as those tomatoes could be sold for enough money to replenish the cash drawer from which he was supposed to buy the milk and ice and the daily paper.

While he was meditating on these things the air awoke to a series of shrill cries. If Jamie had been blindfolded he would have sworn that there were twenty-five youngsters on the job instead of four. It was no longer possible to tell Fat Ole Bill from Angel Face. The Scoutmaster was lost in a series of wildly revolving gyrations which included deftly leaping over flower beds, dodging behind trees, circling bushes, crawling belly to earth. A hail of arrows pinged against the fence, and presently, the wilder the excitement grew, the straighter the arrows seemed to be aimed, and tomatoes began flying far and wide. In the midst of the din a particularly well-aimed arrow hit a particularly large tomato rather from below and jarred it from the fence. Among the wild cries Jamie could distinguish the voice of the Scoutmaster shouting, "Ha! Another Redskin bit the dust!" And return shouts, "Call the ambulance!" "Put him on ice!" Suddenly Jamie sat back and began to laugh quietly, began to enjoy himself. The first thing he knew he was down on his hands and knees. He had gathered a handful of pebbles from the walk before him and then, screened by the jacqueranda, he began shooting the pebbles with accuracy and precision at the tomato hearts of the Redskins. Seeing this the Scoutmaster went wild. "Soak 'em !" came the shout. "Pep up ! This is where the West begins !"

Angel Face sent an arrow over the fence.

"Foul ball !" shouted the Scoutmaster. "Aim below the belt. You'll scalp the early settlers."

Having exhausted his arrows Angel Face disappeared for an instant, and returned to the fray beating the bee drum and shouting : "Atta boy ! Keep your powder dry !"

Flying down the walk came the Nice Child with a fresh instalment of tomatoes.

"First aid to the injured !" yelled the Scoutmaster.

"Ki-yi-ki, yi-ye, huh-huh !" Fat Ole Bill forgot which side he was on and essayed a war-whoop.

"Listen to the rain crow warble !" shouted the Scoutmaster, and in an excess of frenzy, lacking arrows, joined Jamie in throwing stones.

When the last tomato had disappeared from the girders the Scouts appeared breathless and panting before the Scoutmaster, who stood with sword at attention while the Scouts fell in line for orders. "Scouts, our thanks to the noble stranger who has so ably assisted us in vanquishing our ancient enemies."

Three small boys, embarrassed at the unexpectedness of the situation, faced Jamie. Fat Ole Bill hung his head, and with his eyes rolled obliquely, muttered, "Thank you !" The Nice Child looked at him straight and said, "Much oblige !" Angel Face brought his heels together, saluted with dignity, and said, "Deeply obligated, sir !" and the Scoutmaster swept the sword in a wide circle and repeated the hand on the chest bow, and then straightening, faced Jamie. "I thank you ! My Scouts thank you ! Your country thanks you ! Everybody in this darned neighbourhood thanks you ! Scout One, get the hose ! Scout Two, bring the broom ! Scout Three, turn on the water !"

When the line was laid, the Scoutmaster took charge. The water spanged against the white fence. Fat Ole Bill wielded the broom. The Nice Child and Angel Face gathered up the scraps of tomato and carried them back to the garbage can. When they had finished and everything was neat again and the late afternoon sun began with a few last rays to dry and whiten the fence, Jamie noticed in passing close to it that there were dozens of almost invisible red lines all through the white, and he realized that the sham battle was probably a weekly affair in the garden of the Bee Master. So he went back to the bench under the jacqueranda with the feeling that in permitting the encounter he had not exceeded the limit of his privileges. While his back was turned, exactly what happened he was not able to decide. When he turned to take his seat his gaze encountered a heap of flying legs and arms. Arms and legs everywhere. A big ball of humanity was rolling over the gravel walk, and in it the fat, bare legs of Bill, the olive-brown legs of the Nice Child, and the silk-stockinged, kid-shod feet of Angel Face were intermixed. Presently the Dutch bob of the Scoutmaster appeared on top, and the leader with deft hands began separating the mass, disintegrating it, expertly flinging it in different directions.

"Get a pacifier for the babies!" shouted the Scoutmaster. "Grabbing and fighting over a hose like that! I said, 'Scout One, put the hose away!'"

Angel Face was sputtering.

"You didn't said no such thing! You said, 'Scout Three,' and I'm Scout Three myself! You wouldn't a-told One to put it away when you'd told One to bring it!"

The Scoutmaster fell into deep meditation. The sword handle was used to scratch the tumbled head.

"Fellows," said the Scoutmaster, dropping into a confidential tone, "I guess Angel Face is right. I guess, by Gum and by Golly! I *did* tell him to put away the hose; and I guess I told Two to put away the broom, and I guess I didn't tell One to do anything; which is for the reason Ole Bill's so fat it's cruelty to animals to make him move, anyway!"

The Scoutmaster sheathed the sword, combed the Dutch hair with soiled fingers, wiped the face on a particularly dirty sleeve, and stuffed in the tail of a shirt very much in evidence.

"Scouts, use your lipsticks and disband for the day!" came the order.

Then the Scoutmaster walked up in front of Jamie, took a decided stand, and looked at him inquiringly, while Bill and the Nice Child and Angel Face ranged themselves near, their eyes highly expectant.

Jamie, sick though he might have been, Scot though he surely was, remembered back dimly to the time when he was a boy and fought imaginary Indians, and hunted with wooden guns and flourished wooden swords and made weapons with rocking wheels, and carried in his anatomy a stomach that was for ever empty. The stomach that was for ever empty was the keynote of the present situation he felt sure. Jamie rose up and extended one hand to the Scoutmaster and the other to Angel Face, who happened to be such a particularly attractive young gentleman that Jamie succumbed to the light of his eyes and the charm of his smile the first instant he had a square look at him.

"Come on, fellows," he said casually. "Let's go down to the corner stand and clean out the 'hot dogs' and strawberry pop!"

The shrill cheering that greeted Jamie's ears was perfect compensation for the amount of the hole that the treat would make in the very meagre bunch of loose change that he carried in his breeches pocket.

Lined before the stand, while their diverse orders were being attended to, the visiting Scouts looked Jamie over critically. They liked the twinkle in his eyes. They liked the lean smile that crept over his white face. They liked the accuracy with which he had whizzed the pebbles and the dexterity with which he had gathered more when his supply ran short. Above everything else they liked the fact that he had worked from behind a tree. If he had stood in the open and picked up stones and thrown them it would not have meant much to the Scoutmaster and that particular band of Scouts; but the fellow who played the game hard, who played it according to the rules, who made it not a game but a reality by playing it as they played it, was nothing short of a real fellow, and the youngsters crowded close and began to ask questions.

Jamie sat down in the shade of a live oak and put one arm around the Scoutmaster and the other around Angel Face, and saw to it that there was room for Ole Bill and the Nice Child; and while the buns were being toasted and the onions fried, and the wienies split and browned and the mustard beaten smooth and the dill pickles sliced, and the pop brought from the ice, he told the boys something about what scouting meant when a man started on a night as black as a hat, on his stomach, crawling over shell-holes big as a house, through broken rock and the débris of a sodden battlefield, with a rain of shells and shrapnel bursting over him, trying to get close enough to steal a secret from the enemy, searching for the odour that attached to a beloved Buddy, hunting for the body of an officer.

The Nice Child and Ole Bill came and pressed close to Jamie's knees. The Scoutmaster leaned the Dutch head against the wound on his breast and strained unblinking eyes on him, and Angel Face laid violent hands on his arm and paid not the slightest attention when the stand man said: "Your 'hot dogs' are ready!" and the popping of corks began.

"Tell us some more!" they shouted in unison. "Tell us some more!" And Fat Ole Bill kicked the olive shin of the Nice Child and said: "Gee! we never got a chance like this before, did we? He's been where the ground's all soggy with real blood, and swords and things cuttin' into him, and shootin' goin' on above him! Gee, ain't he wonderful?"

It was Jamie himself who wrecked the party with his sensitive nostrils. He had talked about vitamines and calories. He had agreed with Margaret Cameron that they would start a régime that he would follow religiously, but since the régime had not started as yet, and since it seemed to him that he never in all his life had smelled anything quite so alluring as the odour of the "hot dogs", he reached a long arm over the heads of the youngsters and with one hand gathered up the plumpest "hot dog" he could see, and with the other a particularly pink bottle of pop. What he said was: "Fall to chow! Help yourselves, Buddies!"

Half an hour later he came up the grassy sidewalk past Margaret Cameron's door and grinned at her. His white face was flushed peculiarly, and Margaret Cameron peered at him over the load of clippings she was carrying and then stared reprovingly. "I'll wager two bits you went down to the corner stand and ate 'hot dogs' with those youngsters," she accused.

Jamie smiled at her joyously.

"You win!" he said enthusiastically. "Holy smoke! but they were jewlicious!"

CHAPTER X

BECAUSE OF GOD

THE next time Jamie answered the telephone he got his call to the hospital. At two o'clock the following day he again boarded the trolley for the city, and with no difficulty whatever made his way to one of its largest hospitals. Almost immediately he was shown to the room of the Bee Master, a big room where the sun shone in and the wind played through and the air was tinged with the perfume from a bowl of yellow roses. The instant Jamie saw those roses he realized that if they were not from the bush that grew beside Margaret Cameron's door, they were from some other bush that belonged to the identical family and species. The yellow of the roses, the faint sweetness of their perfume was in his nostrils as he rounded the screen by the bedside and stood facing the Bee Master.

Exactly what he had expected to see he did not know. What he did see almost broke his heart. The man whom he had supported to the davenport, whom he had helped to the ambulance, had been ill; he had been in a sweat of agony; but he had been a man alive, with a chance for life manifest by the strength of his frame, the firmness of his muscles, the light in his eyes. It seemed to Jamie that the frame stretched on the bed before him was not tenanted by life, but by a spirit, a spirit that might flicker out and make its passing at any minute. There was not much strength left in the white hand that reached out to him. The voice that greeted him was scarcely above a whisper. The eyes that searched his face and rested on him were tired almost beyond endurance.

To cover his shock, his sense of pity, Jamie drew up a chair and began to talk about the thing he knew would be of most concern to the Bee Master.

"First of all," he said, "I must tell you that I believe I'm bee immune. I've worn your coat, and used the mint and the cinnamon pinks and the Madonna lilies prescribed by your partner, and they have been effective even above the dressings I'm carrying on my side. I can fill the water pans and gauge the right amount of salt and go past any of the hives with safety. I haven't had much length of time to study, but in so far as I know your bees are flourishing. Your partner sends you word that they are all right, and the youngster really seems to know."

"Certainly," said the Bee Master, "my partner does know. My partner knows bees rarely and finely well, even to performing the delicate operation of clipping the wings of a queen."

"All right, then," said Jamie; "you can take it that the bees are fine. Margaret Cameron sends her love and her assurance that your flowers are flourishing, and I can tell you that your house is being cared for lovingly. I lock it carefully if I leave it, and I live in it sympathetically as behoves a man who treads on antique rugs and touches antique furniture. You will find everything exactly as you left it when you come home again."

The Bee Master smiled. "I divined that would be the case when I hailed you from the road," he said. "You appealed to me, even in that hour of agony, as a man of fine perceptions and right instincts. I knew that I would be safe in leaving even my most cherished possessions with you. I had not any sense that you were a stranger. You seemed to me rather an instrument that had been sent to serve my dire necessity. And the little Scout? My little partner?"

"Your little partner comes to the garden, but I doubt if the garden is much of a garden without you. There are two things that I have to tell you."

Jamie dipped in his pocket and produced the price of the "hot dog" and the strawberry pop and laid the coins in the outstretched hand of the Bee Master.

"My instructions," he said, "were to have the bun fried, the 'hot dog' split and cooked crisp. The onions were to be browned. The exact amount of mustard was specified. I was to superintend the construction of that 'hot dog' personally and with care. I'll go now and see that it is made according to specifications, if you think Doctor Grayson would not cane me."

The Bee Master smiled. He closed his fingers over the money, the identical pieces that his little partner had counted out for him.

"That money was carefully selected," said Jamie, "from a collection of buttons and buckles and dice and moonstones, and it happened to just about clean out the treasury. There wasn't much left. But your partner won a bet that was going to bring in two bits, so bankruptcy is not looming. I happened to be a witness to the winning of the bet. An accurately directed stream of saliva hit a bumblebee at about ten paces and knocked it off a red creeper."

A dry chuckle shook the frame of the Bee Master.

"Good work!" he said heartily. "My partner can be depended upon to hit 'most anything that happens to be the mark that's aimed at."

"And your partner," said Jamie, "has got a heart that's filled with love for you, love so deep and of such a nature that I truly believe that the offer to give a right hand that would be needed in riding a horse, in paddling a boat, in managing the Scouts, nevertheless, the offer freely and honestly made, of that same right hand in your behalf if it would ease the pain and bring you home safe and well."

The Bee Master shut his eyes tight and lay there fingering the dime and the two nickels. By and by he smiled stiffly at Jamie.

"You need not doubt the loyalty or the sincerity of that offer," he said. "And you need not doubt that it would have been heroically fulfilled had necessity arisen. And you need not doubt, on my part, that in all the world there is no one left half so dear to me as the little fellow. One of the reasons I'd like to live is that I might go on further in what I am trying to teach that particular youngster about the keeping of bees and, incidentally, about the keeping of a soul that I happen to believe is immortal. Anything my partner has got from me will do no damage. In fact, I have a feeling that the damaging things of this world are going to go past a mind that is fully occupied with something legitimate and constructive. Don't tell my partner that I dare not have the 'hot dog' or the strawberry pop. Say that I am mighty thankful to be remembered. Give my love, and if you feel that I would not be too much of a shock, next time bring the little fellow along."

"I'd be only too glad," said Jamie. "And now, can you give me any instructions before I go? Doctor Grayson specified that I must stay only a few minutes."

"I think there is nothing but to go on as you are. I'd be glad if you would put in your spare time among the bee books. It would help you with your job. It might interest you to an extent that would carry you on during the time of my weakness, provided your own strength is sufficient. Grayson wants to see you in his office here in the hospital before you go, and if you will pull out that drawer there on the left and put the envelope in it in your pocket, that will afford you at least some compensation for what you have done for me in easing my mind about my home and my belongings and my business. Tell Margaret that they will not allow me to write, but that I love the roses she sends and her notes are much company to me. Tell her I hope she will continue to indulge an old man until—let's say until I reach home again, since I possibly have some chance. I will say good-bye now. I want you to know that I am thinking about you almost constantly in my waking hours. Be sure to see Grayson. He is mighty fine. He might be able to suggest something that would make you less white and help you to gather strength. Now it's good-bye."

"Good-bye," said Jamie, "and rest easy. Among us, Margaret Cameron, the little Scout, and myself, we can manage the bees. There is no difficulty whatever about the flowers and the trees. I've already got that routine."

Then Jamie went down and found the office of Doctor Grayson, and half an hour later he went home with a big bundle of antiseptic dressings and without a drop of medicine. He had been advised to follow his impulses. If his body cried out for cold salt water, to indulge it. If the demand was to lie in the sand in the sun, to go ahead.

"Since a year of the best care they could give you at one of our finest Government hospitals didn't budge your trouble, try doing exactly what Nature tells you she wants you to do," said the doctor, "and see what results you get from that. I am not sure but salt water and sunshine and clean air are not the best doctors in all the world, anyway."

In the office Jamie sat on a bench to rest a few minutes and decide what he would do next. He was thankful for the dressings, because he had not known exactly what would be the best things to use. The doctors and nurses had done what they pleased to him, but he had not known very much about what they were doing. Now he would have the assurance that what he was using could at least do no damage.

He thought about some necessaries he wanted, and he wondered if the envelope contained enough to replace the sum he had borrowed for a ring and the marriage licence, and so he opened it. Then he sat in dumbfounded amazement. It would not be a wise thing to go back and enter protest in the room of the sick man. He counted up the days that he had been on the job in the garden. He figured that he had had his room and his board and the use of the clothing he required, but it was not right and it was not reasonable that he should be paid any such sum as that envelope contained for what he had done. He sat there wondering if men all over the country for common day labour were being paid any such sum as that. He felt the money between his fingers. He spread it out before his eyes. He studied it searchingly. He could replace what he had borrowed and he could spend the same sum two or three times over, for only a few days of the protection of his presence about the bee garden.

That was practically what his services had amounted to. He had kept the house open. He had given it the effect of someone on the job. He put the money in his pocket—in a pocket where he could slip his hand into and feel it. He left the hospital and went on the street, and still he kept fingering that money. If a sick man could earn that much merely by "sticking around", as the little Scout had expressed it, what could he not do if he were well? Doctor Grayson had said that salt water and sunshine and clean air might possibly be the best doctors. Very well, then, he had the Pacific Ocean full of salt water. He had the whole sky full of sunshine. He had air, absolutely dustless and clean, wafting softly from the ocean every hour of every day, coming all the way from China. If there were dust in the air he breathed, Jamie reflected that it would have to be star dust.

So he squared his shoulders and with one hand he felt the money, with the other he felt his breast. He touched it deliberately, as probingly as he could through his clothing, and he discovered that since he had recovered from the strain of his tramp it was not quite so tender as it had been. If he could earn money like that, if he had a garden of wonder to work in, if he could earn the Bee Master's confidence, if he could daily make worth-while friends, if he had a wife, if there were going to be a child to bear his name, what was the use of dying? There might be something very well worth while that he could do in the world. At any rate, he could get an unlimited supply of interesting work and interesting amusement out of the bee garden and the little Scout.

So Jamie went to several stores, and bought some things he needed with the assurance of a man who has the price in his pocket. Then he went home and for the first time in two years he changed his occupation; he was thinking about life instead of death.

He put away the things that he had bought and then headed straight toward the bench under the jacqueranda at the top of the blue garden. He found on the bench, curled up like a kitten, the little Scout sound asleep. In an effort to step lightly that he might not disturb the child, his foot turned on a stone of the border that had rolled from place and the slight grinding awakened the little Scout. Instantly the youngster was up, smiling ingratiatingly and stretching two sleep-misted eyes to the widest extent in an effort to prove that sleep had not touched them since the previous night, at any rate.

In further effort to prove that a Scoutmaster was always awake and fit, the youngster stepped forward and inquired brusquely: "Now what shall we *do*?"

Jamie sat down on the bench and drew the little Scout down beside him.

"I'm tired," he said. "I've been in to visit the Bee Master, and he is feeling fine. He sent you his love and he was very much pleased with your gift, and some day soon he wants you to come to see him."

The little Scout nodded in acquiesence.

"But if you're tired, what can we *do*?"

Jamie smiled.

"Must you have something active and vigorous to do every waking minute in your life?" he inquired. "Can't you occasionally sit down and rest and commune with your soul? If you are so very anxious to do something, let me make a suggestion. I have everything to learn about bees that you already know. How would it work, if you have an hour to spare, to spend it on my education?"

The little Scout studied Jamie intently.

"You mean that you want me to wise you up on all I know about bees, when there's all the Bee Master's books in there on the shelf to learn from?"

"But didn't the Bee Master study out a world of things for himself? Didn't he know enough to fill a book of things that he had figured out in a lifetime of experience with the bees? Maybe some of it was original with him. Maybe you know things that are not in the books."

The little Scout chuckled.

"Well, there's a good many things that are not in the books that we would *like* to know. Somebody's got to do a lot more studying about bees before everybody knows everything there is to know."

"Well," said Jamie, "suppose you begin wherever your fancy strikes you and tell me what you think I should know about bees."

The little Scout leaned forward, laid a pair of hands, not so clean as usual, palm to palm, and dropped them between a pair of knees that gave evidence of active service in recent contact with the earth. Then suddenly an intent little face with eyes of deep introspection was turned to Jamie.

"Guess," said the little Scout, "guess the first question I ever asked the Bee Master about bees?"

" 'Why do you keep bees?' " suggested Jamie.

Slowly the little tan and brown head moved in negation.

"Nope! You're all wet!" said the little Scout. "You're not even warm. First question I ever asked was, 'Why is the bee garden blue? And I'll have to tell you the answer because you would never guess it in a thousand years. The answer is, 'Because of God.' "

Jamie's face betrayed the astonishment he felt. His brow wrinkled in thought; his eyes narrowed. He stared at the little Scout and repeated softly: " 'Because of *God*?' "

"Yes," said the little Scout. "That's what makes bees so interesting. About half the things you'll have to learn are because of God, and why the bee garden is blue is the very first thing. Now you listen and I'll tell you the reason."

With uplifted hand to caution silence, slowly and deliberately the little Scout repeated the explanation that had been given to the first question concerning bees.

"The bee garden is blue because blue is the 'perfect colour', and bees are the most perfect of any insect in the way they live, and the most valuable on account of the work they do, and so blue would be the colour they love best, and it *is*! If you don't believe it, *watch* them. And because why—the nearest we come to a perfect insect loves a perfect colour *best*, why, that's because God made them as they are!

The little Scout looked hard at Jamie, and Jamie's face was non-committal.

"I guess you don't get it," ventured the youngster. "Well, wait a minute and you *will*. The first thing you've got to learn is some figures. Because you are big, and maybe been to college, you ought to learn 'em if I can. For one thing, there's four thousand five hundred different kinds of wild bees. That's one thing for you to remember. Another thing is that one hundred thousand kinds of plant would not live any more if all these bees were blown away or burned up or something, because, you see, a plant has to grow where the wind carries its seed or a bird or a squirrel sows it, and if one plant happens to be a male and another happens to be a female, they can't get up and walk to each other and do their courting and make their seeds come good, now *can* they? So they have to have something to carry the pollen back and forth to make the good seed.

"Now *here's* something to remember about a bee itself—say a worker bee, because if would be the one that would carry the pollen. First you can remember that in every one of the little tubes on its nose a worker has got five thousand smell hollows, so it is no wonder it can pick you out if you got a scent about you that isn't *right.* Then a worker bee has got six thousand eyes on each side of its head so it can see the flowers that it wants to get the pollen and the nectar from. And a worker bee has got two stomachs, a little one more inside for itself, and a way bigger one more on the outside for the hive. Back on its abdomen every worker bee has got four pockets to secrete wax, and every worker has got baskets on its legs to gather pollen in, besides the nectar that they carry in their stomach for the hive. Every one of them has got a good sharp sting that it can use if it doesn't like your scent, or if it thinks you are going to hurt it or do something you shouldn't around the hive. Every one of them is covered with hair that is long for a bee, and it is soft and fine, and when the workers go down into Mr. Male Iris to get nectar for their two stomachs and to fill their pollen baskets, the hair all over them fills with the pollen too, and it is the law, because of God, that when any bee starts out to gather nectar and pollen it never *mixes one flower with another*. If it *starts* on iris, it keeps right on going to *iris*. You can see it now, can't you? When the worker bee gets the pollen from Mr. Iris all over his hair and then goes on to get pollen from Miss Iris, the hair is going to scatter the pollen for her that's going to make the good seed come, because the bees do the flowers' courting for them. That's a reason besides honey as to why bees are so useful.

"One time I asked the Bee Master if I couldn't *see* God and if I couldn't *touch* Him, how I was going to know that He was *here*. And he said, 'Because of the hair on a bee!' So that's *one* of the ways *you* can know.

"Then there are a lot of ways you find out about God on account of how He made Queen bees. A beehive is just full of miracles and signs and symbols and wonders. The Bee Master *said* so. But perhaps the biggest wonder in the whole hive is just about the Queen. There is a lot about God mixed up with a Queen bee. Workers may only live five or six weeks, but a Queen may live five or six years. She is a way bigger than a worker and she looks different. She is long and slender and has bigger wings, and she has a big abdomen 'cause she may lay a million or two eggs. She has only about half as many eyes as a worker, 'cause she only needs them when she goes out to find her lover, or maybe a few times more when she has a great hive full of one hundred and twenty pounds of honey and so many bees they are in one another's way. So when she gets everything ready she tells part of them to come with her to found a new hive, and leaves the others to refill the old hive after the Bee Master takes his share of the honey.

"The way a Queen comes to be a Queen is this way: In a little cell all fixed up for it the Queen bee of a hive puts an egg, and she tells the workers 'I want this egg to be a Queen.' Then the workers get busy and make the royal jelly. That's another thing the people who write the bee books haven't found out. They don't know just what royal jelly is or how it is made. But the *workers* know. God showed 'em how when He made 'em. So they make the royal jelly and they feed it to what comes from the egg that the Queen said should be another Queen. It grows to be a white nymph, and when a white nymph is ready to fly it is a young Queen. With different food they feed what comes from each egg in each different cell, and out of each cell there comes the thing that the Queen says she wants to come. For fear something might happen to the Queen, 'cause there can't any hive get along without a Queen, she lays a whole lot of eggs that she says she wants made into Queens, and then she lays quite a number for males and some for nurses and thousands and thousands for workers. Remember this: Bees make four different kinds of cells.

"Now when the Queen has her hive full of honey and enough white nymphs to be sure that the hive will always have a Queen, and lots of bee bread to feed the nymphs and all the other bees that are shut up in the cradles, and when everything in the hive is just right, a thing happens that nobody understands about. Right here is where the Queen takes her ladies of honour and her architects and her masons who make the combs, and her workers who bring in the pollen and the nectar, and she takes some males and she takes some nurses, and she goes right away and leaves all the work that all of them have done so carefully. The thing that nobody knows is who decides, or how it is decided, who shall stay in the hive and who shall go. But it looks like two-thirds of them go with the old Queen.

"Before the old Queen starts to leave the hive with the swarm that goes with her, all of them except the Queen go to the honey vats and take honey to last them five or six days, so they will not starve while they're finding a new home, and so the wax that they can distil from the honey will be right along with them to lay the foundations for the cells to begin work in their new home.

"Then the Queen walks out of the hive, and the ones that are to go with her all come too. She flies a little way and settles on an orange branch, or maybe on a fig, or a jacqueranda, and close around her come her ladies of honour and all her swarm that are taking care of her. They hide her away down among themselves so no bird can get her, or hawk moth, or anything, and the scouts go out to hunt a new home. When the scouts go to hunt a home they hunt a place in the rocks up in the canyon, or a big dead limb in a live oak or a sycamore. But if the bee master is truly a bee master, he has known for several days, by how busy the hive is and by the things he hears the bees say to one another, that they are going to leave their home and find a new one. So if he wants to keep his bees and make his garden get bigger and bigger, he has some hives standing back, all ready, and he watches; and when the Queen comes out of her door and starts to fly he takes his bee drum, and slow and easy and deep, drum, drum, drum, he beats it. The bees wonder what that strange sound is. They forget just what they were going to do, and settle on the nearest limb and hide the Queen like I told you, and quick the bee master goes and gets his smoker and smokes them just a little bit to keep them quiet and easy. If he loves his bees he doesn't smoke them very much, because a bee hates smoke the worst of anything in the whole world.

"Then right quick he cuts off the branch or he sets the hive under it, and with the hand strips off the bees and tumbles them in. He always has to be sure that he has the Queen and that she is all right. Then he takes the hive and sets it on a new stand and puts it in his bee garden. If he wants to he can put it right beside the hive the bees came from, and they will not ever go back in the hive that they lived in before. They will always stay with the Queen and live and work in the new hive. The Queen never in all her life goes out again unless she wants to found another new hive. Then she goes just the same as she did this time. So that is the way the bee master gets new hives of bees.

"Back in the old hive that's left they're feeling pretty blue, because along comes the bee master and takes his share of the honey, and their beautiful Queen is gone, and lovely, golden boxes of comb that fill the hive almost full are empty except for what the bee master leaves, and everybody stands around and feels blue and waits. The workers don't go out after nectar like I get from the Madonna lilies, nor for pollen. They won't hardly even clean up after the lazy old drones. It is the bluest time the hive 'most ever knows. So they all go and they gather around the cells that the old Queen laid the eggs in to make more Queens. The old Queen knows when she leaves that out of one of these cells pretty quick there is going to come a new Queen. So just when everybody in the hive is getting pretty well discouraged, one of the white nymphs sticks up her head and eats open the lid of her cell and comes walking out. The nurses go rushing to her and help her clean up and comb her hair and polish her wings. They kiss her 'cause they are so glad to see her.

"Another thing that God has done in a beehive is not to let one young Queen come out alone, because when she gets all ready and fixed she is going to go out into the great big world to find her King, and if a beebird or a kingbird eats her up, why, then the hive is in a worse trouble than it was before. So maybe the same day, or a day or two later, another white nymph sticks up her head and eats her way out of her cell and comes walking out. But nobody goes to her help or helps her very much, 'cause all of 'em are betting their money on the first one out.

"When the Queen that came out first sees another Queen has left her cell, it makes her awful mad. Right there the fight begins. They just go at it like I go at the Nice Child and Angel Face when I can see back in their eyes that they think maybe they're going to mutiny on me. Only I stop when I got 'em licked. The young Queen doesn't stop until she's got the other Queen killed deader than anything, and the workers carry her out to the bee cemetery.

"Then the young Queen wants to go on and kill every white nymph that's sleeping in the rest of the cradles. Right then and there she wants to do it. But the workers and the scouts and the guards step up and they say, 'No you can't do that. You have to go and find your King and come back ready to be the mother of the hive before you can do that.

"So the young Queen rests up a few days and gets all ready, and one day when the weather is all bright and sunny, in the morning when the dew is on the flowers and the lark is on the wing and everything, like that morning Browning wrote about—the Bee Master made me learn it : that one about 'God's in His Heaven and all's right in the world' ; I expect your mother made you learn it too—why, the new Queen goes to the door and she walks out of it backward. She goes away a little piece and she comes back to it three or four times. God told her to do that so she would be mighty sure when she came home from the first long flight she has ever made she would know her own door.

When she is sure she knows where she belongs, why, then she starts this flight, and God's in the way she can fly too, because she hasn't had a chance to use her wings ever before. But when she does use them she goes up and up away up into the sky, she goes up higher than the trees. She goes up higher than the birds. She goes up so high that the men who write the books can't ever see how high she does go.

"When she starts out, all through the line of the hives the something that the bee books call 'the Spirit of the Hive', or Instink, or Nature—but that the Bee Master says is just another name for God—tells all the male bees that a young Queen has gone out to search for a King. They can't ride a milk-white charger to find her; they have got to use their wings. But they are some punkins on looks. They are big, swaggery fellows. On their heads they wear helmets trimmed in black pearls, and tall plumes. They have yellow velvet belts and long mantles, and they walk over everybody in the hive. They don't even pay much attention to the Queen—till they start out to court her. They have been a big nuisance all their lives. They won't work a lick. They don't go out and hunt any honey. They just walk up to the cells that the workers are filling and eat all they please. They go out and curl up in the tulips and in the lilies, and wherever they can find a beautiful flower cradle, and lie there and sleep in the sun for hours. Then they come back and eat some more, and they are too lazy to live like the other bees do, but the worker bees know the hive can't go on without them, so they clean up after them. Nobody likes them very well, but nobody says a word *because they are part of God's plan.* It's all right for 'em to have a good time while they've got the chance; they don't know a little bit about what's coming to them.

"So when the young Queen goes out, all the males think they would like to court her, and from all the different hives they go swarming up after her. They spread their wings so wide and they fly so hard and fast that they get all swelled up and get more air inside them than they ever had before, and they get different from the way they were before they started. It takes a good, fine strong one to go as high as the Queen does. Finally, when some of them get 'way up mighty close to heaven, all alone up there where the sky is blue and the day is sweet and everything is so nice and fine, the Queen says which one may be her King. Then they get married. They don't have but a little bit of a honeymoon, for the Queen says she must go straight home and go to work. So she doesn't even wait to say good-bye to the King; she just gives him a big push, so big and hard it kills him, and he falls down to the ground deader than anything. And she goes home and goes into the door, and she's lucky if she gets home and gets in the door 'cause on account of birds and things. That's why there are more white nymphs waiting, so that if the young Queen doesn't come back, another one can be got ready and sent out. You see how it's all fixed up from the beginning to keep things going! That's why *God's* in it, because it is such a wonderful plan, and it is things that *men* couldn't do in any way at all. It takes just God to plan life for the bees.

"If the Queen gets home everybody is so tickled when she comes through the door that they kiss her and they comb her hair and they polish her wings and they fix her all up fine. You wouldn't think there was a thing but love and goodness in their hearts.

"Then what do you think the workers do? You couldn't ever guess, not in days and days, so I'll have to tell you. All the white nymphs that they have been feeding royal jelly, and that the nurses have been taking care of so fine, get *stung*. Can you beat it? You know how when any man cheats in business and loves another man up and makes him think he is his friend, and then turns around and takes all his money and maybe kills him, why people say the good man 'got stung'. Well, right there in the beehive what happens is 'cause the reason why they say that. All the white nymphs that have been loved up so good and fed on the royal jelly, the minute the young Queen gets home all safe and sound, why, the white nymphs that would be Queens if they got a chance, they all get stung to death, and maybe there's forty or fifty thousand of them—that's how sure the bees want to feel about having a Queen. They are so dead that the workers carry them out and put them all together with the dead ones.

"The next thing they do is for all the workers to get together and every big, bluffy drone that has been lazing round the hive and getting waited on by five or six worker bees and everybody has stood everything from him, why, every one of them gets stung too. When it happens in the observation hive you can sit with the glasses on 'em and see their faces, and they look so surprised and scared you can't help feeling sorry for them. They don't know what they've done and they don't know why what's happening to them happens, and they can't understand why workers that waited on them, just a whole army of workers, mad as Alice's March Hare and the Hatter out of Wonderland, come roaring at 'em singing a war song and whooping battle cries. The old Mr. Drones get their wings pulled off and they get their eyes stung out and they get punkshered everywhere, and every last one of them gets killed good and dead, and pushed out of the hive.

"There's not anybody left but the young Queen and the maids of honour and the workers and the nurses that are going to stay with her. If there's any danger, all of them make a shield and cover up the young Queen. If it is a hard winter they get close around her to keep her warm ; and if there isn't enough food they all go hungry and feed her. No matter what happens to them, every one of them, as long as they are alive, takes care of the Queen, because it is the eggs she lays that make the new brood and keep the bees alive in the world. So something tells every bee, 'No matter if you die yourself, take care of your Queen, so that bees will not vanish off the face of the world like everything did that time of the flood.' The thing that tells them, that's God *again*."

The little Scout looked Jamie straight in the eye.

"You begin to see now, don't you, why the Bee Master said the hair on a bee was God ?"

"Yes," said Jamie, "I begin to see. It is the most wonderful thing I've ever heard about in all the world ! Go on and tell me more. Tell me every least little thing you know."

"There isn't much more to tell," said the little Scout. "There's more figures I could tell about—how the old drone males have got just oodles more eyes and more smell hollows than the workers. The old drone males have got thirty-seven thousand eight hundred smell hollows, and that is so they will be dead sure to find the Queen, and *that's* God again. And the old drone males have got thirteen thousand eyes on each side of their heads. That's so they can see better than anybody else and be certain to find the Queen, 'cause they've *got* to find the Queen, and they've *got* to get married, and the Queen has to lay her eggs to keep the world having bees, and to make the nice, sweet honey for everybody, and to keep the hundred thousand flowers alive.

"When the bee master gets the old Queen and her family in a new hive, he sets it up in a nice place. The scouts come back to where they left the Queen and they hunt until they find the new hive. They know their family and they go in, and then everybody goes to work. The workers build the cells, and the old Queen lays all the eggs and tells the workers what she wants to come out of each egg. They go straight ahead just like they did in the hive they came from. The workers clean up everything and the old Queen fills the cells again with eggs that she wants to be Queens and drones and workers and nurses, and maybe scouts, and they go on making more honey and hatching out more bees, until the hive gets so full that the old Queen says they will have to bring out a young Queen and turn the hive over to her while they go out and start another family.

"The Queen keeps giving orders all the time about what she wants done. She may rule for five or six years. She lays eggs all the time. You couldn't believe how many eggs—maybe as many as two millions. She has only got seven or eight thousand eyes 'cause she's a stay-at-home lady. Right-on-the-Job is her first and last name, both all two of them. But she hasn't any wax pockets, and no brushes and no pollen baskets. She doesn't like light and she doesn't know how Madonna lily nectar tastes, 'cause all her food is digested for her before she eats it. If I could work that scheme on 'hot dogs' you wouldn't think they were so bad, would you ?"

Jamie laughed.

"Go on," he said.

"Well, the Queen just keeps right on laying eggs all day, maybe all night for all I know. Anyway, she lays 'em. I tell you, boy, she *lays* 'em ! And every time she lays an egg she says what she wants it to be, and her nurses go right to work to feed the royal jelly to the white nymphs, and bee bread to make more drones, and to make the workers and the nurses, and the scouts, maybe, like I said before. And some of the workers are builders and some are masons and some are dancers. It's the dancers' job, when the hive gets very hot inside, to dance and wave their wings until they start a breeze to cool the cells. And sometimes they dance the queerest dance for the white nymphs.

"That's *part* of what I know about bees. I couldn't tell all I know about them 'cause I can't think of it all at once. There's too much of it to tell right hot off the bat. But you can watch 'em in the observation hive and pretty quick you can see which cells have got the big, soft, white nymphs in them, and which ones have got the big fat drones, and which ones have the little workers and the nurses, and the scouts, maybe. After what I've told you, you can see the old drones crawling around over the cells eating honey where they please, and being as dirty and mussy as ever they want to. Then you can see the workers go and clean up after them. You can see the cells where the eggs are being taken care of. You can see the cells that are being filled with honey. You can see the cells that have gold and red and purple pollen in for wax. Next time I come I'm going to ask you about the figures that I told you, like the Bee Master asked me. You have to be ready and not make any mistakes, because if *I* can remember, a big man like you ought to remember !"

The little Scout stood up, pushed down the tail of the green shirt that seemed habitually to work up, tightened the belt buckle at the waist, and drew a deep breath.

"I don't know as I've told you so very well. In there in the library you can find books like I showed you that tell what people *used* to think. The books that are the bunk. Then you'll find the books like Lubbock and Swammerdam, which have the wonderful pictures, that will tell you what really happens. Then there are the books like Fabre and Maeterlinck that the Bee Master says are three things at one time. First they are the truth, and next they are poetry, and third they are the evidence of a Master Mind that plans every least little tiny thing. He says the only name for that Master Mind is God. He doesn't see any use in trying to dodge God and side-step Him and call Him 'the Spirit of the Hive' and Instink and Nature and things like that. He says a great scientist, one of the best, almost went crazy trying to do that very thing. His name was Charles Darwin, and the Bee Master says C. D. would have been a heap bigger Injun if he'd been willing to put God in where He belongs. He says when God does anything 'with such care, and puts so much thought in it, and deals out such splendid justice' as there is in a beehive, that a *wise* man will just take off his hat and lift his eyes to the sky and very politely he will say, 'Just God.' "

Then in a lightning-like change, the little Scout kicked a high-standing pebble with fine precision against a mark several yards away, plumped down on the seat beside Jamie, and inquired casually, unconcernedly: "What do *you* say?"

Under the spell of the magic of the story he had heard, Jamie ran his fingers through his hair. Then he cupped his right hand over his knee, and put his left arm around the little Scout and drew the child up to him closely. He dropped his lips against the tow hair, worked down through its bleached exterior, down through the dark strands underneath, and close to the small ear he brought his lips and whispered very reverently: "I say, 'Just God!' "

CHAPTER XI

THE AROMA OF A SPIRIT AND A FLOWER

A FEW days later Margaret Cameron came to Jamie with a pair of jackets that she had fashioned from unbleached muslin. A broad band fitted neatly around his chest and fastened with flat buttons. A pair of straps, easy when sitting, sufficiently close-fitting to keep the bandages in place when moving around, crossed the shoulders. When his wound was dressed and he slipped on one of these contrivances and buttoned it, he felt like a man who had just been redeemed. The bandage was so much lighter in weight, so much easier to wear than what he had carried for two years. Above all, it served his purpose and did not constantly remind him, by its weight and the ceaseless chafing across his shoulders and under his arms, of the fact that it was there.

For a week he and Margaret worked together, "fixing their fences" they called it. They planned the best time of day to do the sprinkling. To the extent of the knowledge of either of them, they watched over the bees. As slowly and easily as possible Jamie went about everything that week. He kept religiously to the diet that they were working on, and every morning at ten o'clock he put on the Master's bathing-suit, and armed with an old blanket to cover his feet and towels for his head and arms, went down and boldly marched into the Pacific Ocean. After the first few ventures he discarded fear and walked in until the waves broke over him, and before a week had passed he discovered that by lying on his right side, stroking with his right hand and using his feet, he could trail his left arm and swim a few strokes. This fact so delighted him that merely the feeling of exhilaration helped the circulation of his blood. When he was thoroughly chilled from the tingle of the cold salt water, then, in a spot he had selected beginning in a mound of gold primroses and sloping down to the sands of the beach facing directly to the south-west, he stretched his long frame on the hot sand, disposed of the blanket and towels to his comfort, and fell sound asleep. When he awoke he would be thoroughly warm from the heat of the sands beneath him and his body would have dried while coated with the salt water.

Then he went through the quaint gate and slowly climbed the winding stairway that led to the back door. During these climbs he discovered that he was developing a familiarity with every flower that grew on either side of the path. Those that he did not know, Margaret Cameron did, from her years of work that she and the Bee Master had put upon their gardens together. He found himself studying the flowers, watching which bees went most frequently to which flowers, and when he discovered that the Black Germans were paying more frequent visits to the nasturtiums than to any other flower, Jamie sneered. He remembered from botanical days Nasturtium officinale. That was cress, but nasturtiums were of the same family. The boys in the classes had always called nasturtiums the "official nose twister", and wasn't it like anything doing business under the title of Black German to select for an especial favourite an "official nose twister?" This and other whimsies began to occupy his mind.

When he reached the house he went straight to the bathroom for a shower, applied fresh dressings, and clothed himself, and by that time Margaret had brought his lunch. After he had eaten he wandered about the grounds for the twenty minutes prescribed, and then deliberately lay down on the Master's bed and to the music of the rhythmic breaking of the waves he slept another hour. From that hour he came to a brimming glass of cold orange juice. As regularly he took the tomato juice in the morning, and, instead of either tea or coffee, he drank milk with his meals. When he had finished his nap he did as much work in the garden as he could do without tiring himself. Then he went to the bookshelves, but in his new resolve to fight to be of some good in the world he passed by the tempting volumes of romance and Ancient Natural History. He laughed at them and talked to them and repeated in their faces rich phrases from their unique pages.

"The bees pluck their young from the air and place them in cells, do they? The honey falls from the heavens, does it? The best bees are small, round and variegated, are they?"

So Jamie had his joke with the ancient naturalists and then he advanced on the moderns and sat down with a book of rules for men who would be the keepers of bees.

Back in the depths of his mind Jamie decided that when the

Bee Master returned he would be so weakened that it might be a year at least before he would be able to go on with his work, and during that time he would stay on the job, if the Master wanted him, and he would learn everything there was to know about bees. The more he thought of it the more it appealed to him that, since there was not the chance for forestry in California that there was in the East, he would do better and extract fully as much enjoyment out of life working with bees as he would with trees.

It was after ten days of religious following of this schedule that Jamie awoke one morning and, instead of arising immediately, lay still to take stock of himself. He stretched his right leg as far down in the bed as it would go and wiggled his toes. Fine! There was not a hint of soreness. He tried the left leg with the same results. Then he tried the right arm and then the left, and then he stretched his whole body and threw his weight on the back of his head and his heels and drew up his shoulders and eased them down, and the result of the exercise so delighted him that he tried it over again. He decided that it might not be a bad thing to work out a form of exercise and put himself through it every morning on awakening.

So for himself, and merely of his own volition, he began a practice which a very great doctor of health recommends for all men and women who would be physically strong. It was considerably a matter of stretching and squirming the first morning, but during the days that followed there developed a sort of rhythmic exercise that stretched and twisted every muscle in his body. After it he lay resting half an hour or so, and went to the work of the day with a feeling in his body and an uplift in his heart and brain that a few short weeks before he had never expected again to experience. He was beginning to realize that the heat and the nerve strain were in some way being eliminated from his system. He was beginning to experience a calm satisfaction in the pit of his stomach as if there were cooling streams running through his veins instead of torturing poisoned blood. The result of this feeling was that he could accomplish very much more in a day among the bees and with the flowers than he had been doing.

At that he realized that the time was coming speedily when he must have help. When it came to examining the hives and ascertaining for sure that each hive had a healthful and happy Queen, that no disease had crept in, he would need help. There was the question becoming imminent of removing the honey, and it seemed that there might be too many Queens. So the next time he went to the hospital for a visit with the Bee Master he asked where he could secure help when the day came that he would need it, and the Bee Master gave him the address of John Carey, another keeper of bees with whom he had occasionally exchanged work in times of honey collecting and swarming.

As Jamie sat beside the Bee Master's bed and watched him, it seemed to him that each day that passed marked a distinct point in the ravages of the disease that was devastating the lean frame before him. Each time he went he could see that the Bee Master had not quite his old strength of voice, that he was slightly weaker in the clasp of his hands.

When he had finished copying the address and listened to the instructions that the Master gave him, Jamie sat looking at the fine old face on the pillow, the skin like parchment, the silken hair, and it seemed to him that daily a great peace and a quietness were growing on the brow and in the eyes, and he thought of what the little Scout had said about the beautiful kind of death that came softly in the night, and he wondered if any night now that experience might not befall the Bee Master.

It was while these thoughts were dominant in Jamie's mind that the same thought must have been passing in the brain of the Bee Master. His voice was very low and quiet and his eyes seemed unusually tired as he said: "Jamie MacFarlane, suppose you begin away back at the beginning and tell me all about the mother who bore you and your father and what kind of home you were reared in."

Now these were subjects upon which Jamie MacFarlane could speak eloquently on slight provocation, because he had loved his father and mother with good reason. They had been full Scot stern, but they had also been overflowingly Scot gentle and loving and tender, and his memories of his home and his childhood were something beautiful. Jamie, seated beside the bed with the light from the window falling on his face, spoke slowly with the deliberation that searches for the salient points, with the loving impulse that puts in the small details that round out the full picture. When he had finished with the final description of how he was brought home from the war to the shock of the knowledge that both of them were gone and there was nothing whatever, he sat very still, looking through the window, and it was the voice of the Bee Master that called him back.

"And from there on?" he suggested.

So Jamie began again and finished the story. He told it truthfully, with no deviation whatever except that he omitted the night of the storm and its subsequent results.

When he had finished, the Bee Master smiled at him, and

then he said: "And what about the bees and the weeks that you have been among them in the blue garden?"

Jamie answered: "So far as my mind is concerned, the time I have spent in your home trying to take care of your bees and your flowers and your trees has been the most beautiful time of my whole life. I began with a gnawing fire in my breast and a bitter blackness in my heart and brain; but some way, owing to something the little Scout said to me, and the clean air and the crisp sunshine and the beauty all around me, there is a sort of corresponding beauty that's crept into my heart and my brain, and I think it's smothered a large part of the bitterness. I was so desperately tired when I staggered across the road to you to try to help you reach the hospital that I am in no position to say what my physical or mental condition was when I came. But I know that to-day I have done about twice the work in the garden that I could manage the first day I really tried to look after your interests."

The Bee Master moved his lean hands over the coverlet. A rare smile illumined his face.

"That's fine!" he said. "Fine! And would you feel, then, that if they carry me out of here one of these days and bring me home, a wreck of a man unable to stand on my feet and carry on my work, would you feel that you would care to remain with me, that you would try learning bees from the egg onward?"

"I'd love it," said Jamie. "I'd love to wait on you and help you back to health over the same path that I've laid out for myself."

Then he explained to the Master what path he had laid out for himself, and again the gentle old voice cried: "Fine! Couldn't be better, and what's more, I can see that you are making it. Each trip you make to cheer the old man up a little, I can see that your skin is taking on a healthier hue, that the blue lights of pain and discouragement are fading out of your eyes. You even speak with a stronger voice, with the assurance of a man who is captaining his own soul. I am staking my money that you're going to win through to health and happiness in the garden that has come the nearest to bringing me consolation of anything I ever have tried."

The Bee Master lay still and waited a long time. Then he said to Jamie: "It may seem to you that such confidence as I asked from you should be met with equal confidence, but I find that my weakness has made a coward of me. Some day, if you ever want to know what there is to know concerning me, ask my little side partner. There was an hour of exceeding blackness in which the little Scoutmaster swung over my side fence and walked into my heart and into my life so securely that when this bitter hour came, almost before I knew what I had done I had laid the whole of my burden on the shoulders of a child, only to learn that however keenly a child may think, however deeply a child may feel, there does not seem to be a large capacity for shouldering burdens. Children are so occupied with growing, with amusing themselves, with exploring the wonderful world around them, with following their impulses to explore and to fight, that there isn't much possibility of weighting their young shoulders with responsibility for anyone else unless, by chance, you take them from their companions, from their play, and load them with sickening burdens of heavy responsibilities that are unnatural and that often breed rebellion in their young hearts. The little Scout knows why I left my home and a goodly circle of friends and came out here alone, and from two acres of rocky land and a few hives developed two acres of beauty and made homes for millions of little denizens that swarm in the garden. The little Scout knows my troubles, but God knows I don't believe I am equal to telling that story again! If the day ever comes when you feel that you need to know, tell the little Scout that I said you were to be told, and you will get an accurate account of what brought me here, of the bitter pain I have endured, and of the surcease I have found in the glory of the sunshine and the song of the sea, in the healing of the lilies and the consolation of the roses, in absorbing work with as interesting a branch of the evolution of life as the whole world affords. I have investigated rather deeply. I will guarantee you that in the evolution of any living species in the whole world there can be found no life processes more complicated, more absorbingly interesting, more nearly human than in just the development of bees. I hope that you are making good use of the bee books."

"Yes," said Jamie, "to the exclusion of everything else. The little Scout started me on the books that, to quote literally, contained the 'jokes about the bees'. The jokes were so absorbingly interesting that they held me. But if I would render honest service for the wage I accepted, I realized that I must work intelligently. So I soon dropped the jokes and went on to the reality. I have advanced to the place where I can recognize a Queen, and I know an Italian Queen from a German Queen, and I am also able to distinguish a nurse from a drone and a drone from a worker. Through long hours of studying the observation hive I've pretty thoroughly familiarized myself with what must be going on inside of each of the hives in those other long rows. As

I told you, I had intended to study tree surgery, but I figure that if there is such a possibility as that I may become a well man, and since I have no ties, I had better remain in the same kind of air and sunshine that seems to be working the miracle that I need to make a whole man of me."

Slowly the Bee Master assented.

"Yes," he said, "I think you're right. I think you're right. I think you can find even a greater amount of interest in the intricate and delicate life processes of a bee than in work with the insensate trees that grow because they must, for however interesting they may be, and however beautiful they may be, the fact remains that they are not carrying out life processes that border so nearly on thinking and on reasoning as do the bees."

"I have quite decided," said Jamie, "that I am going to study hard. I am going on carefully, and if you give me the opportunity I will make my work among the bees."

"About the location, now," said the Bee Master. "How do you feel about my location?"

Jamie smiled.

"I know the Atlantic seaboard and quite a bit abroad. I've seen the coasts of England and France and I've gone all the way across this continent. The bay below your place constitutes my whole experience with the Pacific, but I am fairly sure that in all this world there is nothing to be found much lovelier than your garden of perfect blue. You remember that the ancient Chinese called blue the 'perfect colour'?"

The Bee Master nodded corroboratively.

"There have been days in that azure garden, laddie," he said, "when God has really given me surcease, when for a minute a gold-haired vision of childhood has dropped from my mind, when for a minute the pain of the sin I committed against the woman I loved has been obliterated. If it can do that for a man carrying the burden that has been my portion, there is a prospect that a young man with health in his body and a heart without secrets might find the same great blessing in daily beneficence."

Jamie looked at the Bee Master and winced. For one second he sat with his lips open and his tongue ready to fashion words, and then he reflected that he had no right to tell a secret unless it were his secret alone. He had no right to describe the Storm Woman. He had no right to tell any man of the shame baby he had covered with his name. If there had been anything magnanimous in his deed, it would lose the fine flavour, the beauty that such a deed might have, if he talked about it. If he lived, there might possibly be something more to that phase of his adventure. If he died, he would face his Maker more of a man if he kept his mouth shut concerning a subject that drove so noble a specimen of womanhood as the woman he had married to the course she had taken.

"The next time you come," said the Bee Master, "make it on Saturday, and bring the Scoutmaster with you. That little Scout gets under my cuticle so deeply that I am hungry for the odour of horse and the tang of dog, and all the outdoors that carries wherever the Scoutmaster goes."

Jamie leaned forward with a broad grin on his face.

"Just between us," he said, "could you give me any accurate information as to the sex of the Scoutmaster ?"

The Bee Master leaned back.

"I could go no farther than my own conclusions," he said. "And it wouldn't be fair to the Scoutmaster to deal in surmises. Did you ever have any conversation on the subject ?"

"I asked point-blank," said Jamie.

"And what were you told ?" inquired the Bee Master.

"That if I could not tell, it didn't make any difference."

The Bee Master's head rolled back on the pillows. He laughed until a nurse came racing. As he wiped his eyes with the handkerchief she gave him, he said: "Well, really now, isn't that about the truth ? Does it make a particle of difference ?"

"I don't know that it does," said Jamie. "I'm sure it doesn't seem to have made any with you. I see no reason why it should with me."

He rose to go.

"We'll make it Saturday," he said, "and I think you'll be asked if I got your 'hot dog' right."

The Bee Master reached under the pillow and pulled out a small envelope, a tiny prescription envelope.

"In case I am," he said, "the one thing I've never done is to lie to my little partner. I'll tell the truth. I'll show the money waiting under the pillow until the doctor says I may have the treat."

"I see," said Jamie, "and I think you're right. I don't believe we get very far with the lies we tell children."

"We get nowhere," said the Bee Master sternly. "We get nowhere. They see through us or discover our deception later every time."

Jamie arose and went over to the side of the bed and took the Bee Master's hand, and suddenly he bent down and laid his lips on his forehead, and before he realized what he was doing he found that he was on his knees beside the bed. He heard his voice saying: "When I was a youngster my father and mother taught me to pray. In the intervening years I got so sure of my own sufficiency and efficiency that I grabbed the bait and ran, but lately, when I got to the place where I could truthfully say, in the language of the old hymn, 'Other refuge have I none,' I've been on my knees creeping back toward the foot of the throne. I am asking, if it's consistent with the divine plan, that I may be given back my strength and my youth, that I may be of some help in making my country a good place wherein to live, to work, and to love. I am going home and I am going to kneel beside your bed, and I am going to ask God if it is the best thing for you to let you come home, to let you have more life, more time to enjoy the beauty that you have created; and if that is not His plan, then I am going to ask Him to give you the surcease that the little Scoutmaster says was vouchsafed to little old Aunt Beth."

The Bee Master smiled.

"I heard that story," he said. "I was told about it when it happened. It was a very wonderful thing that those two children could have got such a lovely conception of the journey to the Far Country, and I am very sure it is the right conception."

Jamie kissed the Bee Master on the forehead, and then he lifted to his lips the slender hands of the sick man and, turning, went quietly from the room. As he went, he passed a beautiful blue bowl filled to overflowing with more of the yellow roses that he had seen growing only in the garden of Margaret Cameron.

All the way home Jamie rode in deep thought. Would the Bee Master ever be able to come back to the house with the gracious face turned to the roadway, with the luring garden looking to the sea? Would he ever again sit in his great chair by his fireside and read from his loved books? Jamie realized that he was not waiting to reach home and the side of the Bee Master's bed to offer up his petition. He was asking God as he rode through the turmoil of the streets of the city, crowded on either hand by people absorbed in the affairs of life, to grant even a short respite to the man he was rapidly learning to idolize.

When he left the car he walked slowly up the roadway to the house of the Bee Master. He entered it and stood irresolute for a minute, and then he walked to the telephone and, from a list he had made, selected the number that the little Scout had given him. When he called it, the rich, sweet voice of a woman answered.

Then said Jamie, "This is James MacFarlane of the Sierra Madre Apiary. Is the Scoutmaster at home?"

"Not at this minute," came the reply.

"Would you contract," asked Jamie, "to deliver this message? I've been to the hospital for a visit with the Bee Master. He is homesick to see his little partner. He has asked particularly for a visit the coming Saturday. I thought I had better tell you about it before arrangements were made with the boys for a scouting party or some kind of a hike."

"Yes, that's a good idea," said the voice at the other end of the line. "I'll make a note of the message and I'll see that it is delivered. I should be interested in knowing how you found the Bee Master."

"It is difficult to say," said Jamie. "He seems so frail that a strong draught of air coming in the window beside him might carry his breath away."

"Too bad," said the gentle voice. "That is too bad. The children dearly love him. Anyone can see that he is a noble specimen of manhood."

"Yes, I think that too," said Jamie. "His home here, his library, his room, the pictures on his walls, the furniture he uses, everything seems to indicate that he could not be finer."

"I've heard about you," said the voice over the wire. "If you're fine enough to appreciate the Bee Master to the fullest extent, it means that you are pretty fine yourself. We'd be glad to have you come in with our little person some day and take dinner with us."

"Why, thank you!" said Jamie. "That's awfully kind. I've been pretty seedy and I've been shunning people for quite some time, but I think, if there's an evening when you would not be having guests, I'd enjoy coming with the Scoutmaster and sharing your fireside for an hour."

"All right then. Come any time you choose," said the voice, whose every cadence Jamie liked. "There never was a time when there wasn't enough food on our table for one more and room to squeeze in one more chair. Come right along any time you'd like!"

Jamie hung up the telephone and looked around him. He was not in the mood for reading. He stepped into the kitchen and drank his daily quota of orange juice, and when he reached the back door there was a call in the air, a call that he answered with his blood. He went down the back walk and out of the gate and to his particular mound of beach primroses. He stretched himself on the sand, pulled his hat over his eyes to shade them from the sun, fitted his figure into the curves of the mound, and presently he was unconscious in the unconsciousness of deep, sound, refreshing sleep.

By and by he awoke, and even before he was fully conscious, sniffed the air with questing nostrils. "That's strange!" said Jamie to himself. "I chose this mound for its particularly inviting curve, but I didn't see any sand verbena on it."

Jamie drew a deep breath to be sure that he had not been mistaken as to the odour that was mingling with the primroses around him. He realized that so near to evening the verbenas would be opening to distil their sweetest fragrance. Then he opened his eyes and straightened up to look around him, and he discovered that his right hand was full of verbena blooms. He stared down at it; then he whirled to his knees and took a long survey up the beach and down the beach, and then he shifted over and scanned the sand with eager eyes.

There it was. The footprint of a woman—not the peaked-toed, pointed heel that he sometimes saw tilting over the sand. The imprint of a foot intended for business, shod in a shoe reasonable in width, unusual in length, with decidedly a common-sense heel. Jamie sprang up and, clasping his flowers, followed that row of footprints straight down the beach to the throne. With wildly beating heart and head awhirl, he climbed the throne and peered over, and he found that he was sickeningly disappointed that it was vacant. He took his own seat to the far south to think. He remained there, carefully sniffing the rock beside him. The tang of sage, the odour of verbena, a whiff of primrose, were distinctly discernible. Not to lose time, he made his way down the rock. But the track that led to it did not lead from it. Gravel and fine stone and rock over which footsteps could not be distinguished formed the way from the throne to the roadway above. She must have gone that way. So Jamie followed. But when he reached the road he could not see a trace of anyone that looked in the very least like the figure of the girl whom he was seeking. He went back to the throne and over the path he had come, and at the primrose mount he took up the trail and followed it south along the beach until he lost it among the entangling primroses and verbena, among the sea figs. Just at the point where he lost it Jamie discovered the reason why he had lost it. It had become obliterated by the tramping of dozens of little feet, funny little tracks, all of them the footprints of children. Blindly Jamie followed down the beach, and once he found a spot where the footprint he was searching for stood plain in the sand beside a spot where the sand verbena grew, and all around it there came again the obliterating fleet of childish footprints.

Then Jamie went home. He opened the gate and carefully

closed it after him. Half the length of the steps he sat down. For the first time he brought the little bunch of flowers he held around to the range of his vision.

"Can you beat it!" said Jamie to himself. "Can you beat it! That close, and I *slept*! I must be more of a log than I am of a man."

He sat staring at the delicate pinkish-purple flowers that, as was their wont in the evening, were opening wide with the heat of his hand and distilling all around him the exquisitely subtle and delicate odours of their particular perfume. Once Jamie looked out toward the sea.

"Then I'm right," he said. "She does live somewhere near here. At least she haunts this beach. And she knew me even with my face covered. For that matter, at a pinch I might know her form better than I do her face! But what's the object in filling my hand with the most appealing little flowers in all the world if she hasn't any use for me in any other way?"

Jamie thought that over carefully, and then he told the Pacific Ocean about it.

"Come to think of it," he said, "I've filled my purpose with her. She has the name she asked for. She has the ring and she has the certificate. She hasn't any further use for me, but this does prove that she has me on her mind, that at least she didn't use me and forget me."

Then Jamie dropped the Pacific as being rather impersonal and confined himself to the flowers. He held them daintily in his slender fingers and looked at them with absorbed, questioning eyes.

"I wish," he said, "that you could talk. I wish your little faces could tell me what you saw in her face when she gathered you. I wish that I knew exactly what was in her heart. I wish I knew whether she is very sure that she has finished with me, or whether there's something more that I could do for her."

Then Jamie shook himself and sat straight.

"By gracious!" he said, and this time he addressed a particularly tall, particularly straight, unusually handsome yellow hollyhock growing beside the pergola. "By gracious! I'm not so sure that she'd get me any farther if she did want me! It's one thing to offer a name you haven't any use for and a body that's not going to last so very long as a sop to dry a woman's tears, not of repentance, but of fear, a fear that the world is going to shun the leper of disgrace, fear that the accusing eyes of a child are going to look into her face and find her wanting—it's one thing to do what you can when your time for doing anything is strictly limited. It's only a few days now until this month is going to be passed, and if Margaret Cameron looks at my breast and can truthfully say that the fire is dying out of the wound there, if I am not deceiving myself in thinking that I am infinitely more of a man than I was thirty years ago, that's another proposition. That's a proposition that I hadn't figured on when I essayed the bridegroom stunt. And that's a proposition that's going to take a lot of thought. It doesn't behove any man to assume an 'I am holier than thou' attitude, but, at the same time, a man certainly has to do considerable thinking before he makes up his mind as to whether he wants to assume the rearing of a child fathered by a man who had the streak of yellow in his make-up that made him neglect to give his child honourable parentage."

Jamie thought that over. He thought for a long time. He thought deep and hard. He thought from the background of Scottish prejudice. He remembered personal pride. He thought from the background of public opinion. Then he cast them all aside and thought straight from the shoulder. From somewhere a legal phrase crept into his brain. "Mitigating circumstances." He could not think of the form of the Storm Girl as he had held it tight in his arms, he could not think upon the silkiness of her hair and the perfume of her breath and the wild odours that clung about her, he could not force himself to think that she was anything but fresh and young and healthful both of body and of mind. It was not compatible with ordinary reason that she should have polluted her body and smirched her soul, that she had broken the laws of God and broken the laws of man, and risked, not only for herself but for the life that was to come, that blinding, blighting thing which has been so comprehensively designated as the finger of scorn.

"Whoever," said Jamie to a particularly intelligent mocking-bird that happened at that minute to be perched on a brace of the pergola near him, "whoever invented that little phrase about the 'finger of scorn' didn't make it half strong enough. What they should have called it was the red-hot poker of scorn, the iron that can be thrust against the breast of a woman and that all her days can sear her soul and be set scorching anew at any unforeseen moment, and all because for a minute she probably loved a man so infinitely better than she loved herself that she risked her soul and lost it, so far as the world is concerned. It is a blessed thing that she did not lose it with God, for there was the Magdalene whom He forgave, and the Magdalene was an old-timer who perhaps deserved what the mob gave her. But after all, God did forgive her, and it wouldn't do to allow God to be kinder to a woman than a Scotsman would be."

The mocking-bird flirted his tail and cocked his eye and said, quoting an oriole on a plum tree in the garden, "Once more now! Once more now!"

Jamie grinned.

"Have I got to do better than that?" he said. "Well, how would it do if I said that I'd break my word not to try to find the Storm Girl, and start out with the deliberate intention of finding her? And how would it do if I said that I honestly and truly felt the 'mitigating circumstances' to be mitigating, and if I really turned out, say in about a year from now, to be a sound man, maybe she could overlook my scars and maybe she could explain, and maybe we could find something really beautiful in life together?"

Then the mocking-bird remembered a particularly brilliant performance he had heard on a date-palm down in Mexico from a bloody-red bird, and threw a repetition straight at Jamie's head. "Good cheer! Good cheer! Good cheer!"

So Jamie looked at his flowers again and saw that they were beginning to droop their lovely heads. He got up and hurried to find the little copper bowl in order to put them in water. When he had very carefully arranged them in the bowl, he carried it to the bedroom and set it on the stand beside the bed that could be drawn close to his pillow.

All the rest of that day Jamie stumbled as he walked, not because of weakness, but because he was dreaming a peculiarly absorbing dream.

CHAPTER XII

SEEING THROUGH VEILED PLACES

THE remainder of that week, outside of the time consumed in carrying out the régime Jamie had laid down for himself, he spent in the garden and with the books. With the trees and flowers he had a sure hand. He had learned how to make flowers thrifty and healthful in the meagre climate of New England. With water to lavish, with almost uninterrupted sunshine, with warm days and cool nights, very frequently foggy, Jamie found himself facing a reversion of all he knew about gardening. He very speedily learned that in a land so lavish with sunshine and water, his task was going to be, not to stimulate flowers to growth, but to cut back the growth in order to draw the strength of the plant more directly towards the production of flowers. Much garden lore he accumulated from Margaret Cameron—practical things that she had learned through experience: how to loosen soil; how to fertilize; how to water discreetly and to the purpose. Jamie already knew how to cut back effectively. What to do to secure flowers instead of leaves he soon learned.

All that week he was looking forward to Saturday, planning for the day on which he and the little Scout should go to visit the Bee Master. He had set the hour for their starting at two o'clock. It was fifteen minutes past two when the little fellow swung over the high board fence and came racing down the walk. Jamie was rather surprised. He had expected, from the casual and business-like manner with which the little Scout had conducted the fight with the Indians, that equal promptness and executive ability would be displayed in keeping a date.

He was waiting on the bench under the jacqueranda when the small figure sailed over the fence. Scanning the little Scout closely, Jamie thought he detected traces of recent tears. The eyes were suspiciously red of rim; the cheeks smeared with the undisputable evidence of childish grief. Instantly Jamie's heart went out in protest. Who had any business to hurt the little

Scout? What was it, beside the sting of a bee, that could bring tears to so valiant a small soul? Without taking time for thought, Jamie stretched out both hands. Without an instant's hesitation the little Scout walked straight into his arms and laid a confiding head on his breast, and Jamie's arms closed up tight.

"You didn't have a fall and hurt yourself, did you?"

Jamie could feel the shake of negation on his shoulder and the gulp in the throat.

"I'm sorry," said Jamie," but if we're not to keep the Bee Master waiting we must clean up your face and be on our way."

The little Scout instantly stood erect.

"Clean up! Clean up! Can't you tell by one look at me that I've been parboiled and scoured and curry-combed?"

"You do give evidence of having had a bath," said Jamie. "It's only the region of your eyes that needs slight attention."

"Oh, well, then," said the little Scout, "if you say I need it I reckon I do. I had so everlastingly much trouble with mother and the princess that I thought I never should get started. Women make me dead tired!"

"What's the matter with the ladies?" inquired Jamie as he led the way to the bathroom, moistened a wash-cloth, and began operations in order to make sure that they were properly conducted. To his surprise the youngster stood still and lifted a submissive face, and, as Jamie operated, the child continued:

"Oh, mother is always nagging about cleaning your nails and spooning out your ears, and wild hairs in your eyelashes and ingrowing toe-nails! You'd get to be a burden to yourself if you'd try to pay any attention to all the things that woman wants done. When it comes to the princess, I'd give my best jack-knife if dad would fire her."

"Fire a princess?" said Jamie. "You're suggesting an unseemly proceeding. A princess is supposed to be treated with a very high degree of consideration."

The youngster shrugged lean shoulders and sniffed.

"Well, this princess we've got in our kitchen hails from some little cross-road in Europe, and she's used to being waited on herself, and so she knows too darned well how to wait on other people. All of us got to go through too much pollyfoxing. It's too familiar to call us by our first names and say anything in plain English. You've got to beat around the bush like a scoutin' Indian to put it across that you'd like a little more butter on your toast, or the strawberry jam just ain't. What's the use of all the fuss? When it comes to clothes, both all two of 'em make me sick! That's what this row was about. I wanted to wear my clothes, so when I got back I could meet the fellows and go down on the beach for a sham battle. Mother would have it that I couldn't go with you and I couldn't go to the hospital without being all rigged up until I looked like"—the little Scout stopped and dug an enraged toe in the rug before the wash-bowl, and then concluded—"until I looked like such a sissy that the Bee Master wouldn't 'a' owned me! And to tell it like a want ad., I was just forced to dress the way they wanted me to and at the same time I had to steal out the things I meant to wear and hide 'em in a hedge down the street a house or two, and then I had to duck the hedge and get the bundle and find a place where I could change, and I'm none too sure my things will be where I left 'em when I go back. Always making a lot of time-killing and a lot of worry!"

"I see," said Jamie slowly, "but didn't you *want* to be dressed in the best you had when you went to visit a very fine gentleman, whom you love as you told me you love the Bee Master?"

The little Scout drew up and heaved a deep breath. Into play came the gesture that had now come to be inseparable from the Scoutmaster's personality.

"About loving the Bee Master—that's a thing that it ain't very good to talk about. That gets down among your feelin's where you want 'em covered up, where things ain't much of *anybody's* business. If it was anything that would do the Bee Master any good, I'd stand fire and water to do it; but when it's just nonsense, what's the use? The Bee Master likes me or he wouldn't have sent for me, and he never in his life saw me as dolled up as I am right now!"

The Scoutmaster squirmed, thrust forth a stocking-clad leg and a patent-leather shoe.

"Look at that now! Wouldn't it make you sick? What's legs for if you can't use just leg? Who invented stockings, anyway? Scratchy, itchy things, and in a country where you don't *need* 'em! I'll tell the world I'd 'a' shed the socks too, but I knew I was late. Come on, let's go!"

Jamie hung up the wash-cloth, used the towel, and started to apply the comb. The Scoutmaster backed away with outthrown hands.

"No, you don't!" cried the little Scout. "I'm not allowed to use other people's combs. They might have tarantulas or Gila monsters or octopuses on 'em!"

Jamie laid back the comb and reached his hand. The Scoutmaster laid a hard, scarred, wiry hand in his and walked sedately beside him until they passed through the front gate.

Then the child looked up and remarked: "Now I guess we better release the clutch. If any of the fellows would see us, there's just a possibility that I'd get toppled off my throne. My Scouts are about all I can handle some of these days, anyway."

When they reached the street car and took their places, Jamie looked down at the figure beside him and decided that it was too lean, that the physical condition was not what it should be.

"Do you mind," he asked, "telling me how old you are?"

"No," said the Scoutmaster, "I don't. I'm ten years old, and lemme tell you, I've lived 'em! I've lived 'em all the way from the Atlantic Ocean to the Pacific Ocean, and I've lived in cities where you had to be for ever dodging the police, and the bandits, and the kidnappers, in mother's imagination. You couldn't get a kidnapper to touch me with a lightnin' rod. They'd take me for a regular roughneck!"

Jamie decided that the best way to get information was to keep quiet, so he said nothing.

"I've ridden on ships and boats and launches and paddled canoes and travelled on trains from the New York Limited to the Missionary, and believe me, I've had my eyes open and my ears open all the way! Last time we came out we missed the Limited we had reservations on and we had to take the Missionary or stay five days in Chicago, and none of us could stick that so we took the Missionary. The rest of 'em like to died, but I had heaps of fun, and lemme tell you, I swelled my roll something pretty. I'd just go through the cars and nice and polite I'd say to the hot, dirty folks: 'For five cents I'll get you a nice, cool drink of water.' If they looked like a Rolls-Rich I'd make it ten, 'cause more of 'em got caught than us. You ought to 'a' seen 'em fall for it! I got so much I had to bank in my suitcase in our drawing-room, and Nannette saw me and baa-ed like a sheep, and I thought 'all was lost'——"

"Well, was it?" inquired Jamie.

"Not total. You see, dad and mother wasn't in that load. First our Personal Conductor looked a mixshure, but finally she got to laughing 'cause I told her the funds was the result of the idle rich grindin' the masses, and she's a dead sport. She said if I'd go fifty-fifty with the Orthopaedic Home, I could keep it. I was lief as not on that." The little Scout paused. "Ever thank God for good legs?"

Jamie said, "I have!" fervently, and the little Scout grinned and continued, "I've gone a good deal scoutin' round with the Scouts, and of course some of it at school would stick to me by accident. My mother's not so slow, and let me tell you there's things you can learn from my dad! Maybe you think he hasn't been a giddy ranger! Boy! He's been city editor of a big newspaper, and he's been two years in a scoutin' plane over Germany, and he knows about making pictures. My dad's a reg'lar leapin' tuna!"

"I am going to meet him one of these days," said Jamie.

The little Scout looked up quickly.

"Where?"

The inquiry was terse and forceful.

"When I called your telephone number to tell you about to-day, your mother invited me to dinner."

The little Scout's face fell.

"Aw!" The ejaculation was too laden with disapproval to escape notice.

"Of course, if you don't want me to come——"

"Now that's another one of them unpleasant issues," said the small person. "Sure I want you to have grub! You can live on casabas and lobster and home-brew for all of me. But what's the use of draggin' mother and dad and Nannette and Jimmy and the Royal Family of Denmark into our affairs? Why ain't it good enough for us to go on being friends just the way we are?"

"All right," said Jamie. "I wouldn't think of coming if you don't want me."

"There you go again!" said the small person. "Did I ever say I didn't want you? Did I ever say I didn't fall for you hard? Did I ever say I wasn't hittin' on six cylinders every time I see you? No, I never did! But just because I say there's places I want to see you and places I don't, you go and make it look like I didn't want you any old time and any old place! I thought from your mug you'd be a guy that'd play the game square!"

"Well, I try to play the game square," said Jamie.

"Well, you're out of luck, you're all wet!" said the small person, "if you think you're playin' the game square when you tell me I don't want you just because there's certain places I don't want you! Couldn't a fellow have reasons? Couldn't there be some things a body wouldn't want to bleat all over the pasture?"

Jamie reached down and put his arm around the small person

and drew the little figure up against him and found that the frame he was holding was quivering from head to foot.

"The days are fairly long for you, aren't they?" asked Jamie.

"Oh, I reckon the days are all right," answered the little Scout. "They're the same days other kids have, and a lot of 'em get fat on 'em. Cast your optics on Fat Ole Bill if you don't believe it. It's just that there's times when I pretty near know that my job's about all I can handle."

"What's the trouble?" asked Jamie.

"Well I reckon you know how to get to be a Scoutmaster, don't you?"

Because he wanted information, Jamie said he was not sure.

The little Scout shrugged exasperated shoulders.

"Well, I'm sure! I'm darned sure! You get to be a Scoutmaster by *mastering* the Scouts, that's how! If they are jumping, you jump the farthest. If they are swinging, you swing the highest. If they are running, you spread your white wings and beat 'em to it. If it's bicycles, you just lie down over the handle-bars and paw the air for dear life and let the rest eat your dust. If it's canoeing, your canoe makes the waves the rest of them upset in. If it comes to a slugging match, you got to have your jewjits so thoroughly in practice that you can sling any of the bunch in any direction you want 'em to circulate. Being a Scoutmaster means mastering the bunch; and Fat Ole Bill is getting to the place where I'm goin' some if I handle him! The Nice Child is easier, but let me tell you, Angel Face is putting on muscles these days! He didn't used to be so well. He was fussing around with appendicitis. Anywhere in the region of his right side even a little crack would knock him out and make him sweat blood. But now he's kicking out of it in fine shape. He's going to make a great big strong man. In just about a year more he's going to find out what I know already, that if he knew as much as I do, he'd know it's only luck if I handle him now. And whenever they find *that* out they'd mutiny, and the fellow that *can* handle the bunch is due to usurp the throne. I got that out of a history book, and it's good stuff. It sounds unpleasant, but it's a plain statement of facts. Scoutmaster and The Limit is the same thing."

"In other words, you are working too hard," said Jamie. "You are trained down so fine that you are on the edge, and while the rest of them are gaining, you are losing. Is that the point?"

The Scoutmaster meditated.

"I guess the real needle-fine point of it is that there's one of me and there's three of them, and sometimes they beg so hard that we let in two or three more that I can't eat 'em raw ; I got to roast 'em or quit. And on those days I finish up just about out of ammunition. Nannette says that I keep on fightin' and rollin' and kickin' until I horn in on her territory sometimes, but she ain't got anything comin' on me. I never had the hysterics and bellowed out in the night until I waked the family just 'cause the turtles didn't eat *all* of anything !"

Jamie tightened his arm around the Scoutmaster and slumped his body into an inviting curve, and in three minutes he held against him a youngster tired to exhaustion at the middle of the day and fast asleep.

When they reached the hospital Jamie gently shook the Scoutmaster, and instantly the youngster was up with blinking eyes and an ingratiating smile, ready to prove that unconsciousness of what was going on was for someone else ; that particular fellow always was and always had been wide awake. The instant they were inside the hospital the Scoutmaster reached for Jamie's hand, crowded up beside him, and walked to the elevator and down the long halls cat stepping.

Evidently they were expected. The Bee Master's door was open ; a screen shielded the bed from the view of the passers-by. The Scoutmaster sent one look across the room and to the open window and nudged Jamie with a sharp elbow.

"Have you noticed how Margaret Cameron's roses have fallen off in bloomin' lately ?"

The whisper was sibilant ; but Jamie caught it and smiled as he noted the flowers, and then he heard a further whisper.

"She's always cottoning up to him. She's got the idea that he's her personal property. There's been more than one day when she'd about given her eyes if I'd 'a' gone home, but as long as the Bee Master says 'Stay', I'm staying !"

Jamie rounded the screen and the Scoutmaster followed and stood back until Jamie shook hands with the Bee Master and stepped aside. Then the small Scout walked up before the Master's bed, wide-eyed, and took one good look and changed colour, changed slowly from red lips and tinted cheeks to a spreading white. But the heels came together with a click. The figure stood very straight. The salute was according to rule and snappy to the superlative degree. The grin that overspread the small features was ingratiating. The Bee Master held out shaking hands and suddenly—Jamie thought he never had seen a movement quite so sudden; he wasn't sure how the intervening space was cleared—the little figure simply rose in a leap and dived into the bed. The Bee Master made a good catch, although he caught his breath at the same time, because he was shaken by the suddenness of the plunge. But he had the little Scout tight in his arms, and the child was thoroughly draped over the chest of the Bee Master. A small hand was gripping the old white head on either side, and from forehead to chin a shower of short hot kisses was raining over the Bee Master's face. The little Scout sat straight up on the bed and suddenly big tears shot one after another across the childish face, and a little sharp wail that cut deeper than a knife piped out, "Oh, God! I wish you didn't have to suffer so!"

The Bee Master's chin pointed toward the ceiling. He lifted his right hand and gathered his lower lip into folds and gave it outside pressure to reinforce it.

"Yes, Buddy, I've thought about that myself," he said, "and I've sort of wished it, but it seems to be in the divine plan, or through some negligence of mine in taking proper care of the machinery as I've come along, and so I have to take the consequences. But don't you mind."

"Well, I *do* mind!" said the little Scout. A hand was jerked backwards in the direction of Jamie. "He's all right. He's a good scout. He had sense enough to get behind the tree and use what he could find when the Redskins attacked us. He's good stuff, a sure fire thing, but he don't think himself that he's *you.*"

The Bee Master glanced at Jamie and their eyes met and held.

"Take a chair," he said to Jamie. "Draw up close here. I want to tell you something, but first I want to ask you something." He looked straight at the Scoutmaster. "You're fairly sure," he said, "that the man I left to keep the bees is the right kind of a man?"

"Yes, I'm sure," said the Scoutmaster promptly. "You couldn't get him to do a low-down, mean trick to save you!"

"That's all right, then," said the Bee Master. Then he turned to Jamie. "And you," he said, "have you become rather well acquainted with my little partner here?"

"Oh, we've made a start," said Jamie. "We haven't had so much of a chance. The little Scout is in school, you know."

"Well, what I'm interested in knowing," said the Bee Master, "is whether you've got a feeling that my little partner plays the game square, doesn't do any mean tricks, is willing to help the other fellow, knows how to salute and to revere the flag of our country, and has a proper reverence for the Great Giver of all good and perfect gifts."

Jamie thought an instant, and then he nodded assent.

"Yes," he said, "yes, I think we've come pretty close to at least touching on all that ground. I think if you had searched the whole world over you couldn't have found a more genuine little human being to make your partner in the keeping of the bees."

"All right, then," said the Bee Master, "that's all I wanted to know. Merely if you liked each other. If you are getting along well together. In case I should have to stay here for quite a time, or in case I should get better and have to make quite a long journey, I just wanted to know if you would keep the garden growing and keep the bees happy. You know it's something of a trick, if you have been studying the books carefully; you know it isn't a thing that everyone can do, just keeping two acres of bees happy, two acres of life thriving."

Then he addressed Jamie directly.

"There will be times when you must have help," he said. "I told you about the right man the last time you were here. If you will call Mr. Carey and tell him the circumstances when you find in your examination that the last cell of any hive has been filled, and the bees are growing restless, he will come and help you harvest the honey. He will show you how. Then you can render him the same service, and that way you will neither one be put to the expense of hiring a party who may not be compatible to the bees. He will teach you what the first signs of foul brood are and how to go to work on it, and so far as the rest is concerned, my little side partner here can tell you anything you need to know in taking care of the bees. Can't you, Buddy?" asked the Bee Master, tightening his arm.

"I sure can!" answered the youngster. "I have put him wise to every single thing you ever told me about a bee. I haven't forgot the first word of anything you told me, and I can pretty near hit the bull's-eye on anything you ever read me from a book. I might not have just all of the big, high-soundin' words, but I pass on the proper meaning."

"Yes, I think you could," said the Bee Master. "I will bear you out in that. I never read anything to you that you failed in getting the proper meaning."

"And, too, you know," said the little Scout, "that you read sompin' wonderful! You go very slow, and you pronounce your words so that almost anything you read is like poetry, and you put in little explanations where the language gets extensive. Most anybody could understand what you read."

Then with a sudden rush the Scout slid from the bed and, turning around, smoothed the coverlet and dipped deep in a trouser pocket and brought forth a grimy, round-cornered pair of dice. With a flourish of triumph these were laid before the Bee Master.

"I won't get you all het up throwin' against you to-day," said the Scoutmaster. "This is the luckiest set I got. I'm goin' to leave 'em with you so as if times come when you can have a pillow propped up, you'll have 'em to play with. Would a nurse be too puddin'-headed to throw with you ? Could you teach her just how to roll the bones right ? Could you teach her ?" The Scoutmaster stopped suddenly. "If a woman's got sense enough to take care of sick people and give 'em their medicine right and bathe 'em and rub 'em and take away the pain, I reckon she can throw dice. So of course you'll have somebody to play with you. I just kind of got the feeling that there can't anybody do anything just exactly the way *we* do it."

The Scoutmaster looked at the Bee Master and the Bee Master looked at the Scoutmaster and each smiled a smile so rarely beautiful that his whole face was transfigured.

"Well, as a secret between us, and not letting that tall, lean Scotsman there hear what we are saying, of course, such old friends as we are, people that have been so many years with each other, we *do* have ways that nobody else can quite understand. We *do* satisfy each other a little bit better than anyone else could. I have a very nice nurse. She will play with me, and I can't tell you how fine I think it is of you to leave your *best* set with me. I'll take great care of them, and if it just happens that the nurse *is* so puddin'-headed that she can't roll the bones right, I'll ask Jamie to bring them back to you one of these days."

The Scoutmaster nodded. Then from a hip pocket was brought out a small roll done in tissue paper. This was spread on the bed and opened up, and before the amazed eyes of Jamie and the Bee Master there billowed over the bed yards and yards of gaudy silk and satin flowers, plaided, and striped ribbons. The Scoutmaster ran appreciative fingers through the gaudy mass and shook it out.

"You wouldn't guess in a frog's croak how I got these. A few years ago, before all the girls took to painting their mouths and their faces like the Indians, and all of them got the shingles, they was addicted to ribbons. Ribbons just raged. You couldn't get 'em bright enough, and you couldn't get 'em broad enough and you couldn't get 'em stiff enough. Nannette used to look like the ribbon counter at Wanamaker's or Marshall Field's or Robinson's when she'd come down to breakfast. And then, just like that"—the Scoutmaster snapped a thumb and second finger with a spang to show how instantaneous "that" was—"just like *that*, ribbons were *out*, and Nannette had spent all her pin-money on ribbons until she had a lean and hungry look every time she passed a hot-dog stand or an Eskimo-pie wagon. Ain't they the prettiest things! I liked to see Nannette wear 'em. She couldn't get 'em too bright to suit me, nor too broad, nor too flowery. She had a whole drawer full of 'em. But when she shingled I asked her if I could have 'em. She's got a business head on her all right! She soaked me two bits, but I paid it because I knew what they were worth. Then I took 'em down to the princess in the kitchen and I told her she could have two that she liked the best to make her cases for her embroidery silks if she'd wash the rest of 'em and iron out the creases and make 'em pretty for me. I wasn't too *lazy* to do it myself, but I wasn't right sure how much soap to put on 'em, or what kind, and swingin' an electric iron is a profession you got to learn. You can't flip the dust off your shoulder into anybody's eye unless you've had a good deal of dust there to flip, and that's the way it is with swinging an electric iron. You've got to know how to do it before you get results."

The Scoutmaster shook out the ribbons.

"Now, one thing you can do is to take 'em one at a time and just slip 'em through your fingers and look how silky they are, and how lovely the flowers are and what beautiful colours there are in the stripes and how they run into each other."

Before the eyes of the Bee Master there was held up one ribbon of delicate hues.

"You know," said the small person, "the man who invented that—if it wasn't a woman—whoever did it—had rainbows on the brain. See the violet and the orange and the purple? See how the colours mix and blend? That's about as good a rainbow as God ever set in the sky to make a sign to His people that He would keep His covenants with man. S. S. That means Sunday School."

With fingers busy with the ribbons, the Scoutmaster glanced over towards Jamie.

"Do you know the Bible pretty good?"

"My father was a minister," said Jamie. "I know the Bible from cover to cover."

"Then you know that about rainbows?" asked the Scoutmaster.

"Yes," said Jamie. "I know."

"Do you know anything prettier?" asked the Scoutmaster.

"No," said Jamie. "In any literature of any language I ever learned to read, I know nothing more beautiful than the promise that is symbolized by the rainbow."

The Scoutmaster stood still. Lean brown hands dropped among the ribbons. A pair of deep, expressive, tender eyes lifted to the eyes of the Bee Master.

"Do you reckon," said the Scoutmaster, "that that covenant between God and man is a little like our covenant about the bees and about our secrets?"

The fine old eyes of the Bee Master were tender and solemn and his voice was loving as he said to the little person: "Well, you know a covenant is an understanding; it's an agreement, usually only between two people, an agreement about something important and something worth while."

"Well, then," said the little Scout, "that's what ours was, and I'm keeping it, and I am going to go on keeping it. And this one, now this one is a regular flower-bed with the bouquets all made up, and this one is Roman stripes like Ben Hur had for his sash when he drove Atair and Aldebaran and Antares and Riegal. Oh, joy! Oh, boy! Wouldn't it be great stuff if we really had an honest and true amphitheatre and horses like that and races like that now? These dinky little races around here where the riders come and sell out the race before they run it, and they draw cuts in the morning to decide who gets to win that day, oh, bah! don't it make you sick? The world's getting so rotten they don't even run the ponies fair any more!"

"I am sorry to say," said the Bee Master, "that you are about right in your statements. If we don't call a stern halt, if we don't make a right-about, if we don't come to our senses pretty soon, we won't have very much of the ancient honour, that obtained among men, left anywhere in this world concerning sport or business, either one."

Then noticing the arresting hand and the grave face of the little Scout, he added: "Are you holding the Scouts level these days?"

There was an instant of hesitation on the part of the Scoutmaster.

"The Nice Child is all right, but Fat Ole Bill and Angel Face are eatin' too much raw meat. If they mutiny one at a time I can handle 'em. If the day comes very often when two or three of them go bad in a heap"—the Scoutmaster straightened up and lifted a face contorted by a wry grimace—"woe is me!"

Jamie and the Bee Master could not keep from laughing, much as they respected the mentality of their small partner.

"Now, as I was telling you," continued the little person, "you can look how beautiful they are and, too, you can *braid* 'em. Just by getting a nurse to give you a pin and starting with two and then workin' up and down and across like this, you can make a coverlet big enough for your shoulders to keep the cold air out, and you can make them run in waves, and you can make 'em go in loops. I don't know anything you can play at easier or get more combinations out of when you are sick and have to lie in bed than just a bunch of beautiful ribbons. It keeps your mind on what you are doing, but it isn't like solitaire or some of the things you can play alone that still make you think hard enough to send you to the mat if you wasn't already there. Now I guess we'd better go. The Bee Master will be tired. Mother said I wasn't to stay long enough to make a sick man tired, and I wasn't to talk enough to make him worse, and what else did she say? Oh, I know. I wasn't to look like I wanted anything to eat, 'cause there wasn't anything to eat at a hospital."

The Scoutmaster, with a lingering stroke pushed back the gaudy ribbons, eyed them an instant covetously, and then bent above the Bee Master and dropped a feathery kiss on his forehead, ran a hand over his hair, and said:

"You be a good boy and take your medicine and sleep when you're told and come home quick, just as quick as you possibly can!"

With that the Scoutmaster whirled and marched brusquely from the room.

Jamie waited for a few words and then followed. Once outside of the hospital and on the street again, the Scoutmaster lifted an enigmatical face.

"You've seen a good deal of hospitals yourself, haven't you?"

Jamie assented.

"Yes," said the Scoutmaster, "you seem to kind of fit a hospital right now, but not so much as you did the first time I saw you. The first time I saw you, you looked like you *were* a hospital all by yourself. But now you don't look much more than half a hospital. You seem as if you might belong to the garden just about as well as to the hospital. I suppose they are necessary, but, oh, boy! ain't they fierce? Everything so slippery and so quiet and so clean, and everybody on tiptoe an whisperin'. If I had a mint of money, if I had gobs and stacks of money, I'd build a hospital where all the windows opened on to a race track and you could see a horse-race and a motor-race twice a day, and I'd have bands and radios and moving pictures. Gee, the hospitals they have these days make me sick when there's nothing the matter with me!"

Then suddenly the Scoutmaster took Jamie's hand and looked up at him.

"Say, what's the matter with Mrs. Cameron? What makes her cry so much, and what's the use of her lookin' like a funeral without anybody dead, and *why* don't Lolly come home?"

"Now look here," said Jamie, "you're asking me questions I can't answer. In the first place, I didn't know that Margaret Cameron was crying. I didn't suppose anything could happen that would wring tears from a woman so self-contained as she is. And in the next place, what could I know about Lolly?"

"Well," said the Scoutmaster, "she *is* crying a lot these days 'cause she's right at the end of the car line where I get off with the Scouts to play brigand in the canyon, and robbers' cave in the mountains, and sand fights on the beach, and to go bathing. She's right where I see her every time I come past, and nearly every time I see her lately she's wiping her eyes. It might be about the Bee Master, but there ain't any use for her to spill the brine when he might get well and he might come home. If she knew he wouldn't ever, I could understand it. I reckon it's about Lolly because she don't seem to come home and, of course, when she isn't at home, Mrs. Cameron doesn't know whether she's sick or well, and she ain't goin' to feel comfortable so long as she doesn't know."

The Scoutmaster paused in intent thought a minute and then continued: "I reckon that's kind of a silly thing to say. Lolly's teaching school and, of course, when she's teaching school she can't come home, at least not until it's time for vacation. If it was vacation and she could come and didn't come, why, that'd be a horse of a different colour, and there'd be some reason for getting droopy."

Merely to carry on the conversation, Jamie inquired: "Is Lolly a pretty girl?"

The Scoutmaster scuffled along the sidewalk, glancing from right to left, dodging pedestrians, watching passing cars for their numbers and direction, and replied en route: "Oh, joy! Maybe you'd call her pretty. If you like taffy molasses hair and big blue eyes and pink cheeks and a baby smile and about as much notion of whether you're going to do it or whether you ain't as a wave coming in, why, Lolly's a pretty girl. But if you ask me, I'd tell you that if you want to see a pretty girl, if you want to see a right loyal, high-steppin', cat's-whiskers kind of a girl, just turn you optics loose on Molly!"

"This sounds interesting," said Jamie. "Can you give me any instructions as to where I'd have to be in order to 'turn my optics loose on Molly'?"

"No," said the Scoutmaster, "not during the school season I couldn't. Vacations it's easy, unless the coming vacation is going to be different from all the vacations that have gone before. All that have gone before Molly comes home, at least part of the time, and then we have picnics and she tramps with us and scouts with us, and we sure do have a real time when Molly's on the job."

"Her home is near here?" inquired Jamie, beginning to take interest.

"Well, how goofy!" exclaimed the Scoutmaster. "Have you lived over a month beside Mrs. Cameron and she hasn't told you a word about Molly and Lolly and about Don?"

"It just happens," said Jamie, "that when we've talked together we've talked about bees and flowers and food. She hasn't told me so very much about her children."

"Well, they aren't her children," said the Scoutmaster. "At least Molly and Donald aren't. Molly and Donald are twins and their father and Mr. Cameron were brothers, and when both of them went down in the boat the night of the big storm, why, Mrs. Cameron brought the kids home to her house and she helped both of 'em to get their schooling, so Molly could teach and so Don could work. He's electricity. He knows a world about radio and he puts in wires in different places. I think you call it 'installations'. 'Installations' would be the right word, wouldn't it?"

"It sounds right," said Jamie. "And who's Lolly?"

"Well, Lolly belonged to Margaret Cameron before she was married. Sometime, somewhere, she must have been married to some other man, and I dunno whether he went by the graveyard route or got eliminated by a divorce judge. Sometimes I think I'd like to be a divorce judge. It'd be fun to hear all the folks telling what's their troubles and why they can't pull even and who's to blame, and sometimes I see women that I'd just naturally separate from any man. I see a lot of 'em that don't look like they were keeping house or tending to their babies or could come within a mile telling whether their kids' toe-nails were cut or their ears spooned, and things like that, that my mother's always fussin' about. And, of course, journeying along I do at times see men that need suppression."

The hands went down and out. The men who needed it were suppressed at that instant.

"There's some men, you know, just so trifling and just so full of home-brew, or some other kind of brew, that no woman could live with 'em and think anything of herself. Maybe I wouldn't like it. Maybe it would be kind of a painful job. I don't know that I'd want it. But I'll tell you this about things I do want: I'll go to my grave disappointed if I don't ever get to drive across this country from ocean to ocean in a motor-car! One of the kind that's got front seats that let back and make a bed, and a little cupboard and an ice box and a pantry on the running-board, and sleeping-rolls and everything. Maybe I'd have a trailer. Maybe I'd pick up some things along the way to bring home for mother's garden. I don't know just what I'd do, but you mark my word, I'm goin' to twist it around some way so I get to go before long! Of course, the best thing about it is camping by the wayside and sleeping on the ground, and meeting different people and seeing the country when you got time to look at it. You can't get much being whizzed through on a railway train, and all the places you think might be a little bit interesting or have a bear or a deer, or there'd be an Indian or bandit or something, those are the places you are whizzed by the fastest."

"That's the truth," said Jamie. "That's quite the truth."

Their car came down the line and the Scoutmaster was on the platform before Jamie had really convinced himself that the number and destination were right and could follow suit. Again on the way home the Scoutmaster frankly leaned over against Jamie and waited for his circling arm, and went sound asleep until the point came that brought the inevitable awakening.

On the way near the hot-dog stand at a corner toward which Jamie felt a slight propulsion on landing from the car, he said to the Scoutmaster: "Do you know, youngster, you are doing what the big folks call 'burning the candle at both ends'?"

To his amazement, the Scoutmaster tuned in:

> "But ah, my foes, and oh, my friends,
> It makes a lovely light!"

"That may be all right," said Jamie, "and it may be a brand of philosophy that will do for grown folks, but that's rotten for the kiddies. There isn't anything you are doing that's worth stunting your growth for."

"Stunting my what?" said the Scoutmaster.

"I mean," said Jamie, "that you are exercising too hard and sleeping too little, you are going such a pace that you are not so big and strong as you should be. You are on such a strain mastering those three big boys you play with that you are not getting the strength in your own arms and legs that they have in theirs. If you don't go a little slower and eat more properly cooked food at home and eat less hot dogs while you are scouting, just what you prophesied will happen to you. If you take such pride in being the Scoutmaster, you'd better remember that you can't hold that office unless you are physically fit. You'd better cut out some of the hiking and some of the fights and a whole lot of irregular eating."

"Sky Pilot!" scoffed the Scoutmaster. "You sound like I had the hoof-and-mouth disease."

And thereupon Jamie was treated to a countenance of such solemnity, to folded hands and uprolled eyes—for one instant he caught an expression with which he had been familiar in his boyhood—that he could not help laughing.

"You know," said Jamie very soberly, "that I've been thinking lately that being a preacher wouldn't be such a bad profession. You might do a whole lot worse things than try to teach other men to come clean, to shoot straight, to ride hard, to be real men spiritually as well as physically."

The Scoutmaster shuffled ahead and beat Jamie to the hot-dog stand. Also the price for two was forthcoming.

"My treat to-day! And that looks kind of rotten to let you treat the last time when there was five of us and take it myself when there are only two. It'll be my treat the next time and a half."

Jamie stood staring.

"You figure your finances to the penny?"

"I do," said the Scoutmaster. "About the worst mess you can get into in this world is the one you get into when you don't keep your millions straight. Dad says he guesses all the trouble in the world that is not about women is about money, and mostly if it's about one of them it's about the other one too."

Having settled the financial end of the transaction, the Scoutmaster gave undivided attention to the hot dog. The combination struck Jamie as about what he wanted also. It appeared to him further that he had no business, at that critical period, to partake of the combination that was entailed by the Scoutmaster's idea of a perfect treat. He hesitated over it a second, then came off triumphant, although slightly humiliated to fail in being a good fellow.

"You know," he said to the Scoutmaster, "I've been very sick and I'm not long out of the hospital and the doctors' care. I think I won't put my stomach up against that combination of yours. I'll just go home and take a glass of orange juice instead."

It touched his heart with particular appeal that the Scoutmaster said instantly: "Well, I'd go and take the orange juice with you, but I've got this started and I can't waste it, so I have to pay for it and eat it, but the next time we'll take the orange juice together, if orange juice is your limit until you get well."

And then, trotting along the street beside Jamie, past a mouthful of the tantalizing combination, the Scoutmaster said: "Oh, gee! Ain't it goofy to be sick? I don't know what I'd do if I couldn't have a hot dog when I wanted it. Of all the things there is to eat in the whole world I don't know of anything I like better. Mother likes them too. Dad doesn't come in so strong on them 'cause he's got a stomach himself every once and a while. City editor and war did it. But as yet, glory be! they haven't either of them put the grand kibosh on me. The day they do, I'll leap from the pinnacle (I got 'pinnacle' in geography) of the highest rock in the bay and go out with the undertow."

"That would be pathetic," said Jamie. "Why do you want to cause your friends such grief and deprive the Bee Master of his partner and me of about the only friend I have on earth, unless the Bee Master has decided to be my friend."

"Of course the Bee Master is your friend," said the little Scout. "I knew the Bee Master was your friend the minute I faced up to the jacqueranda and saw you sittin' on his particular bench. Didn't you notice me keep straight on coming?"

"I certainly did," said Jamie. "I registered that fact in my mentality with great pride and pleasure. I shall always remember that when you caught your first view of me you kept straight on coming."

"It was the same way with Molly," said the Scoutmaster. "First peep I ever got at her I kept right on coming. I walked right up to her and into her just as far as I could get at the first séance. Do you know what a 'séance' is?"

Jamie said he did.

"All right, then. A séance is so goofy that I didn't know but I'd have to tell you about it like bees and other things you need educating up on. But getting back to Molly—there's something about her that's got a pull. Every one of the boys just took to her like you take to buckwheat cakes and maple syrup or waffles that you get from the waffle man on the beach, or anything like that that you want all you can hold of when you think about it and want to go back in a few days for more. Molly's like that. Something that you want awful bad when you see her and every few days you want her just as bad."

"Tell me about Molly. She sounds interesting," said Jamie.

By this time they had reached the gate. Jamie opened it and the Scoutmaster led the way to the seat under the jacquer-anda.

"Well, telling about Molly is a pretty long story. Molly had hard luck. She didn't have any mother to begin with, and then she lost her father. Then there was a good while that she had the devil's own time with Don. He just seemed bound and determined to do everything in the world except the thing she wanted him to. She thought she was never goin' to make any-thing out of him. She thought just dead sure he'd go some way that wouldn't get him anywhere, and I don't know whether she ever would have got him pulled through or not if there hadn't always been Lolly in the background. There never was a time since I've known 'em that he didn't think she was just old peaches and persimmons, alligator pears, and everything squashy like that. When he wouldn't do anything 'cause it was honest and square and straight and 'cause it was what he *should* do 'cause Molly wanted him to, why that very same thing he'd do for Lolly if she'd give him a kiss or pat him a little or laugh at him or coax him along with a petting party. I like Molly 'cause she ain't any all-day sucker. She just comes to the point and she knows what the point she's coming to is before she starts for it. There ain't any meandering about Molly!"

The Scoutmaster showed in deft handwork the straight way that Molly went.

"And I reckon, if I was grown up and wanting a job to earn money at, that I'd rather have the job Molly's got than any job in the world."

"You surprise me," said Jamie. "You astonish me! I'd have thought teaching school was the last profession in the world that you'd choose."

"Yes, but in these days there's different kinds of teaching school," said the Scoutmaster. "The kind that Molly does isn't the kind you're thinking about. It isn't shut up in a room and staying in one place and doing the same thing over and over. The kind Molly does is called 'teaching Americanism'. Did you ever know how good-looking and how interesting a lot of little round-the-world children can be—a lot of little Italians and Greeks and Spaniards and Indians and Hawaiians and Japanese and Chinese, cutest little brown things with big round eyes? You ought to hear 'em sing 'My Country 'tis of Thee!' You ought to see 'em salute the flag! You ought to hear 'em learn the words that mean that there isn't any country in all the world so big and fine and nice to live in as the United States. You ought to see 'em learn that their heads are made to think with, and their hands are made to work with; their feet are made to march with; their eyes are made to see with, to see straight, to see all there is. Oh, gee! I *like* Molly's job! I like to help her when she is having a picnic on the beach with 'em."

"I think that school sounds mighty fine, myself," said Jamie. "Would you take me some day when Molly's teaching Americanism on the beach?"

"Sure I would!" said the Scoutmaster. "Molly would be *glad* to see you. Molly's always glad to see anybody that believes in America and believes in God. She's strong on both of them. Anybody that shoots straight and rides hard and plays square like I told you. You ought to see her shoot and ride. If I was a millionaire and had money to burn, the first thing I'd get, after I got the kind of a horse that I'd like to have for myself, would be the kind of a horse Molly would really *like* to have."

The Scoutmaster rose.

"Just about now I speed for home with barely time left to shift to my other wardrobe, provided it ain't been bandited and left a dark cloud hanging over me."

"Anything I can do to avert trouble?" inquired Jamie.

"Not a thing, old dear," said the Scoutmaster. "Not a thing. But I thank you, I thank you heaps for your good intentions."

The Scoutmaster cracked heels, laid a palm over the region of the pit of the stomach, and bowed low. Then, with a whirl, the youngster started down the walk. Only a few steps had been covered when the small figure turned and the Scoutmaster called back: "I didn't have time to-day, but remind me the next time I come and I'll do the Lame Duck and the Wet Hen for you. I made 'em up myself. I have to have a bathing-suit and a dock to do 'em right, but I could pretend I had on a bathing-suit and the walk was a dock and off of it was water, and show you how it goes. I'm nifty about the Wet Hen. I think I do her spiffy."

"I'll remember," said Jamie. "I'll surely remember."

He waited before turning to the house because he liked to see the agility, the free sweep, the unfailing grace with which the little Scout skimmed the line fence between the grounds of the Bee Master and Margaret Cameron.

The next morning, before Jamie took up the line of march for the beach, he called his neighbour. Since she said nothing herself he ignored the fact that her eyes were red and her hands tremulous, but he did wonder. He wondered exceedingly whether it was the Lolly he had not liked so particularly well from the Scoutmaster's description, or whether it was the illness of the Bee Master that worried so fine a woman as Margaret Cameron.

Jamie stretched himself on his bed and laid his hands on the dressings that covered his side. Then he looked up at his neighbour.

"Margaret Cameron, you are on oath!" he said. "Your right hand's in the air and you are solemnly swearing that you are going to tell me whether or not one month of the best régime we could devise has taken the colour and the fever out of this wound any. I haven't had the nerve to look myself, for I cannot face it very well except in a mirror, which is not altogether satisfactory. Let's go!"

Jamie did not know, as he shut his eyes he did not know that the skin of his face was tightly drawn across its bonework. He did not realize that his hands were trembling as he raised them to uncover his left breast. Margaret Cameron came to the side of the bed and leaned over him and looked intently.

"Turn slightly toward me!" she ordered sharply.

Jamie's eyes popped open, and at what he saw on her face his heart began to leap and to bound, and before he knew what he was doing he was upright and he had both her hands.

"Oh, Margaret!" he cried. "Are you sure? Are you sure it's *that* much better?"

Margaret was gripping his hands as tight as ever she could.

"Oh, Jamie boy," she said, "it's well-nigh a miracle the way the colour's fading out, and as sure as you are six feet high, it is drawing together at the bottom! It is coming clean, and there is more flesh over your ribs and across your chest! You're not so lean! I've been thinking I could see it on your hands and in your face, and at that we haven't been trying so much for flesh-building as we have for blood purification. If we can get the blood-stream clean, 'most any time we can begin flesh-building. Jamie boy, I'd say you are going to make it. I'd say, if you hold steady and keep it up six months, you can close that ugly spot. It's going to leave a nasty scar, but scars are the aftermath of any war. If your blood will purify, if you can get in working order, there is nothing to stop you from being the man God meant you to be when you were born."

Then Jamie took Margaret Cameron tight in his arms and kissed her over and over again on the top of her head. Then he released her and looked after her wonderingly, because she was going from the back door, her shoulders shaken with sobs deeper and longer than the most motherly of women need shed over the joy of a step in the right direction for even a highly considered neighbour.

Slowly Jamie turned from the back door. Slowly he went back to the bed upon which he had lain. Slowly he got down on his knees and clasped his shaking hands and laid his forehead on them, and then, reverently, deeply, from the bottom of his heart he thanked the Lord.

Then he headed straight for the ice box and drank a pint of tomato juice.

CHAPTER XIII

THE KEEPER OF THE BEES

THERE came a stretch of days during which the awakening of each morning was a small miracle all by itself to Jamie. To awake rested, refreshed, to awake with hope in his heart, to look down the irregular stretch of the garden and on the ceaseless lapping of the sea and to say to himself, "To-day I will transplant the lilies. I will trim the poinsettias. I will plant some tomatoes." To be able to tell himself that he would do something constructive, with the knowledge in his heart that he would have the strength to do it and the uplift in his spirit that would give him joy in the doing; because from that period on, each morning awakening was in a way a new miracle. It seemed to him that he could feel the purity, the cleanliness of the blood that was flowing through his veins. He knew that the heart in his breast was calming down, was throbbing with a regularity and a surety that he had not known in a long time; it had ceased to flutter, even at a stiff climb. He knew that strength was gradually forging into his limbs and his hands, that his brain was clearing. He was no longer a pusillanimous creature creeping around wondering about how long he could live. He was an upright man with a hopeful outlook, with a definite purpose of beating the game if it lay in the power of himself and Margaret Cameron and California to win. It was a big game that he was playing.

It is in the blood of humanity to fight for life. Anything but death. Jamie sat on the side of the bed and meditated upon how strange it was that human beings should complain of pain, of poverty, of disappointment, of defeat of every kind, and yet the instant death, death that the little Scout said was beautiful, became imminent, humanity armed against it and fought to the last ditch, as he was fighting. He admitted that he might be mistaken, that he might be over hopeful, that Margaret Cameron's vision might even be coloured by her hopes for him. But one thing he could not be mistaken about. His body was not so lean; his hands were surer; he could walk without his legs bowing under him; and he had quit morbid introspection. He had reached the place where several times alone in the evening he had laid aside the bee books and picked up the greatest of all books and read chapter after chapter, and he realized that never once had he done this without closing the sacred volume with the feeling that in some way he had gained something; there had been possibly only one word, some thought, something that remained with him and helped him to fashion the coming day.

Then Jamie arose, picked up a pencil and drew a circle on the calendar around the previous day, and from the circle he ran a line to the margin and lettered it "M.C." That meant Margaret Cameron, and the date was the day on which she had found him better. Another month he would continue the same régime with even more exactitude, and then she would look again, and he registered a vow as he put on his clothing that she should find him better.

As he arranged the dressings on his wounded side, he looked closely at the pad he had removed, and then suddenly Jamie found himself doing what the little person would have called pirouetting. There was barely a faint pinkish seeping. He had felt for days past that the stains were not so large and not so angry. That morning there was ocular evidence that could not be done away with. Too plain for words to dispute it, lay the proof before him that Margaret had been right. Before Jamie realized what he was doing, he found that he was dancing around the bedroom with much less reserve and more enthusiasm than the little Scout had danced down the garden walk. He was actually laughing to himself as he drew on his clothing, and when he heard Margaret Cameron in the kitchen with his breakfast, he opened the door and called to her, "Lady of Scotland!"

His voice rang out with a tone Margaret Cameron had not previously noticed.

"Step this way," said Jamie. "Yesterday you had Exhibit Number One. This morning cast your optics on Exhibit Number Two!" And Jamie picked up the pad from a basket that was being filled for the incinerator and pulled it apart that Margaret Cameron might see.

"A month ago," said Jamie, "those pads were pretty thoroughly soaked with brilliant colour. This one I just removed is barely damp and the faintest pink. Oh, Margaret, woman! I *am* going to make it! I *am* going to be a whole man again!"

"Sure you are!" said Margaret Cameron, and for the sake of a good cause she was willing to throw even more assurance into her tones than there was in her heart. But the boy was better. Anyone could see that. There was noticeably more flesh on his bones. The skin over his face did not look so much like parchment. There was a faint colour creeping into his cheeks and his lips, and it might well be that half the battle lay in having him merely believe that he was better. At any rate it was infinitely preferable to the doleful attitude of considering his days as numbered and spending most of his time deciding on the highest number.

That month both of them worked and held frequent consultations. They repeatedly revised the diet lists, making the food that they felt was right and beneficial recur most frequently, omitting things that were not helpful and sticking religiously to the tomato juice in the morning, the orange juice in the afternoon, and the best milk that could be found in as large quantities as Jamie could take it. That month was one in which they neatly walked. Sometimes they spoke softly. For Jamie it was a month filled to the brim with joyful thanksgiving. Every day he could positively see and feel the progress that he made. Each day he could accomplish slightly more in the garden. Each day he knew more about the bees.

That month he developed the habit every night of picking up the Bible the last thing before he went to bed and reading a few verses, and from thinking a prayer and from thinking thanksgiving, he advanced to the place where he boldly, in the silence and serenity of the little room, got down on his knees and prayed the prayer of thanksgiving. Then he followed it by the prayer of asking. He found himself asking God to take care of all the world, to help everyone who needed help; to put the spirit and courage into every heart to fare forth and to attempt the Great Adventure on its own behalf. When it came to cases, he asked for strength to keep the bees and the garden safely; he asked for help, physically and morally, to be a man of whom his father and mother could justly have been proud. Then he asked God to take care of Margaret Cameron; to ease whatever trouble it might be that seemed to be resting in her heart. Then, from the first time he actually had gone on his knees and lifted his face to the throne, Jamie had included the little Scout. He told God about what a fine spirit he thought the little fellow had and what a bright mentality; how unselfish the child was and how overly-developed the sense of fairness; and he asked that the little fellow be taken care of and guided right and given the opportunity to grow into such a citizen as would be a benefit to the nation.

When he reached the Bee Master, Jamie laid hold on the foot of the throne, and he begged the Almighty that if it were at all consistent with the divine plan of things, to spare the Bee Master, to let him come back to his home and the homely, simple things that comprise the spirit of home, to let him have a few more years in his garden with a brilliancy of colour to comfort his waking days and the song of the sea to soothe his pillow. Last of all he reached the Storm Girl, and for her Jamie begged safety, mercy, and the power to give her help. Then he arose, in some way fortified, a trifle bigger, slightly prouder, more capable, more of a man than he had been the day before. He had asked for help and he knew that he was *receiving* help, and he knew that never again would he be ashamed to face any man, or any body of men, and tell them that he had asked for help and that help had been forthcoming, and that the same experience lay in reach of every man if he would only take the Lord at His word ; if he would only do what all men are so earnestly urged to do—believe.

That was a good month for Jamie. Before the close of it the pads covering his side were coming off dry and clean. He was using them now more as a protection to tender, freshly formed flesh covered with skin so thin it seemed as if a breath would rend it, than because of any seepage. When Jamie went into the sea he stroked with his right arm only. When he lifted a heavy load he protected his left side. If a high reach was to be made he made it with his right hand. But never for an instant, during the day or in a waking hour in the night, did there cease in his soul a little, low murmuring song of thanksgiving. Over and over, all day he sang it, but there were very few words. It ran "Life ! Life ! A useful life ! I thank thee, Lord, for a chance at Life, for a chance at beautiful work, for a chance at beautiful friends. I thank thee, Lord, for life !"

Each time he went to the hospital he carried flowers from the garden, and sometimes fruits and loving messages from the little Scout, and quaint gifts ranging all the way from a battered jack-knife and a stick to whittle, to a well-worn deck of cards with which to play solitaire.

One day as he went into the hospital he met Margaret Cameron coming out ; so he knew that she had been to visit the Bee Master and had not told him that she was going, and he knew by the whiteness of her face and the pain in her eyes that the Bee Master was not improving, that he was not gathering strength, that the chances might be slowly lessening, day by day, of his ever returning to the friendly house so beautifully encircled by a garden of love.

Jamie went up to the Bee Master's room and read the truth for himself. The Master was scarcely able to speak. There was a white look across the noble brow that seemed to Jamie to indicate that the fine old soul before him was very near to being ready for transfiguration. When he arose to go he had extreme difficulty in keeping his voice even and his eyes clear.

"I want to tell you," he said, "how much I thank you for the chance you've given me to get back my manhood and to learn work that each day I am growing to love more and more. I want to thank you for giving me in your home the opportunity to get back to a confidential understanding with God, to find out the peace and sustaining power that He is willing to give to every man who can muster the manhood to receive the gift."

Jamie leaned over and kissed the Bee Master on the forehead once.

"That's for the little Scout, who sent you a truck-load of love."

Then he kissed him again, and added whimsically: "And that's for Jamie. He's brought you the same amount."

The Bee Master held Jamie's hands very tight for a minute, and then, in barely a whisper, he said: "Thank God that you've learned to lay hold on the promise of the Master. I am thankful that you have learned to accept His gifts, and I believe, too, that you have learned enough of life and enough of love in my house and in my garden that you will be ready to accept any gift which love and confidence may bring to you."

Jamie went out wondering what that meant. The next day he learned. The call came early from the hospital. The Bee Master had found that beautiful crossing that the little Scout had so understandingly described. With his hands folded on his breast, in his sleep, he had answered the call so lightly given that the nurse found him as she had left him. His instructions had been that his remains were to be shipped immediately to an address he gave in the East. He wanted to be laid for his final sleep beside the two Marys, the one he had loved and married, and the one to whom their love had given life. All three of them were gone now, and Jamie put it into the next prayer he uttered that that hour might find them hand in hand wandering amid greater beauties than the little garden had ever contained, even among the splendours of the fields of Paradise.

In telling him, Doctor Grayson had asked that he come to the hospital for a conference, and when Jamie reached the hospital an hour later he was dumbfounded to have placed in his hands, ready for execution, the last will and testament of the Bee Master. It set forth that, on account of love and affection, the property therein described was given, devised and bequeathed to the present occupant and caretaker, James Lewis MacFarlane, and to his first assistant, Jean Meredith. Said property was to be equally divided between the two beneficiaries, the acre on the right hand facing the street with the beehives contained thereon to be the property of Jean Meredith. The acre on the left hand facing the street to be the property of James Lewis MacFarlane with all the improvements thereon. There followed the further provision that the two beneficiaries were to draw cuts for the possession of the residence, the one drawing the short cut to become the owner of the house, which was to be removed to the property of the winner, the expense of moving to be paid from funds in the banks belonging to the estate, which were also devised, share and share alike, to the beneficiaries of the will. From these same funds there was to be drawn sufficient money to duplicate the house, or to build one having the same number of rooms, general appearance, and conveniences on the property of the loser. The remainder of the money in the bank, after these transactions were made, was to be equally divided between the parties benefiting by the will.

When this amazing document was thoroughly explained to Jamie he sat looking rather bleakly at Doctor Grayson. He was not in the least ashamed of the big tears that were running down his cheeks.

"But I can't do that," he protested. "I haven't earned that place. There must be someone who is nearer to the Bee Master than I."

"Well," said Doctor Grayson, "in case there is, don't worry. You'll hear from them. If there are people living who feel that they have a better right to that property than you, they will put in an appearance. In the meantime, we will go on the supposition that the Bee Master knew his own mind and his own business and that, in giving you the place, he wanted it to go into the hands of a man who would appreciate it, who would love it, who, in all probability, would keep it as the Master left it."

Jamie sat staring, thinking deeply, and then he knew what the Bee Master had meant when he had said the night before that he should learn to accept any gift of love as well as the gifts of the Heavenly Father. The Bee Master had known that his time was imminent, that his crossing was near, and he had meant in a way to prepare Jamie for the fact that the little house and the bees and the bright garden were going to be, in part at least, a gift of love to him. Suddenly Jamie sat up and repeated a name slowly.

"Jean Meredith."

Then he realized that he was still in the dark. He didn't know any more than he had before. Jean might be a boy or might be a girl. He looked at Doctor Grayson.

"Does Jean Meredith know about this ?" he asked.

"The Bee Master gave me the telephone number and I called the parents. Yes, the Bee Master's little friend knows."

"And will the parents accept that gift on behalf of the child ?" asked Jamie.

"Most assuredly," said the Doctor. "Why not ? There probably was no one on earth to whom the Bee Master was so attached as to the little person he always referred to as his side partner. There is no reason, since he had no child of his own, as to why he should not leave his property to anyone he chose. There was every reason as to why he should leave it to a man who had cared for it in his absence, in whom he had faith, and to a child who has perhaps relieved the tedium of more dark hours in the Master's life than all the rest of the world put together. It seemed to me eminently right and fitting that the Bee Master should do precisely what he has done. I forgot to call your attention to a last provision and an afterthought in the form of a codicil as to the furnishings of the house. Everything in the living-room and the books go to the little Scout ; the remainder of the furnishings are yours."

Jamie arose. He offered his hand to Doctor Grayson.

"I am going out in the air where I can walk and think," he said. "But I'll tell you right now, there's no use to probate that document. It was made by a sick man——"

"It was made by a man fighting for life after an operation," said the Doctor. "His mentality was as clear as yours or mine when I said good night to him at ten o'clock last night. There isn't a court in the land that can touch that will."

"It's simply impossible," said Jamie. "I will not even consider it."

"Oh yes, you will," said Doctor Grayson, "because if you don't probate that will, I'll do it for you and you can rest very largely assured that Mr. Meredith will see that his child's interests in it are taken care of. You will take it whether you want it or not. If you don't want to keep it, once it comes to your hands, if you'd rather see someone the Bee Master would have hated go into the little house and commercialize the garden, that's up to you, so far as your half of it is concerned. You can make up your mind when the time comes. Since you are so in doubt about it, I think I had better turn the document over to Mr. Meredith, but the chances are he will want you to co-operate with him."

"Well, I will not!" said Jamie stubbornly. "I will not accept a thing I haven't earned!"

"Oh, damn the Scots!" said Doctor Grayson impatiently. "I'm glad I'm English and willing to take all I can get, and you're the first Scotsman I ever saw who wasn't willing to take all he could get, no matter if it did come as a gift. And as for not taking things you haven't earned, you'd better stop breathing, you'd better stop soaking in sunshine, you'd better stop eating the fruits of the earth. They are all gifts that you have accepted, and were mighty glad to accept!"

"A gift from God is one thing," said Jamie. "A gift from a man I have known such a short time is something different."

"There is no difference in the gifts," said the Doctor. "They are both gifts, and I reiterate you are a fool if you don't accept them with a thankful heart!"

Jamie shook his head and, turning from the office, went down to the street and then back to the house and to the blue garden that the love of flowers and the love of beauty in the heart of a sentimentalist had built around a home. He stepped softly as he entered the door. He carried his hat in his hand and looked around for some place, not too intimately connected with the Bee Master, where he might lay it.

What was it that amazing document had said? One acre of valuable soil crowded to the limit with wonderful planting, a row of white hives running the length of it, something in the bank, plenty of comfortable clothing that fitted him, a bed whereon to sleep, and they were his if he cared to stretch forth his hand and take them? Jamie suddenly discovered that he was not so strong as he had thought he was, because he was shaking until his teeth chattered and the tears were rolling down his cheeks until he was exhausted. So he got up and went down the back walk the extreme length of it, and opened the gate and stepped into the footpath that led down to the white sands of the sea. There before him his eyes encountered an amazing sight.

Backed against a rock, making feeble efforts at self-defence, were a couple of children, and before them there was a small figure working a sand shovel with the precision of a rotary plough and the velocity of a whirlwind. The victims against the rock were clawing their eyes and gasping for breath and making an ineffectual effort to return the compliment. To Jamie it was evident that the flying sand was very nearly smothering both of them. A few long strides brought him to the rescue. He grabbed the little Scout by the belt and pulled hard.

"Gently, partner! Go gently!" he said. "You're smothering those children!"

The little Scout lifted the shovel and raised a face of outrage with the offered explanation: "They began it! They picked on me! I wasn't doing a thing until they threw sand on me half a dozen times!"

"No doubt," said Jamie. "No doubt, but that is not any sufficient reason as to why you should smother them. You're going at them like a whirlwind!"

The little Scout drew to full height. A deep breath filled a heaving chest. There was no disputing the argument offered. "Again, I threw as much on each one of them as both of them could throw on me; I *had* to be goin' some!"

Jamie took that in slowly.

"Perhaps you did," he said. "Is that shovel yours or theirs?"

"It's theirs," answered the little Scout. "I took it from the biggest one, and you will notice he is taller and huskier than I am. So that's that."

"You come with me," said Jamie. "Let's go up here to the rock and sit down and look out on the ocean. When were you home last?"

"Left right after breakfast," said the little Scout. "It's Saturday, you know. I was comin' to help you with the bees this morning, but you wasn't there, and so I came on down to the sand and thought I'd look around and see if I could start anything, and right away those kids began picking on me, so I thought I'd better show 'em a few."

Jamie headed toward the throne and the little Scout scuffled along beside him.

"If you've not been home since breakfast," said Jamie, when they were finally seated facing the ocean, "if you haven't been home since breakfast, Jean——"

"*Who* told you my name was Jean?" cut in the little Scout.

"Doctor Grayson," said Jamie. "He told me at the hospital this morning that your name was Jean Meredith."

"What else did he blab about me?" inquired the little Scout. It was evident to Jamie that the whole of the small figure beside him was suddenly imbued with defiance, drawn up for battle.

"He didn't say anything," said Jamie, "except that you would have the sense to accept a very wonderful gift that's going to be offered to you."

"Is it a horse?" asked the little Scout instantly, the defiance beginning to fade.

"No," said Jamie, "it's something worth more than a great many horses. Never mind that right now. There is something else I want to tell you. I've just come from the hospital."

Slowly the little person drew away from Jamie. Slowly the grey eyes widened. Slowly the hands clenched. Slowly the narrow chest heaved up and sank back again.

"Aw!" said the youngster harshly, "aw! he ain't gone and slept the beautiful sleep, has he?"

Jamie sat still and looked out across the ocean. It was a blow he found himself powerless to deliver. Slowly his eyes turned to the horrified face of the child beside him, and suddenly the little Scout launched a quivering figure into his arms and buried a twisted face on his breast, and for a short time Jamie had difficulty in holding the writhing body in his arms together. A curious thought struck him. That rock that he had called the throne was not very well named. It seemed to be a place where people brought their troubles. In an earlier experience with it he had held the body of a woman tortured to the extreme limit of endurance. Now he was holding the body of a child so lean and slight that he could scarcely manage his long arms to give the support that was needed.

"Don't!" begged Jamie. "Don't take it like that! Let me tell you. It was like your Aunt Beth. It was in the night without even awakening the Bee Master. His hands were folded on his breast too. There was a wonderful smile on his face, exactly the smile that you described, the smile that seemed as if there were a great secret that those closed lips could tell if they could open."

Jamie fumbled for his handkerchief and turned the little Scout's head and wiped the streaming eyes and cupped a big hand under the quivering cheeks and held on tight.

"Don't cry like that," he begged. "You are tearing yourself to pieces! The Master wouldn't like it. Don't you know that you said all the angels would be glad when they saw your Aunt Beth coming marching, straight and tall, with a sure step, down the flower ways of Heaven? It's going to be like that with the Bee Master. You are selfish when you cry like that,

You are not thinking about him; about his going home to Mary and his wee girl; you are thinklng about yourself."

Instantly the little figure straightened.

"Sure, I'm thinking about myself! Why shouldn't I think about myself? I got myself to live with, haven't I? Who's going to be hurt when I've got a pain or ain't strong enough to handle Fat Ole Bill, or when I can't make anybody understand *any* of the things that he always did understand? He ain' the only one that spilt the beans. When he told me all there was to tell about things that went wrong with him and the people who ruined him, he didn't do *all* the talking. He knew just as much about me as I did about him, and now I ain't got a living soul to go to that'll understand! What am I goin' to do? Just answer me that! *What am I going to do?*"

Suddenly Jamie found himself taking the woebegone face before him between his hands; he found himself laying it against his face, first on one side and then on the other; he found himself hugging the frail body until he knew he was almost cracking the bones in it, and deep and husky he heard his own voice saying: "You come straight to me! When you've got a secret you want kept, when anyone doesn't seem to understand and some of the bunch will not play fair and things go wrong, you come to me!"

Instantly the little Scout struggled away from him. Jamie met a level gaze of such depth and appeal as he never before had encountered in human eyes.

"Honest to God?" said the little Scout. "Tear out your heart, cut it in pieces, and cast it to the four winds of the heavens?"

"Whose lodge ritual have you been reading?" asked Jamie.

"Dad's," said the little Scout calmly, "only we made ours as much worse as we could." Then his fingers tightened again. "Honest? On the level, do you really mean it?"

"Honest. On the level. Swear over my heart," said Jamie. "Hold up my right hand and take the oath before the Almighty! I'll always be your friend. I'll keep any secret you tell me. I'll do anything in all the world that I can at any time, at any place, to help you."

A steady hand was thrust at him.

"Shake!" said the little Scout. "All that goes for me. All what you said about me, I'll say about you. I'll come to you like I been goin' to the Bee Master. We'll be partners like him and me was. I'll help you all I can. But, say, what's going to become of the bees? What's going to become of the garden? What's going to become of that nice house?"

Jamie hesitated. Someone had to tell the child. They were there. It was his opportunity. He wanted a childish viewpoint. Why not?

So he said quietly: "Would you believe there was anyone in all this world that the Bee Master loved any better than he did you?"

"I don't have to waste any breath on explaining beliefs on that point," said the little Scout. "I got acshal information, and I got it from the Great Mogul; I got it from the Man Higher Up; I got it right up against the Bee Master's heart; I got it with a tight kiss and it's a sekert I ain't tellin' anybody except the man that takes his place. Reckermember you're under oath and this is the first one I'm goin' to tell you because it was our sekert between us. There might have been folks that wouldn't have liked it if they'd known it. There *was* folks that wouldn't have liked it. Margaret Cameron wouldn't have liked it, for one, 'cause I've got my doubts if she cared any more about Lolly than she did about the Bee Master. What I know about her, the way she cleaned after him and waited on him! I guess I seen mother cottoning up to dad. I guess I know a *little* about married folks, and what I know about her is that she'd have been tickled to pieces if the Bee Master had said to her, 'Wilt thou?' You just bet she'd have 'wilted'! She'd have 'wilted' all over him! But he didn't ever ask her, and he didn't ever *intend* to ask her. He never loved any woman in all the world but Highland Mary, and he let one other woman make a fool of him when he was so lonesome after she was gone, like a chicken tryin' to peruse around with its head cut off—Say! That's a sekert, too! I seem to be spillin' all I know on you all at once. You might get 'em in line better and hold on to 'em tighter if I told 'em one at a time, and it'd be more sense if I'd tell my *own*, anyway. He might not like it if I told his. I didn't mean to either. Just sayin' that about Margaret Cameron made me think how I could've told her, any time she was whirling like a button on a barn door, that there wasn't nothin' to it except that he thought she was clean, and he thought she was fine, and he'd rather play cribbage or checkers with her than to sit and think about the awful thing that happened to the woman he liked best and to his little Mary. No, she needn't ever thought it was her he liked best, 'cause it wasn't. It was just 'as is' little old me! And why I know it is like I told you before. 'Cause he *said* so! And he wouldn't have to say so if he didn't want to. Nobody asked him. Nobody pushed him off the springboard. He took the high dive all by himself."

"Well, then," said Jamie, "if he loved you like that, and you know he loved you like that, and if he was going on his long journey and had something very dear to him to leave, who do you think would be the person to whom he would leave it ?"

So long as he lives Jamie will remember the reaction of the little Scout to that question. The flat shoulders squared. The head lifted to an extreme height. The chin drew in. The eyes batted. A hand was laid on the chest at the base of the throat ; the mouth opened and the eyes closed, and the little Scout went through the pantomime of swallowing the biggest morsel that could, by any possibility, be forced down a small æsophagus. Then it came straight from the shoulder, as Jamie was beginning to learn that everything came with the little Scout.

"Why, he'd just naturally leave it to *me* !"

Calmly, casually, convincingly, the words came from lips of assurance. "He'd leave it to me, and maybe he'd leave *some* to you because you stuck on the job when you wasn't hardly able, and you faced down the bees like a real man would, and you been square about taking care of things. You can write down my answer to that question : He'd leave some to me, and if he played the game square, like he always did, he'd leave some to you."

"Well," said Jamie, "you're a good guesser, Jean ! That's exactly what the Bee Master has done. He's left a writing that Doctor Grayson thinks will hold in the courts, and this writing says that the west acre of the garden of wonder up there, and the hives that are on it, are yours ; and the east acre and the hives that are on it are mine. For yourself you are free to do whatever you and your parents think best. For me, it seems to be a gift that I cannot accept."

"How come ?"

The little Scout shot the phrase at Jamie forcefully.

"Why, I haven't done anything to earn it," said Jamie. "All I've done here is a drop in the bucket compared with the value of an acre of land down that slope, planted as it is, peopled with the bees. It's simply stepping into a home and a comfortable living and a profession that I feel sure I have brains enough to master with a few years of loving and painstaking work, and there are all the books I need and all the material I need, and the name of a man who will help me. It's too easy ! It's a fairy-tale ! It's a dream ! Things don't happen that way in real life."

The little person thought that over.

"Look here," said a confident voice, and a small hand was laid on Jamie's cheek and his face was turned straightly to meet the gaze of the speaker. "Look here! Maybe you think the bandages you're wearing don't show through the shirt on your back; but when you stoop over *they do.* You're pretty game about it and you don't bellyache, but of course you wouldn't be all harnessed up like that if you didn't have to be. And that means that wrong things and things that hurt you and hit you awful hard came your way, and it was for all of us, for 'Our country 'tis of thee'. But you bucked up and you stood your hurts, and you didn't complain, and you pulled through 'em. And you just know, all by yourself, that ugly things, and mean things, and maybe things you didn't deserve at all happened to you. Now, why ain't that just the same as if something that was wonderful and lovely happened to you? Why couldn't a beautiful thing happen to you just as well as a bad thing? Why couldn't gettin' an acre of land with beehives and flowers happen to you just as well as gettin' a rip-snorter that nearly tore your heart out? Laugh that off, will you?"

"Well," said Jamie, "come to think of it, I have heard of the law of compensation. The law of compensation means that when things have gone about as far as they can go in one direction, sometimes they turn around and go equally far in the other direction."

"Sure!" said the small person. "That's the dope! That's the way to look at it! Don't sit there and talk about not understanding things and not being worth things. 'Course you're worth 'em, or you wouldn't have got 'em! All your life there's been something in you, and I expect it was born in you just like it was born in our baby. Ever since they brought him home from the hospital you can see there's things about him that's like dad, and you can see things about him that's like mother, and I hope to goodness there'll be one thing about him that'll be like *me*! When I went on a boat past the cave in the rock where, if you look through, you can see the light, Molly said, when I saw the light, if I'd wish for the thing I wanted most in the world it would come true. So I made a wish and Molly wanted to know what I wished, and I wasn't goin' to tell her. I like Molly, but everything ain't all of her business. I like her, but she ain't the keeper of my sekerts like the Bee Master was and like you're going to be now in his place. So I'll tell you what I wished for my little brother when I saw the light that makes wishing come true. I thought of it just the minute I saw the light, 'cause even worse than I want a horse I want the thing I wished for my little brother. So just as quick and just as hard as ever I could say it, right in my heart and looking straight at the light, I said:

'I wish that our Jimmy will not ever grow up to be a cad!'"

Jamie arose and took the little Scout by the hand.

"Come on, Jean," he said, "let's go home."

The little Scout bounded expertly from crag to crag down the rock in front of him and waited for him at the base.

"You seem to like my name."

"Well," said Jamie, "there couldn't be a lovelier name. It's something to know about you definitely, and at that it doesn't tell me whether you're a boy or a girl."

Jamie saw the mutiny that instantly dawned in the eyes raised to his.

"Still harpin' on that old no-sense thing, are you?" demanded the little person. "Still fussin' over trifles when you are satisfied with the big thing. If I'm your partner and you're the keeper of my sekerts, and we're goin' home together, ain't that enough for you?"

"That ought to be almost enough for any man," answered Jamie.

So they started up the path toward the back gate. Halfway there the little Scout paused and looked at Jamie speculatively.

"Am I to call you the Bee Master now?"

"No," said Jamie. "You aren't going to call me the Bee Master, maybe not for long years yet. The Bee Master is a title that has to be won by painstaking work and fine thought and delicate operations. It's a title that properly belonged to the man who's sleeping now. He could wear it with grace and dignity. It's too big to fit my case. We'll have to find a title for me that means stumbling along plainly and simply, every day studying my job and making the most of it, going at things with all my heart and putting the best I have to give to them, just sticking on the job because I like it, as you told me I would."

Registering among the mental pictures that endured, there registered on Jamie's consciousness the upward lift of the shoulders, the backward slant of the head, the elevation of the chin, the outward gesture of both hands, and on his ears fell the dictum: "Oh, well, then, if you want to be plain and simple, if you want to get right down to brass tacks, you better just answer to what you are—the Keeper of the Bees. That's a good enough name for any man."

"I heartily agree with you," said Jamie. "That's a fine title. That satisfies me fully and completely, better, in fact, than any title possibly could that was of German origin."

"Is the 'Bee Master' of German origin ?" queried the little Scout.

"Yes," said Jamie, "that title is of German origin."

"Was the Bee Master a German ?"

"No," said Jamie. "Never! The Bee Master was British by breeding and training. He happened to be located in our country, but he was of British ancestry if he didn't go farther and be of British birth."

"Well, he didn't go that far," said the small person. "That's another thing he told me himself. He was born in Pennsylvania, and he found Mary there and he was married there and he lived there, and the awful tilting rock was in the mountains there."

"The tilting rock ?" asked Jamie.

The little Scout looked down.

"I guess I'm kind of broke up to-day," was the conclusion reached. "I guess I've said two or three things I'd better kept still about. We won't talk about that rock to-day. Maybe some day I'll tell you. It's pretty awful, and I don't sleep well if I get to thinking about it. If I get to thinking hard about it, I can't very well quit. I want to see him before they send him away. I want to straighten his hair and fix his tie and fold his hands myself. I want to fix his feet comfortable and easy and I would like to put his slippers on him too."

Right there Jamie broke down. By that time they had reached the bench under the jacqueranda. He sat down on it and buried his face in his hands and sobbed aloud. The little person stood beside him and put stout arms around his neck.

"Aw," said the voice, roughened with emotion, "they didn't go and send him right away ? They didn't put him on a morning train ? They did not give me a chance ? They didn't let somebody *else* fix him ?"

Jamie straightened up.

"Honey," he said, "I'm afraid they did."

"Well, I call that a dirty gyp!" sobbed the little Scout. "It ain't giving the Bee Master any show, and it ain't giving me any show! When he liked me the best, he would have wanted *me* to fix him. Mother would have come with me and so would dad. Doctor Grayson knew all about me, and I'm goin' to tell him what I think of that kind of business! I've called him on the 'phone maybe half a dozen times and got him here and run as tight as I could lick to get what he wanted and to heat water and to help him. He knew darn well who the Bee Master would want to fix him up to go to see God! It ain't fair!"

Then the little person collapsed, and Jamie had his chance

at comforting. By and by, when both of them were calmer, they sat on the bench side by side and dried their eyes on the same handkerchief.

"Did he divide things the way you'd like to have 'em?" asked the small person, in abrupt change, as was habitual. "Did he give you the side of the garden you'd most rather have?"

"Why, I'm perfectly satisfied," said Jamie. "I don't see any difference."

"I do," said the little Scout. "If I'd got to take my choice, I'd 'a' said the east side."

"What difference does it make?" asked Jamie. "There are as many hives on the west side as there are on the east. If there aren't, we'll count them and make them exactly even. I'm perfectly willing to move the Black Germans over and give you them as a bonus. Was it the Black Germans you wanted?"

"No," said the little person, "it wasn't the Black Germans I wanted. It was the Madonna lilies. I can beat the bees to 'em every crack. I just love to suck the honey out of 'em! It's the real thing, straight from the fountain, and I like the real thing! And that panel of fence where we make the Redskins bite the dust, I'd like to have had that mighty well."

"But won't a west panel do as well?"

"Oh, I reckon it'll *do* as well. The only difference is that I ain't *used* to the west panel and I am used to the east, and so is Fat Ole Bill and the Nice Child and Angel Face. All of us are *used* to the east, but I reckon we *could* use the west just as well."

Then the little person looked at Jamie speculatively.

"I'm kind of disappointed in you."

Jamie sat straight.

"I don't know what I've done," he said.

"That's just edsactly it," said the little fellow. "'Tain't anything you done. It's something you didn't do. When you said it didn't make any difference to you, and I showed you good and plain that it made the difference of the Madonna lilies and our Indian ambush to me, you might have offered to trade sides with me! Prodibly I wouldn't a-done it. Prodibly I wouldn't a-had anything but what the Bee Master wanted me to have. Prodibly I would a-saved up my money and got some Madonna lilies and planted 'em on my side for myself, but I *thought* you'd *offer* to trade."

Slowly Jamie digested this.

"I beg your pardon," he said. "That must have been a thoughtless streak in me. My head is a lot older than yours, and

I knew that we couldn't trade without going to court and having measurements and making out deeds and paying officers for making the change, and I suspect that knowledge kept me from saying that I'd trade when it really wouldn't make any difference to me which side you had or any particular difference if you had both of them."

"But I wouldn't have both of them," said the small person promptly. "If the Bee Master had said both of them were for me, I wouldn't have taken but half, because it wouldn't be square, when I asked you to stay and did all I could to get you to stay. It wouldn't be fair to take all of it."

The little person looked at Jamie again inquiringly.

"What's goin' to become of all the money he had in the bank?"

"Well," said Jamie, "according to the word of the will, after his funeral expenses and his just debts are paid, whatever remains in the bank is subject to provisions in the will that your dad will explain to you when he has thoroughly studied the document. I can tell you this: that there is money provided to pay the cost of moving the house on to the grounds of whichever one of us draws it, and there's money to build another little house that will cost the same as the value of this one, and whatever is left is to be divided evenly between us."

"Hm-m-m-m," said the small party slowly. "You think it's likely the Bee Master gave me some money as well as the bees and the flowers?"

"I know he did," said Jamie, "if that will holds good. If there doesn't turn out to be some blood relatives somewhere, who can prove that they are relatives and are entitled by law to have possession. You mustn't set your heart too hard. You must go at this with the feeling that the Bee Master intended you to have it, but there is a large possibility that somewhere in the world there may be a man or a woman who can take it from you, and who very probably will when they learn about it, because, after all, blood is thicker than water, and in this case anyone related to the Bee Master would be blood and you and I would be water."

"Yes, I get that," said the little person. "I follow through. But in case the Bee Master knew his business and the judge would say things were ours, then would there be money coming to me?"

"Yes," said Jamie, "I think there would be, but I doubt if it could come to you before you are of legal age. I think probably your father would have to handle it for you and conserve it for you until the law says you are old enough to have it yourself."

"Aw!" said the little person. "Aw, there it goes again!" and the small feet kicked the pebbles of the walk until they flew yards away. "*There* it goes again! Always havin' to wait and wait, always havin' to be disappointed!"

"What was it you especially wanted?" asked Jamie.

"What's the use to tell if I don't get it?" said the disgruntled little person. "What would you think I'd want?"

"Well," said Jamie, "if I was taking a random shot at it I'd say that you would want a horse."

"You said it, son!"

The little Scoutmaster leaped in the air.

"You said it! If I ever wanted anything, if I ever really wanted anything in all this world, I want a horse! I want my own horse! Queen's wonderful and Hans is wonderful, but I want my own horse! I want to put my arms around his neck and love him personal. I want him to know me and follow me like dad's dog. I want him to come when I call. I want him to learn my way. And I don't want anybody else, not Nannette, not little brother, not anybody, to ride him ever but just me! I want him for one thing that's mine and nobody else's. I want to be just as selfish as ever I can be with him!"

"Well," said Jamie, "never having met your father and your mother, I don't know, but it seems to me, from the tones of your mother's voice when she talked with me over the 'phone——"

"Yes, I know her telephone voice," said the small person. "I like it myself. I stand and listen sometimes when she's talkin' just to see how much sweetness can be put into the way she says things."

"And about your father, because he is your father I'd think it would be my judgment that if this money and this land is a gift to you from the Bee Master, I should think——"

"Of course you should!" interrupted the little Scoutmaster. "Anybody would think that they'd let me have a horse out of it. Couldn't we keep him here?"

"I don't know how far the city limits extend," said Jamie, "but we'll investigate. We'll keep that a secret between us and we'll investigate it. We'll see what we can do. If you think it isn't likely that they would agree to your having a horse in town, don't say anything about it. Let's just keep it under our hats and see what we can figure out ourselves."

"All right," said the little person. "I won't say a word to them. We'll see what we can figure out. And I believe now that I'd better go home. Maybe Doctor Grayson telephoned dad. Maybe he's waiting for me. Maybe mother would like to see me. And just maybe they haven't taken him away yet."

"I'm sorry," said Jamie. "I'm awfully sorry, but I happen to know that they have. You mustn't build any hopes on that. I happen to know that he's gone."

The little person stood still staring hard at the zinnia bed, struggling hard to hold steady lips and to keep dry-eyed. Then came the habitual lightning-like change of subject.

"I hope," said the little Scout, "I just hope that the Bee Master didn't have very *much* money in the bank. I hope there's only going to be a little of it."

"But why?" said Jamie.

"Oh," said the little Scout, "I can't see the use of people havin' so much money. It don't seem to do anything but make a lot of trouble. I been lookin' on for a good many years, and seems to me most of the fightin' and the fussin' and the lawsuits and things going wrong is among the people that've got a whole lot of money. Why can't folks be satisfied with a reasonable amount?"

"Well," said Jamie, glad to change the subject, "what would you say was enough? What would you think would be about the right amount for *us* to have?"

The little Scout thought that over and then announced conclusively: "I'd say that anybody that's got the east acre or the west acre of this place, and a long row of beehives and lots of fruit trees and flowers and flowers and worlds of flowers, and the sand and the sea, and a little house that yells 'Come on in!' clear across the road to you, I'd say if they had enough to own that, and get the bread and butter and the strawberry pop and the hot dogs, I'd say they didn't need another thing on earth—clothes, of course, I forgot about enough clothes to cover 'em up with——"

"And didn't you forget about a horse?" said Jamie.

"Oh, well, now, of course I meant a horse. I meant a horse most before anything else except a place to keep him. You can't have a horse without a place to keep him. That's been my trouble for years. I could a-had a horse almost any time. There wasn't any stable for him and not any alfalfa or oats or anybody to keep the stable clean. That's been my trouble all along. A horse, of course!"

"And a boat, of course," suggested Jamie. "The ocean isn't very much good without a boat, now, is it?"

The little Scout hesitated. "Oh, well, of course, with the ocean at our back door, of course, now, we *could* use a boat. The Bee Master told me once why he put the fence where he did, but he said he owned clear down to the water. A man wanted to buy his shore-line and put a hot dog stand there and he decided he couldn't have it because we could get hot dogs down at the corner. The Bee Master said that one of the finest men who ever lived in England, one of the biggest credits to that fine old land was a man, and his name was William Blackstone. He made me say over and over about the hot dog stand what William Blackstone said. I'll tell you now."

The little Scout stepped in front of Jamie, brought small heels together, squared lean shoulders, lifted a chin, and accomplished a nobility of countenance that was startling. Jamie did not understand how it happened that a tear-smeared face, that sand-filled tow hair, sanded brows and ears could take on the look of dignity and serenity that was on the face of the youngster in the delivery of this sentence: " 'Thou shalt not obstruct thy neighbour's ancient light!' "

Suddenly, with the flashing change habitual to the little Scout, the entire figure slumped, came back to the bench, sat down beside Jamie and leaned against him.

"That means," said the little Scout, "that 'ancient light' means the sunshine and the moonshine and the clean air clear from China. The Bee Master used to go down and lie on the sand by the hour and let the ocean tell him things that comforted him. He said if he sold that the man adjoining him would be the owner, and *he* would be the *neighbour*, and he didn't want his 'ancient light' all mussed up with a hot dog stand, and he didn't want his inheritance of well-salted, dustless air right fresh off the sea all fogged up with hot dogs. Didn't make any difference if they did make your mouth water, we could get ours down at the corner."

Then the little Scout put a pair of arms tight around Jamie's neck and closed in almost to the point of suffocation, and the Keeper of the Bees got his second little hot kiss firm on his lips.

The little Scout said: "Thank you for taking his place with me, and I'm glad that you've got the Madonna lilies and the fighting ground, and I'm glad you've got the east acre and half the bees. I'll take the Black Germans if you don't want 'em. And I'm glad, if the Bee Master *had* to go, I'm gladder than I can tell you that you are goin' to stay and keep the bees!"

CHAPTER XIV

THE HOME-MADE MIRACLE

ONLY a short time was required for the settlement of the estate of the Bee Master. All he owned was the two acres of mountain-side and beach and the money that he had deposited in the Citizen's Bank. Because he was so thoroughly familiar with the Bee Master's wishes, Doctor Grayson consented to act as executor. The determination as to whom the house should belong had been decided after the manner prescribed, and it had fallen to Jamie. It was agreed that the house should be appraised, its value should be set aside to accrue interest for the little Scout until such time as it was desirable to erect another house on the west acre. It was agreed that the home should remain where it was until Jamie desired to move it. A fund sufficient to cover a contractor's estimate of this expense was set aside to Jamie's credit. The little Scout was to have the complete furnishings of the combined library and living-room on demand. The remaining money in the bank was divided equally, Jamie's half being set aside to his credit, the little Scout's to begin compounding interest until legal age was attained. The proceeds from the honey and the garden were to be divided equally after the wages of any help employed had been deducted, the child's share to be placed in the bank. The Bee Master was reaping the reward that the Almighty has in store for a man who has kept the faith, and from his earthly opportunities has made of himself a scholar and a gentleman.

After the inheritance it was noticeable to Jamie and the family of the little Scout that ownership had brought problems and responsibilities to the youngster. There was an inclination to eat fewer hot dogs and save more dimes, and very speedily it developed that the first improvement the little Scout planned for the west acre was a fine large bed of Madonna lilies, and the bulbs of these are expensive in comparison with hot dogs. It would take much self-denial to plant a bed from which a satisfying amount of money could be obtained in the raw. Jamie frequently noticed the child going carefully over the ground, apparently in search of a level spot that would have access to the road and not disfigure the premises, and he knew what that meant. Plans were being made for housing the horse that was the secret desire of the youngster's heart.

As for Jamie, he was frankly bewildered. It was very true that he had been born in this country, that his education had started in our public schools and ended in one of our best colleges. It was true that he belonged to our country by birth and environment. But it was also true that the blood of a man and a woman both of whom were born and reared in Scotland was in his veins, and the habits and characteristics of the Scot were strong upon him. All the Scotsmen with whom he had ever come in contact had inherited what they owned from their parents, or earned it by hard labour. Jamie was not accustomed to gifts. He could not recall that anyone ever had given him anything in particular. Then why, all at once, and out of a clear sky, should an acre covered with fruit, carpeted with flower brilliancy, humming with bees that were doing the work that provided the income upon which to live, be presented to him? There might have been a feeling in Jamie's heart that his Government owed him something; there was no such thought concerning the Bee Master.

Jamie said frankly to Doctor Grayson, to the father of the little Scout, to the probate judge, that he could not feel that he had any right to a half-interest in the garden of the bees. Under pressure he agreed to assume the responsibility of taking care of the same tentatively, but he said firmly that if any relative of the Master's nearer kin turned up and claimed the land, he should abdicate immediately. For this he was rated roundly by three very intelligent business men. Doctor Grayson pointed out that the Bee Master knew what relatives he had and where they were, and if he had desired that they should possess his property he would have left it to them. It was the Doctor's opinion that what the Bee Master desired was that a man of fine perceptions, of trained mind, of high capabilities and appreciation, a man who cared for colour, for music, for the small graces and beauties that go to make up the refined excellencies of life, should reside in the blue garden.

Mr. Meredith said that he was only slightly acquainted with the Bee Master, but it was his opinion that he was a highly cultured gentleman, that he knew his own mind, that his brain was extremely clear, and what he had seen fit to do with his own property was good enough for him. The probate judge said business was business. The records to the property were clear; the beneficiaries were before him; there was nothing on his part to be done but to follow the customary processes of the law. Whether Jamie wanted it or not, the east acre of the garden was his. That and the house belonged to James Lewis MacFarlane. It was up to him to assume the responsibility of ownership, to pay his share of inheritance tax, and to be ready for the property taxes that would be assessed according to the regular processes of the law.

So Jamie went back to the garden, his mind in a turmoil of bewilderment. There was much sprinkling to do, and he could think while he sprinkled. He could wonder why things happened as they did as he trimmed shrubs and used a hoe. When it came to caring for the bees, they received his undivided interest. But when he had accomplished all the work that he had been doing daily in the garden, giving perhaps a little extra attention to the west side merely because he was Jamie, then he applied himself to the régime of diet and exercise that he and Margaret Cameron had evolved. In the long evenings, by the hour he pored over the bee books, and then went out in the daytime and tried to apply what he had learned to his personal experience.

He was not responsible for his mind in those days. It flew off at queer tangents, and he found himself developing a habit, when he had any time of leisure, of taking a book and, from beneath the shade of a certain orange tree at the foot of the garden, alternately reading and keeping an eye on the shore-line. He had a feeling that some day, sooner or later, a tall girl with the free stride of a boy was going to pass along the beach and climb the back entrance to the throne, and when that happened Jamie wanted to be there to see. The letter in his pocket was exactly the same letter it had been from the first time he had read it, and he had read it times uncounted since and pored over every stroke of each letter. He could reconcile the letter with the girl that he had held in his arms, with the woman who had stood shoulder to shoulder with him and taken the marriage vows. But he could not reconcile either of these people with a girl who had complicated her personal affairs to the extent of being in dire need of the outward signs and symbols of chastity.

The longer he mulled over the situation, the more his mind became at least open to the conviction that the girl of the canyons and the mountains and the desert, the girl to whom there persistently clung the odours of sage, whose step was alert, who had the far-distance look in the eye of the outdoor person, would not have been subjected to the allurements and temptations of the girl who loves her life at the high pressure of cities. Jamie could see how any girl who was daily dreaming of herself, of fine clothing, daily frequented over-sexed and vulgarly sexed picture shows, nightly attending dance-halls indiscriminately peopled with whoever chose to appear, from whatever condition of life they happened to come, could get into serious trouble. He could see how the mad dash in motor-cars from one place of amusement to another, how irregular eating of highly seasoned foods, how the loss of sleep, the constant contact with men who had not been rigorously trained in the habits and customs and ideals of a generation or two back, might have resulted in disaster to girls too young to realize how they were abusing their bodies or imperilling their souls. The more he thought of it, the greater grew his wonder that any girl in such circumstances escaped with her virtue or with sufficient health to finish even a reasonable lifetime. And what benefit a girl bereft of virtue and health was going to be to a home or to a nation, he had not much idea. The only thing he knew definitely was that such girls were the kind that he wanted to keep a mile away from.

Standing before the glass one morning intently studying his left breast, holding in his hand a pad he meant to apply and strap in place after his inspection, Jamie for the first time was paralysed with a thought that had not before obtruded itself. Exactly why he had not thought of that very thing he did not know. After he did think of it, it seemed to him that it was the one thing he should have thought of first. And he had not.

Any Scot gentleman, truly, in the depths of his heart, places his God and his country and his honour and those he loves above everything else, but always deeply ingrained in the heart of every Scotsman is the love of money; the place that can be bought with money; the power that can be purchased with money; the comfort that it will give; the luxury that it will provide for loved ones; the assurance that the cold and hunger and misery of the world will be averted. The very first instalment of money that the Bee Master had put in Jamie's fingers had stirred him to the depths of his soul. He had held it between his fingers. He had stared at it incredulously. The fact was that never in his life had he had money that belonged to him to spend as he pleased. All the money he ever had had in his possession was what his father and mother had given him to buy his clothing and to pay for his education, and it had tried them sorely to get together sufficient means to do the things most desired for him without providing any luxuries. He never had known what it was to have money in his pockets to spend as he chose, and the result was that his first earnings as the Keeper of the Bees spurred him to the fight that it now seemed possible might end in victory.

It was several days yet until the time for Margaret Cameron to make her second inspection. The pad Jamie had removed that morning looked as fresh and clean as when it had been applied. The morning tomato juice, the afternoon orange juice, the soaking in the sea, the baking on the sands, the clean, dustless, salt-laden air, absorbing occupation, all day out-of-doors, a mind with something to dwell on that was holy, that was beautiful—what doctor need hope to compete with such a combination, such an exhibition of Nature's powers for healing? Perhaps it was the clean pad he had removed, the evidence that there was a skin coating over his breast firm enough to hold through the work of the day, the feeling of coolness and satisfaction in the pit of his stomach, the absence of heat and burning in his blood; probably it was a combination of all these things that had made Jamie, standing facing the glass that morning, voice the joyful conviction: "I'm going to make it! As sure as there is a good God in the heavens, I'm going to be a well man again!"

Right there was where Jamie received his blow, an awful blow, a blow from which he shrank and which whitened his face and set his hands to shaking. His voice sounded strained in his own ears because he said it aloud: "*And by all that's holy, I contracted to die! It was part of my agreement to be through with life in six months at the most! I said there wasn't a chance that I'd live, and probably the girl who married me would not have done it if she had not thought that I was practically a dead man.*"

Jamie stood still, holding the pad and staring at it. He could feel the girl's exploring fingers across his chest. He could feel the shudder, perhaps of pity, that had gone through her as he guided her fingers across the outline of the bandages and braces that he was then wearing. He had given her evidence to prove his words. She had accepted the evidence, she had trusted his word, and now he had turned round and he was doing everything in his power, making his utmost effort, to live.

Soberly Jamie laid on the pad and fastened the bandage that held it in place. Soberly he donned his clothing and went out to his work. Every few minutes he stopped and stood staring before him. Fifty times that morning he said to himself: "There isn't a ghost of a chance of my dying in six months or six years, or ten times six years, if I keep on improving as I am now. The only way I could die would be to wreck myself, and if the day ever comes when I meet Alice Louise face to face, and her circumstances seem to be accompanied by mitigation, what will she think of me for being alive?"

Then Jamie's sense of humour came to the surface.

"If matters turned out in such a way that I had a chance to live, I suppose she wouldn't ask me to kill myself if the wound didn't kill me; and if she did, I scarcely believe I'd follow even the dictates of a lady quite that far. I'll tell her I was honest, that that storm night was as black for me as it was for her, that the struggle that raged in my heart was the same thing as the storm in hers or the storm on the sea. I'll tell her that it is my good fortune that the sun has broken through and that there's life in store for me. I'll tell her that I called on God and He came to the rescue and made it life and work and a chance for happiness. I'll tell her that if she will call on God it will be in His power to straighten out her problems as mine are straightening. I'll tell her that it is not my fault that I'm alive. No, I can't very well tell her that either. It is at least halfway my fault that I'm alive. God gave me the opening. It is to my credit that I took it. I suppose I could have gone on eating the wrong food combination and carrying a black load on my shoulders; I could have gone on eaten up with self-pity and reeking with poison. I'll take enough of it to myself to stand responsible for the resolution and the ability to do the things necessary when the way was opened. Dad used to say in the pulpit that the days of miracles were over; that to-day God gave us our chance, and if we wanted miracles we had to perform them ourselves." It took the greater part of a day to get this problem straightened out, but it ended in Jamie reaching the conclusion that he was honest in what he had said, honest in what he had done, but different circumstances had altered the case.

Margaret Cameron would be overjoyed the next time she examined his chest. He found himself so elated, so full of hope that day, that he was very careful to protect his left arm and his left side. It seemed to Jamie that if anything happened to break that frail coating of skin across his chest and set the bright stains to reappearing on the pad he wore he could not endure it. He knew if it happened that it would break his mental reserves until he would sit down and cry like the veriest baby. At any cost he had to keep that delicate, tender coating intact.

In the beginning of his work Jamie had very seldom left the premises. He had scarcely ever gone to town, never unless it were imperatively necessary. Now the necessity seemed to be imperative that he go frequently. There was always something occurring about the settlement of the Bee Master's affairs, or a reason why he should go to see Doctor Grayson or the probate judge or the banker who was holding the funds of the Bee Master's estate. Added to this he was falling into the habit of paying an occasional visit to the man with whom the Bee Master had exchanged work. He found John Carey an interesting man, an entertaining man, a man of whom it would be worth while to make a friend. Sometimes he would not exactly understand the instructions of the bee books. Carey could make everything plain, and do it so quickly and so effectively that he was worth knowing from a business standpoint alone. So more and more frequently the Keeper of the Bees hurried through with his work and went to spend a few hours in the apiary of another man.

Soon he began to realize that, from her work about the house and in her own garden, Margaret Cameron was watching him. He was brought to the realization by the fact that every time he came home from one of these absences he found a house in order, dustless furniture, fresh bed-linen, a spotless kitchen, a bowl of flowers on the living-room table.

One day he came home to find a shining house. That morning Margaret Cameron had examined his breast for the second time and had told Jamie what he already knew, that however faint it was, however frail it was and delicate, however liable to crack on slight strain, nothing altered the fact that there was a tissue coating of skin entirely covering the wound on his breast. Margaret Cameron was old enough to be his mother. She had thrown her arms round his neck and kissed him, and they had performed a crude dance of exuberant joy in the small bedroom. Margaret had arranged her yellow roses in the bowl. She had drawn forward the Bee Master's chair and set before it the slippers that Jamie had been wearing. It was her way of inviting him to take his place as the master of the house. She had set a table with the daily paper on it beside the chair, and every other vase and pitcher in the house that ever had held flowers was flower-decked.

Jamie smiled with pleasure as he glanced around the living-room. He thought how few men there were in the world who could take insensate objects and make a room so livable as the Bee Master had made the room upon which he had indelibly stamped his tastes, his mentality, his artistic tendencies. Then Jamie swung open the door and stood as still—as still as the last pause before the breaking of a great storm. The sleeping-room was dusted; there was fresh linen; it was shining; it was reeking with the odour of sage—an odour that never in any faintest degree had attached to Margaret Cameron—and on the night stand beside the bed where the light stood and the thermos bottle for water, was the copper bowl, and the copper bowl was overflowing with sand verbena. The exquisite flowers, with the refreshment of water at the evening hour, as was their habit, were rolling up and spilling abroad their faint, delicate incense, the most beautiful flower perfume, Jamie thought, in all a world of flowers. He walked over and picked up the bowl. He looked under it. He looked on the table carefully. He looked over the floor. He lifted the pillow. He searched the four corners of the room. There might have been a note, and a breath of wind might have blown it away. Then he headed straight for Margaret Cameron.

He found her in the garden. He took the pruning shears from her fingers and led her to a rustic seat under the sheltering boughs of an acacia that a few months before had been a stream of flowing gold, liquid gold that spilled and poured and dripped. Then he sat down beside her and captured both her hands and turned her face toward him.

"Margaret," he said, "you know how much I thank you for all the thoughtful things and the motherly things and the kind, heartening things that you do for me. You probably understand the cleanliness, the immaculate, scrupulous state of scouredness of my boyhood home. You know how I appreciate and luxuriate and grow stronger and feel better with the kind of housekeeping that my mother would do for me, had she not been forced to make her crossing before my return. I think my house is the most wonderful house in all the world to-day. I wouldn't trade it for any house of any millionaire anywhere in the State of California. The little Scout is right in thinking that it's possible to be satisfied with what you have; that if you have a house and a flower garden and the assurance of daily bread, it is enough. Life is wonderful to-day, Margaret, very wonderful. I've had an interesting time with Carey and his bees. I've made up my mind that if the Bee Master wanted me to have the house and garden, I want them as badly as he could possibly want me to have them. There never was any question of my *wanting* them. I merely had the feeling that I might be usurping the rights of some other man. If it happened to be a woman whose rights I was usurping, then, of course——"

"Of course, you'd be puddin'-headed enough to get up and get out and leave what rightfully belongs to you!" said Margaret Cameron.

"If she could convince me that she really had a right to the place, naturally, however much I loved it, I'd clear out," said Jamie. "But clearing out isn't what I came over here to talk about. Margaret, you've made my living-room wonderful with a world of flowers. Now, tell me truly, did you put the flowers in my bedroom?"

Margaret Cameron turned toward him a face of frank astonishment.

"No," she said, "I didn't. I never want a bedroom cluttered up with flowers. I don't like to sleep with stronger flower perfume than comes through the windows. I don't think it's healthy to lie all night in a surcharged atmosphere. I didn't put any flowers in your bedroom."

"All right, then," said Jamie, "if you didn't put them there, you are the only one who has keys and access to the room. You can tell me who did."

"That's exactly what I cannot," said Margaret Cameron, "because I haven't the least notion."

"Has the little Scout been here?" asked Jamie.

"Not that I know of," said Margaret Cameron. "Of course, I don't pretend to keep tally on the comings and goings of that youngster, and I wouldn't take oath that a window wouldn't form a more suitable mode of entrance than a door. You know there's a gate between us, and you know that you never saw the little Scout do anything but jump the fence."

Jamie grinned.

"I know. That's part of a code of exercise. By this time I know the little Scout fairly well. In the first place, the youngster is not addicted to gathering flowers. In the second place, these flowers have been very carefully clipped with scissors or a knife, and in the third place, they are arranged with a grace and a beauty to which the little fellow has not yet attained. Some of the stems are long and some of the stems are short, and some of the heads are upstanding and some, having a few leaves, spill over the edge of the bowl and creep out on the stand cover, and altogether they are sufficiently artistic to please the senses of the most discriminating artist of Japan. If the little Scout had gathered them they would have been wadded into a tight bunch and chucked into the bowl in the most effective way to get them there. Don't you believe it?"

"I think it very likely," answered Margaret Cameron.

Jamie smiled his most ingratiating smile.

"Margaret," he said, "you *would* tell me if you knew, wouldn't you?"

"Why, I think I would," answered Margaret, catching his mood and smiling back at him. "I can imagine no reason as to why I shouldn't. I think I'd tell you if I knew; but honestly and truly, Jamie, I haven't the faintest notion who would compose the very artistic combination you've been describing so enthusiastically. Have you made friends with any of the neighbours?"

"You know I haven't!" said Jamie. "There aren't any neighbours on the west. Neighbours are something to acquire in the future, and you are my neighbour on the east, and beyond you I haven't penetrated. Straight down, of course, there are hundreds of people daily on the beach, but aside from more blue, this garden probably looks like every other garden running down to the sea. It's had no visitors so far as I know. The truth is, Margaret, that there's something about the house to-day that puzzles me. The bouquet in my bedroom was one thing. The Bee Master's chair pulled to the hearth-side with the slippers I've been wearing before it—— While we are on the subject, did you do that?"

"No," said Margaret Cameron, "I didn't. I've felt that the Bee Master's chair was something sacred and devoted to him, and I've respected the fineness of your nature that kept you from appropriating it. I've got to bring myself to the place where I don't mind seeing some other man using it. Frankly, I'd rather see you use it than any other man I know, but I couldn't see you sitting in it just at this minute without resenting it."

"I thought you'd have that feeling," said Jamie. "I had, and a desire to be more worthy to attain more years and more knowledge, to make of myself the level best it was in me to become; not until I have climbed to near my limit dare I aspire to occupy that chair. You told me that you had a daughter away teaching school and that you had a niece who came to see you frequently, and I wondered if either of them might have been with you and might have arranged things differently from the way you would."

Margaret Cameron shook her head.

"Lolly went far up state with the school she accepted, clear to Sacramento. She can't afford to come back and forth until the term's out. I don't mind admitting that the house is like a grave without her, and I've had some tears to shed because in one or two of her recent letters she has insinuated that she might not come home for her summer vacation, that she might go with a camp of girls up into the Yosemite. To tell the truth, I felt sort of peeved at Molly. Right down in my heart I know that she was instrumental in getting my girl the school away from home, and I can't see why she did it. The plea that she would get more salary doesn't take into consideration the fact that she'd have to spend such a big share of her salary for food and a room, when, if she taught in the city, she could use the car line and be at home over nights and over Saturdays and Sundays. I haven't dared say anything to Molly because, a few months ago—it was at the time I was away when you first came—I went into the city to her. She had had an awful shock. She hadn't but one near relative on earth, her twin brother Donald, and from the time their father and my husband were drowned at sea at the same time, I've had them in my home until they were far enough along with their education to get work and go out for themselves. They'd all been friends. Don and Lolly had been better friends than I'd wanted them to be. Don didn't have Molly's backbone; he didn't have her view of life. I thought he was kind of shiftless and weak, and for a few years we all had a fight to keep him from getting into a lot of things that he shouldn't have drifted into. It was always Lolly that could hold him and manage him, if anybody could. I was kind of glad of it when he got work and went away, but having Molly at her school work in the city left this house so emptied out and lonesome that my girl just packed up and went too, and in my heart I knew that Molly planned it, and I didn't like it.

"Then, like a clap out of a clear sky, Molly called for me to come quick, that she was in trouble, and when I got to her I found her worse broken up than I'd ever thought she could be. Word had come that Don was dead. They had got him work, a fine place, in the big powder plant at San Joaquin, and he seemed to like it and was doing fine. I don't know enough about electricity to know how the thing that happened could happen, but he did something wrong, and as quick as electricity can do it he was gone. We sent for Lolly, but she didn't come. She sent word she felt so bad she was sick in bed and she couldn't, and I could see how she would feel bad enough to make her sick in bed. You know, Lolly's my girl. I had her by my first marriage. She wasn't really related to the children. Mr. Cameron was her stepfather, and she might have thought a lot more of Donald that I knew she did. Anyway, Molly and I had to lay him away alone. Molly felt so bad I 'most forgave her. Besides, I didn't actually know that she had planned to get Lolly away from home. I just felt she had. The whole thing has upset me a good deal of late, and Molly hasn't been here so often as she used to come. I don't know why, because the truth is I thought a lot of the boy myself and I could have been honest and sincere in mourning him with her.

"Now come these letters from Lolly hinting about going further north in the state for a summer vacation and only being home a few days at the very last, and going away again to teach the coming year. The whole thing is just the way it shouldn't be. I wonder sometimes if I've been too clean and too particular about where the girls went and what they did. The way things seem to be going among the youngsters these days, it doesn't look as if a mother *could* be too particular, but if she is so particular that she drives her young folks away from home, I don't know that that gets her anything except a good big heartache. No, there wasn't either of my girls with me. If there's a feminine touch in your house to-day that you don't understand, I'm telling you truly I don't know who the female is or where she came from."

Jamie thought deeply.

"All right," he said at last; "if you don't know, why you don't, and that's all there is to it. I'll have to do my own Sherlocking."

He said it jestingly, but the idea persisted. He went home and down the back walk. He lifted the latch of the beach gate with exploring fingers. He followed the hard clay and gravel path down to where it met the sands of the sea, and he stood and looked very intently, very carefully, over the sands. By and by he thought he began to distinguish the impress of a foot, and a few yards further he found what he was looking for —an imprint that he had seen before, the same shaped shoe, the same width, the same broad, common-sense heel. Then he knew without any doubt whatever that the Storm Girl had been in his home.

He went further along the beach toward the south, following the footprints, and finally he found the sand mould on which the verbenas had grown. He found the severed stems from which his flowers had been cut. Then a thought struck Jamie, and he whirled and almost ran in the direction of the throne. With palpitant heart he climbed the ascent leading to the crest, clambered over the rocks, and came about facing the place where he and the Storm Girl had endured the storm together.

That evening the sun was dropping into the Pacific in a

circle of red glory. The clouds above were almost blood-red in its light; the water, a deep indigo-blue out on the way to China, an exquisite light emerald near the shore, and wavering over the surface and coming in slowly with the light waves were exquisitely shifting colours of lavender and old rose. The foam of the beach and the very sands were delicately coloured with it. Somewhere very close a mocking-bird was singing and white gulls were passing in homeward flight, and a few little sandpipers were quarrelling down on the shore-line. There was a whole world of things for Jamie to see and to love and to thank God for, but what he did see was the fact that the Storm Woman had sat in her place and arranged the flowers that she had brought him. Tiny withered leaves of sand verbena lay on the rocks at his feet, discarded blooms that were too old had been dropped there. Jamie took one step further and looked, and in his place there lay on the rocks three exquisite heads of bloom, a long trailing stem and a medium and a shorter stem twined together deftly, braided past the leaves and laid in the place upon which he had sat as one would lay an exquisite tribute on the grave of the dead. That very thought came to Jamie.

"Good Lord!" he said; "I wonder what she'd think if she knew I am about ten times the man that I was the day I married her! I wonder if she'd think I haven't played fair if she knew that I was working with all my might to be a whole man. And I wonder what she'd think if she knew that I'm not keeping my promise not to try to find her. I wonder what she'd think if she knew I broke it when I went to Margaret Cameron to see if she could tell me anything, and I broke it again when I went along the beach trailing a footprint that I know. I wonder what she'd think if she knew that right down in the depths of my heart I just about adore her. I wonder what she'd think if she knew that there haven't been very many minutes since the night that I held her in my arms that I haven't held her in memory and haven't wanted her and haven't ached for her and haven't worked for her and haven't thought about her, until I've got to the place where I don't much care as to why she needed my name. And I wonder what she'd think if she knew how often I've read her letter and how I've appreciated it, and I wonder what she thinks when she gathers sand verbena and puts it into my fingers and carries it within a few feet of my pillow. By Jove! I wonder if I married her with sufficient assurance to stamp a little bit of my individuality on her! I wonder if she feels that I really am at least half a man. I wonder if days of trouble are coming near and if she needs a man who could take care of her and comfort her and do what he could to fortify her. I wonder if those flowers beside my pillow are her way of asking me to break my word, to search for her, to find her, to help her? I wonder if they are her way of saying that she needs more from me than my name?"

Jamie sat until dusk, then slowly arose and made his way home to his supper. As he crossed the back porch a thought occurred to him. He went down the walk and round to his bedroom window, and as he examined it closely a heap of sand verbena lying on the ground came to his notice. Margaret Cameron had told true. She did not know who the Storm Girl was. She had not furnished the key to give entrance to his house. The Storm Woman had done what she was so perfectly capable of doing. In the seclusion of the shrubs, screened from the streets and the neighbouring houses, she had slipped up the back walk and stepped into his window. So that was that, and it did not help Jamie any on his way toward dying. As a matter of fact, it gave him more food for thought and more reasons for living than ever before had possessed him.

After that Jamie lived in hourly expectation. Some day surely she would come again. Some day he would be in the garden when she came through, or he would find her on the throne. He was almost tempted to write a note and leave it there, but the knowledge that many people climbed the uncertain path leading to the top of the jagged rock deterred him. He could not take the risk of anyone else finding the message that he intended for the Storm Girl. He could not help in his heart thinking of her as he had seen her, strained and unhappy in the glare of the lightning, or with quivering lips and staring eyes as she had left him. He could not help trying to picture how her face would appear if it were afire and alight with happiness; how her eyes might shine if she were pleased and interested; what a wonderful companion she would be breasting the waves or climbing a mountain, or working in a garden, or sitting opposite a hearthstone. Whatever he might have thought of her in the nebulous character of a woman he had seen, a woman whose race and blood were manifest in her face and bearing and the tones of her voice, a woman to whom his blood had a right to cry out because they were of common nationality, each only one generation removed, the fact remained that she never could be nebulous to him. She was stamped on his memory in his consciousness in a different way from any other woman.

"Because before the Lord and by the law she is my wife," said Jamie, "and I cannot get away from that fact, and she cannot get away from it. She cannot marry any other man without making herself known and divorcing me."

Then Jamie got another blow that knocked him speechless and almost senseless for a moment.

"What's more," he said to himself and to all and sundry when he gained sufficient breath with which to speak, "what's more, James Lewis MacFarlane, *you* can't marry any woman, you can't have a real home, you can't have a hearthstone so long as you are legally married to a girl who wants only your name, or to one who doesn't want you in person at all!"

Jamie sat down suddenly and admitted that he was possessed of a single-track mind. He had been on the track that led to death and elimination when he had done this fool marrying stunt. Now he was on the track that led to a home, to work in the world, to the things that all men desire when they are sane and healthful, and he was bound as tight as the law could bind him by records in the office of the Marriage Licence Bureau of the country in which he lived. That was something more to think about. So Jamie went about being the Keeper of the Bees, the master of the house, the partner of the little Scout, with several problems very persistently in the forefront of his mind.

CHAPTER XV

REAPING THE WHIRLWIND

THE days began to slip by rapidly. As Jamie became more familiar with the work he was supposed to do, he found that constantly he could see things of his own volition that no one had told him about, yet they were things that increased the activities of the bees, things that added to the beauty of the garden, things that resulted in producing a larger amount of different kinds of vegetables. He found, too, that a number of fruit and vegetable stands not far from his location were willing to pay him worth-while prices for anything he had in those lines that he and Margaret Cameron could not use. Then he began filling baskets for the little Scout to carry home that there might be no question of unequal division.

There had been ten days when he had scarcely seen the little Scout, and then there came a joyous day when the child came whooping into the garden followed by Fat Ole Bill and the Nice Child and Angel Face. They had made merry, and Jamie's ears rang and his sides ached with laughter. They were celebrating the close of school. They were planning for a long summer that was to comprise more mischief than probably ever before had been crowded into the same length of time.

Jamie found himself mighty thankful to have the little Scout around the garden. It was not only that he received much efficient help with the bees, with the pruning and watering; it was that he had fallen deeply in love with the youngster. As he became more firmly fixed in his regard for the child, he worried, grew obsessed with the feeling that things were not as they should be; that of the Scouts it was the Master who was not attaining the height and developing the physical strength that the exercise all of them took should have resulted in producing. Several times Jamie had seriously considered calling on the Scoutmaster's mother and asking her if she did not think Jean was exercising too strenuously, taxing brain power to the breaking point, making of each day a round of never-ending activity. From a word dropped here and there Jamie realized that the child was not sleeping any too well of nights. Sometimes the little Scout slipped into the living-room and stretched on a davenport, or into Jamie's room and, across the foot of the bed, slept for hours as the dead are supposed to sleep.

As Jamie's own strength grew, as the tissue coating of skin across his breast strengthened in thickness and faded in colour, as the continued careful diet, the salt baths, the sun treatment, and the tomato and orange juice worked their will, so Jamie's mind cleared in proportion as his body strengthened. A feeling of power, of executive ability, began to develop in him. He ceased almost entirely to think of himself. All the thought he had he needed to concentrate on his work, on the little Scout, on Margaret Cameron, and he found that there was no hour of the day in which his mind was not battling back and forth, pro and con, concerning the girl he had married.

He wondered if he should start a systematic search for her; if he found her, whether she would be pleased or turn from him in anger. He wondered if there might not be assistance he could render her. He wondered if there might not be mitigating circumstances. Jamie could not force himself to think of the Storm Girl as a girl who had broken the laws, the laws of God and the laws of man.

In those days he had an ever-present worry concerning Margaret Cameron. He had learned to respect his neighbour highly. He had learned to appreciate deeply the many kind and thoughtful things she did for his comfort. He felt that if the whole world were filled with mothers who were willing to remain at home, to shoulder the duties of caring for a home, to stick to sound common sense and reasonable judgments as Margaret Cameron had done, there would be more boys and girls willing to remain at home, willing to find entertainment there instead of on the beaches and in the canyons and in cheap public dance-halls. Then he reflected that Margaret Cameron's trouble at that present minute, as nearly as he could figure it, was because her only child had left home and was deliberately remaining away from home. Margaret had told him only that morning that Lolly had definitely decided to go with a party of young people who had planned to hike through Yosemite and Muir Woods. She had written that she would try if possible to get back for a few days before school began in the autumn, so a long, lonely summer was stretching before Margaret, and she frankly admitted to Jamie that there was an unrest, an apprehension hanging over her that it was quite impossible for her to dispel.

So when Jamie thought of Margaret, he thought sympathetically, wonderingly, and much of the time with a fair amount of indignation. He could but feel that something was due to parents who kept the home fires burning, who weathered the years, who had doctored their children and worked over them and prayed over them, who had used the utmost of their strength and bestowed the deepest of their love, who had unselfishly given, and given all they had to give, and still had earned, seemingly, nothing whatever, not even gratitude. Jamie could not believe that the attention Margaret was paying to him was touched with the depth of devotion and tinged with the quality of consideration and love that she had given to any of the three youngsters she had loved and devoted herself to until they reached the point where they were able to fend for themselves. Now it was vacation. It was the time that other children were coming home, and neither of Margaret Cameron's were coming, not the girl to whom she had given birth, nor the girl to whom she had given shelter. Why did not both of them come for a few weeks? Why did they not plan and come one at a time so that Margaret might have her vacation when other people were having theirs? Why did they not make some plans for her? Why did they not do something to break the monotony, the sacrifice, and the hard work of her life?

He resolved that he would work very hard. Then he would take a few days off and he would ask Margaret Cameron to go pleasuring with him. They would go where people were resting on the beaches. They might go somewhere on a boat. They would go into the city and hear some wonderful concerts, to see some worth-while pictures, or to an interesting play. For his share of what she was making life mean to him, he would try to make some material return. That he settled on definitely.

One day Jamie mentioned Margaret's children to the little Scout, and found that the child was as indignant as he was.

"There isn't any tellin'," said the little Scout, "as to when Lolly will get here. She doesn't think about much except herself and she does mostly what she pleases, but Molly will come. Her job's a hard one and she may have to rest up a few days. She may have to close her rooms and get somebody else in them, but if Molly doesn't come she's got a mighty good reason, and when she comes the camp fires and the picnics will begin, and there'll be something worth while doin' around these parts. When Molly comes she has greased her bearings and she's hittin' on six cylinders, and we *go* !"

The little Scout used both hands to illustrate how they went when Molly came home.

"There's a lot of fun in Molly to the square inch ! She wears a big kid grin on her face and she ain't afraid of dirt. And she ain't afraid of water, and she ain't afraid of work, and she ain't afraid of spending a penny. Talk about persimmons ! Molly's them !"

"I'm waiting anxiously," said Jamie, "to know Molly."

"Well, go on waitin'," said the small person. "Stick on the job, and when she does come, if you care about girls, why, there's a girl that's got some juice in her !"

"I believe you," said Jamie. "I think you should know, and I've every confidence in your judgment."

The little Scout was crumbling bread along the edge of the back walk for a hen mocking-bird that had nested in a date-palm beside the pergola. A large chunk of apple from one that was being consumed in scarcely-masticated chunks was laid beside the bread. In three more bites the apple disappeared, core and all. Juicy fingers were wiped on the seat of unusually soiled breeches, and the little Scout took a hold above the hands Jamie had gripped around the stems of some iris he was transplanting. The added strength that was brought to bear loosened the roots from the ground, and the Scoutmaster and the Bee Keeper rolled promiscuously over each other and down the side of the mountain until they came to forceful impact with a grape-fruit tree. They got up laughing, and Jamie gathered up the iris. The Scoutmaster stood daintily poised. A deep inhalation of breath, an indrawn upper lip, an outshot lower one, blew the dust from the deep grey eyes. A shake like a dog coming from the water was supposed to be sufficient to dislodge accumulated dirt. An ecstatic expression toned to idiotic sweetness settled on the small face. With the thumb and second finger of the right hand a very real piece of dirt was flipped with exquisite execution from the left shoulder. Then in pantomime Jamie's condition was inspected through skilfully manipulated eyeglasses that Jamie saw perfectly even when they were not there.

"Aw, weally," said the little Scout. "I hope you didn't dawmadge yourself permanently."

"No, I didn't", said Jamie, "and I entertain the same lively hope concerning you."

"Aw, thanks awfully !" said the little Scout, and with a

continuation of the same breath. "I betcha——" A hand dived into a pocket, brought up some small coin and inspected it carefully. The price of a hot dog and a strawberry pop were laid aside and the remainder estimated. "I betcha seven cents I can hang by one foot from the beam of the pergola right there!"

Jamie looked the sitation over.

"I'm not taking your bet," he said. "If your foot slipped and you came down there you'd knock your brains out."

"I wouldn't if I hit on the *ground*," said the Scoutmaster.

"You would if you struck the stones within six inches of the ground."

"Yes, and that's the kick to it," said the small person, "just to find out what I would hit on!" and immediately started scaling the pergola.

"Look here," said Jamie, "cut that out! You aren't going to hang from one foot from that cross section. I don't know how long that pergola's been built, and there's been a lot of water thrown on it to wash the vines. It may be as rotten as sin."

Steadily the Scoutmaster climbed upward and presently sat on the second bar, bouncing up and down on it to ascertain its stability.

Jamie looked belligerent.

"I told you not to do that!" he said provokingly.

"I ain't goin' to do it," answered the Scoutmaster serenely. "I heard you. There's nothing the matter with my ears. I can pull another one just as good, and if I come a smasher 'twon't break any more than my *leg*. I'm going to hang by my little finger!"

Before Jamie had time either to say or to do anything, the body of the Scoutmaster was dangling and it was supported by the little finger of the right hand and nothing more.

"All in!" shouted the swaying youngster. "Look out! I'm coming down! I'm aimin' for the dirt. Call Grayson if I hit the stone!"

Down came the Scoutmaster, landing deftly and with perfect precision on the freshly-watered soil of the garden, perhaps four inches from the stones that might very easily have broken a leg.

"Now, look here," said Jamie. "I told you I wasn't feeling as good as I might one time, didn't I?"

"Yes, and you didn't need to tell me!" said the Scoutmaster. "I could see it for myself, but I can see now that you're about as husky as they make 'em. You could drive a steam plough or run a stone crusher or swat a bandit if you wanted to. I won't do it again."

Then the Scoutmaster planted a small pair of feet squarely in front of Jamie and looked at him with the very devil dancing in the depths of the deep eyes.

"Got your goat, didn't I?" taunted the little Scout. "Thought you'd have to go to the telephone and ring up mother to come with the ambulance. By gracious! There goes your telephone!"

Jamie had got past the place where the ringing of the telephone was an event, it rang so frequently in those days. It might be Carey calling for help. It might be Grayson to explain some new legal technicality that he had encountered. It might be the bank calling. It might be the Scoutmaster's mother wanting her offspring at home. Jamie wiped his hands on his trousers and walked to the telephone and lifted down the receiver. The Scoutmaster sat on the stone that had failed to serve the purpose of breaking any bones, and with loving pride inspected the west half of the garden in which they were working and which constituted a beloved personal possession.

Looking over the length and the width of the acre that stretched down to the sea, said the little Scout: "When I get through high school I'm comin' here to live. They may take their darn colleges and gamble 'em and smoke 'em and drink 'em and Bolshevik 'em straight to the devil! I'm goin' to get my education out of the books that the Bee Master put in his library. What was good enough for him is good enough for me, and while I read his books I'll be thinking about him. One of the reasons I'm going to keep clean and walk straight and be decent like he was is because I'm going where he went, and we're going to see what we can get out of heaven together like we got a good deal of fun out of earth. And, oh, boy! I wish he knew how I miss him!"

In the house, before the telephone with a face sheet-white, hanging to the instrument for support, shaking in every part of his being, shorn of his new-found strength, torn to the depths of his soul, stood Jamie. He had lifted down the receiver and said "Hello!" as casually as any man ever had said it, and then answered in the affirmative to the inquiry: "Is this James Lewis MacFarlane of the Sierra Madre Apiary!" Then the voice had continued: "You are wanted immediately and most imperatively at the Maternity Hospital, corner of Irolo and Seventeenth Streets."

"Yes," panted Jamie.

The voice went on: "Your wife last night gave birth to a fine son, but she is not reacting from the anæsthetic as she should, and we are growing alarmed. We found your address among her effects. Kindly see how quickly you can reach her. The probabilities are that she will be asking for you very shortly."

Jamie hung up the receiver, picked up a pencil and wrote "Irolo and Seventeenth Streets" so that he would not forget. Then he reeled to the bedroom and began seeing how quickly he could put on suitable clothing to make his appearance on the street. As he worked he called for the little Scout, and when the youngster appeared he said: "Lock up quickly. Have the front door key ready for me. I have an urgent business call to the city and I don't know when I'll be back."

"Aw!" said the little Scout, in disgusted tones. "I came to stay *all* day! There was a lot I wanted to get done on *my* property."

"Yes, I know," said Jamie. "Maybe to-morrow. You better call the gang and play the rest of the day on the beach or run along home."

He was out of the door, locking it behind him. Then he made a headlong plunge down the walk and down the street toward the car line.

The little Scout stood looking after him.

"'Important business!' Well, I'll tell the world it's important! The house is on fire, the dog's bit the baby, Ma's lost her vanity case, the Government ain't survivin'. God's dropped out of heaven, and there ain't a darned thing right in the whole world! Leap to it, Jamie! Fix it all up fine! Oh, boy!"

The little Scout walked around the house, climbed in the back window, punched up Jamie's pillow, and lay down on the foot of his bed.

Jamie sprinted to the nearest street car and rode to the city, getting instructions on the way as to where Irolo and Seventeenth Streets might be, and when he landed some distance away he took a taxi. Once seated within it, he felt for the cheque-book he had stuffed in his pocket and all the emergency change that lay in the little box on the top left-hand shelf of the working library of the bees. His thoughts were whirling in chaos. The Storm Girl. She had come to her hour of agony, bravely, without help, as she would. She had asked no help from him. She had brought a child into the world, a son. "A fine baby", the voice had said, but it did not sound as if she were all right. The report had sounded ominous to Jamie. He had not known that anæsthetics were a part of the birth of a child. A great many things had happened in the past six years that Jamie did not know about. He had not known anything worth while in the beginning as to how human beings entered the world, but he had been told, he had deciphered for himself the fact that it was not an easy journey either for the mother or the child, and at this hospital that he was going to there was a little living boy, and the ceremony Jamie had gone through had been for the purpose of covering the child with an honourable name. That "fine little fellow" he had been told about was James Lewis MacFarlane, Junior, and the fine girl, the Storm Girl, the girl of the deep eyes and the broad chest, the girl of the cold wet face and the clutching hands, the girl of the quivering lips and the staring eyes—what was it ? She had not rallied from the anæsthetic ? She was not regaining consciousness as she should, and among her effects they had found his address, and he was on his way to her. A minute more and he would be in the room where she was. He would see her forehead, and the wealth of hair streaming over the pillow, and her white throat.

Jamie knew what he was going to do. That was definitely settled in his mind. He was going to take her hands and hold them tight. He was going to draw her face to his as she had voluntarily yielded it to him once. He was going to cover it with a passion of suffering kisses. He was going to tell her that he did not give a darn what had happened or how it had happened. He never could and he never would believe that dishonour had touched her or ever could touch her. He was going to make her well, and he was going to take her home, and he was going to take care of her. They were going to live together and love together, and they were going to make something very wonderful of life. The new blood, the fresh blood, the clean blood surged up in Jamie until the hair was almost standing on his head. He was wringing his hands without knowing what he was doing.

"They aren't efficient ! They aren't doing what they should ! I'll kill the doctor and wring the neck of every nurse in that hospital if they don't get a move on them !" threatened Jamie. "Birth's a natural function. You can't tell me that a big, strong girl like that wouldn't live through it if she had the proper care."

Jamie raced into the hospital and to a desk and down a

hall and into an elevator and then into a small room. He stood beside a bed and took one long look. Then he turned his ashen face from the doctor waiting beside the bed, holding the wrist of the gasping woman, to the nurse.

"I have made a mistake," he said. "They've given me the wrong number. This isn't my wife."

The nurse stepped over and from the contents of a drawer picked up a marriage certificate that he had seen before.

"James Lewis MacFarlane," she read from it, and replaced it in the drawer.

Jamie took a grip on the foot of the bed and leaned over. The girl lying on it was not a girl he ever had seen, not a girl who, by the wildest stretch of possibility, could have been the Storm Girl. Jamie gripped the insenate wood harder and bent lower and stared wide-eyed. What did it mean? How could this have happened? Why should this girl have in her possession the certificate which symbolized the marriage that he had entered into with the Storm Girl?

He made his way to the side of the bed and looked intently at the left hand lying nerveless on the coverlet. There was the ring that he had bought, on the third finger, the cheap little wedding-ring. He picked up the hand and examined the ring until he made sure. He knew that both the doctor and the nurse were watching him.

The doctor spoke. "How long has it been since you've seen your wife?"

Jamie opened his lips to say that never in all his life had he seen the woman before him, and stopped with the words unsaid.

If he said what he was thinking, if he repudiated her, if he left her to life or the greater mercy of death with the avowal that he did not know her, that he never had seen her, then where was the beauty of the deed that he had tried to do in covering a woman who needed a name with his? After all, it had not made any difference to him, the night of the storm, what woman bore his name if with it she recovered self-respect and a decent heritage for an unborn child—"a fine little fellow", the doctor had said. If he opened his lips the fine little fellow would no longer be fine. He would be a shame baby, a thing to be pitied, to be scoffed at, to be shifted around from one charity organization to another. He would be thrown on the world defeated in the right to a home, to love, to the proper kind of rearing. It would be no marvel if any wave of crime or of shame that anyone could imagine should engulf him.

And the girl. Jamie stared hard. He realized that if there were blood in the china-white face, if there were colour in the lips, if there were lustre in the hair, if those transparent eyelids would reveal pain-filled, beseeching eyes, she would be lovely. Possibly there was a man in the world who could have repudiated her. Jamie could not. Not Jamie MacFarlane. The words died without utterance.

"You mean," he said thickly, "that it's strange I don't recognize her? Maybe it's the pain, and it's been long months since we were married."

"I've learned," said the doctor, "that there are a good many curious and some inexplicable things in this world, but I can't help expressing the opinion that you've been a poor sort of a husband if you've allowed your wife to go through anything so crucial as the nerve strain and the physical strain of approaching maternity and delivery and given no sympathy, extended no care. It scarcely seems human."

Jamie licked his lips and took his medicine. He could not say anything in self-extenuation that would not cast a reflection on the girl before him, and in the few minutes that he had stood staring down at her he had realized that her every breath was coming shorter. The hand he was holding was a weight in his fingers. He gripped it and began to chafe it.

"For God's sake!" he cried, "try to do something! Forget about lecturing me now! Do something! Don't—don't let her slip away like this!"

The doctor looked up at Jamie and said quietly: "There is nothing known to medical science that three of the best doctors in the city have not been trying all night, and some very excellent nurses have performed their duties carefully. You might as well understand that it is very near the end. I thought possibly she might rally. I thought possibly she might have something she would want to say to you. I thought you ought to be here in the event she needed you, and I told you the truth when I said your son is a fine little fellow. He is a beautiful specimen of physical babyhood. There's the makings of a fine man in him, and we are needing men in this country. We seem at the present minute to have an overplus of hounds."

Again Jamie took his medicine. The taste of it was bitter on his tongue, because he was not a "hound". He never had been. He had not the smallest obligation to the woman before him, other than the obligation that any man owes all women, to love them honestly, to care for them gently, to respect their bodies as the vessels through which the world must be populated. That was a thing that had been hammered into him from the hour that he was old enough even remotely to understand its meaning. He must always take care of the women. He must always be polite to the women. He must always be kind to them. They must be taken care of because they were to make homes; they were to mother little children. They must be respected. They were the vessels that contained the seeds of life. From their loins must come the presidents and the senators, the governors and the business men, the captains and the sailors and soldiers and the tillers of the soil and the ministers who filled the pulpits and the teachers who moulded the minds of youth in our schools.

Here lay a woman dying: dying in youth; dying in beauty; dying, in her own thought of herself, in shame, in scorching anguish, because some man, somewhere, had held her body lightly and violated it and consigned it to months of mental suffering, to hours of pain-racked anguish, to the loneliness of unloved death. Jamie reeled on his feet and the nurse thrust a chair under him.

She looked at him penetratingly and then she said deliberately: "Doctor, there's something about this I don't understand, but I will not join you in the belief that there is anything unmanly attaching to Mr. MacFarlane. In the few days she was here before the child was born, Mrs. MacFarlane seemed to adore him. She had no unkind word to say against him."

"What's that?" asked the doctor sharply.

"I am telling you the truth," said the nurse. "She said that he was the noblest man, the finest man in all the world. She said that he had done one thing so big and shining that no other man would have done it. She said that she had a feeling that she would not survive the birth of the baby. When she showed me her marriage certificate, I supposed she intended me to send for him. I looked up his residence. She said that if her baby should live, provision had been made for it, but she expressed a wish to me that so fine a man as he might have it. I don't know how to explain the fact that they haven't been together these months, but I do know that the fault did not lie with Mr. MacFarlane."

"In that case," said the doctor to Jamie, "very likely I owe you an apology. I am seeing so much these days that is exactly as things should not be in this world, that I am getting fairly raw. I do apologize if I have said something I shouldn't.

About your son and provision having been made for him, that's up to you. If you want the child, of course, in the face of this marriage certificate the law will give him to you."

Jamie turned to the nurse.

"What did she say?" he asked.

"She said once," answered the nurse, "that it was impossible, but if it were possible, she would give her life gladly if she knew that you would take the baby and make of him the kind of a man that you are."

"All right," said Jamie tersely. "I will take the baby. You may get him ready. I have a comfortable home. I can see a way in which he can be well cared for. I will do my best to make the kind of man of the boy who bears my name that his mother wanted him to be."

Then Jamie and the doctor and the nurse were astonished and bewildered. A low laugh broke from the lips of the girl on the pillow, a low, exultant, caressing laugh, a laugh full of wonder and delight and unbelief; and with it ended the last remnant of breath from the tortured body, and the bright head on the pillow rolled back and lay still.

Jamie covered his face and sat silent, and when he looked again he saw a sheeted straight line. He looked at the nurse with pitiful eyes.

"Have you instructions," he asked, "for necessary arrangements?"

The nurse nodded.

"Everything has been provided for and, most unusual, all expenses were paid when Mrs. MacFarlane entered the institution. In such an event as this we were ordered to prepare her body and send it to her family."

"All right," said Jamie, arising and mustering his strength. "Where is the boy?"

The doctor looked dubious.

"You have someone competent to take charge of a new-born baby?" he asked.

"I have," answered Jamie. "A fine, cleanly woman who has reared three children to maturity."

"All right, then," said the doctor. "Give him the baby."

The nurse disappeared and presently returned. She put into Jamie's arms a bundle odorous of castile soap and boracic, a thing that was warm and alive and moving. Convenient to his reach she set a suitcase, and Jamie put on his hat, crooked his arm around the live bundle, picked up the suitcase and walked from the room.

The nurse looked at the doctor and the doctor looked at the nurse, and they said to each other: "Well, can you beat that?"

"What do you suppose came between them?" asked the doctor. "If she said things like that about him, why should he leave her, never to see her again, without a tear of remorse, without a touch of affection? I've had a good many peculiar experiences in thirty years' practise of medicine, but this beats everything. I don't understand it!"

"Neither do I," said the nurse, "and what's more, I don't believe he does. I must go and put in the calls for the party I was told to send for in the event she died. I think she must have been very much under the weather all the time. I think she came with the feeling that she would not survive, and I think she had that feeling because she did not in the least care whether she did or not."

The nurse picked up a towel and wiped her hands vigorously. "I get so mad at this sort of thing sometimes," she said, "that I want to go out and stand on the platforms and in the pulpits and I want to tell people some of the things I've seen and heard. I'd like to talk for one solid day to the *girls* of this country. I'd like to tell them of the heartache and the disappointment and the pain and the shame that they are fixing up for themselves in their future lives when they undertake to leave the straight and narrow path and allow themselves voluntarily to become the playthings of men; to let their honour be taken from them; to let their efficiency be wiped out; to let their years of training and the loving care that has been expended on them all go for nothing; to bring shame and disgrace on their parents, and do to their own souls and to their own bodies what this poor dead girl has done to hers."

"Evidently," said the doctor, "you are one of the people who still believe in hell-fire and damnation."

"Yes," said the nurse, "I do. And I believe in hell at its hottest and damnation at its damnedest for the men who are responsible for such anguish as we have seen this girl suffer and for such a death as we have watched her die. I'd like to take the men who cannot wait for honest marriage and a time when they are able to support a woman and give her a home and fortify her body to serve the functions of wifehood, of motherhood and home-making, men who upset everything and ruin everything for their own personal immediate self-gratification—I'd like to take them all out and hang them as high as Haman. Sometimes I think I just hate men!"

And to his amazement the nurse broke into tears and used the towel on her eyes.

"But look here!" said the doctor. "You spoke up for Mr. MacFarlane. You said he was not responsible for this."

"And I'll say it again!" said the nurse. "Can't you see by what she told me, by the way he came in, by the way he left, that he'd never *seen* the girl before, that he didn't know who she was? Because some arrangement had been made by which that child was to bear his name, he assumed responsibility for it. But good Lord, you can't convince me in ten years that he had ever seen that girl there on the bed before, or that the marriage certificate I packed among her belongings so that child could have it was a *legal* document! Don't you think it!"

Then the nurse went her way and the doctor went his way, and the Keeper of the Bees climbed in the taxi and gave instructions to be driven back to the blue garden.

CHAPTER XVI

THE PARTNERSHIP BABY

When he dismissed the taxi and started up the front walk with the bundle and the suitcase, Jamie was surprised to find the little Scout sitting on the front steps beside a bottle of milk half consumed, with crumb decorations prominently on the face lifted inquiringly in his direction.

"Well, look who's here!" said the little Scout. "My gracious, you look edsactly like dad when he brought Jimmy home from the hospital!"

"Well," said Jamie, "that's a very good way for me to look. Have you been sitting here ever since I left?"

"No," said the little Scout. "I went through the back window and lay on the foot of your bed and slept about three hours, and then I was hungry and I went over to Margaret Cameron's to ask her for something to eat, and I run into her just as she was leaving. She said Molly had telephoned her to come in for a few days. I am waiting at the choich to tell you you'll have to get your food the best you can until she comes back. Didn't strike me until after she was gone that I'd forgotten to ask her for something to eat myself, but I knew she wouldn't care, so I climbed in at the back porch window and got a chunk of bread out of the bread box. The milk's yours—all that ain't used. Say, Bo, honest, *what* you got there?"

Jamie sat down suddenly. His solution of what he was to do with James Lewis MacFarlane, Junior, had been to transfer him to the care of Margaret Cameron. He had planned to ask his neighbour to take the child and care for it until he could find the right kind of a woman to undertake the job. In the back of his head there had been a hope as he had driven out that Margaret would use on the baby the same cleanliness, deftness, and expert care with which Jamie had not a doubt, from her brand of housekeeping and cooking, she had reared her own family. Of all the bad luck that he had experienced in his unlucky days, nothing had been much worse than that Margaret Cameron should have chosen to go pleasuring, should have selected the day to start a vacation when he needed her the very worst. Jamie set down the suitcase and produced the front door key.

"Unlock the door," he said to the little Scout, and together they went in.

Jamie laid the small bundle on the davenport and then he stepped back and drew his hands over his perplexed face and said to the Scoutmaster: "I wish you'd tell me what I am going to do."

"What's eatin' you?" inquired the small person casually.

Jamie pointed to the bundle.

"That's a baby," he said; "a live baby that needs nursing and feeding and loving, and I thought Margaret Cameron would be the woman who'd do it. Are you sure she said she had gone visiting and she would be gone no telling how long?"

"She didn't say 'no telling how long'," said the Scoutmaster. "She said 'a few days'. I should think a few days would be a week, maybe."

"And what," demanded Jamie, "what am I going to do in 'a week maybe' with a live baby?"

"Aw, feed it to the birds and let's get on with our work! We're wastin' a lot of time on the garden," said the little Scout.

"You look here!" said Jamie. "You aren't talking about a crust of bread. That's a baby in that bundle, a tiny boy who wants his chance to live and to grow and to paddle a canoe and to ride a horse and to be a Scoutmaster just as bad as you do!"

"Aw," said the disgruntled small person.

Then the Scoutmaster walked over and lifted a square of fine flannel with a border of forget-me-nots and peered down at what was beneath it. Suddenly the Scoutmaster dropped to a kneeling position, leaned forward and looked intently. Then a softened face turned to Jamie over a lean shoulder.

"You'll have to get a baby bottle," was the verdict. "*'Tis* a nice baby. It's an *awful* nice baby! It's the cutest little thing. It's as pretty as our Jimmy was the first time I ever saw him, and I thought there wouldn't ever be another baby as nice as he was. But they is. Far as I can see, this baby has got just as nice clothes and just as pretty a face and just as cute little hands as our baby had. Say, *where'd* you get him!"

"He's mine," said Jamie. "His name is James Lewis MacFarlane, Junior."

"Well, I'll be darned!" said the little Scout. "Ain't the world gettin' full of James and Jamies and Jimmies! I know about two dozen. Dad's name begins with James, and our baby's Jimmy, and this baby will be Jamie and you're Jamie. You wouldn't think, with all the names in the back of the dictionary and names by the yard in the Bible and fool names that people invent, that so many folks would have to run to James. Say, *what* are you going to do with him?"

"That's exactly the question," said Jamie. "What *am* I going to do with him?"

"Hm-m-m-m!" said the little Scout. "Lemme think."

Jamie had the impression that he came closer to seeing thought than he ever had before. The face of the youngster was drawn with thought. First the body sank back on the heels, and then the heels curled under and the floor made the seat. One arm leaned against the davenport. One hand, from fingering the blanket, crept up and closed over the little red fingers of the new-born baby. The little Scout looked up.

"Pull down that window blind," came the order. "You got to have a dim light. Their eyes are riley for the first few days. They can't see. If they get too much light they go cross-eyed."

There was a return of a few minutes to thought. Then the little Scout began to think aloud. "My, ain't we accumulatin'! Talk about compound interest! I'll say things are compoundin' for this partnership! Here all unbeknownst to ourselves we get a house and flowers and trees and bees and now, by gracious, we get a baby! And, of course, if we got it and it's yours, we got to take care of it. Say, *where's* his mother?"

Jamie hesitated a second and decided that the truth was the quickest and the easiest.

"I hate to tell you, Buddy," he said. "I hate to tell you, but the truth is this baby hasn't any mother. The task of getting him into the world was too big for her. She paid for his life with hers. You will be glad to know that she was like your Aunt Beth. She went over to see what heaven had in store for her laughing, laughing out loud, laughing the gayest laugh of contentment and exultation."

From the floor the little Scout stared up at Jamie with wide eyes and slowly nodded a corroborative head. "I know: that was Aunt Beth's smile come true. It's the kind of a laugh that the smile she had would have been if it had broken through and come out loud. I told you being dead was beautiful, but I don't see what's going to become of this little new Jamie.

You never saw the amount of oiling and bathing and bandaging and changing and dressing and weighing—you never saw anything to equal the things mother does to our Jimmy."

Then suddenly the little Scout came up to one knee and then the other, and then slowly assumed an erect position; then, from the depths of preoccupation, stumbled to the telephone and took down the receiver and gave a number. Jamie stood breathlessly, fearfully, and listened to a one-sided conversation.

"I want Mom."

"Hello, Mom, is that you?"

"Say, Mom, we got the dirtiest gyp out here this morning! We got a little splinter new boy baby just like Jimmy when he first came from the hospital, just as nice and sweet and everything. And, Mom, this is the dirty part of it. Getting him here was too much for his mother. She went dead on us and we ain't got her, and we sure got the baby, and his name's Jamie after his dad—just like our baby! And, Mom, we thought Margaret Cameron would take him and take care of him for us and that's another dirty thing. She's gone off on a visit an' she won't be home for three or four days, and we ain't got a thing to feed him!"

The little Scout clapped a hand over the mouthpiece, turned to Jamie, and in a strained whisper inquired: "Have we got any clothes?"

"I think so," said Jamie.

The small person turned back.

"We got oodles of clothes. Everything we need. What we need is somebody to do the oiling and the feeding and the changing——"

Then the little Scout sprang straight in the air and gave a shout.

"Bully for you, Mom! I *knew* you'd come across! Do you see why I didn't *ask*? I was givin' you your *chance*! I knew all the time you would. Least, I was dead sure you would. And say, Mom, take your roadster and step on the gas! Any minute he may begin to yell, and we don't know what to do. He just came in the night. Jamie's too big, and I'm afraid. Take the shortest cut, and if a speed cop mixes with you, bunt him and come on!"

The Scoutmaster hung up the receiver and turned to Jamie. The shoulders drew up, the chin lifted, a gloating look passed over the features, an indrawn breath was shot out suddenly.

"Um-hum-m!" said the Scoutmaster. "Ain't she the Lallapasooza! Did you get that! I didn't even have to *ask* her! Right off the bat, just crack! Babe Ruth couldn't of hit it cleaner! She says, says she, 'I'll take care of him for you'—just like that!" Both hands waved outward and onward in a curve of exquisite grace. "Just like *that*! Whenever you go to bet on the right royal high-steppers, I've got two bits I'll chalk up on my mother!"

In the interim Jamie replaced the blanket over the face of the sleeping baby and looked dubiously at the suitcase. What was it the nurse had said about having put in personal belongings for the baby? He had better get those things out and take them into his own keeping. So he picked up the suitcase and carried it to the bedroom, opened it on his bed, and pulled out a drawer in the dresser, pushed aside the clothing it contained, and began emptying the case. He removed little nighties and dresses and all sorts of queer soft garments and square-folded stacks, and when in the bottom of the suitcase he came across a package wrapped in a cloth, he pulled it open enough to see that it contained strings of beads and bracelets and trifling feminine adornments.

He had not had time as yet to think of the Storm Girl. When he did think of her he realized that the time had come to find her, and the time had come to settle a fairly long score with her. This was not playing the game. She had not been fair.

"And of all the women in the world, I wouldn't have selected her for a liar!" said Jamie, and that minute his sense of outrage was so strong that he forgot the relief he should have felt over the knowledge that the woman he had rushed to the hospital to help was *not* the Storm Girl. Scot materialism, Scot integrity, Scot bulldog stubbornness, not alleviated by enough American environment to tone them down perceptibly, surged up in Jamie.

"She'd much better have a clean heart and be where the baby's mother is than to be going around in the world high-handed and strong with a lie on her tongue," said Jamie, and he slammed the package down and pushed it back and dropped some of his clothing on top of it, and shut the drawer with a bang.

Then he went back to the bed and carefully repacked the baby-clothes. There was lace on some of them, and the fabrics were so fine that they stuck to his work-roughened fingers and clung to them so that he had to shake some of them off. At any rate, they seemed to be warm things, there seemed to be enough for two or three babies, and even to Jamie's unpractised eyes they seemed to be fine things, carefully made things, lovingly fashioned things, with tiny buds of pink and forget-me-nots of blue and wee yellow daisies showing here and there. As Jamie slammed shut the suitcase, he stood erect and addressed the back window. Possibly he was speaking to the ocean that glinted blue and gold beyond.

"Right this minute," said the preacher in Jamie, said the judge in Jamie, said the stern critic in Jamie, "right this minute, between the two of you, *I'm* thinking most of the dead woman!"

He carried the suitcase out and dropped it on the floor beside the sleeping baby. Then he sat down and turned back the face blanket and worked back the clothing and pushed away the hood strings tied under the chin, and looked long and intently at the baby. He did not remind him of anyone. He was very small. He had eyes and a nose and a mouth. He was extremely red. The girl on the pillow was not reproduced in him in so far as Jamie could see. Then, as the Scoutmaster had done, he examined the hands. He got more from them than he did from the face. They were perfect hands, fashioned exquisitely; long, slender fingers, beautifully tapering fingers, with little nails finished and extended beyond the finger-ends, perfect workmanship; and they were such fingers as paint pictures and play violins and lovingly handle the kind of books that the Bee Master had bequeathed to the little Scout.

Jamie turned, saying, as he did so: "Did you notice how beautiful his hands are?"

He got no answer, and turned farther. The little Scout had crossed the porch and gone the length of the walk and opened the gate, and was hopping from one foot to the other in the nearest wheel-track, looking with undivided attention toward the city.

In an unbelievably short time a nifty sports model, a beautiful car suitable for the show piece of a motor-car exhibit, swung to a deft stop, and almost before it stopped the little Scout was on the running-board. Jamie could see that the dirty arms were thrust inside and the face lifted to the face of a woman moving toward the door. He could not hear the conversation that ensued. Something was asked on the part of the Scoutmaster, and that something met a laugh that sounded mellow and sweet on Jamie's ears. But the door was barred, the Scout was insistent, the hand that reached out to open the door was covered by a grimy hand, and then Jamie distinctly caught the phrase: "Aw, please, Mom, *don't*!"

And he heard the answer: "All right, then."

The little scout hopped off the running-board and opened

the door, and there stepped down a woman who seemed to Jamie to appear the way any woman ought to look to be just about exactly right, a radiant picture of wholesome health. A head of golden-brown silken curls, bobbed short for comfort, sensible clothing, dainty and pretty, of extreme style in cut. Briskly across the stretch of sward, through the gate and up the walk toward Jamie she came, the little Scout scuffling ahead. The screen door was pulled open as Jamie stepped back, and the little Scout darted through.

"Mom, this is Jamie!"

Jamie made his best bow and stood for inspection. He got it. Careful, incisive, but not offensively long. A firm hand was held out to him.

"I've been intending to come for some time," said the mellow voice that Jamie recognized as the one he had frequently heard over the telephone. "I've had my hands reasonably full with our little Jimmy and a Danish Princess presiding in our kitchen, and keeping the children in school. I think I took it for granted that anyone the Bee Master would leave in charge here would be all right, and so I haven't got around to make friends as I should have done. But, of course, our little Scout has been all right with you."

It happened that Jamie's eyes were on the face of the little Scout when the expression was used, and he saw the deep breath of satisfaction that swept from the lips of the child. Then past him hurried the woman that the little Scout had called "Mom". She dropped on her knees before the davenport. She turned back the blanket and laughed softly. The face she lifted to Jamie was beautiful, a Madonna-like face, the face of a woman fashioned for motherhood.

"I am sorry," she said, "if your baby has cost his mother her life. I am sorry. But I must congratulate you on the baby himself. You'll have your compensations. He is a beautiful child, really a beautiful child!"

The pair of deft hands, glittering with sparkling rings, slipped under the baby and lifted it, and the mother who had it in her heart to be a mother to any baby, to all babies that needed her, sat down in the Bee Master's chair, its first occupant since his going, and lifted the baby and held it against her breast and to her face, and laughed to it and said sweet little words of utter nonsense and praised it and curved around it and cuddled it up, and then paused and looked at Jamie.

"I didn't know," said the soft voice, "that you were married."

"I hardly knew it myself," said Jamie. "It was such a very

hurried marriage on account of circumstances I may explain to you some day. I'd been overseas and I brought back a wound, and there were reasons as to why we had not been much together. I am shocked beyond expression that the baby's mother lost her life. I had not even once thought that such a thing might occur, and I had depended on Margaret Cameron. I didn't know that the child had been born until they telephoned me from the hospital. I decided I'd stay with the baby and let his mother's family care for her. I could not leave the garden, and I was sure of Margaret, and got back to find that she had been telephoned for to go on some kind of a jaunt and she'd started suddenly. Before I knew what the little Scout was doing, you had your call. I'm afraid it's too big an imposition for words."

The face that met Jamie's was a laughing face.

"Don't bother about that," Mrs. Meredith said. "I'm willing to give a few days' time for a lovely baby named Jamie. It will be like having my baby over again. You needn't worry in the least. Have you clothes for him?"

Jamie pointed to the suitcase.

"Enough for two or three babies, I'd judge."

To prove his statement, Jamie opened the case. Across the baby a pair of interested eyes explored its contents.

"Why, those are lovely things, exquisitely made! I almost hate to use them. I could use some of Jimmy's things just at first when there is so much oiling, and a tiny baby is rather a mussy proposition."

"I imagine those things will be more carefully handled in your hands than at the hospital or even by Margaret Cameron," said Jamie. "Go ahead and use them. When they are gone little Jamie shall have some more."

"That's fine!" said Mrs. Merdith. "That's fine! You will have something of your very own to work for now."

Jamie felt something of a hypocrite as he assented to this proposition, but in the presence of the little Scout that was not the time for dissent, so he let the statement go and closed the suitcase, and when the lady arose he escorted her to the car. There they met a difficulty.

"I can't drive and hold the baby too," said Mrs. Meredith.

The little Scout made a clean leap to the front seat and held eager arms.

"I can hold him! I can hold him edsactly like you do and keep the face cloth down. I *want* to hold him!"

Jamie smiled quizzically.

"And if Fat Ole Bill and the Nice Child and Angel

Face come trooping down the street and see you holding a baby——"

"Now, you look here!" broke in the little Scout. "Fat ole Bill and the Angel and the whole bunch can just *fry* in their own fat! All of 'em's gettin' too fat, anyway. Great big softies! Anybody that's got any objections to anybody else holdin' a little bit of a new baby that ain't got any mother and that wants his dinner can have the best lickin' I've got in my system, and they can have it quick! Step on the gas, Mom, and let's get him home before he cries!"

The Scoutmaster tightened careful arms around the little bundle and called back: "I'll telephone twice a day. I'm goin' to stay at home and do all the care-taking myself except the feeding and changing and bathing. You call me when Margaret comes and you get your arrangements made."

Jamie went back inside the house and sat down suddenly on the first chair he saw. He tried to think constructively, reasonably, humanely. Such an unexpected experience, such a startling experience, such a pitiful experience, he had not bargained for in his Adventure. It had come, and Jamie could not figure exactly why.

"I suppose," he said at last, "that when God made trees and fruit and grain, He knew how He was going to use them. He didn't intend that they should stand around and fill no purpose, and when God made men, very likely it was His intention to use them. That is a wonderful hand little Jamie brought into the world with him. It may be a useful hand as well as a beautiful hand. It may be that, if it's carefully trained, there is work in the world that such a hand can do better than any other hand that ever has been fashioned. Once in a while there does come into the world one hand that can do work slightly better, a trifle finer, than any other hand ever has done it. There is one thing about this experience that is dead sure. So long as there is blood in my veins and marrow in my bones, there is not going to be any taint of shame attached to this baby. He is going to have his chance, no matter who was his mother. And as for that little mother herself, with that unexpected and wonderful laughter on her lips, stepping across the boundary to meet her Maker . . ." Before he knew what he was doing, Jamie had slid to the floor and he was on his knees. His hands were clasped, his face was lifted, and he was praying: "Oh, God! Great God, Creator of the Universe and of men and of women and of all that this world contains; Oh, God, have mercy, have mercy on the girl who is coming before you this morning! Whatever her frailty was, whatever her fault was, remember the suffering and the price she paid and have mercy! Take her to your heart, take her to your everlasting home where there is safety and cleanliness of body and purity of mind, take her with my father and my mother and all the holy angels and teach her that there is a better way than the way she chose. Have mercy, O Lord!"

Stumblingly, Jamie arose and went to the bedroom. He sat down on the side of the bed and put his hands over his face and cried until his lean frame shook, cried his heart out. After a long time, when the storm had passed, he wiped his eyes and discovered, as he reached the back porch, that he was hungry. So he went across to Margaret Cameron's kitchen and burgled his way through a back window. Into the basket she used he packed everything he could find that would spoil in her absence and carried it home with him. Then, for the first time, he really went about the business of trying to cook food for himself. He knew where he could take the street car and find a small café not so far away, but somehow he was in no mood to meet men. He was in no mood to face women. He wanted to be alone. He wanted to think. He wondered where what remained of Alice Louise was going to be laid. He wondered if a small stone was going to be erected above her and if his name would be carved on that stone. He wondered if it would read, "The beloved wife of James Lewis MacFarlane".

Then he wondered what the name of the baby's mother might have been, and it occurred to him that he had a way of finding out. The first time he was in the city he could go to the Marriage Licence Bureau and ask to see the records on some excuse that he could think up by that time. He could find out what name the Storm Girl had written in to fit with Alice Louise. Jamie never in his life had examined a marriage certificate. The one in which he had been interested had been compiled by the clerk, a line shown Jamie to sign on, and then the Storm Girl had signed her name and taken prompt possession of the document.

When his thoughts reached the Storm Girl they immediately grew chaotic. Exactly why, he had not as yet time sanely to figure out. He had the feeling that he had been made a dupe of, that he had been a good deal of a fool, and yet he knew that feeling was not fair. The girl had not asked him for anything. He had put up as strong a case of special pleading as he knew how to build before she had told him in a few brief words exactly what it was that she needed. Wherein Jamie felt aggrieved was that she had not been square. She had not told the truth. She had said what she needed; she had left him to feel that the offer he had made and which she had accepted was on her own behalf.

This morning had proven that she had used him not to serve her own needs, but those of another woman. Jamie realized that he would have done what she wanted. In that storm, facing his own reckoning so shortly, as he had felt at that time that he was facing it, he would have given any girl who had happened to appeal to him in distress the benefit of his name and what protection he could offer her. It would not have made any difference who the girl was when her needs were so very great. It was just that he had gone to the hospital and had raced to the room expecting to kneel beside the bed and take the hand of the Storm Girl in his and fight for her life in a fight that some way he felt certain he could win. When he had seen a strange face the shock had been so great that he had sat down tamely and submitted to what the doctor and the nurse had said was inevitable, without even making the beginning of the fight he had meant to wage for the woman he had thought he was going to see.

He had been defeated. She had slipped away from him again, and this time he was angry, genuinely provoked. He had had only a short time in which to think, and in that time he had told himself repeatedly: "She didn't play the game square!" In Jamie's eyes that was almost the worst sin that anyone could possibly commit. His feelings on the subject had only grown stronger during his months of contact with the little Scout. The little Scout thought as keenly about playing the game square as he did, and was absolutely scrupulous in every practice indulged in. Jamie remembered with some amusement and a throb of pride that when he had asked the question of sex directly, the answer had been neither a lie nor an evasion, but straight from the shoulder: "If you can't tell, does it make a darn bit of difference?" That was fair dealing. That was leaving the field open. That was the kind of thing that Jamie liked.

Before he went to bed he called Mrs. Meredith. The baby was fine. It was no trouble. It had been oiled and fed and rolled up warmly, and the little Scout was on the job, said the voice that Jamie thought was the sweetest voice he had ever heard over the telephone. "None of us are getting much of a chance at the little new Jamie. Our little Scout has taken possession of him and is on the job. I think you will need help with the bees seriously before you get it for the coming few days. There seems to be a feeling of responsibility that none of us understand. I think perhaps it's all of a piece with the pride of possession, with the ownership of an acre of ground and a line of beehives and a fine showing of orchard and garden. I notice that the little Scout says proudly: '*Our* baby!' "

When he had gone back to his bedroom, Jamie was still thinking.

"Well, anyway," he said, " '*our* baby' isn't a shame baby. He has a perfectly good name standing for him on the records, and he's going to have a perfectly good chance, and as for the Storm Girl, she can go hang! I'm *through* with her!"

Then Jamie turned out the lights and lay down on his pillow and decided that he would go to sleep very speedily. Out of the darkness a voice said to him in the vernacular of the little Scout: "What's eatin' you? Did you want *her* to be dead? Did you want *her* to go to the horrors that are facing the beautiful body of Alice Louise?"

Jamie turned over and buried his face in the pillow and cried: "Oh, my God, no! I didn't think of that! I don't want her heart broken! I don't want her dead! What I want is to know who she is, where she is, to have her depend on me, to be able to do something for her, to be released from my promise not to seek her. No! No! For her I want life; I want happiness!"

CHAPTER XVII

THE INTERLOPER

If the little Scout had not been taking a double share of responsibility for the new baby Jamie, very likely the thing that happened during this period never would have happened to Jamie the elder, who did not come far from being considerably of a baby himself under the right circumstances. To begin with, Jamie had not yet been able to reconcile himself to the fact that he owned an acre of California and a house beautifully furnished with the exception of one room. He had not been able to take it in that a world of flowers, an orchard of fruit trees, a garden of vegetables, and a long row of hives of bees yielding the most delicious of honey, a very large percentage of it having been gathered in the delicate blue garden of the bees and in adjoining gardens—he had not been able to realize that the most attractive small house he had ever seen and half of the Sierra Madre Apiary, were his. He had not been able to bring himself to feel that it was either just or right that all these things should be his.

He was still looking upon his possessions in a state of bewilderment. It was true that he had been before the probate judge; he had fulfilled the requirements of the law. The property had been transferred to him and Jean Meredith according to the exactions of the law. Money had been drawn from the bank and the inheritance tax paid as the Bee Master had provided. And still Jamie did not feel that he really owned the acre that was standing in his name. He had the feeling that if he had stayed there for a long period, say ten years, and had studied the bees and had worked faithfully; if he had taken the place of a son to the Bee Master for that length of time, and then the Bee Master had made his crossing and left his property to him, knowing him thoroughly and feeling that he could depend on him, that, to Jamie would have been a right and reasonable transaction. He did not realize that anyone who met him and who was a judge of human nature, in one good look from Jamie's head to his heels, would have been able to say definitely what he thought concerning him with very nearly the same degree of truthful delineation as could have been rendered at the end of ten years' acquaintance.

Jamie was the kind of a man that women and children and other men and dogs trusted without asking any questions. Jamie was the kind of a man who could forget the biggest problem preying on his mind to bind up the broken leg of a dog, to heal a hurt for a child. His present predicament was proof of what he would do for another man, glowing proof of what he would do for a woman. He had not been accustomed ever to think seriously of himself until the shrapnel wound tore his breast, and then for two years he had been forced to think. In the régime of hospitals and medical treatment, he had faced for such a long period the thought that the end of him was not so far away that it had become an obsession. Gradually the garden had worked its magic until now Jamie was once more a man, a man who was thinking for the little Scout, for Margaret Cameron, for a girl who had risked her life and lost it and, dying, had left him a second inheritance, one that Jamie was more willing to accept than the first.

In the absence of Margaret Cameron he was cleaning house. His thrifty mother had trained him to be her assistant in childhood. He knew how to sweep and dust, how to arrange furniture, how to keep a house immaculate. He was using the broom on the entrance porch when a taxi stopped before the door. A very smartly dressed young woman stepped from it and verified the house number. She looked over the premises with approving eyes and a smile of reassurance on her lips that caused panic in Jamie's heart. He had not felt that he had earned the property; he had not felt that he had first right to it; but he was quite certain that God Himself did not know how much he loved it, how much he wanted it; and when this attractive young lady with the smile of assurance, that was almost too assured for the best degree of breeding, looked the premises over and inquired: "I am not mistaken in thinking that this is the residence of Mr. Michael Worthington, am I?" Jamie shook his head.

"I think," said the young lady confidentially, "that I could have selected papa's house from any on this street. It looks so exactly like him."

Jamie had thought that he was fortified for this very thing, but when it happened he learned that he had not been prepared in the least. He felt precisely as if someone had slugged him over the head with a very substantial piece of extremely hard wood. He had only brains enough left for an observation that he was too polite to make at hazard, so he said to himself: "Well, it may be that this house looks exactly like 'papa', but God knows that you don't!" He went further: "And I'd always been taught that there was a strong probability that girls would resemble their fathers."

What Jamie did outwardly was to get his heels together, square his shoulders, and manage a bow.

"Am I to understand," he asked, "that you are a daughter of the Bee Master?"

The young lady looked at Jamie and smiled, probably the most attractive smile she could muster.

"I am not only a daughter," she said, "but I am his whole family. Of course, when the news came of papa's having died so suddenly and unexpectedly, it was necessary for me to spend some time seeing that he was laid away as he would have desired to be and doing everything that I could to comfort mamma."

Jamie suddenly found himself putting up what he considered a fight.

"I had understood from the Bee Master," he said, "that both his wife and daughter were dead."

"I don't know much about his first marriage. Of course his first wife was dead before he married mamma, and I think they did have a child. I seem to have heard it mentioned, but of course that was long before I was born."

"Oh, I see," said Jamie.

"And I might as well tell you, if you are in charge here, that mamma and papa never could agree. They were always having difficulties, and at last she was forced to secure a divorce. She could not live with a man so irritable and exacting, a man who never wanted to do anything but drone over a book or occupy himself with some kind of highbrow stuff that nobody human ever could have been interested in. I didn't blame her a bit. I was entirely on her side. After she got the divorce, papa went somewhere. She never knew where he had gone. He did not communicate with us directly. His lawyer sent the money for my support, and I suppose it is to him that I shall have to appeal to secure the property which rightfully belongs to me as his only child, his only living heir."

"Has nobody told you," asked Jamie, "that the Bee Master left a will in which he bequeathed this property to a partner he has had for a period of several years, and to me?"

The young lady laughed pleasantly.

"There was a rumour. Somebody said something about there being no effects—possibly a letter from a nurse at the hospital where papa died—but, of course, when people here know that I am Miss Worthington and papa's only child, there isn't going to be any question as to whom the place rightfully belongs."

Jamie looked very hard at the young person before him. He could see no reason as to why he should not believe what she said, but she did not in any way, in any faint degree, resemble the Bee Master; not a mannerism, not a word of speech, not in the shaping of hands or feet, not in facial formation or expression. At the same time, if she carried with her credentials to prove who she was and that her claim was just, it was nothing more than he had expected, nothing more than he had been insisting would happen, so he said: "If you furnish proof that the Bee Master was your father by blood, if you furnish proof that you have a legal claim to this property, there is no contesting the fact that it is yours; but the Bee Master was very clear in his mind, according to the testimony of his doctors and nurses, until he made his crossing, which happened in his sleep, and he was very emphatic in his statements that he had no heir of his immediate blood. What you will have to do is to show your proof, establish your identity, and make your claims convincing to the Probate Court of this county. In case you can do this, there is no question but that the property is yours. In the meantime it is standing on the records in my name and in the name of the Master's partner, and I am in charge here and I am going to remain in charge until your identity is established and your claims substantiated."

"And where," cried the young lady, "am I going to remain? If I have to go into court and make a legal fight of this it may require weeks or months even, and I had barely enough funds to bring me here. The allowance papa made me never was half what it should have been."

"I know nothing about that," said Jamie. "I have nothing to do with it. But I do know that there is a small fortune in the bees and the trees and the flowers of this property, and that its value depends upon the bees being watched, as many of them are swarming at the present time. There is honey that must be removed to save the bees from starting robbing, and always in California the watering must be strictly attended to. In the event that what the Bee Master wished and intended can be substantiated before a court, I do not propose, for the sake of his partner, who is now mine, and for my own sake, to have value depreciate, as it will if I step out and leave the place to the care of a stranger."

Then the first really ugly streak showed in the disposition of the young woman. She laughed disagreeably.

"Well, there will be no question about your stepping out," she said, "and about your stepping very speedily. There is not a court in the world that would cut off an only daughter and an only child and leave a man's property to an almost perfect stranger. That would be a little bit too low. And since this house is papa's, I think I have every right to remain here."

She turned toward the street and beckoned to the taxi-man.

"Bring my trunk and bags!" she ordered.

The taxi-driver shouldered a small steamer-trunk, carried it into the house and set it in the middle of the living-room, placing upon it a suitcase and a dressing-bag. He was paid for his services and he climbed into his taxi and drove away, and a strange young woman with a very determined countenance took off her hat and looked round.

Jamie was worsted in the first round. He should not have allowed her to come in the house. He should not have permitted the taxi-driver to leave the trunk. But she had said that she had very insufficient funds; there was a possibility that a judge might substantiate her claims; whatever Jamie did or did not do he had to be a gentleman. He thought swiftly and he thought correctly. He thought: "Margaret Cameron is away. If she were here in this emergency she would give me a room. She would let me sleep in the bed that belonged to her nephew, and since I know positively that this is what she would do, why shouldn't I climb in her back window and take possession? I will water her garden and see that her flowers are carefully kept until her return, and in her kitchen I can cook me something to eat."

So Jamie went into the bedroom and gathered up the clothing in which he had come, the things that he had bought since his occupancy, and the package containing the personal belongings of Alice Louise. He made them all into a bundle and went down the walk, through the side gate, burgled a back window, and established himself in the room that he felt certain, from the wall decorations and its location, had belonged to Margaret Cameron's nephew. Then he went down to the corner grocery and purchased some food with which he filled the ice-chest. He hung up the "Ice Wanted" sign and removed the milk and tomato and orange juice he had in the Bee Master's ice-chest, and inside an hour he was dispossessed; but he was still holding the job, still weeding, still watering, trimming, and keeping careful watch on more than the bees.

As he worked it appealed to him that the first thing he should do was to call Mr. Meredith and let him take what action he chose in his child's interest. So he went to the telephone and, after hearing all the latest particulars which were enthusiastically delivered concerning little Jamie, he asked for Mr. Meredith. He was told that he was out of town and would be away for a week or ten days. Right there Jamie hesitated. He could take care of his little partner's interests in the same manner as he would his own. He could see what legal action was taken and report it when the time came. There was no necessity for setting Mrs. Meredith and the little Scout to worrying when there was probably nothing they could do. So Jamie hung up the receiver without saying that at that minute the apiary was in the hands of an interloper.

As Jamie worked, this same interloper came down through the garden on a tour of observation. She had changed her dress for another, light and attractive. With the stains of travel removed, she seemed more like a world of girls such as Jamie saw everywhere every day. The difficulty was that she seemed so much like them that Jamie was not interested. It had to be an unusual girl, someone different, someone giving at least slight evidence of having a human heart, mental culture, and consideration for others, to make Jamie look twice. This young party evidently was thinking mostly of herself. Jamie watched her advancing toward him down the back walk and the first thought that came to him as she was sharply delineated in a patch of sunlight was: "She looks hard".

Persistently he went on with his work. The girl was now within a few yards of him. She stopped and studied him intently.

"I've been thinking," she said, "there's nothing here that can suffer greatly in the few days that will be required to arrange the papers so that I can come into possession of my property. I prefer that you leave me in undisputed possession."

Jamie looked at the girl and smiled, and it was a winsome smile, a bonny smile.

"Don't you think," he said, "that you are asking a good deal of human nature? I've been caring for this place for quite a while now; I've been thinking it was my own for some time past. You are confident to an unusual degree if you think I am going to walk out and turn over property that stands on the records in my name without having seen any proof you have to offer, without knowing whether you can establish the claims you make before a court. Do you mean that if you came into possession of this property you would live here, you would make your home here?"

The young lady glanced around her. Jamie's incredulity irritated her.

"What kind of a back number are you?" she asked. "As we came here I thought we were going about twenty miles from the station I came in at."

"And so you were," replied Jamie. "You are a good guesser."

"And what would a girl, just when she has a right to have a good time, want to be marooned in a place like this for? If there is anything I am afraid of it's a bee. If there's anything I hate it's a mountain. If there's anything I hate worse than a mountain it's the sea. If there is anything I can't abide for a few hours at a stretch it is such stillness as this, such deadening, sickening silence. Does anything ever happen here?"

"Yes," said Jamie; "*you* came, and the bees are beginning to swarm every few days. There's fruit to be picked. There's sprinkling to be done. There's hoeing and cleaning and work a-plenty, more work than any one man can do as well as it should be done."

"In other words," said the young woman, "you are proposing to stay here and keep an eye on me."

"You said that," said Jamie. "What I said was that I was proposing to stay here and take care of the property, to do the sprinkling, to hive the bees."

"I'm not such a fool that I don't know why you will not go," said the young person.

"Draw your own conclusions," answered Jamie. "This side of the garden needs watering to-day. I am going to water it." And he quietly went on with his work.

The young woman stood still a minute and then she said: "I want the keys to the chest papa always kept his papers in. Undoubtedly there are things there that will help me to establish my interests."

"Tell that to the probate judge," said Jamie. "If he wants that chest unlocked and the papers that it contains turned over to you, he will send a clerk to go through them with you and to make a record of them and place them in evidence before they are tampered with."

It happened that Jamie was keeping watch—oblique watch,

but nevertheless a sharp watch—on the face of the girl when he made that statement. He saw the arrested breath; he saw the whitened face; he saw the tense pause and the deep thought, and the voice that sometimes talked to him inside himself said to him: "Now she doesn't like that. She doesn't want anyone present when that chest is opened. She doesn't want a record made of those papers. She doesn't like the idea of asking the probate judge to send a man to go through them with her."

Jamie immediately attached another length of hose and drew his work up the slope until he was opposite the window that gave the best view from the living-room.

In this manner time went on. He had occupied Margaret's house and kept his eye on the young person for two days and one night, and he was fairly well tired out when the young lady passed Margaret Cameron's and Jamie watched her take the car for the city. He went over to the house. He did not see how it could wear the same expression on its face that it had always worn. It would have comforted him if it had looked very much disgusted and displeased, but it did not. It smiled on the roadway and the mountain-side on which it looked with exactly the same serene, placid smile of invitation that it always wore for him. He tried its doors, but they were all locked. He looked in the window, but he could see nothing except that the trunk was standing in the middle of the living-room and the wardrobe of the young lady seemed to be mostly draped over the Bee Master's chair. He decided that this would be a good time to work Margaret Cameron's garden, so he went over and turned on the hose. He was busy there when he heard the light padding of beach shoes behind him and turned to face the little Scout.

"Oh, hello! How's everything?"

"How's everything at your end of the line?" parried Jamie.

"Fine!" said the little Scout. "I'm doin' all those things that I told you I'd do for our partnership baby. He's going to be an awful nice baby. Mother's crazy over him. She cuddles him up and takes care of him edsactly like she did Jimmy, but she ain't much stuck on this bottle business. She says it's an awful nuisance to fix the bottle, and she says it's an awful pity that any baby should have to lose its mother, because she says that a baby, when it's a little thing like that, gets more from its mother than just milk. She says it gets a steady stream of love. She says that a baby that lies on its mother's breast and looks in her eyes and lays one little hand on her neck, gets with its food something that it knows about all its life. She says it ain't natural and it ain't right for a baby to be laid all alone on a pillow and any old bottle propped into its mouth. It ain't propped with Jamie, 'cause I hold it, and it's a good thing this happened while there's no school, 'cause I'm tellin' you that you wouldn't believe all the things I do when there ain't anybody looking. I can hold the bottle, and I put my arm around Jamie so's maybe I can kind of fool him into thinking he's got the same stream of love along with his milk that our Jimmy got. I tell you, our Jamie is just keen. My goodness! There I've gone and used Nannette's word! That's the only adjective Nannette knows. Her shoes are keen, and her dress is keen, and her hair-cut is keen, and the party is keen, and the picture is keen, and I've heard it so much I hope to goodness I ain't goin' to go and get keen too!"

Jamie laughed.

"You don't have to 'get keen', Mr. Scoutmaster," he said. "You've been perfectly keen ever since you've been born!"

The little Scout was evidently pleased. There was a slight increase in height; there was a funny toss of the head.

"Well, who's going to shake dice with the right kind of a swing, and manage a bunch of Scouts, and do a whole lot of other things that I been up against all my life, and not be pretty keen? I'm keen on this place, I can tell you that! I'm about dead for it. I was telling mother this morning that the very minute I get through 'readin' and writin' and 'rithmetic', I'm going to come here and get on my job. She says I'm going to college, but there are a whole lot of things about me that she doesn't know as well as she might, and college is one of them."

Then the Scoutmaster amply proved to Jamie the claim that had been made. He felt himself being subjected to a long look. He felt the length of a small figure pressing against him. He felt a hand unusually clean slipping up over his left side. He heard a voice so soft and sweet that it reminded him of a certain telephone voice that he knew.

The voice wailed: "Oh, Jamie! Your side didn't *tear*, did it? You ain't got it all to do *over* again, have you?"

Jamie put his arm around the little Scout.

"Why, no," he said, "my side's fine! It's getting better every day. I have it in the back of my head that in two or three months more I will not even have to wear the lightest kind of a pad or a bandage."

The Scoutmaster looked up.

Then *what's* the matter?"

Jamie hesitated.

"Your face looks pasty and your eyes are dead tired. You look all beat out. You look just like I do when the Scouts go to rough-housing and I've had to lick the bunch. Sometimes I look at my face when I brush my teeth and I can see just how big my job is. Right around my eyes I can see it. And I can see things around your eyes now. What's the *matter*?"

Jamie thought swiftly. He did not want to tell the little Scout what was the matter, in Mr. Meredith's absence. He did not want Mrs. Meredith worried with a legal complication when she had undue care of the baby for whose welfare he had assumed responsibility. He thought fast and hard and let the moment slip.

"You are all right, little Scout," he said. "You *are* rather keen. I was worried last night and I didn't sleep well. I was kind of keeping watch over our place and Margaret's."

"Isn't Margaret back yet? Things look all shut up," observed the Scoutmaster.

"I imagine she's gone into the city to have a vacation visit with the Molly you're always talking about," said Jamie. "I'm taking care of things for her while she is gone."

"I guess I'll go over and take a look at my property," said the Scoutmaster, grinning broadly at Jamie.

"All right," said Jamie.

Neither of them had noticed that the interloper had passed Margaret Cameron's while they were watering her garden and had unlocked the front door and entered the house of invitation. The Scoutmaster flew over the fence, trotted down the gravel walk, waved a salutation to the jacqueranda, and took the curve passing the front of the house for the very natural reason that the one acre which stood on the county records in the name of Jean Meredith lay on the right-hand side of the house as one approached it from the entrance. As the child crossed the walk there was a noticeable movement in the living-room, and the whiff of an odour that acted on the little Scout as a stiff breeze of formic acid acts on the wild. With a large fund of assurance the Scoutmaster crossed the porch in a bound, swung open the front door, and faced the open trunk, the dresses draped over the Bee Master's chair; faced, also, a young woman with an unduly bleached head and over-painted face, a young woman who, to the eyes of the Scoutmaster, was a fine combination of everything in the world that a nice young woman should not be. The youngster stared in amazement.

"How come?" was the greeting shot at the interloper. The suggestive hands were thrown out, one in the direction of the trunk, one of the chair.

"Hello, Kiddo," said the young person. "You're sure my luck! Take this dime and run to the nearest grocery and get me a bottle of milk, and when you bring it back I'll give you a nickel for going."

The Scoutmaster stood still and looked hard at the young woman, looked long and intently and remembered something and could not tell exactly what.

"You're not—you're not Jamie's mother, are you? But of course you couldn't be Jamie's mother 'cause Jamie's coming made her too sick and she had to go across whether she wanted to or not. Who are you, and what are you doing here?"

"That's nothing to you," said the young lady. "Run along and get my milk, and then I've got about fifty other errands I want you to do. You can pick up quite a bit of my small change in the next hour or two if you move so that you stir the dust at all."

The Scoutmaster stood still. With hard, almost feverish eyes the face of the woman was scanned. The eyes especially were studied deeply. The trunk and the clothing, the abominable odours of cheap soaps and vile perfumes, all registered adversely on the child's mind. This woman in the house and Jamie at Margaret Cameron's, and doing nothing about it! That was exactly like Jamie. It had been the private opinion of the little Scout for some time that as a fighter Jamie might hold his own among the Germans, but he did not show much inclination to hold his own when somebody tried to give him a wonderful piece of property. Vaguely the thought that had begun stirring in the back of the Scoutmaster's head stirred deeper and cleared up and took form. The small hand was thrust out.

"Give me your dime! Sure I'll do your errands for you!" said the little Scout.

With the dime tightly gripped in one hand the Scoutmaster sailed over the fence and landed almost at the feet of Jamie, and there the child stared at him belligerently.

"*Who's* the Jane in the crooked make-up and the dirty skirt?"

The demand was brief and to the point.

"Is there anyone in the house ?" asked Jamie.

He was so taken aback he reverted to his father's childhood and said "hoose".

"I'm telling you there's someone in the 'hoose !' " cried the little Scout. "There's a comedy queen in the 'hoose' ! A Jane like that draped all over the Bee Master's chair and her trunk open in the middle of the floor ! What did you let her in for ?"

"She walked in," said Jamie.

"And wasn't you big enough to keep her out ?" demanded the little Scout, tilting up a head to look to the full extent of Jamie's six feet plus.

"Yes, I was," said Jamie, "if I had used force, but I'm not given to using force on the ladies."

"So you cleared out and came over here and you turned over *our property* to that peice of Limburger cheese !"

"I'm afraid I did," said Jamie.

"Well, you put the biggest crimp in my style that anybody ever did," said the Scoutmaster. "I bet you just walked out like a milk-fed turkey an' never put up one warlike gobble !"

"I told her," said Jamie, "to tell it to the probate judge."

"Aw !" said the Scoutmaster in the hoarsest, roughest tone Jamie ever had heard issue from the small throat. "Aw, what's the use of the probate judge ? You *knew* the Bee Master, and you know *he* wouldn't do anything that wasn't fair and right. If you want to lop over like a California Christmas candle, you can just do it ! You can give her *your share* if you want to, but believe you me"—the hands were in action—"believe you me, Mr. James Lewis MacFarlane, you will not give away *my* half of that bee garden, 'cause that was the only chance I've ever stood of getting a horse. The reason I didn't get a horse wasn't 'cause there wasn't enough money in the family to buy a horse ; it was 'cause I couldn't keep a horse in a city. Out here I don't see why I couldn't. There's no neighbours on my side to object. I'll see that flax-wig in there doing me out of my horse !"

The little Scout thrust forth a hand and disclosed a dime.

"I'm going to the grocery to get milk for her, and then there's 'fifty other errands'," suddenly the little Scout changed to the woman in the house and in an exact imitation of the tone and manner that Jamie recognized, he heard, " 'Kiddo, there's about fifty other errands you can do for me.' " There was another change. "You can stake your roll 'Kiddo' is goin' to do the errands, 'Kiddo' is goin' to find out some way to get that Jane out of there and get her out pretty quick. 'Kiddo' happens to know a whole lot of things that you don't, and 'Kiddo' is just beginning to get wise to *who* that party is!"

Both hands flew out, one of them widespread, the other gripping the dime. "Let me tell you, 'Kiddo' is savin' a last arrow for that party right in there! 'Kiddo' owes it to the Bee Master to puncsher her until you can see daylight clear through her! Maybe you think I ain't got her number now. Maybe you think I don't know who pushed little Mary and broke her spine and made her die! You watch me! If you ain't going to fight, I *am*. How did you get in this house?"

"Walked in," said Jamie.

"All right," said the little Scout. "I'm going to telephone mother and I'm going to get my scouts on the job, and you put your ear to the ground and listen for a rumble. 'Kiddo' is letting loose the dogs of war, believe you me!"

The Scoutmaster brought both feet down with an emphatic slap, and presen ly Jamie heard the ringing of the telephone and he heard, too, the voice of the little Scout.

"Say, Mom! Margaret Cameron's away and my partner out here needs me. I'll prodibly have to cook his dinner for him. I may not get in till late. If it's too late, he'll bring me. Don't worry about me. I'm all right, but this big baby out here needs taking care of worse than baby Jamie. I'll tell that to the assembled multitude!"

The receiver hit the hook hard enough to break both, and the Scoutmaster went through the front door and started on a skimming run in the direction of the corner grocery below. Jamie sat down and began to think. Then he went to the telephone and called John Carey. He asked if, in the event any of the bees threatened to swarm the next day, he could depend on him for help. The reply was that he could. Carey would come over in the morning and they would look the hives over and get some fresh ones ready for swarms to occupy.

Presently Jamie saw the Scoutmaster enter their front gate and go up the walk with the bottle of milk. After that he saw a bunch of papers and odds and ends carried to the incinerator. Then he watched the gathering of tomatoes and vegetables, the picking of fruit that was carried to the kitchen, and when he went over to get a better idea of what was going on, he saw in passing a window that the Scoutmaster was standing in the middle of the living-room fitting dresses over the Bee Master's coat-hangers and hanging them up in his closet. Presently the little Scout came out to him.

Jamie was surprised at the expression on the small face. It had become absolutely inscrutable. It did not remind Jamie of anything he ever had seen. It was a trifle white, a trifle set, immobile to the last degree. It was only by looking closely that Jamie saw that the entire figure was tuned up like a fiddle string, stretched and taut and ready to respond to the note it would be called on to deliver. Suddenly in Jamie's heart there leapt up a feeling of confidence. The Bee Master had said that the little Scout knew. Thereupon it appealed to Jamie that it would be a wise thing on his part to stand guard while the little Scout went into action on the basis of whatever knowledge would furnish the grounds for action.

Said the Scoutmaster: "She is trying every key in the house on my chest and pretty soon she will find one that fits, and that chest is just wadded full of things that ain't any of her business. That's got Highland Mary's things in it and little Mary's things. It's got marriage certificates and deeds. It's got business papers. It's got the signed-up settlement that settles that little flapper in there for life. I know who she is. I know what she thinks she will do. And believe you me, she can *do it* if she gets that chest open, and that chest belongs to me. What are you going to do about it?"

"Where's the key?" asked Jamie.

"My dad's got it," said the little Scout. "It's among the things the Bee Master had at the hospital with him, and the day things were settled the probate judge gave 'em to dad to keep till I'm of age. It's in his desk at home. I could get it by making a run in, but I ain't going to do it. That reminds me that she ain't going to unlock that chest with any key she'll find around the house, nor any key she will get made, 'cause that chest's got a private kind of a lock in it and there's a leaf in the carving where you've got to press a spring before the lock will work. Days when I had done everything else and I was getting ready to go home, and the Bee Master was so lonesome for something alive and something to talk to him, he would let me work that combination and show me the things and let me look at the pictures and let me see the things that were in there that belonged to Big Mary and Little Mary. And that's what's been working in my head. There's a picture in the chest of that Jane when she was little, and she looked just about as measly as she does now. It's got a name and a date on it, too, that will kind of fix her if she don't look out what she tells the probate judge. She can't get in that chest unless she splits it with an axe, and if she ever does that—zowie!"

The face lifted to Jamie was the face of a small pagan dealing justice. There was not a hint of mercy; there was not a hint of tolerance. It was as inexorable, as immobile as the face of the figure of Justice holding the scales above the judge's chair in the office of the Probate Court. A cold shiver crept down Jamie's back. For the first time he addressed his small partner by name.

"Jean," he said, "Jean, be mighty careful what you do. I am not claiming that I haven't got an awful wrench in the prospect of being driven from the garden, of giving up what the Bee Master meant me to have, but however much your share of it means to you it cannot mean what it would if you did some terrible thing and got yourself put in prison or blackened your whole life. There is only one way to manage these things, and that is to let justice take its course."

"Edsactly what I think!" agreed the little Scout. "I'm not believing that there isn't justice in this village, and I'm not believing it ain't goin' to take its course if I spring from ambush like Chief Running Horse at the right time. I told you before, I tell you now, you keep out of this and you watch my dust!"

The little Scout wheeled and went back to the house. Facing the interloper, in tones of suave politeness, this message was delivered: "Mistaw MacFarlane says to tell you that the keys of Mistaw Worthington's chest are in the care of Mistaw Meredith, and that Mistaw Meredith will be out of town for several days and they cawn't be delivered until his return."

"Well, I have no time to wait!" said Miss Worthington. "I've got to go through the papers that belong in that chest. I've got to open it if I smash it!"

The little Scout smiled.

"Mr. Worthington said that chest came from across the ocean with his grandfather's housekeeping things and it was hand-carved and it once belonged to a queen. If you tried to break it open and damaged it, and if what you found didn't satisfy the probate judge as to who you are and what you are doin' here, you'd get yourself into pretty serious trouble,'cause here in California we begin to train the babies along with their bottles—which are ag'in Nature and I don't recommend 'em, but I thought they'd sound more polite than mentionin' the other way—anyhow, we begin to train 'em that early to pull off their hoods and wave 'em when anybody says 'Antique'. We swat 'em on the dome impressive if they don't. We adore antique chests and tables and chairs and rugs and things, and you better look sharp, 'cause California wouldn't *like* it if you abuse anything antique."

"Say, look here!" said Miss Worthington. "Who are you?"

"Oh, I'm a kid round this neighbourhood. What's your next?"

"Drag that trunk into the bedroom."

The Scoutmaster advanced and stooped to one end of the trunk, looked around and about and said politely: "Kindly take the other end. These rugs are also antique and furniture can't be dragged over them, and besides that, your trunk is about twice my size, even if it is a steamer."

Miss Worthington hesitated a minute and then took one end of the trunk and helped to carry it into the Bee Master's sleeping-room. The little Scout looked at the open closet from which Jamie's clothing had been removed, at the open drawers from which he had taken his belongings, and a wave of anger surged up that very nearly upset the brand of self-possession that the Scoutmaster was trying to maintain. The thought that was at that minute in the small head was whether fists that were sufficiently hard, muscles that was sufficiently tough, were not equal to the task of pitching this interloper through the window down a particularly steep piece of mountain-side leading toward the sea. But the mentality of the little person spoke up.

"Go on and pitch her! Chances are big soft Jamie would be standing outside and catch her in a blanket and bring her in and put her to bed and stand up all night himself watching to see whether she was going to open that chest or not, and he prodibly wouldn't stop her if she did. What's the use if I did pitch her? It wouldn't get me anywhere. I better just stick around and stay on the job and see what she's going to do."

So the Scoutmaster ran innumerable errands and watched with blood literally at the point of boiling while the house was searched from top to bottom. Drawers were emptied, books shifted on shelves. At last the little Scout lost patience.

"Say, what's eatin' you?"

Miss Worthington fairly jumped.

"Think you're going to find the Kohinoor or the Drums of Jeopardy?"

"Whadda you mean?" demanded Miss Worthington.

"Sounds too funny," said the Scoutmaster, "to hear you say you are Miss Worthington and then say 'whadda'. I should think the Bee Master would have taught you when you was about two years old to say 'What do you', and I didn't suppose you *would* know what I was referring to, but it's strange he didn't teach his own child. He's the one who taught me that the Kohinoor is the biggest sparkler in the world, and the Drums of Jeopardy are the biggest emeralds. I got that out of a picture show. It was a hair-raiser too. And it had the prettiest girl in it, a girl with dark hair and eyes and a *reasonable* amount of lip-stick and her make-up on straight, and she could act too! She was just a humdinger, I'll tell the world!"

"If you are so carefully educated," said Miss Worthington, "why do you use the slang that you do?"

The little Scout laughed.

"Oh, I've got to sling that brand of gaff to keep in favour with the Scouts. If I talked among them the way dad makes me talk at home, I wouldn't be Scoutmaster with my bunch very long. When we play we're Indians and bandits and pirates and things like that, we talk that way 'cause it makes it realler, and anyway, nobody expects a ten-year-old kid to talk the way a woman of thirty would."

"I am not thirty!" snapped Miss Worthington.

"Excuse me," said the Scoutmaster, "I knew you were close to forty. I only said thirty for politeness."

"I'm done with you now," said Miss Worthington. "You may go home, but you'd better come around again in the morning and see if there's anything you can do for me."

"All right," said the Scoutmaster. "I'll be right here, and I'll start home whenever you pay me for what I've done to-day. I've been flying pretty lively all afternoon, and I'm getting hungry enough to eat up every hot dog on the corner stand!"

"I'll pay you in the morning," said Miss Worthington.

"I'll take my pay now," said the little Scout. "I happen to be out of change and I'm tellin' you I'm hungry."

Miss Worthington produced her pocket-book, and taking some small change from it dropped it into the outstretched hand. The little Scout counted it twice.

"Say, you ain't throwing your change to the birds, are you?"

But the inquiry was good-humoured. The Scoutmaster had decided to be on the job in the morning.

"What time do you want me?"

"Better make it about nine."

"All right," said the Scoutmaster; "maybe I can get here an hour sooner and wipe up the dust on the furniture or straighten things out for you, or clean your shoes. I often clean my mother's shoes. I know how."

"That's fine," said Miss Worthington; "come as soon as you want to."

"I'll be right here," said the little Scout, "and for your own sake, 'cause I'm so fond of you, I'm just telling you before I start that you better remember how California feels about antique furniture."

The little Scout closed the door and went down the path and scaled the fence and said to Jamie: "I can't chase up a reason for staying here any longer, and I'm about sick hungry. If you can hang out the night and do something to scare her off about getting into that chest until morning, I'll go on the job again pretty soon after seven and I'll stick at it until I see if I can't make *something* happen."

Then the line of march was taken up to the nearest hot-dog stand. A few rods away the little Scout turned.

"Let me wise you up to this: if she gets desperate in the night like the hardened criminals do, she may try breaking my chest. Be a good idea for you to take the axe or anything she could pry with out of the tool-house and fasten the windows on the inside where they latch and lock it on the outside. If she can't find anything that just suits her to attack with, maybe she will let it be until morning."

And that was what Miss Worthington did. She was tired herself. Being too lazy to cook, she ate bread and milk, took a bath, and went to bed early, and she was still asleep when the Scoutmaster arrived in the morning. Depending on the assurance that he would be called if needed, Jamie, reeling for lack of sleep, stretched himself on his bed and went over the edge. The situation for that day was up to the little Scout.

CHAPTER XVIII

THE LITTLE SCOUT ON THE WAR-PATH

UP until ten o'clock the little Scout served as kitchenmaid, lady's maid, housemaid, errand boy, anything the interloper required. Then a load of worthless paper was sent to the incinerator which stood in the middle of the lower portion of Jamie's side of the garden, halfway between the hives of the Black Germans and the long row of the Italians. As the Scoutmaster scratched the match and lighted the papers and stood a few minutes to watch them burning, an ominous rumbling that came from somewhere in the direction of the Italians became noticeable.

"Um-hum m-m," said the little Scout. "Dunno but I better call Jamie. Some of his bees are going to swarm."

Coming back up the walk there was a pause of a second beside the hydrant. The Scoutmaster had intended to set a few drops trickling to keep the mint bed happy, but the heaviest hose was attached and stretched up the walk. The nozzle could be seen lying above one of the jacqueranda trees, open enough to let a tiny stream drip no faster than the earth would absorb it for the watering of the tree. That jacqueranda tree seemed to be particularly precious because, under its lacy shade of serene blue, some of the very happiest hours that the Bee Master had ever conjured up for the amusement of the little Scout had been spent. So the Scoutmaster left the back walk and circled around the house, and turned the nozzle one faint degree wider open, and laid it down in a new place as a slight expression of devotion to that special jacqueranda.

As the nozzle touched the earth there came from inside the house a splintering crash. The little Scout straightened suddenly, eyes wide open, muscles tense, and with a lighter step than ever was used in the fairest pirouetting, the ground was covered to the side window. Carefully drawing the weight of the body upward, the little Scout peered through the open window in time to see the lid of the antique chest wide open. The axe, that must have been secured and hidden somewhere in the house before Jamie had locked up the previous night, lay on the floor.

Breathlessly the Scoutmaster clung to the window and peered in. The time was past for diplomacy. War had been declared. The enemy had invaded the most sacred stronghold of the Bee Master, of the little Scout, of the Keeper of the Bees. It was time for action. Clinging to the window-sill with eyes wide open and mouth considerably wider, the little Scout watched while the wastepaper-basket that belonged beside the Bee Master's writing-desk, the big Indian cooking-basket, was filled indiscriminately with everything that could be gathered up from the contents of the chest that was a picture, a paper that looked as if it might contain the slightest record of any transaction. Nothing but playthings, jewellery, ornaments, laces, and scarves were left. The basket was heaped to the top. Then Miss Worthington arose, possessed herself of a handful of matches from a dish over the mantel, and picking up the basket, started toward the back door.

Deftly the Scoutmaster dropped from the window-sill, raced to the jacqueranda, caught up the hose, and darted down the side of the vine-laden pergola until the hydrant was reached. There was a pause to shut off the hose and turn the hydrant until the hose swelled and writhed like a snake. Beyond the thickest wall of vines the little Scout crouched and hung on to the hose, both eyes trained on the incinerator, still smoking and with fire in the bottom of the papers that were smouldering. Peeping through the vines of the pergola the Scoutmaster could see the girl was not yet coming, and again the soft buzzing called attention to the neighbourhood of the incinerator. The little Scout leaned low and peered from side to side, and stepping lightly, remaining screened to get a clear view, watched for the girl's approach. Then in an ominious roar almost at one and the same time from two hives of Italians there came streaming swarms of bees that were leaving their hives, honeycombs filled and bee crowded, to seek new homes at the behest of the old queen.

The little Scout's eyes opened wider. The hose dropped from the small fingers. One leap carried to an opening in the pergola. A twist carried through, and small feet raced wildly up the back walk and to the back porch and shaking hands grabbed the bee drum. One glance in the kitchen showed Miss Worthington on her knees beside the basket with nervous fingers sorting out the papers and the things that she had thrust into it with small discrimination.

"For a little time," said the Scoutmaster, grabbing up the drum, "I sure am thankful." And a wild race began for the region of the incinerator, and softly on the morning air broke the slow rhythmic "Drum, drum, drum-drum-drum," and the bees that were swarming in the air began to gather. The drum led them first to an orange branch within three yards of the incinerator, then headed off another bunch and guided them toward a fig branch on the opposite side. "Drum, drum," the little Scout stood with bulging eyes and parted lips in a cloud of bees, watching first one swarm and then the other. The air was still thick with them, but it was apparent to experienced eyes that the queen of each swarm had settled and that was all that was necessary.

"Drum, drum, drum-drum-drum." The eyes alternated between the bees and the back porch. There she came; the basket full to overflowing, one hand circling it full of matches, the other hand full of the papers that it was most essential to destroy. Keeping under cover of the trees and the flowers and the pergola, stooping, on silent feet, the little Scout slipped back to the hydrant, made sure that it was wide open, dropped the drum, and picked up the nozzle of the hose that operated with the pressure of water carried at such force as a running current flowing through pipes large enough to motor on with a small motor-car and carried in many places straight down mountain-sides, would attain.

The hose twisted as if it were a living thing, and the little Scout eased off the hydrant a trifle in fear that the hose might burst.

The interloper hurried down the back walk as fast as her feet would carry her over its winding and precipitous way, and dumped the contents of the basket into the incinerator. On top of it the precious papers were thrown, and then the match was scratched and held a second to make sure that it was blazing before the papers were touched off at the top. As the hand holding the match reached toward the papers, a stream of water that shook the incinerator on its base struck it and began speedily soaking its entire contents, and a shrill voice, keyed to the top note of wild excitement, shouted: "Look you careful there! You've got swarming bees on each side of you! You'll be stung to death in just about one minute, 'cause God knows *your* scent ain't *right*!"

How much Miss Worthington knew about bees was debatable.

One thing the little Scout recognized : She knew enough about them to be afraid. She looked to the right and then to the left and decided she would risk it, though the bees were coming closer.

"Turn off that hose !" she shouted. "Turn off that hose !"

"Not on your life !" retorted the little Scout. "You ain't a-goin' to burn up those papers ! They don't belong to you. Don't you touch 'em. Don't you touch one of 'em ! If you do, I'll hit you with this hose until I knock you spang into the nearest of the bees behind you ! You don't know mountain water pressure, but I can do it !"

"Turn off that hose !" cried the young woman, clinging to the side of the incinerator and looking with bulging eyes at the two swarms of bees milling so alarmingly near, looking up at the air above her gradually filling with the roaring wings of bees scenting something they did not like, bees already nervous with the strain of leaving the hive in which they had been reared and following their queen to a new location.

"What are you trying to do ?" cried Miss Worthington.

"I'm not trying," shouted the Scoutmaster. "I'm doing ! I'm going to have the truth out of you or I'm going to set two swarms of bees on you, and they will sting you until you are the deadest of anybody that ever went dead, just the horrid way you ought to go to pay for little Mary. I know you ! I've seen your picture ! You've got it there in that incinerator. You ain't the Bee Master's daughter any more than you are mine ! Your mother had you when she vamped him into marrying her. You are trying to play you are Mary. You are trying to cheat to get this lot. See 'em closing in on you. See 'em coming closer ! Hear 'em roar !"

The terrified girl looked on every side of her. Escape was cut off to the rear, the roaring hose was menacing her in front. If she left the incinerator with the papers she had consigned to it unburned there was no hope for her claim, no chance for any proof she had brought with her to be effective. She must get the papers or be defeated. But the little fiend at the end of that roaring hose—— Resolutely she bent over the incinerator and began with shaking hands to gather up the papers. In that instant the little Scout trained the hose, running full force, squarely in the back of the hives of Black Germans, trained it and so held it that they rocked on their foundations and there came pouring from them in distracted hosts the vilest-tempered bees that the history of bee-keeping ever has known. The object most prominently in front of them was the smoking incinerator, and the taint that was carried on the air, the most maddening taint that their experience knew, was the taint of the human being exhaling from every pore the odour of formic acid—the odour of fear. The Black Germans began to rise with a roar. The little Scout set the water-tap wide open and manipulated the hose nozzle to its full strength and watched it beat a hole into a bed of marigolds, tearing them out of the earth. And above the roar of the bees, and above the rush of the water, the voice that matched the face that Jamie had seen the night before, the voice of a small pagan intent on wreaking justice, carried high and shrill: "Now you are surrounded! Now you got 'em on three sides! Now you got 'em all around you! Now you'll get it! I'll give you just one chance! Drop those papers!"

The girl looked up. Within a few yards of her roared the Italians on one hand. At her back another swarm was even closer, and down on her from the front came the Black Germans.

"Turn that hose on me!" she shrieked. "Cover me with water! Beat 'em off with it!"

Then the little Scout stepped out in full view on tiptoes and kept the hose precisely where it was.

"Turn that hose on our bees, nice innocent bees, tending to their own business, making sweets to feed the world? Them bees is *friends* of mine! I'm the Bee Master's partner. Half of this place he gave to me. You think you are going to steal it! You think you are going to burn his papers! Come clean now, or the bees will get you, and it will not be five minutes until you'll be deader—you'll be deader than any liar or anything ever was before! Look out! They are in front of you! Come clean! Say you ain't the Bee Master's daughter!"

Clinging to the incinerator, the girl cast a terrified glance around her. She was in a circle of bees and she had heard of Black Germans. She knew them when she saw them. There had been bee gardens in her childhood when she had been an inmate of the home of the Bee Master. She screamed at the top of her voice.

"Stop your noise!" said the Scoutmaster. "Come clean, I say, come clean! Say 'Michael Worthington was not my father.' "

At that instant the first Black German hit its victim on the head not far from the right ear and went into execution.

"No! No!" shrieked the girl. "He wasn't my father!"

"Say you are trying to steal this place and you've got no right to it," said the little Scout.

The girl righted herself and tried to take a step forward. Another Black German hit her squarely on the forehead.

"Yes! Yes!" she cried. "I am trying to steal it! I have got no right to it!"

"Um-huh!" said the little Scout. "Now say you are trying to burn those papers to get rid of all the evidence that would keep you from being the thief you are trying to be! Say it, and say it damned quick!"

"Yes! Yes!" panted the tortured girl. "I'll say anything! For God's sake turn that hose on me. Clear a way through! Quick! Quick, or you will be too late!"

"You will tell the truth about one thing more first," said the little Scout.

At that minute the boiling hose was beating a hole big enough to have drowned a calf right in the marigold bed. The little Scout danced from one foot to the other, hanging to it with all the strength of a pair of unbelievably tough young arms.

"Tell the truth about little Mary yet! Say you pushed her! I *know* you did. The Bee Master knew you did, but he couldn't prove it. I'll let 'em sting the everlastin' liver out of you if you don't tell the truth about that!"

The third German got in its work in the tender muscles close to an eye.

"Yes! Yes!" panted the shrinking creature. "Yes! The hose for God's sake! Turn the hose on me!"

"Drop flat on the ground!" shouted the Scoutmaster. "Get on your belly and crawl! Crawl like the *worm* you are! I won't turn the hose on our bees. Get down, Nebuchadnezzar, get on your belly and eat grass! Eat dirt, for all I care! Then you can start inchin'! You can start inchin' along like a poor inchworm! Head for me and I'll juice you up enough that they'll not get you! Turn the hose on my *friends*, I guess not! Hold your nose! It's going to snow."

Full force the hose struck the miserable object grovelling on the ground, struck her, played over her and knocked a few bees that were flying low out of the way. A pitiful creature came crawling up the mountain, gasping for breath, one eye slowly closing, the pain of three stings on the head almost unbearable torture, bees by the thousand roaring above her. Slowly the little Scout backed up the mountain, dragging the twisting hose, pausing every few seconds to play it again on the victim. By and by sufficient distance was reached to permit an armistice.

"Now you stop right where you are!" commanded the

Scoutmaster, with a deft twirl cutting down the water. "Stop right where you are !"

"No !" cried the girl, struggling to her knees. "I'll not stop where I am ! I'll get you and I'll wring the head right off of your neck ! You little devil ! You vile little devil !"

Flip went the nozzle, spang came the water squarely on the girl's head and shoulders. Down she went.

"So that's how you feel about it ? That's the way you thank me for savin' you, all lyin' and stealin' like you are ! You didn't know I could magic bees, did you ? You didn't know I could run around on the other side of them and spray 'em gentle until I'd drive 'em on you, did you ? You didn't know I got a better trick than *that* up my sleeve, yet, did you ?"

Once more the girl rose halfway to her knees, and once more the hose came roaring threateningly near.

"Now you pause," said the little Scout, "pause in your mad career edsackly where you *are* until you get me *right.*"

From the soiled string around the neck of the little Scout the police whistle came into play. In reply to its shrill note there burst from behind the lilac bush, from behind the poinsettias, from behind the plumbago, three wild-eyed, wildly dancing young fiends tuned by what they had seen to the spirit of battle.

The Scoutmaster stuck the police whistle in the front of a soiled blouse.

"Scout One !" came the terse order, and Fat Ole Bill drew up and saluted.

"Scout Two !"

The Nice Child bounded into place.

"Scout Three !"

Angel Face ranged in line.

"Scout Three," said the Scoutmaster "get a-hold of this hose ! It's about wiggled the wind out of me. Help me train it close to the head of the young lady doing her devotions in our presence. My neck's going to be wrung. 'I shall holler for assistance. I shall meet her with resistance !' "

"Yes, your neck's goin' to be wrung !" puffed Fat Ole Bill. "Yes, your neck's going to be wrung ! Let her try it ! Let her try it ! What will she get, fellers ?"

In unison the Scouts shouted : "The Limit !"

It was at that instant that the police whistle and the commotion awakened Jamie, and it was an instant later, as he came around Margaret Cameron's house from the back, that he met John Carey coming around it from the front.

He said to him: "There's something going on over in the bee garden. I think maybe the Scouts are having a sham battle. Keep behind the bushes and follow me. You might be interested in what you see and hear. Sometimes it gets good!"

So the two men slipped through the gate and, under cover of the shrubs and bushes, came down very close to the flower wall behind the jacqueranda, where they paused.

"Scout One!" commanded the Scoutmaster, "tell it to the probate judge. Did you hear the witness before you say that she was a liar?"

"I'll tell the world I did! And she said she stole the papers, and she was tryin' to burn 'em so she could steal this garden. You bet I'll tell the judge!"

"Scout Two!" said the Scoutmaster, and Jamie and John Carey, with eyes as wide as the eyes of the youngsters, leaned forward and peered through the bushes.

"Sure! Sure I heard her!" said Angel Face. "Sure I heard her say she lied, and she was trying to steal this place and she pushed little Mary. Sure I heard her! Sure we saw you set the bees on her! Sure we saw 'em ping her on the dome! Sure we know she got what was comin' to her! Sure we'll tell the judge!"

"Scout Three," said the Scoutmaster. "What are *you* good for? Put it in mamma's hand!"

In the excitement the hose was yielded to the manipulations of Scout Three, and he had all he could do to manage it. The little Scout reached over and lowered the pressure.

"Same as the rest. Everything. From start to finish I heard it all. Sure I can. All about the lies. All about the stealing. All about the little girl she pushed. Sure I can tell any old judge!"

The Scoutmaster rocked from heel to toe and bent up and down and cupped a hand over each bony knee and emitted a war-cry that would have reached fairly well around the circle of the globe had it been properly delivered into a rightly tuned radio transmitter.

"And I'll tell the world what the Bee Master told me, and the stuff in the incinerator is *safe*, with three swarms of bees standing guard, and if four of us can't handle you, I know where to get somebody that can! Get up, worm. Get up, liar! Get up, thief! Get up, you nasty thing! Get on to your feet! Scout One, go to the telephone and call 0075. Call the taxi the Bee Master and I always take to come here quick. Scout Two, stay with Scout Three. Scout Three, you keep the hose right where you got it. If she moves let her have all of it. Don't be skimpy. The lady doesn't like California; it's too rough. So she wants me to pack her trunk. Excuse me!" and the Scoutmaster disappeared into the home of the Bee Master.

When the telephoning was finished, between Scout One and the Scoutmaster the steamer trunk was dragged to the middle of the living-room and the clothing of the interloper was thrown into it. Off Jamie's dresser the toilet articles were swept into the toilet case. A hat and coat were snatched from the closet and the travelling paraphernalia was dragged on to the front porch, and with wide eyes behind a wall of honeysuckle, Jamie MacFarlane and John Carey stood half paralysed and watched the proceedings.

Sooner than they would have believed, the taxi drew up at the gate and the Scoutmaster, stepping like a half-drunken dandy doing an Irish reel, with a swagger and a sweep from side to side, and arms set akimbo when the hands were not busy distributing elaborate gestures on the atmosphere, gave the command: "Put that trunk up on the seat beside you. Put that suitcase and that dressing-bag in back. I'll direct this picture just like my dad directs in the big studio. Mr. Taxi-man, take this coat and put it on the lady and take this hat and put it on her, and put your arm around her, and if she can't walk, carry her out and put her in the taxi. Take your taxi right down to the Santa Fe Station and, if she needs help, help her get a ticket to any place in Pennsylvania she says she is going, and be darned quick about it into the bargain!"

The Scoutmaster stood still until the taxi disappeared, then turned and said: "Scouts, I thank you! I'm off for to-day. I got business, but I'll not forget that it's my treat and I'll make it a double header! I'll tell the world I'll make it a humdinger. A dollar won't touch it. And don't a one of you *forget* a word of what you've *heard* or what you've *seen*. There's a slim chance that this may be the real thing. There's just a chance that you go to court and tell it to the probate judge like I said, but just for this minute I'm through with you and I want you to disband and speed. I'll settle your score to-morrow and you can all step mighty high, 'cause this day there ain't been no make-believe. You been Scouts, and you been *real* Scouts, what's done a *real* job, and done it up brown! They's just one thing. Remember your sakerd oaths. Remember your vitals and all that. Remember if you *tell*, you'll be cut an' cast. Take my blessing and disband. And Scout Three, if you would run down and turn off the hydrant before you go, I'd be glad, 'cause I don't care if I tell you fellows that this has been *some* skirmish and I'm all in ! Now furnish your own music and march to it."

The Scoutmaster stood straight, watching the gate and down the road until Scout Three and Scout Two, and Fat Ole Bill bringing up the rear, all gesticulating, all talking at once, disappeared. Then, headlong, the little Scout fell face down in the dirt and began to cry right out aloud, sobbing, shuddering, shrill little screaming, terrified cries that broke Jamie's heart, and he tore through the honeysuckles and gathered the little Scout up in his arms, and sat down on the bench under the jacqueranda and held his small burden tight and rained uncounted kisses all over the little face and head.

The tongue of a Scotsman is usually rather stiff, but in that tense instant Jamie's ran away with him.

"You little thing !" he said. "You brave little thing ! You've done it. You've saved the Bee Master's gift for us. John Carey was with me back there and both of us saw and heard enough to send that woman to the penitentiary. So don't you cry any more ! Let me hold you tight and rest a minute. It was a big strain. It was too much for you, you poor little darling !"

Just for an instant Jamie thought the burden in his arms was going to spring entirely from him, the stiffening and the straightening were so abrupt.

" 'Little darlin' !' " scoffed the Scoutmaster. " 'Little darlin' !' Next thing I reckon you'll be callin' me 'Kiddo' ! That's what she called me. If anybody ever calls me 'Kiddo' in all this world again I'll kick their teeth in. That's that !"

The Scoutmaster hunted for something that would be good to dry eyes on, and failing to find it, sat very still while Jamie used his handkerchief.

"I don't know what you are goin' to do with me," gulped the little Scout. "I reckon I've just about wrecked the marigold bed, and it was on *your* side of the line."

"Well, never mind the marigolds," said Jamie. "We can make up the bed and sow some more seed. Never mind the marigolds ! Tell me what happened."

"It was just all I could do," said the Scoutmaster, "to handle that hose when I had it turned on full, and I was scared of my life it would bust. It just wriggled and twisted like a snake, and I had to keep it close to her because, if they really began to close in, I *had* to beat 'em off, but I wasn't going to do it for pinging on the bean only *two* or *three* times, 'cause she *had* to be hurt *some* or she wouldn't 've come clean. I wouldn't 've minded if it had 'a' been on my own side, but I hated awfully to tear up yours. You can take the hose right now and go over to my side and beat up a hole just as big as I tore up on yours."

"You surprise me," said Jamie. "A head as level as yours usually is! How would it help me in getting back my marigold bed to tear up a hole as big as that on your land? It wouldn't be sensible."

The little Scout thought it over, then looked up at Jamie with wide, tired eyes.

"Well, I can see how it would be *just*," came the reply.

"Possibly," said Jamie, "but justice and good hard common sense don't always agree."

Suddenly the little Scout brightened.

"Well, anyway, you aren't the only one that got some ruination worked on you. Look what she went an' did to the Queen's chest! Just go in and look what she went and did to *my* property!"

"To the 'Queen's chest'?" said Jamie. "What do you mean?"

"What do I mean?" cried the little Scout. "I mean she had been to the shed before you locked it up, an' got the axe, and she had hid it in the house. She broke open the Queen's chest, prying it with the axe."

"Oh, boy," said Jamie, "that's rough! But don't you feel bad. I'll have it repaired so you will never know the difference if I have to have the whole front reproduced."

"She busted the top around the lock and where the secret spring went," said the little Scout. "The thing about it is that I don't *like* things smashed and patched up. I like 'em when they're whole and the way you've got 'em give to you by one you love."

"Well, don't you mind," said Jamie. "There couldn't have been anything new about that chest. I think it must have been about five hundred years old to begin with, and, anyway, people can do things so wonderfully these days in such repair work. If it's only around the lock, I'm sure we can get it fixed so nobody will ever know it."

The little Scout used Jamie's handkerchief on a pair of red eyes.

"All right, then"—the assent came with one of the youngster's lightning changes—"all right, then. We'll get it fixed, but we didn't need a patched chest to remember her by. We got the whole garden for a souvenir of that lady!"

Suddenly the little Scout began to laugh.

"My! Didn't she look wonderful when the taxi-man put her hat and coat on her? Wasn't she a spiffy lady? I wonder, if Nannette had seen her, if she would have said she looked keen?"

Jamie roared.

"No," he said; "I don't think Nannette's favourite adjective would have worked. I don't think even she would have thought the lady on her departure looked keen."

"She'll have to make a straight shot for the dressing-room," said the little Scout, "and put on her war-paint and feathers the best she can."

"Do you really think she will go?" asked Jamie.

The little Scout heaved a deep sigh.

"I don't give two Apache war-whoops whether she goes or whether she stays. The pony I'm bettin' my money on in this race is one that tells me that that lady ain't never comin' back to the Sierra Madre Apiary. She's had her dose of treat-'em-rough, and I bet she ain't weeping for more, not a mountain pressure hose, nor Black Germans in the eye, nor nothin'! She got her share, if I did have to tear up your marigolds to give it to her!"

"For goodness' sake don't worry about a hole as big as a wash-tub when you have just got through saving me an acre!"

"All right, then," said the Scoutmaster. "If *that's* the way you feel about it, it suits me. Do you mind if I just fool around a little while?"

Jamie knew what that meant. It meant that his little partner would go and creep up on the foot of his bed and fall sound asleep, and he thought that would be the best thing that could possibly happen. So he said he did not mind in the least, because he and John Carey were going back to hive the bees. The Scoutmaster slid to the ground. Suddenly Jamie felt a pair of small, wiry arms around his neck that hugged him up so tight he did not know but that his head was going to be decapitated. Then, for the third time, squarely on his mouth, he got another little hard, hot kiss of a brand and delivery that he knew he was never going to forget.

The little Scout started toward the house, but only a few yards had been covered before there was a halt, and the small person whirled. "Quick! How goofy! We forgot the incinerator! There's Highland Mary and little Mary and all the valuable papers soaking in the ashes and maybe some fire under them! You got to get 'em quick, if I have to turn the hose on you while you're doin' it! Whatever it was she wanted to burn up so bad, why that's edsackly what we must have to prove that what's give us is ours. You can't tell it to the probate very good without the papers in the incinerator, and it doesn't seem as if you'd be placid enough to tackle the incinerator right now without riskin' a mixshure of Black Germans and Italians—an' Germans can shoot straight!"

"You go on to your fooling around," said Jamie. "I'll jump in to the bee clothes. Maybe I'll put the old raincoat over them, and I may take the bee mask since things are so stirred up, but don't you worry, I'll reach the incinerator and I'll get everything in it. I'll not stop to hive the bees until everything is on the kitchen table and spread out to dry."

Jamie raced to the back porch to prepare himself, and, as he rounded the corner of the house, John Carey came walking up the back steps trailing ashes in his wake, and set the incinerator on the back porch.

"I thought I'd better get this and start the stuff to drying out. I didn't want the job of taking anything out for fear somesomething might be lost or missing. I want you to do that yourself."

So Jamie stepped to the living-room door and called in: "John Carey has got the incinerator for us. He's a right real bee immune!"

"I'll tell the world he is," came the voice of the little Scout, but it sounded muffled as if it were coming from fairly deep in a pillow.

The two men gathered up some soft towels and, working swiftly, dried the documents, the bank books, the valuable papers, the letters and the pictures that they found, and spread them on the kitchen table. Then they hurried to the shed to arrange new hives for the swarming bees. By the time they reached them, the two swarms that had gone out were weighting down the branches around their queens and only needed a slight smoking to numb them so that their transference to the hives could be easily managed. As for the Black Germans, they were still nervous, but they were a distance away, the hot sun was rapidly drying the water around their hives, the roar of the hose had ceased, the scent they disliked had been removed, and so they were calming down as speedily as might have been expected of bees of their irritable temperament.

As they worked, the two men talked to each other, breathless exchanges, exclamations mostly. What a listener would have heard, ran like this:

"Can you beat it! That little Scout tackled her single-handed and made her come clean! I'd give a fifty-dollar bill to have seen the whole show!"

This from John Carey.

"Wager it would have been worth more"—from Jamie.

"Chances are you've been saved a lawsuit that might have dragged for months and cost a lot of money and made a lot of rotten publicity."

"When we get these bees up I'll go over to Margaret Cameron's and straighten everything up and bring home my stuff. I was going to camp there until Margaret got back."

"You were a fool ever to have allowed that creature inside the house, to have walked out and turned things over to her!"

Jamie smiled, a slow Scot smile.

"You know," he said, "we are no so verra well acquainted with ourselves in this world. I thought I had not earned this property; I thought I had no right to it; I thought it belonged to someone of blood kin; I thought I had not set my heart on it, and when I had walked out and started trying to give it up I found it was almost going to kill me to do it. You can trust me—there'll not be any more walking out for anybody, and that's that!"

So they hived the bees that had swarmed, and went over the other hives to clip old queens and destroy queen cells and to search for moth-webs on the comb, and when everything was in proper shape John Carey went home, and Jamie took a shovel and commenced repairing the damage to the marigold bed. After that he went over and cleaned up Margaret Cameron's house, and brought home his belongings with a heart so full of thankfulness that he remembered to go on his knees and thank God.

When the little Scout awoke in mid-afternoon, Jamie was waiting to return his possessions to the chiffonier and closet. They went into the kitchen and gathered up the Bee Master's effects, which the crisp, dry air had done its work upon, carefully returned them to the chest, pushed the splintered wood into place, and took stock of the damages. Jamie thought he could find a man who could make the repairs so skilfully that no one ever would know that the beautiful thing had been broken. Then he went to his room to hang up his clothing and replace his things in the chiffonier.

No one had ever known the little Scoutmaster to waste very much time. There were no lazy bones in the small body. Jamie had assistance in folding the papers and putting them in the chest. He was now being assisted in returning his shirts, underclothing and socks to their proper places. When they came to a small package, carefully pinned, the Scoutmaster ran a pair of small hands under it and lifted it, then looked at Jamie with speculative eyes.

"Feels like woman's stuff."

Jamie smiled at that comment.

"It is 'woman's stuff'. It's things that belonged to wee Jamie's mother."

The little Scout stood very still holding the package toward Jamie, and Jamie saw the lips open and he knew that the question was going to be: "May I see?" And someway he did not feel that he could stand to touch those things. So he reached his hand and said quickly: "Some day I'll let you see what's in that package." It did not occur to the little Scout that Jamie did not know what was in it himself. So they put the package back in the drawer and covered it with clothing, and then they went down to the corner grocery and bought what the little Scout called a "party".

After they had finished the "party", and Jamie had been told every detail of what had occurred in the morning, the little Scout arose from the table and helped to put away the food and wiped the dishes.

'Now what shall we do?" inquired Jamie.

"Well, I don't know what you're going to do," said the small person, "but I know what I'm going to do. I'm going home to Mom and Jamie. I been taking care of him so much the last few days that he knows me better than he does anybody else, and he likes me better. I know how to fix his bottle now, and get his milk just right with the thermometer and everything. The rest of the way I could take care of him myself if I had to. I'm pretty near doing it, anyway."

"But that's girl's work," suggested Jamie.

"Yes, I know," said the little Scout, "and if it's what a girl really ought to do, it's kind of funny that I'd want to do it, but I *do* want to take care of Jamie. I want to take care of him so bad I can't hardly bear to see mother touch him. It's the funniest thing. I thought I liked a horse better than anything else in the world, but I don't. I like our Jimmy better than any horse, and I like your Jamie about as well as I do ours. I don't know but *just* as well, and I don't care a bit who sees me takin' care of him. And that's strange too. Girls don't interest me. I have nothing in common with them. I never can think of anything to say to them. I don't know how to play with them, and I don't like the things they do, anyway. They're so sissy. They got no pep to 'em. They got no kick and bang. They won't play Indians or robbers or policeman or Scouts."

"Now, back up there," said Jamie. "You're mistaken. Girls *do* plays Scouts. They not only play Scouts, but they *are* Scouts, and *being* is better than *pretending* any day. There are Girl Scout camps and there are girls that can ride and shoot straight and fish and do everything that a boy does, and do some things even better than a boy does, and are all the prouder because they are girls."

The little Scout did not seem deeply impressed.

"Aw, girls! I ain't got any use for girls! But I'm going home and take a girl's job 'cause I'm going to see for myself that Jamie's all right. He's so little and sweet. My! You're goin' to love him! My! You're going' to be *glad* you got him!"

"Am I?" asked Jamie.

"Sure you are! You ought to see my dad with our Jimmy. He's just crazy about him. He says that our Jimmy has got all the rest of the babies on the map lashed to the mast."

"And you think my Jamie stands a chance of being as fine a baby as that?" asked Jamie.

"I don't think anything about it," said the little Scout. "I'm well acquainted with both of 'em and there ain't a thing the matter with your Jamie. He don't cry and he's no fusser. He just takes his food and goes to sleep and lies there so little and so still it most breaks your heart 'cause he can't help himself any, and no mother to cuddle him. He's got some service due to him, and I'm going to see that he *gets* it."

"Yes, I thought about that too," said Jamie. "He's certainly a helpless little duffer."

"Yes, he is," agreed the Scoutmaster heartily. "He's a helpless little duffer. And that's where we come in, and so we got to get on the job and take care of him."

"All right," said Jamie, "we'll get on the job and take care of him. Do the best you can for a few days more until Margaret Cameron comes."

At the mention of Margaret Cameron they both looked her way, and at the same time they both saw her going in her back door and moving through the back part of the house.

"Why, there she is now!" cried the little Scout. "Shall I go over and tell her about Jamie and ask her if she will take him?"

"No," said Jamie, "let's give her time to take her hat off and set her house in order, and maybe what I consider straight she wouldn't think was straight. Some time this evening I'll talk with her, and then I'll telephone you what she says."

"All right," said the little Scout.

Possibly in those two words lay the secret of the thing that made the little Scout so many friends; such an adorable little Scout. In the small person's cosmos there was no time to argue. In training the Scouts the same teaching had been applied to personal experience. The Scoutmaster had learned how to obey. So Jamie watched the receding figure on the way to the car line, willing in one instance to take a girl's job, because the "little duffer was so helpless". Jamie smiled whimsically and started to interview Margaret Cameron.

CHAPTER XIX

THE PROVINCE OF A FRIEND

JAMIE stood in Margaret Cameron's back door and called cheerfully: "Oh, neighbour, where have you been for the past fifty years ?"

Margaret Cameron stepped to the living-room door and braced herself with a hand on each side of the casing, and Jamie was shocked to the depths. He found himself crossing the room and in a sweep catching her in his arms.

"Oh, Margaret !" he cried. "Margaret !"

He held her from him and looked at her, and her face was the face of a stricken woman. She was there. She seemed all right herself. There was only one thing to think.

"Lolly ?" he questioned. "What happened to your girl ?"

Margaret Cameron opened her mouth, but no words came. Jamie helped her to a chair and rushed to the kitchen for a glass of water. Then he knelt on one knee beside her and took both her hands and stared at her with questioning eyes.

"Tell me, friend of mine," he urged. "Tell me what I can do for you. Where can I go ? Whom can I get ?"

Slowly the woman shook her head, and at last her voice came, a hoarse, rasping voice with which he was not familiar.

"She went on that hiking trip up in the northern part of the state. She fell over a bluff and hurt herself terribly. Nobody knew how bad it was. They were where they couldn't get anything. It must have been appendicitis or peritonitis. Her body was all bandaged. Anyway, Lolly is beside her father out in Pinehurst Cemetery."

"Oh," cried Jamie. "Oh !"

He dropped back on his heels and possessed himself of both Margaret Cameron's hands and sat staring at her.

"I had a 'phone call," she said presently, "from my niece

Molly, to come to her place in town quick, that she was worried about Lolly. She just said that to make it easier for me to get there. They must have sent her word from the start that Lolly was gone. Molly had written her a letter and they got the address off it and sent Lolly to her. They were always, not like sisters, more than sisters. If they had been sisters, they'd not have got along half so well as they did. I've been kind of sore at Molly for a good while. I thought she had a good deal to do with Lolly going away, but maybe she didn't. Maybe I was so hurt at her going that I just imagined it. You know, a mother has got a lot of time to think, and her children are so bone of her bone and flesh of her flesh that to save her she can't help worrying over them. But I needn't worry over Lolly any more. There's nothing more I am ever going to do for her."

She sat still in dry-eyed resignation.

Jamie gripped her hands.

"Go on and cry! Cry your heart out about it!" he said. "Put your head over here on my shoulder and let me hold you tight. If it tears you to pieces you had better cry than to sit dry-eyed like that."

Margaret Cameron shook her head.

"I think I am cut too deep for tears," she said. "I am just about killed. I wish to God I had something to do beside the routine of the house, something different, somebody who needed me! I wanted Molly to come home with me, but she seemed to have things keeping her in town, and she wanted me to stay with her; and awful as it seems here now that Lolly is never going to come again, I don't seem to be able to even think about leaving. I am hit pretty hard, losing my neighbour and all the light of love and laughter that there was in my life and in my home. I don't mind telling you, Jamie, that the Bee Master did not care anything about me. His heart had been broken on the question of women.

"I don't know all the details, but I know this much. He had had a first wife that he idolized, and after her death he had let another woman fool him into the idea that she would take care of his child and make a home for him and comfort him. But she wasn't the right kind of a woman and she had a child of her own, and there was a tragedy about the Bee Master's little girl. I don't think he could prove it, but I think he knew in his heart that the other child had pushed her, and when they got to her, her spine was injured and she never could walk again. Her agony was fearful and she couldn't stand it long. When she died he turned everything over to the woman but enough to buy this place, and asked the courts for his freedom and came here. He was free and he could have married me, but he did not want me. He did not want any woman in that way. He had had his punishment. He was worn out with sorrow and disappointment. He didn't love me, but oh, Jamie! I did love him! I couldn't help loving him. Whenever I look at his chair beside the fireplace, I see his white, silken hair, his noble forehead, his lean slender face fine as parchment, always gentle, always patient —I would have given my life to have comforted him! And just when I knew this couldn't ever be, Lolly went, so suddenly and so needlessly.

"Jamie, I *can't* understand it! There was no reason why she should have left home. Her grades were always good. Her school work was fine. She was offered positions here at the close of the war when teachers were so scarce, when so many girls preferred the freedom of the shops and offices to the confinement of teaching. I can't get away from the fact that she went because she didn't *want* to stay at home. She didn't want to be around me, and I can't see why. I spent my days and I lay awake at night trying to think of things that would please her, but I couldn't keep up with the procession. I can't think that a lot of things the youngsters are doing are right. I can't think that they won't end in humiliation and pain and maybe death, and now death's come to her just from a little foolish accident. She must have slipped on the mountains, and I can't understand that. She was sure-footed as a goat. She'd been in the mountains all her life. Oh, Jamie, it's all so useless. What am I going to do?"

Jamie hesitated.

"Margaret," he said, "I came over here to tell you a tale of woe, but what I have to say seems feeble compared to what you are enduring."

Margaret Cameron straightened in her chair. She drew her hands from Jamie's and laid one of them on his head.

"Oh, my boy, my poor boy!" she cried. "Has that awful thing gone and broken open again? Have we got it all to do over again?"

"No! No!" Jamie hastened to assure her. "No, it isn't that. My side's fine. I'm fairly sure I won't have to wear either the pads or bandages more than two or three months more. I haven't been able to stick to diet so well since you've been gone because I'm not much of a cook, and I haven't been in places where I could get what I needed."

Margaret Cameron went on smoothing his hair.

"I guess you're about all that's left to me, Jamie," she said. "I guess you are my job. It's fair hell to stay at home, and it's blacker hell to try to leave it. I doubt if I can go to Molly. If she wants to be with me, I guess she will have to come here. And as for you, lad, if it isn't your side, what is it that's hurting you?"

With Scot brevity Jamie told her.

"About the time I came here, I married a girl. A few days ago her baby was born at the Star of Mercy Hospital and she was not strong enough to make it. All I have to show for her is the baby."

Margaret Cameron pushed him back and looked at him quietly.

"Why, Jamie," she said, "Jamie, I can't understand that. Why didn't you bring her here to the garden? Why didn't you let me take care of her too? Maybe if her diet had been right and she had been cared for as a woman can care for a girl, maybe it wouldn't have happened."

"'Maybes' don't do any good now," said Jamie. "The circumstances were such that I couldn't bring her here. The point is that she is gone and there is a splendid boy baby and his name is James Lewis MacFarlane, Junior."

"At the hospital? He's at the hospital?"

"No," said Jamie. "She told them before I got there that she wanted me to have him, that she wanted him named for me. They had him all ready and they put him in my arms, and without knowing what I was going to do, I walked out with him. I am the same kind of a dog that you are, Margaret. I came home, to the only place I've got, to the only place on earth that knows me or wants me. It hasn't been long, but as long as I live this spot right here is home to me. So I came home with a little raw new-born baby."

Margaret Cameron rose.

"You have him over at the house?" she asked. "*You're* trying to take care of him yourself?"

Jamie shook his head.

"No, I couldn't do that," he said. "I'm too big and clumsy. I don't know enough. The little Scout was there and went to the telephone and had a conversation, and half an hour later Mrs. Meredith came. She has a small person of her own and it seems that one more didn't bother her."

Margaret Cameron made a curious sound, a dry intake of breath which might have been a short laugh if she had not been too unhappy to laugh.

"No," she said tersely; "one more doesn't bother that

woman! I've heard about her. At the birth of her first child there was a charity baby and a little millionaire baby at the same hospital and both of them were starving, and for the length of time she was there, along with her own baby she nursed the others and she saved both of them. She got them past a critical period where they could take proper nourishment and retain it, and then they could go on feeding them. And when her next baby came there were a couple more starving babies and she took them under her wing and shared the nourishment for her own baby with them. And when her third one came there had been a Caesarean operation a few days before and the baby lived and there was no milk for it, and she nursed it as well as her own. Mrs. Meredith doesn't stick at doing anything for any baby, that you can depend on. It isn't hard to see where the little Scout gets a large bunch of lovable qualities, but if she's got a little person of her own she doesn't need yours. Maybe that's the job that I was looking for. Maybe something alive that will put in a demand will be the thing that will tide me over. Go and get your baby, Jamie, and bring him to me."

Jamie rose and went to the telephone. He called Mrs. Meredith and asked to have the baby brought home. Margaret Cameron had returned and was willing to undertake his care. In only a short time a small brown car apppeared down the street. Jamie stood at the gate and watched it coming. The car was the colour of the hair of the woman who drove it. Her eyes, wide and bright, shone out smilingly. On the front seat beside her sat the little Scout, carefully holding the bundle. Jamie looked at it curiously and wondered what he would think and what he would feel if that child were truly his.

In an effort to spare Margaret Cameron he stretched his arms for the baby, but Mrs. Meredith was a genial person. She had to deliver the baby herself. She had to spread out his wardrobe and explain how she had used the things. She was dubious as to whether Margaret Cameron, who had not had a baby in more than twenty years, was going to know enough to oil a baby and put the right kind of clothing on it and handle it properly in the present year of our Lord. Twenty years is a long stretch, and science figures out numerous things in that length of time. She was so full of good nature, so full of high spirits, so pleased with herself for having taken care of the baby until Margaret Cameron came, that she did not notice the white, drawn face of the woman, a woman whom she scarcely knew to begin with. She shocked Margaret's old-fashioned soul by putting into her arms a baby that was wearing no flannel, whose feet were bare and kicking, whose dress was no longer than the feet. It seemed to Margaret Cameron the only thing Mrs. Meredith did that had been done to old-fashioned babies was to watch that the little eyes were screened, that strong lights did not penetrate.

Margaret lifted her voice in protest.

"Where are his flannels?" she said, and Mrs. Meredith spread a pair of expressive hands in a gesture that both Margaret and Jamie recognized immediately.

"There ain't going to be no flannels!" she laughingly quoted. "California babies have graduated from flannel. It's too hot for them and chafes their delicate skins and makes them fret and cry."

Then she sat down on the davenport and opened up the baby-basket she had brought and displayed the implements she used in the morning toilet of James Lewis MacFarlane, Junior.

Margaret sat and stared. She listened to what was said. She watched what was done. She looked the baby over and then slowly shook her head.

"Jamie," she said, "if I take this child and try to take care of him in this way and he dies, are you going to hold it against me?"

Jamie and Mrs. Meredith laughed unrestrainedly.

"No," promised Jamie, "I won't lay it up against you, and since Mrs. Meredith seems to have had fine success with a baby of her own that isn't so many months older than our Jamie, let's try what she says. The things she has here are the things the baby's mother made for him. You see they are short. She intended to use the little dresses and clothing she had made."

"Why, yes," said Mrs. Meredith, "all these things are what Mr. MacFarlane brought from the hospital." She turned to him. "Are there any more?"

"Yes," said Jamie, "there are. But the nurse said the small package was personal belongings of the baby's mother. It is in the middle drawer of my highboy, Margaret. Any time you need anything you haven't got, maybe it's there. I haven't reached the point of trying to go through it myself, but I don't mind your looking enough to see if there are any other things that the baby might need."

"Well," said Margaret, "I must say frankly that this beats me! I'm sure he'll be killed. I'm sure he'll take cold and die of the croup. I thought babies and flannel were inseparable."

"Just cut off the 'in'," laughed Mrs. Meredith. "Cut off the 'in' and make it 'separable'! My baby is the best baby you ever saw. He isn't roaring with the colic and keeping us awake at night. He is getting so fat his face is round like a full moon. We never know he's in the house unless he is hungry or needs attention, and he is the kind of a little gentleman that lets me know instanter when he does need attention. Aside from that, I haven't got a baby for all I know. You try the new way on this other little Jamie; try it on him, and if he isn't a better baby and an easier baby to take care of, less trouble in every way, and happier, why, then you can call in a doctor and figure out what you think would serve better."

She turned to Jamie.

"You must fix up some kind of a bed for him. It wouldn't be a bad idea to get a clothes-basket. Put a couple of pillows in it and fold something over for a padding. Our little Scout will bring you out a really soft pillow for his head. Our Jimmy has two or three. He can always divide with another baby, and I think he has enough little covers that we can spare a couple, and there is a world of clothes in that suitcase. He won't be needing anything for months, unless he grows so fast that he walks out of them.

She rose and went to the telephone, picked up a pencil attached to a string, and on the margin of a list hanging there wrote a number.

"That's my number, and a ring will find me at eight o'clock in the morning, or twelve at noon, or six in the evening. If anything goes wrong, call me and I'll come right out and see what I can do to help you."

Then she picked up the baby and held it tight to her and kissed its little face and its hands and finished with its feet, and handed it to Margaret Cameron. Jamie escorted Mrs. Meredith and the little Scout back to the car. As he closed the door, the Scoutmaster leaned forward and laid a hand on Jamie's and lifted a pair of lips that had something to say. Jamie brought his ear in range.

"May I tell mother about that girl off the Santa Fe buttin' in on our garden?" came the whisper.

Jamie drew back and looked at the small person in surprise.

"Haven't you told her?" he inquired.

The little Scout shook a vigorous head.

"No. You said it might worry her; not to tell until Dad came, but he's coming to-night."

"Since it's all over," said Jamie, "there's nothing to worry about. You didn't leave the lady a leg to stand on. You got her confession before three good witnesses, and it just happened that there were two more in the background that you did not know about. We have the papers in our possession, and that reminds me that, while the lock of the chest is broken, I'd better go over that stuff and select what really is important and put it in a safe somewhere. I think likely I'd better turn it over to Mr. Meredith."

"What are you two talking about ?" inquired Mrs. Meredith.

"Since I wasn't in on the whole performance," said Jamie, "the little Scout had better tell you from start to finish exactly how things were, and then, if there are any details I can add as to what I saw and heard personally, I'd be glad to furnish all the corroborative evidence that I can."

As the car started Jamie heard the voice of the little Scout saying: "A long time ago, one day when he was blue, the Bee Master told me . . ." and that was all he heard of the story. What he had seen of it was sufficient for him. He went back to the house laughing and without realizing that Margaret Cameron would expect him to be in mourning. He saw the surprise in her eyes and straightened his face immediately. His Scotch honesty instantly asserted itself.

"Margaret," he said, "I am not sailing under any false colours with you. There are some things that I don't want to talk about, because I don't understand them well enough to make them plain to anybody else. But there is this I am going to tell you. I saw the girl I married only once, and very little of her before we were married, and I did not see her afterward until she was at the point of making her crossing. This baby bears my name and has been left to me, and I am going to do the best job I can in rearing him properly, but I am not in mourning for his mother, and you needn't expect me to exhibit any deep symptoms of grief, because I can't when I don't feel them."

Margaret Cameron stood still, looking at the baby.

"That kind of tale doesn't sound like you, Jamie," she said, "but if I understand the province of a friend at all it consists largely in keeping one's mouth shut and doing the things that will be of most benefit. Naturally, I would like to know what this baby's mother looked like and what kind of a girl she was, but I suppose, after all, she looked like the baby since a boy generally resembles his mother, and I can't tell what any baby three or four days old looks like. If she were to be judged by this suitcase of baby clothing, she was pretty fine. These are dainty little things, carefully and exquisitely made. That tells a big story about any mother."

As the days went by, it seemed to Jamie that there never had been a greater blessing afforded a woman than the Storm Baby was to Margaret Cameron. He had the feeling very largely that that tiny bit of humanity had the same pull for Margaret Cameron that it had for Mrs. Meredith and the little Scout. Its appeal to him was strong. Half a dozen times a day he made some excuse to slip into the living-room and look in the basket in which tiny Jamie lay. If the little fellow were sleeping, he covered him up and went quietly away. If he were awake, he leaned over and talked to him and examined his hands and his feet. They were hands that had been fashioned to play music, to paint pictures, to hold rare books, possibly to write them.

Sometimes when he went he found Margaret Cameron busy bathing the small person, or dressing him, or washing little garments, or carefully ironing them. One day he realized suddenly that exactly the thing that Margaret had asked for had been given to her. Something alive, something that she would work for, something different, something that would appreciate what she did. So he ceased to feel guilty over the physical strength he was asking her to spend on the tiny baby, and felt instead that the child might be the greatest boon that could come into her life. He had a difficult time the day he tried to talk finances with Margaret concerning the baby. After a few words she flatly refused to listen to him.

At last she said to him: "Jamie, this baby's been such a blessing to me, loving him and caring for him has so eased the tension in my brain, that I have no way in which to tell you what he has done for me. I could not take money for him. Really, I couldn't! As time goes by, when he needs more clothing or things come up, like a little bath-tub shaped right for a baby, things that he has to have, I'll tell you, and it's your right and your privilege to get them, but as for taking money for what I am doing for him, I can't do it. We won't talk again about it."

"All right," said Jamie, and he walked out of the house and began the process of going over Margaret's grounds minutely to discover what there was he could do in the garden she was neglecting, among flowers she was hurriedly watering, that he thought would be equivalent to the care of the baby.

Presently Margaret realized that this was what was happening, and the arrangement suited her admirably. For a few days she had not cared whether her flowers lived or died. She had not cared whether her house was neat and orderly, or the food in place for the mocking-birds and rosy finches. To-day she cared immeasurably about all these things because very soon little Jamie would be big enough to notice a pretty flower, to throw crumbs to a bird, and always his health must be safeguarded by perfect cleanliness and sanitary conditions around him. So Margaret Cameron became more of a housekeeper and less of an outdoors person, and Jamie found on rising every morning that he had gained enough more strength to add to the labours of his day what was necessary to be done at the house across the white fence.

Religiously he stuck to the tomato juice in the morning, the orange juice in the afternoon, milk as a beverage at meal-time, the diet that Margaret Cameron always insisted she had worlds of time to prepare for him. He was beginning to feel so much of a man, so secure in his strength, so proud of the skin coating that was deepening in colour, deepening in thickness, stretching securely across his left side, so proud of the free, pure blood coursing his veins, so thankful to God for release, for his chance, he found his lips puckering in a little whistled rendition of every tune he knew as he went about his work. Some of them were army songs, things that the boys had sung in camps, but most of them were songs that he had sung in Sabbath School or things that he had heard his mother sing when he was a child. Sometimes he picked up airs that he heard on the streets or as he lay sunning on the beach. Jamie's repertoire ran all the way from "Jesu, Gentle Saviour, Hear Me !" to "It Ain't Gonna Rain No More", and as he used the hose to help produce the most prolific growth of fruit and flowers that he had ever known, as he thought of his healing side and the rare miracle that had been wrought in his cure, it seemed to him that it did not make much difference whether it rained or not. California seemed to be getting along without rain.

But all this was superficial ; all these were things that were going on as a result of the exigencies of life. The deep thought, the thing at the bottom of Jamie's heart, the thing that had sent him reeling on his feet and had made him reel mentally ever since the thing he did not understand and that he could not excuse, was the thing that he had been led into by the Storm Girl.

He had thought from what she had said that she needed his help for herself, and he had given it immediately, freely. But he did not like being lied to. He did not like being deceived. He had married one girl ; he had been invited to assume the responsibility of bringing up a child that belonged to an entirely different girl. It was not fair. It was not honest. If his ring and if the certificate of marriage that had been issued to him for the Storm Girl had been turned over to another girl in distress that she might have them to make her peace with doctors and nurses, he could see how they could have been so used. But if the name under which the marriage had been performed was not the true name of the girl he had married, then the marriage was not legal, and investigation would leave the tiny baby to be a shame baby after all. The thing had been clumsily done. In the condition in which he had been at the time, feeling as he had felt, Jamie would have given his name to any woman anywhere who needed it. He had taken the letter that he had treasured from his pocket and laid it away. It was no longer a personal possession. The whole thing had not been fair.

Then, when his indignation waxed hottest, when anger surged up the strongest, in his heart came a great, throbbing, gushing, overwhelming sense of relief. However she had lied, with whatever motive she had deceived him, one big fact remained on Jamie's horizon. The Storm Girl had fulfilled his thought of her. He had not felt that a woman with sage in her hair and sand verbena and primroses rising like an incense around her knees, her midnight garments trailing in them, he had not thought that the hair of silk binding across his face, that the physical strength, the quick assurance of speech, had not thought that these things possibly could be coupled with a shame woman. He had been ready to accept any excuse, to believe anything. Now there was nothing to believe except that there had been a lie—but, after all, there had been lies in the world that were rather magnificent. There was just a bare possibility that this lie, that this thing that had been done, had a reason backing it that he might be willing to countenance. So Jamie spent largely of his days and somewhat of his nights torn by conflicting emotions.

CHAPTER XX

THE SCOUT MUTINY

It was midsummer in the garden; long, golden vacation days. The bees were happy. Innumerable swarms had stretched the rows of hives not only down the sides of the garden, but well across the foot, and Jamie was beginning to feel that by the coming season some of them must be disposed of or he would have more than he could manage. The flowers were blooming in a mad riot of colour. The trees were laden with fruit. He was so nearly a well man that he was beginning to use his left arm almost without realizing that he was using it. Carefully he was oiling the soft skin. It was still protected with a light pad. The bandages were so nearly negligible he did not even notice them or the soft strap across his shoulders that held them in place. Every day was a day of work that he loved in a location that he loved. Every evening he found refuge in the books that taught him the things that he needed to know to master his new profession, and now he was beginning to branch out to those other books, the emanations of the brightest minds of ages reaching back to the earliest collected beginnings of literature.

With the advent of an income, with the assurance that he would not be again at the mercy of the Government or the public, Jamie had ventured to subscribe to half a dozen of the leading magazines in which he was most interested, and they carried to him wonderful tales of a world with which he had lost touch for a long period. Some of the things he learned from them were interesting, highly educative, and some of them were alarming, and he was set to wondering where our country was heading, exactly what was to be expected as an ending for peculiar beginnings that were being made. Some of the things that he found, which seemed to be casually accepted and written of and to be bandied about in the world in print and conversation, set his cheeks flaming and the reserves of his Scotch soul felt outraged.

There began to be borne in his breast the feeling that it was time for him to go out in the world, to break his bands of security and of peace in the garden, and hunt up the men who were forming the Legion to which he should belong. He began to listen, on slow, sleepy Sabbath mornings, for the tolling of the church bells, and to wonder if there might be such a thing anywhere within a reasonable distance as a Presbyterian church with a minister just near enough to Scotland to have a little bit of a loved burr in his voice. He began to feel that the time was coming very shortly when he was going to fare forth in search of these things.

He was thinking of it very strongly one morning when the hose he was handling had brought him to a petunia bed just across from the jacqueranda tree, and he stooped to flood the roots of the brilliant flowers. His scouting ears caught a rush of feet, a slam of the gate, and there flashed into view the little Scout forging towards him with both arms extended, a distorted face, and clothing fairly torn to ribbons. Jamie dropped the hose and whirled with arms outstretched. He caught on his breast the little quivering figure and eased himself down to the seat under the jacqueranda and held the child tight—a twisting, shaking figure, physically nauseated, tears so big that they gushed and rolled in a torrent. All he could do was to gather up the little bundle and hold it together and wait. He began rubbing his cheeks over the small head, whispering, as best he could, words of consolation.

"Little Scout, dear little Scout," he panted, "tell Jamie what has hurt you so? Oh, what has hurt you so? Little Scout, little partner!"

Then suddenly Jamie gathered the little figure tighter in his arms and thrust his lips down through the hair to a grimy cheek, and with all the intensity in his body he repeatedly kissed the little Scout.

"Sweetheart," he whispered, "darling little sweetheart; tell Jamie, tell Jamie what's the matter."

And by and by, from the huddled bunch on his chest there came a panted whisper: "Who told you?"

"Nobody told me anything," said Jamie. "You tell me. What is it? What has happened to you? Where have you been? If anybody's hurt you——" War rose in Jamie's breast; red war flamed in his eyes. "Did any boy lay a finger on you?" he panted.

The little Scout moved in negation.

"Who, then? What?" urged Jamie. "I'm ripe for murder. Tell me where I'm to go, what I'm to do!"

The bleached little head buried deeper in his breast, the grimy hands gripped him tighter. Something was being whispered. Jamie almost broke his neck to drop his ear to hearing distance.

There came in wheezing gusts: "My Scouts"—another world of tears and another panted gasp—"mutinied on me! They wanted—to go off down the beach, away alone, and strip bare naked and swim, and—and I——"

Jamie held tight and spread his big hands over as much of the little body as he could cover. He leaned low to catch the whisper.

"—I couldn't. And they mutinied on me and they nearly tore me to pieces!"

"Do you mean," asked Jamie, "that those little brutes pitched on to you and beat you?"

The little Scout wormed in his arms.

"I reckon I had it coming," panted the child. "I reckon I've beat them up often enough. But I was tired this morning. I couldn't get the old grip on 'em. I couldn't handle 'em, and they got me."

"What happened?" asked Jamie breathlessly.

"A man came along, a man on horseback, and he reached down and picked me up on his horse and brought me along out of their reach until I said let me off here. Oh, Jamie! I'm killed! I'm going up the rock and I'm going in the undertow where I can't get myself out if I want to."

Jamie held on tight.

"Why, you little idiot, you can't do that," he said. "Think of your father, think of your mother, think of Nannette and little Jimmy! Think of me! You can't do that!"

"I ain't got anything left," sobbed the little Scout. "There ain't anything I want to do. If I can't lead my Scouts, I don't want to play anywhere!"

"Look here!" said Jamie harshly, his voice roughened with emotion. "Look here, darling! You got a wrong start because you didn't like what girls do, and you've been running with the boys until you have about unsexed yourself. And what have you got out of it? Embarrassment and disappointment and a beaten body. You needn't think you are the only girl in the world of your kind. You needn't think that there aren't a lot of others who don't like to stay in the house and do the things that girls are supposed to do. You needn't think that to be a Scoutmaster you have got to be the master of a pack of boys. Damn them!"

Jamie rose.

"You come on in the house with me," he said. "I'm going to clean you up and take you to your mother, and she is going to put some decent clothes on you and we are going off by ourselves for to-day. We are going to some place you will *like*. We are going to do something you will *want* worse than anything in the world. I'll tell you right here and now what we are going to do. We are going to get you the finest little horse that ever stepped! I've been looking for him and advertising in the papers for him, and I've found him. I've got him all ready for you. I was just waiting a few days because I had lumber ordered. I was going to build a stable over on your side next to nobody. John Carey was coming to-morrow to help me, and when I got it done I was going to have the little horse there to surprise you, but he can wait for a stable. We will go and buy him to-day."

The little Scout slid from Jamie's arm and stepped in front of him. An outstretched hand was a mute invitation for the partnership handkerchief. Jamie supplied it and the little Scout used it.

"A real horse, a nice horse, my very own horse that nobody rides but me?"

"Yes," said Jamie, ready to promise anything in the world. "Yes."

"We can buy him, we can buy him to-day?"

"Yes," said Jamie, still ready to go the limit.

"That's the berries!" said the little Scout. "Then I won't go in the undertow. Then I won't care any more *what* Fat Ole Bill and the Nice Child and Angel Face say. If any of them wants to have the sword and all the emblems of office, they can. They can have the robbers' cave and the bandits' den, they can have the Indian fighting. I'll go with you, and I'll have my horse."

"Sure you'll have your horse!" said Jamie. "I'll hike with you, and we'll see what's in the canyons and what we can find that you will be interested in outdoors; and you know, if you would go and investigate, you would find that there are girls' camps where they do all the things in scouting stunts that the boys are doing, and I haven't a doubt, either, that they do some of them better!"

The ex-Scoutmaster straightened up and drew a deep breath.

"Do you think, Jamie, do you think honestly, that they do 'em *better*?"

"Bet you two bits they can!" said Jamie. "I'll find out where headquarters are, and I'll go with you and we'll see. But I bet you two bits that those girls can lay a fire right and make the sparks fly quicker, I bet they can set a tent, do anything they want to do, and do it quicker than those Scouts you have been training with, anyway. I wouldn't have anything to do with free-lance Scouts. They're outlaws. I'd let those boys go hang!" Then the Keeper of the Bees ventured further: "I'd let them go hang, Jean. If I were in your place, I'd find out where there were some girls of my kind and I'd stick to my own kind, and with the training you've had and with the stunts you've been doing, there isn't a doubt in my mind but that you can work up so that in maybe six months you can be the leader. You can do something that isn't play but is real, constructive scouting work, something that gets you somewhere. You can train yourself so you might be able to help stop a mountain fire, or find a lost child, or do something wonderful and worth while, something that isn't just play. And there is your own horse you can have and you can ride. I can ride a bit myself. There are none of the tricks of riding that I can't teach you."

The handkerchief was restored to its owner. Jean Meredith began to feel over her body to see if she had sufficient clothes remaining to cover her.

"Is it a bargain?" asked Jamie. "Are you going to take the car and go down the beach to the stables where this particular horse I am talking about is waiting for you? There are three bully ones. You can take your choice. Shall we go?"

"Oh, boy!" the cry came in almost breathless wonder. "Shall we go? Shall we paint the petunias, shall we put the scent in the roses? Shall we march past the Black Germans? Shall we flip the dirt off our shoulders into the eyes of the first Boy Scout we meet? I'll tell the world we shall! And Fat Ole Bill and the Nice Child and Angel Face can just plumb go right straight to perdition! I wouldn't ever play with 'em again, not if they came and got on their knees, not if they begged me with tears in their eyes. I wouldn't ever play with them again——"

"Yes," interrupted Jamie, "and I'll wager you another two bits. I'll wager you two bits that inside of a week they'll come and ask you to play with them again!"

Jean Meredith stuffed the tail of her shirt inside the band of her breeches. The simper that she marshalled on her smeary, teary face was something exquisite. Her body bent in a curve. The index finger of her left hand lightly touched her lower lip. With the right hand she flicked a chunk of adobe that was not in the least imaginary from the left shoulder.

"Aw, thanks!" she said with the most flapperish of flapper

accents. "Aw, thanks, my deah boys! You are chawming, simply chawming, but I have outgrown you. I've graduated from small folks to a higher class. Kindly amuse yourselves by eating my dust when I ride by on my own horse!"

Suddenly the exquisite flapper became the little Scout again. "Jamie, is my horse a *he* horse or a *she* horse!"

"There are two or three," said Jamie. "I haven't settled definitely. There are two or three I am going to lead you to. I'd like to see if you like the one best that I like best. In any event, you may have the one you want."

"All right," said Jean. "All right. What I was thinking about was that if my horse is *he*, I am going to name him Chief, and if she's *she*, I'm going to name her Swallow, and whichever one it is I am going to get there on it, no matter if it's straight up a mountain-side or right into the ocean. My horse and me are going to swim same as we are going to ride!"

"All right," said Jamie, reaching a hand that was instantly accepted, "let's go!"

When Jean was properly dressed and they were settled on the car headed toward the corral where Jamie had learned there were riding horses being sold several miles farther down the beach, Jamie again broached the subject of horse.

"Jean," he said, "have you any very definite idea in your head as to exactly what kind of a horse you want?"

Obliquely Jamie was watching. He saw a slightly sullen look, a slight stiffening of the figure, and he knew what it meant. There was a minute or two of silence and then, instead of an answer to his question, there came a question on a different subject.

"Ain't you ever going to call me 'Little Scout' any more?"

Jamie thought hard and fast.

"No," he said, "I'm not. Not ever again. I'm going to call you by your *name* after this. It's a perfectly good name and one that I like very much. It's Scotch, and so am I, at heart. So far as I am concerned, you are done masquerading. The rest of the way, when you are with me, you are going to be what you are. You lay pretty stiff stress on people playing the game square in this world. You've got away with it in a good many instances all right so far, but from now on you're getting big enough that you'll strike some pretty unpleasant things if you undertake to keep on masquerading."

"Do you mean that you don't want me to wear breeches any more around you?"

"Why no, foolish!" said Jamie. "I think breeches are the thing for you to wear when you work in the garden and ride, and during play hours, and when you are exercising. What I want you to do is to stop playing with the boys and learn how fine your own sex can be. You needn't think you are the only girl in the world that likes to ride a horse or to climb or to be outdoors or to command a Scout company. I want you to get on your own side of the line, where you belong."

Jean thought that over carefully, as was her custom.

Then she said slowly but in more cheerful tones: "Well, maybe you're right about it, but you'll have to show me?"

"All right," said Jamie, "I'll show you! The first thing we're going to do is to head right straight for a number I have here in this pocket. We are going to join you up to a Girl Scout camp, and I am going to be your escort to a meeting once a week. If they won't let me inside, I'll hang around outside until you get through, but you needn't tell me that any girl joins a Girl Scout camp without being the kind of a girl who likes to swim and paddle a canoe and ride a horse and be out-of-doors. And you needn't tell me that among the number of girls it would take to form a camp there aren't going to be at least two or three that are going to be nice-looking girls, and nicely behaved girls, girls of good families, girls with whom your mother would be glad to have you associate."

"All right," said Jean. "We'll play 'Follow My Leader'. You set the pace and I'll be right after you."

They had no difficulty whatever in finding the number of a secretary who gladly registered Jean Meredith, furnished the necessary cards and equipment, and Jamie paid the bills. When they were once more in the car and headed for the corral, Jean looked at him.

"Jamie," she said, "that was a good deal of money you paid there. I didn't see how much, but it was more than you must pay for me. You must take it out of my share of the next sale of honey. I'll tell dad that you did."

"Never you mind about that," said Jamie. "Your father and I will attend to the finances. You needn't fret about my spending a little money on you, because I haven't started to spend money yet. There are two more things I'm going to do before this day is over. Both of them are going to cost me some money, and it will be the easiest money that I ever spent, because, if you hadn't got my inheritance back for me, I wouldn't have had any money to spend on anything, with the exception of what I've saved out of my earnings this summer. If it hadn't been for you, it wouldn't have taken me very long to be down to bedrock financially, and with little Jamie on my hands in the bargain. So, if I can accept my east acre with all there is on it from you, you can take what I want to give you to-day without making any objections concerning it, can't you?"

"I sure can," said Jean, and the twinkle that Jamie knew crept into her eyes. "You said *two* things. What other thing beside a horse?"

"We'll stop right here and you will see," said Jamie.

Again they left the street car, and this time Jean was led into a tailor's shop where she was measured for a proper pair of girl's riding-breeches and two coats, one having sleeves and one having none, both of them having fitted bodices and skirts with a bit of a flare and nifty pockets. The garments were to be made from a lovely soft blue-grey cloth very nearly the colour of the eyes of the youngster who was to wear them. Then from displayed accessories Jamie selected two silk shirts and a blue-and-grey tie, and handkerchiefs with borders to match the shirts. Little squeals of delight greeted the fitting of a pair of grey boots with soft folds around the ankles and stiff tops, and gloves with cuffs to match them. Jean looked dubiously at the gloves. She wiggled her fingers and told the truth.

"It seems a pity for you to spend money on them. I bet a dollar I lose them the first time I start out with them."

"I don't think that would be showing me much consideration," said Jamie, "to value the first gift I ever made you so lightly that you would lose it. I could do better than that with them, if you made me a present of a pair of gloves."

"Well, you've got a lot of pockets," said Jean.

"You're going to have pockets too," answered Jamie, and turning to the smiling tailor, he ordered: "You're to put inside pockets in those coats, and left breast pockets on the outside, and plenty of pockets in the breeches. We don't want to give this young lady any chance to lose her handkerchiefs and gloves."

As they left the store, Jamie said: "Now, we've done a fair job of getting the cart before the horse. We've bought the accessories. Now we'll buy the horse, and after we select the horse, we'll go to a leather shop and buy a saddle and a sporty riding-crop."

Jean shook her head.

"Don't spend money on a whip," she said. "I don't use 'em! I guide my horse with my hands."

"Nevertheless, young lady," said Jamie, "there are times when the life of any rider is in danger who is not armed with a good sharp whip. If a horse becomes terrified on the mountains and starts to back over a cliff that would land you in Kingdom

Come, and you had in your hand a good stout whip and could lay on a few cuts that would sting sharply, you might succeed in making that horse forget his fright and carry you forward."

"That's so, too," agreed Jean instantly. "I didn't think about that because I haven't ever ridden much where there was real danger. Queen and I have climbed the mountains some, but Queen has too much sense to back on a body."

"I never bank on how much sense a horse has," said Jamie, "because if something comes rolling out unexpectedly and terrifies it so that it jumps for self-protection, the damage is done before a horse really knows what has happened. You are never safe on the back of a real horse without a good stout whip. It is part of the necessary equipment, and whatever your theory of loving-kindness may be, there are some creatures in this world that you cannot manage except by force when they are frightened."

"Just like Miss Worthington," commented Jean. "And I tell you it got my goat to call her 'Worthington', 'cause I happened to know that her name was Young, just plain, red-haired, snub-nosed, freckle-faced Young. I never did see anybody that I couldn't bear quite so hard as that 'Kiddo' person. It wasn't so easy to do it, but I'll tell the world, she got what was coming to her, and I might strike another case just like her. You get the whip!"

When they arrived at the corral, Jamie went round to the gate. He knew so well where the gate was that Jean realized that he had been there before, and she realized, too, that the men who came to meet him were acquainted with him.

Jamie spoke to them and said: "I want you to become acquainted with Miss Jean Meredith, and I'd like to have you show her the three horses that I looked at the other day."

Jean stood entranced as three horses were led before her. They were really ponies, animals the right proportion for her to ride and look well on, and that she would have strength to make obey her will.

"Now, one at a time we will saddle these," said Jamie, "and you may put in two or three hours riding them. You can try them over and over until you discover which one has the gait that suits you. I've looked them over very carefully. They are all of reasonable age; they are all in good condition. There is very little difference in the price."

Then Jamie realized that he was talking to the air. Jean was not hearing a word he was saying. She was standing before the three horses, staring at them. Slowly she went up to the first one and pulled down its head. She ran her hand over its forehead. She looked deep into its eyes. She drew its ear through her hands. Then she slipped her left hand under the chin and with the right parted the lips and looked at the teeth. Then she went around the side and down the neck and over the chest and down the forelegs. She got the spine line in perspective and looked at the sides and the flanks and the tail, around and over. As a surgeon searches for a hidden disease, the youngster examined those horses, and Jamie realized suddenly that she knew more about horses than he did. She was looking for points that he had not thought about. He stood back in amusement and watched her examine the three horses minutely. When she had finished, she stepped out in front of them.

She pointed to one and said: "That one has the best temper, but it is easy and slow. That one has a good disposition. It will go steady and it will go all day. I believe it has good wind."

Then she looked at the last one.

"And this one has got a fine large dose of the devil in him. You won't know when he's going to kick and when he's going to rear, but he won't know when you're going to want to turn a quick curve or slide down a mountain-side instead of walking. So maybe that will be even. He'll go the farthest and he'll keep it up the longest, but it would be a good long while before anybody that owned him could really *trust* him."

"All right," said Jamie, "so far as I know that's probably the way it is. Now, put the saddle on and I'll give you two hours to test them. I'm going to do down to the sand and stretch out in the sun for an hour. I've got so accustomed to it at this time of day that I miss it if I don't get my sun-bath. The salt water I'll pass up for the day."

"Wait a minute," said Jean. "Stay here for a minute."

Her nimble feet went flying over in the direction of a corner stand. On her return she came up to Jamie and handed him a paper bag.

"Thank you very much," said Jamie gravely, as he accepted the bag.

Then he turned to the attendant.

"Let this young lady," he said, "ride each one of these three horses around the track as often as she wants to. By the time she has her selection made, I'll be back to escort her home. Anything she wants, will you kindly see to it for her?"

The attendant said that he would and went to bring a saddle. Jean dug the toe of her shoe in the dust of the corral and then looked obliquely at Jamie.

"What's the use to rub it in?" she asked.

And Jamie did not resort to the subterfuge of asking, "Rub what in?" He happened to know, and he was too much of a Scot to pretend that he didn't know when he did.

"You die hard, don't you?" said Jamie. "But if you have been at this subterfuge all your life, I suppose you can't get over it all in a minute. At any rate, I'll explain to you exactly why I rub in the fact that you are a girl good and hard. I am conceding that you look enough like a boy so that anyone might mistake you for a boy when you are doing your utmost to prove that you are one. The reason I seem to hammer in the fact that you are a girl is because men among themselves sometimes grow pretty coarse and they say things and they do things that they would neither say nor do if they understood that a child of your size among them was a girl. What I am trying to do, Jean, is to give you the same kind of loving care and protection that I'd give you if you were my little sister."

Jean looked at Jamie and studied him intently. Then she almost bowled him over.

"I wouldn't ever be old enough or big enough to be your sweetheart, would I?" she asked, as casually as she would have asked for a drink of water.

Only for a minute there rushed in a tumult through Jamie's brain a picture of the kind of a sweetheart that the child before him might make ten or twelve years hence, and his head went a little wild; but Scotsmen are noted for saneness and sobriety and integrity, and he held himself and answered steadily: "I cannot imagine any sweetheart in the whole world I'd rather have than you, Jean, but it wouldn't be fair to you. I am too much older than you are. Youth demands youth. Nothing else is fair. I have noticed in my experience that things always go wrong when a man is much older than a woman. It isn't fair to a girl to tie her up to a man very nearly old enough to be her father. If I ever marry again, I'm going to marry a woman very near my own age."

"Was Jamie's mother very near your own age?" inquired Jean calmly.

"Well, considerably nearer than you are," said Jamie. "Now you go and ride your horses and I'll go and take my sun-bath, and when you have your horse selected I'll match it up with the saddle, and I'm not right sure that we didn't make a mistake in ordering the clothes first. Perhaps they should match the horse too."

Jean thought that over.

"Well, I don't guess that suit is going to be cut out and made right this minute. Maybe we could change the colours of the things this afternoon by telephone. There was the same cloth in tans and browns as well as blues and greys."

"So there was," said Jamie. "Maybe we'll want to change it. Now think about your horse, and be sure you get the right one. We don't want to find out later that you have a biting brute of a thing that is going to tax your strength every time you go out. You want a horse that will be your friend; that will be some comfort to you; that will love you."

"Yes," said Jean, "that's exactly the kind of a horse I do want. I want a horse that will love me like dad's dog loves him."

"Well, I doubt," said Jamie, "if you will find a horse with the capacity for love that a dog has. A dog has been around man so many centuries and has had so much attention that he has come to be almost human. There are times when I've seen a dog think; there are times when I've almost heard a dog talk; there are times when they have managed sounds that told what they wanted."

"I'll tell the world!" said Jean. "Dad's dog can every time, and so could mother's dog Chum."

Then she turned to the horses and Jamie turned toward the beach.

CHAPTER XXI

THEN COMES A VISION

WHEN Jamie reached the road, he crossed it and started down a steep embankment leading to the hot sands of the sea and the breaking waves. As he was going down, to his right he noticed a stone projecting in such a manner as to make a particularly attractive seat. From the feel of the package he thought he knew what he had. So Jamie went over and sat on the stone, screened on one side by an unusually large toluache, its lilied white trumpets blaring widely from blue edgings. Next to it a rose mallow towered, ten feet tall, a flaunting cloud of rosy-pink accentuated by maple-like leaves of silvery-green. He reached in his pocket, drew out his knife and opened it, opened the bag also, and found what he had expected: two very large, very red tomatoes. It was the time for his morning tomato juice. Jean had been thoughtful of him; she had decided that if he could not have the juice, he could eat the tomatoes and get his vitamines in slightly different form. So Jamie laid one tomato on the paper beside him and with his knife cut the stem end and the core from the other and began peeling back the thin skin in small pieces and cutting out the tomato in chunks. He found that he was enjoying it thoroughly. He had formed the tomato habit. He had got to the place where, if he did not have tomato juice at ten-thirty, his stomach arose and shouted for it.

While he was sitting there enjoying his fruit and watching the hundreds flocking back and forth on the beach, family parties here and there sheltered by beach umbrellas, people in bathing-suits lying on the sands, children playing in the breakers, swimmers floating far out—the everyday life of a beach in summertime—there broke on his ears from behind him a clamour that to say the least was startling, and then there came pouring down the embankment at his left the most surprising aggregation of humanity he ever had seen collected in one crowd. Little Mexico with straight black hair and black eyes, with rosy cheeks and red lips and shining teeth. Sober little Yaqui, with blue-black hair, with square, narrow face, with wide mouth and shining eyes and red lips. Little Italy, the prettiest sight, with tumbling curls and olive cheeks and always the lips of red and the white teeth. Little Spain was there wide-eyed and lovely; and China and Japan and Greece, and shiny little copper-coloured Indian faces with the straight hair, deep-set, watchful eyes, the high cheek-bones and sober faces, with lean, flat bodies and the prideful lift of head of the proudest race that ever walked the earth.

As this amazing combination poured over the embankment around him, Jamie noticed that each youngster either carried a small basket or clasped a small package. Some were boys, some were girls. All of them were shining-eyed, all of them were young, all of them were beautiful, each in its own way, beautiful with the beauty of a perfect thing in the flower of youth.

Those who reached the sand first paused and looked back, and beside Jamie, so near that he could have reached out and laid a hand upon it, there came down the embankment a narrow, arched foot and a slender leg clad in hiking boots. Then came khaki breeches, and in an instant more there stood out, back toward him, a tall, slender girl. The figure never could have been a boy. There were decided calves to the booted legs. There were rounded hips and arms and the profile of a shapely breast. There was a gracefully lifted neck, and it was topped with a shorn head of hair so thick that it stood out at the sides and on the top and turned over in big, soft curls, and sloped down to the neck at the back like the hair of a boy.

When the foot lifted and took one step forward, Jamie looked down into the track that remained in the sand and drew in a deep breath in which he recognized sage and beach primrose and sand verbena, albeit heavily laden with garlic and mangoes and tamales. Jamie's heart stopped right where it was and stood still so long that he did not know whether it ever was going to begin beating again or not. He shut his eyes tight and a strand of wet hair whipped across his face and drew him. Then he opened his eyes to make sure and saw the shorn head, and in his heart he cried: "Oh, what a pity! What a terrible pity! How could she sacrifice her crowning glory, a mane of silk like that?"

He watched the graceful movements of the slender girl as she went down the beach and seated herself a few rods in front of him. The little flock gathered around her. He heard a voice that he had heard before, that he knew perfectly, saying: "Now, children, before we have our lunch and before we begin to play, we must have our lesson, just to see if you are going to remember when school is not in session. What is this before you?"

In concert the children shouted: "Pac-eef-ik O-shun!"

"And what is behind you?"

"Sierra Madre Mountains!"

"And what is above you?"

"Sky!"

"And what is it you are sitting on?"

"Sand!"

"And whose country is this?"

Each little individual shouted for him- or herself: "*My* country!"

"And who of you can recite 'My Country'?"

The air was waving with little hands. The teacher pointed in the direction of a little Yaqui Indian boy.

"Isadore, you try!"

The little fellow stood up, brought his heels together, removed the little straw hat he was wearing, and because he knew what the child was going to say before he began, Jamie could distinguish:

> "My count-ree tissof 'ee,
> Swee' lan' of li-ber-tee . . ."

The teacher of Americanism smiled on the little fellow and said: "Right, Isadore! That's fine. Now, who can tell us what 'liberty' is?"

Again the air was full of hands.

The teacher indicated a little girl of Mexico.

"Maria, you try."

Maria answered promptly, waving her arms like a windmill over the sands and toward the mountains and the sky and the sea: "All this—with no fights."

The teacher applauded. Then she asked: "And who was the Father of your Country?"

Little Japan knew: "George Washeton."

"And who is our President?"

Little Greece and Spain and China shouted in Unison, "Alvin Oolidge!" and the teacher laughed and applauded again.

By this time quite a crowd had collected. Children with fairer faces had gathered and were listening and looking on. Grown people were passing before and behind the group of twenty-one, according to Jamie's count. They went on with their affairs without paying the slightest attention. The teacher opened a book the size of a school atlas, and taking a pencil began to draw.

Mechanically, Jamie finished the tomatoes, wiped his knife through the sand and then on his trouser leg, snapped it shut and restored to it his pocket. Then he arose and walked down the beach until he stood within three feet of the back of the girl he knew and looked over her shoulder in company with several other people.

The girl had drawn up one knee and the big book rested on it. The other leg stretched out along the sand in lithe comfort. The head was bent and with the right hand, in quick, precise movements, Jamie saw there was being crudely sketched the figure of a man. When the work was sufficiently completed that the component parts stood out plainly, the pencil rested on the round head, and instantly most of the youngsters touched their own craniums and shouted, "Head!" Then they proceeded down the anatomy, naming neck, shoulders, arms, hands, body, knees, feet. Then the pencil went back to the cranium and began making upstanding strokes on it and each youngster lifted his or her hands to his or her head and shouted, "Hair!" Then came forehead, and brow, and eyes, and eyelids, and eyelashes, and by this time, as each part of the face was named, the teacher ran a line out to the margin of the paper and whirled it into a circle and inside that circle printed very plainly, "Nose". "Eye". Ear". Every feature of the face was being reproduced and named.

Jamie noticed as this proceeding advanced from the ears downward that the space that had been left for the mouth was large. He stood almost breathlessly watching while gums were placed in the mouth, and then teeth and a tooth. The mellow voice of the teacher was talking almost constantly. She opened her mouth and exposed firm, milk-white teeth. She ran the eraser of the pencil across them to indicate that all of them were teeth. And all the children showed their teeth and ran a finger across them and shouted, "Teeth!"

Then she touched one of her front teeth and said, "Tooth," and held up one finger and indicted one tooth. Then all the little brown children found "a" tooth. She stuck her tongue out, laughing all the while, a very pink tongue glowing with health, not a sign of a bilious coat on the extent of it, and all the little brown people stuck out their tongues and shouted with laughter and immediately fell to making faces at one another. Isadore made such an ugly face at little Mexico that Mexico threw a handful of sand and a scuffie began on the outskirts. The teacher sat laughingly watching. Then her voice was raised to call them to order. Very distinctly she pronounced the word "tongue", and all the little folks kept showing their tongues and telling one another that they were tongues. Then she drew the tongue in the mouth of the figure she was working with, and from the tip of it she swept the pencil over to the margin and rounded the circle in which she meant to write the word.

At that instant there was the slightest movement behind her. Someone knelt at her back. A big brown hand flashed over her shoulder and firmly imprisoned her hand and the pencil it was holding, held it in a grip from which there was no release, and with extreme plainness in the circle she had made, one little ugly word comprised of four letters was printed. She was forced to print it three different times, and under the first writing there was one underscoring; under the second, two; under the third, there were three, very broad and black. The words that were written were:

Lies! Lies! Lies!

Then her hand was released. She was free to go on with her lesson in Americanism.

As Jamie arose from his knees he kept his eyes on the back of the girl, and what he saw was, that apart from the slight tensing of her figure that he had felt as he leaned against her back, there was not the least indication that she recognized the presence of anyone behind her. There had been no resistance in the hand he had held. It had yielded to his use, and he had used it to write the ugly word as forcefully as he could write it. After he had released the hand, he saw the surge of red that flamed up in the cheek next him; he saw the pencil whipped over and the erasure of the words he had written begun.

He was on his feet heading down the beach. He was dying to look back, and he would not. The question that was hammering in his heart and brain was whether she would follow him, whether she would speak to him. If there only were a rock. If he could only stub his toe; if he could only pretend that he had fallen, that he might look back and see whether she were coming. But there was no rock. There was no slightest excuse for looking back unless he did it deliberately, and he was too Scot stubborn to let the girl see, if she happened to be looking his way, that he would turn his head for her.

The whole thing had been so unexpected and so bewildering that his brain was only functioning so far as proceedings had gone. He had not reached the place where he could think progressively, consecutively, conjecturally. He was simply putting distance between himself and a girl who had lied to him—lied outrageously.

He had experienced the satisfaction of letting her know that he knew her and that he had called her a liar about as definitely and emphatically as a man well could, but he had not gone farther in thought than he had in action.

Right there he reached a rocky projection that ran down until the waves were breaking at its base, each wave creeping higher. Jamie was in no mood to stop for water. He went through, and, as he rounded the rocks, it seemed to him that here was an opportunity for a backward glance without being discovered. So he took the backward glance and what he saw stopped his heart again.

Away back on the beach in a sedate circle, mute and wide-eyed, with their lunches gripped tight, waiting the command from their beloved teacher, were the little brown and red and chocolate and copper-coloured children, born in the United States, products of our soil, entitled by our laws and our Government to be educated with our children, to live with them, to love with them, to fight with them, to die with them, all free, all equal before the law. They were huddled there waiting, while their teacher was coming down the beach in flying strides.

Jamie thought in all his life he never had seen anything quite so beautiful. The Storm Girl was running as an Indian runs, perhaps her body a bit straighter, her chin thrown a trifle higher. The ocean breeze was catching her thick red-brown hair and blowing it back. He could see the broad white forehead. He could see the flash of the brown-grey eyes. He could see the surge of red staining the cheeks and the lips and even the throat. He could see the heavy sprinkling of freckles that the sun had drawn out not only crossing the bridge of the nose, but scattered over the entire face. In a minute, with the speed at which she was coming, she would reach him. All Jamie could think of was that he must not be caught peering around a rock. To preserve his dignity he should be striding down the beach with his head up, with his shoulders square, his back toward her. Let the little liar run after him! Let her catch him if she thought she had anything to say to him!

At that moment, with anger flaming hot in his heart against her, Jamie whirled on his heel and looked behind him. He saw that he was standing before a crevice in the overhanging rock that led back to what looked as if it might be some kind of a subterranean passage. Before he realized what he was doing, he had gone plunging into the black depths until he brought up precipitately against walls which would afford him no further retreat. He turned in time to see the shadow of the Storm Girl's figure as she splashed through the waves in passing the opening. Immediately he was back at the entrance. She was still racing down the beach in absorbed pursuit. Jamie darted into the water around the point and did some sprinting on his own behalf. By the time the Storm Girl could have retraced her steps, he was across the road and hidden by the live oak, the madrono, the manzanita, and the sage of the mountain-side. Hurriedly he made his way back to the corral.

He found Jean exactly where he had expected to find her, on the back of a horse, circling the riding course that surrounded the corral where the horses were being sold.

When she saw him, she rode up to the railing and asked: "How do you like this one?"

"This one" was, to Jamie's way of thinking, the poorest horse of the three.

"What are his points?" asked Jamie, and laughed outright at the femininity of the first response.

"Well, he matches my suit, for one thing. You wouldn't have to telephone. And for another, he's got the wind and he rides easy, and he *likes* me. He seems as if he kind of needed to be loved and petted up a good deal. He seems like he could be better-looking than he is if he was rubbed up a lot, and fed right, and ridden with some sense. Most of the kids that get on these horses think they're on a piece of machinery, and they don't care whether they break it or whether they don't, so long as it doesn't belong to them. *This* horse could stand quite a bit of being treated decent."

Jean stood in one stirrup, drew the other leg across the horse and deftly dropped to the ground.

"I haven't put any of 'em to the final test," she said. "Let's try it."

She called to the attendant and said to him: "Bring my horses and stand them along in a row headed toward me. Right along there."

"Right along there" was an imaginary line perhaps four feet in front of her. When the horses were so disposed, Jean stood in front of them. She looked them over carefully. She walked up to each horse, and, one at a time, she laid the length of its head against her body. She cupped her hands around their ears, pressed in at the bases, and drew them through her hands two or three times, and then slid her hands down under each cheek and under the throat and hugged the head tight. Precisely what she did to the throat and muzzle Jamie could not tell. This performance she repeated with each of them, with the horse she had been riding last, and it seemed to Jamie that her touch was lingering, that she hugged it slightly closer. She certainly finished by laying her cheek against its nose. Then she backed away eight or ten feet and uttered a funny little whinnying call, and of the three horses the one she had ridden last stepped forward and immediately went to her and again dropped its head to her touch.

Jean laid her hand on it and said to Jamie: "If this is the horse I think he is, if he is *my* horse, he will follow me."

She gave one more light stroke around the ears and across the nose and said to the horse: "Come on, Chief!" and started down the corral. The horse followed her as she might have been followed by a dog that she had trained for a considerable period.

That settled the horse question. All that remained for Jamie to do was to make the reservation, to set a date when Chief would be delivered and where, to stop on the way home and purchase the saddle and the crop upon which he insisted, and then to make as straight a journey as possible to the garden of the bees, because there was lumber to arrive for the stable and John Carey was coming the next day to help him and the carpenter he had engaged to build a shelter for Chief.

When they left the car line and started up the road toward the bee garden, Jamie, from an impulse whose origin he could not have guessed, faced Jean.

"Everything all satisfactory?" he asked.

Jean stood very still, and finally she raised her eyes and in them Jamie saw precisely what he had seen in the face of the Storm Girl when she had left him without a word and a written letter to say it afterwards; so he understood.

He kissed her again and said: "You run along home now, and I'll telephone you when I have the stable finished and the horse is here. Then you can come out in the car and bring your dad and mother and Nannette and let them see Chief and show them how you can ride him. I'll tell them that the horse and fixtures are my gifts to you for saving me a lawsuit or any disagreeable complications in keeping my property. Will that be all right?"

And Jean the versatile, Jean the ever ready to talk, Jean of the school playground, of the diving raft, of the beaches and mountains, of the picture studio, of city and country alike, turned a small, quivering back, and silent, wordless, walked away.

Jamie went up to his door alone to find out what the premonition had been that had kept him from bringing the child with him.

CHAPTER XXII

THE MAGNIFICENT LIE

As he unlatched the gate and went inside, Jamie noticed that the front door was standing open. That meant that Margaret Cameron, who had a key, was in the house putting things to rights. As he opened the screen and passed through the door he was fairly sure that he heard a low moaning. Swiftly he crossed the living-room and stood in his bedroom door. The first thing he saw was the bed, and spread over it was a queer assortment of beads and pins and rings and bracelets and combs, the little vanities of a girl of the day, and lying open beside them was the marriage certificate he had not yet examined closely himself. A little bundle showing life lay very near to it, and on her knees beside the bed, her arms extended, her hands gripped full of the beads and bracelets, crouched Margaret Cameron, so still that she seemed to be breathing only in faint moans.

The drawers of the highboy were open, and in a heap on top of it lay Jamie's rolled socks and his shirts and underclothing, so he knew that Margaret Cameron had been examining his wearing apparel, hunting out the pieces that needed to be mended. Under his shirts she had found the package that had been given to him at the hospital. The story of what had happened to her and to him lay spread before him, and it read like the plainest print. He could see it all, with that certificate before him reading "Alice Louise Cameron"—Lolly.

Before he moved, before Margaret became aware of his presence, there was one thing Jamie had to do. He must make up his mind whether he would tell her that he was legally married to the girl she had idolized with the double devotion of a widowed mother. He must tell her the truth, or he must live a lie. He must stick to it that the child was his and its name James Lewis MacFarlane. He resolved that this was what he would be forced to do. But if he made Margaret Cameron think that he had been married to Lolly, that he had cared for her in any slight degree, that the child was his, she would expect him to observe at least a period of mourning. And he had already told her that he could not pretend to be in mourning for the mother of the child, that he had scarcely known her. That constituted the first difficulty he thought of. Jamie had to be decent no matter at what price of mental suffering or physical endurance, or to his purse. So he made his decision. He took one step forward and reached out his arms.

"Mother," he said, "Mother Cameron," but he got no farther.

Margaret Cameron, still gripping the beads and the bracelets, pressed her hands against the bed to brace her and rose. She turned toward him, but her face was no longer the set, hard face of a woman in danger of losing her reason. It was a face broken, lined, and creased with sorrow, but a face down which the blessed tears of relief had rolled until the sources of grief were nearly dried. Jamie was so surprised that he did not know what to say. It was Margaret Cameron who spoke.

"Jamie," she said, "you needn't fix up any magnificent lie. You needn't try to make me believe that you are the father of this baby. You needn't try to make me believe that you ever went through a marriage ceremony in person with my Alice Louise. You couldn't have. You didn't know her. I am sure you never saw her. I don't know where you ran into Molly. Down on the sands taking your sun-baths, most likely. And I don't know what you two fixed up between you to try to save the situation, but I do know this: I know as well as I am standing before you that Don was the boy Lolly loved. If she ever was in trouble, it was Don. There wasn't anyone else she was accustomed to being with. There wasn't anyone else she loved with a self-effacing love. I can see now that all their lives together they had cared for each other, and as I think about it, I think there must have been some mistake in some way. I don't just understand this clearly."

Jamie's arms closed round her.

"Margaret," he said, "it is true that I never saw your girl until they sent for me to come to the hospital where that certificate made them expect me to take the baby. I gave Molly the right to use my name. She used it for Alice Louise. I think that will help you to understand."

Margaret Cameron stood still, clutching the pitiful little strands of cheap beads and bracelets, the tears rolling down her cheeks, her eyes fast on Jamie.

"Since Don is the father of the boy, I'd be glad to think the best I can of him," she said, "and I'm glad to have the sore feeling wiped out that I've carried in my heart against Molly for months. I knew that she was at the bottom of helping Alice Louise to go away, but, of course, I didn't know that she was doing it to spare me, that she was trying frantically to fix some way that I might be kept from knowledge that would hurt me so. I didn't know that, but I know it now. There is only one thing that you can do for me. There will be some legal complication maybe. Maybe Louise's doctor can engineer it for you. Anyway, this baby isn't going to bear your name. He shall not be James Lewis MacFarlane. He's going to be Donald Cameron. I have surely got that much to say about it. He's going on the records with his father's name, and, of course, he is mine. Will you have his record changed for me?"

"Certainly I will, if it is legally possible," said Jamie. "I'll talk to the doctor and find out. I think very likely that he can arrange matters as you wish without any great difficulty."

He went to Margaret Cameron and took the pitiful little relics of her girl from her fingers and made them into a heap. The marriage certificate he laid back in the drawer.

"I might need this," he explained, "in accomplishing what you want done. The certificate and these things, I give you my word of honour, I have not seen. I did not know, when I left the house this morning, that it would make any difference if you did run onto that package. I didn't know that I gave my name to help *your girl* until I saw that certificate there on the bed when I came in."

Jamie picked up the baby and the bundle and put his arm around Margaret Cameron and helped her back to her home. As they went, he tried to say to her everything he could think of that might be of comfort, that might be of consolation. When they reached her living-room, she freed herself, took the little package she carried, laid it on the table, and gently tucked the baby in his basket.

"Jamie," she said, "I'm thankful to you for your kindness of heart and for your good intentions. I know you are trying to comfort me, but at the present minute I happen to be a woman for whom there is no comfort. It may be that in years to come I can arrive at some sort of peace of mind concerning Lolly. It may be that in years to come I can love her baby, can take him to my heart and try to get some sort of comfort from him against old age, but I'll tell you right now that it looks to me rather like a hopeless proposition. It seems to me as if in taking the bit between their teeth and running, the youngsters of the present day had, at least in my case, met sickening disaster. Don was a fine chap, and under the pressure of necessity to get out and earn money and earn it quickly that he might marry Lolly, he went to a job that dealt him his death, and she spent her maternity period in torture. How she was tortured is attested by the fact that her health was undermined until a function that should not have hurt her permanently, killed her. That's two dead. Here's a baby without a clear and legal right to a name, and a brand of shame to hang over it for the rest of its life in the knowledge of several people. Here's Molly been tortured almost beyond endurance for months. And here am I, who have lived my life and done the best I could, left to bow my head to a blow that by no interpretation can be made into anything except a shameful blow. All the rest of my days there is nothing left for me but to go softly, to know that there is something that I must hide, that I must keep secret, that never again can I lift my head with the pride of the Camerons or the pride of my own people. There's no use, Jamie. Go home, and if it turns out that you and Molly learn to care for each other, don't get the cart before the horse. Keep yourselves right before God and before the law. Stand by the ancient pride of your race and your clan. Stand by the laws of your country ; and the laws of your church and the laws of God. It may sound like preaching, but who has a better right to preach than I who have had two funerals on my hands, both children I have reared in my own home and by whom I can swear before the living God I did the very best I knew.

"And it was not enough. The youngsters thought they knew a better way, and they disregarded me and left me, and I wish that the good God would in some way make thousands of youngsters all over the land who are thinking about trying the same way, oh, I wish that the good God could show them the two dead faces that I have seen so lately, dead in their youth, dead in their beauty, gone out of life, gone out of love ! Those children cannot face the Master and answer anything but '*Guilty*', and all the rest of life for me I must bear the burden of their sin. I am right when I say that with bowed head for the rest of my days I must walk softly. Go home and leave me, Jamie. This is a thing I have to fight out alone."

Jamie took the stricken woman in his arms and kissed her and left her. There was nothing else he could do. What she had said was true. There was no controverting it. There was no way to get around it. There were no consoling words that he could speak. But he made up his mind that with the young folks with whom he came in contact he would try to use all the influence he might have on the side of God's laws, of man's laws, of the natural laws of physical cleanliness and decency.

CHAPTER XXIII

STILL ADVENTURING

THROUGH the rapidly falling darkness Jamie stumbled home. He stumbled because there was a vision that filled his eyes to the exclusion of everything else, even the walk upon which he trod. All he could see was the lean, slender form of a girl with rounded curves, with flushed cheeks, with wind-swept hair, with the fires of indignation streaming from the brown-grey eyes as she rushed down the beach in search of him. He reflected that possibly it was well for him that she had not found him, that he might stand a better chance with her if she had more time to reflect before he tried to talk to her.

When he reached the bench under the jacqueranda he dropped on it and sat there, a bewildered and a broken man. He reflected that he had run true to the well-known characteristic of the Scots. He had bridled his anger and bided his time and waited long to strike. Then, when he struck, he had struck too cruelly, too hard. There was no use to try to imagine anything else, to think any other way. The whole situation was open before him now. There was no one his Storm Girl could be save Molly Cameron, the niece of his neighbour and friend. There was no one she could be save the little Scout's idolized teacher of Americanism, and he had witnessed what probably was a picnic following the close of school with a group of the young disciples. Vivid before him came the flock of little black faces, the brown faces, the chocolate faces, the copper faces, the red faces, of these children born in America to all the rights of the American citizen. Then there came the absorbed face of the girl who was accepting the situation as it was and making her contribution toward the betterment and the safety of our land by trying to mould and to utilize this strange material into forces that in time would be called on to do their part to help sustain and protect our Government.

It seemed to Jamie in that hour that the men who had gone abroad had done nothing nobler, nothing braver, nothing more worth while than this girl was doing, this girl who was getting her fingers on the very pulse of the situation, who was preparing these children to carry to their homes the seeds that might flourish and grow into mighty trees.

There would be no difficulty in finding his Storm Girl now. He knew her name. All he had to do to locate her stopping-place was to ask Margaret Cameron. He realized, too, as he sat there in the perfumed darkness, with the glinting stars peeping through the lace of the jacqueranda, sheeted for months at a stretch with bloom as blue as the night sky, he realized for the first time precisely the depth of agony that had filled the heart of the Storm Girl the night she had come to him as he sat alone fighting his own battle on the throne beside the sea. He had thought that he was dealing with a wounded heart, broken over her own troubles. Now he realized that what a girl such as he knew Molly Cameron must be would feel for herself was as nothing compared with what she must have felt when she awakened to the galling realization that her twin brother, the only near relative she had in the world, was responsible for the anguish that was beating Alice Louise Cameron to the dust. The certainty that Lolly in trouble would cost the reason, if not the life, of the dear Aunt Margaret who had opened her home to them when they were homeless, friendless, penniless, must have weighed heavily on Molly's soul. Jamie could see how, in a vision of the years, the Storm Girl would sense her obligation to a woman as fine as Margaret Cameron, and he could see why she was frantic to the point were she had resolved to throw herself into the undertow because she could plan no escape, she could figure no way in which to right the wrong that had been done, since a power that no law can sway or divert had reached out and struck Donald down before he had any chance to make the reparation that if he were never so little of a man he certainly would have made. Margaret had said that he was not a bad boy, and it was her desire that his child should bear his name.

Far into the night Jamie sat under the jacqueranda, and when at last he began to be tortured by the aching of his bones from the cold, he got up and went into the house. He lighted the fire and sat down before it in a chair opposite the Bee Master's and stretched his long legs to the comfort of the flames. With his heart in turmoil and his brain whirling so that he could scarcely think consecutively, with all his might he wished for the Bee Master. He wished that Michael Worthington, who for so many years had been the spirit and the life of that small house, could come back to it, that he could sit for an hour in his accustomed chair beside his hearthstone and counsel with him, help him to see the light, tell him what he must do to make his peace with a girl so unspeakably fine that Jamie had no way in which to say what he thought of her.

That day, with brutal force, he had compelled her own hand to write before the astonished eyes of her group of little people one of the hatefullest words that can be found in any language—not only to write it, but to re-write it and to underscore it. He had struck it home as hard as he knew how to strike, and then he had disappeared and left her to be seared with a brand that probably was as repugnant to her soul as any form of torture that could have been invented for her.

Jamie stared across at the vacant chair questioningly. He found himself praying that the Bee Master would come. But he did not come. The chair stood vacant. It was only in imagination that Jamie could see the white head, the slender, face, the big dark eyes, the silken beard, and the slender, probing, delicate hands that accompany sensitive and artistic natures. He did not come. Jamie felt in his heart that he knew why he did not come. The Bee Master would have been so much of a gentleman, he would have been so refined by the crucial fires of his own suffering, he would have been so tender, he never would have hurled that awful word at a woman, he never would have forced her to brand her own heart with it. What the Bee Master would have done would have been to say: "Molly girl, things seem to make it appear that you haven't told the truth, that you haven't played the game square; but since I know you as I do, I know this cannot be true, so won't you explain to me how things really were? What truly occurred?"

Now it was not necessary for Jamie to be told anything. He had learned all there was to know when he looked across the bowed head of Margaret Cameron and the pitiful baubles her hands clutched, to the open marriage certificate lying on the bed before her with his name and that of her only child written upon it.

The grey of morning was beginning to creep in the windows when the Keeper of the Bees threw himself on his bed without undressing and fell into troubled sleep. He did not awaken until he heard Margaret Cameron in the kitchen with his breakfast. Then he rose and went out to her. She took one look at him and then she said: "Jamie, you haven't been undressed, and I doubt if you've been asleep all night!"

Jamie replied: "Neither have you, Margaret, so you haven't any grounds upon which to base your right to scold me."

"Yes, I have," said Margaret. "I've almost never been sick a day in my life with real illness. I've no scar over my heart that must be nursed with extreme care for months yet. I carry my scars where the world can't probe into them."

"Don't!" cried Jamie. "Don't be bitter, Margaret. We don't know why, we never can know why things happen in this world exactly as they do; but this we know: We know that God is in His heaven, that He is merciful to the extent of ordaining mercy; we know that if we disobey and take our own way and run contrary to His commandments, we are bitterly punished. And it is the most pitiful of laws that no man or woman can take their punishment *alone* in this world. It is the law that none of us can suffer without making someone else suffer, but in some way it must be that everything works out for the best, even if we can't possibly see how that could be when things are happening that hurt us so. I thought when I rose and walked out of the hospital that I was embarking on a Great Adventure all my own. I got a great thrill out of standing on my feet and doing what I pleased for a few days, out of taking my own orders. Before we get through with what has happened to me, it may prove that God told me to get up and walk out and test the mercy of the road in order that I might be truly thankful when shelter came to me; and it may be that He needed me here to offer what comfort I could to a stricken girl's heart in the days when things were going so pitifully wrong for her."

Margaret Cameron was setting the breakfast-things on the table and the big tears were running down her cheeks, tears for which Jamie was unspeakably thankful. Reason may be depended upon to keep its balance when God gives the surcease of tears in time of trouble.

"Now," said Jamie, "I'm going to eat my breakfast and take a bath here at the house. Then I am going to dress myself the best I can and go in search of Molly Cameron. You could do a very great deal to make that search easier for me if you would give her me address, if you would tell me where I might find her."

"How long is it," asked Margaret Cameron, "since you have known Molly?"

"Almost ever since I've been here," said Jamie, "only please understand that I didn't know that she was my next-door neighbour, that she was your niece, until yesterday."

"There is this I can do," said Margaret Cameron. "I can call her on the 'phone and ask her if she will be at home to-day and if you may come to see her and at what hour she will see you."

"Would you be so kind as to do that ?" asked Jamie.

Margaret sat down until Jamie finished his breakfast. Then he walked over with her to carry back the things, ostensibly to see little Donald, in reality to suggest the telephoning and to learn what the answer would be. When he did suggest it, Margaret Cameron called two or three times and had no reply. The telephone could be heard ringing distinctly at the other end of the line, so they knew that Molly was not at home. Margaret said there was nothing to do but to wait until she returned. So in disappointment Jamie went home. Instead of bathing in the tub as he had intended he went down to the sea, and in its cold, saline waters he drew some of the soreness and the tiredness from his body. Then he lay on the hot sands and almost instantly fell asleep.

He slept until nearly noon. Then he went back by way of Margaret Cameron's, and this time he copied the telephone number and carried it with him. He meant to keep the wires busy until he had a response. After his first failure, he laid out the most attractive clothing he could find among his own things and those he had been given by the Bee Master. With more care than he ever before had used, he selected the finest silk shirt of a delicate lavender with a deeper-coloured tie to match. He put on the grey trousers and black shoes and laid out the black coat. He had the feeling that he wished to appear at his level best. There was enough on the record against him that it behoved him to enhance his personal appearance to the extent of his ability. He was standing in his shirt-sleeves before the highboy, carefully labouring with the tie he meant to wear, when he heard the screen of the front door open and close and then a clear voice, faintly blurred with accents that he loved, call "Keeper of the Bees, are you here ?"

Jamie stepped to the bedroom door, and across the living-room faced Molly Cameron. He was so taken aback he could not even say, "Oh !" to indicate that he was surprised. He felt that he was crazy for thinking that he detected a twinkle in the grey-brown eyes, half a laugh twisting the red lips of the wide mouth. Molly Cameron, in boots and breeches as she went afield, the bobbed hair tumbling in the wind, her cheeks flushed with exercise, or was it anger, stood before him.

But it could not have been anger because, so surely as he had ever seen anything, Jamie MacFarlane saw laughter on Molly's face as she demanded: "Jamie MacFarlane, are you still firm in the conviction that I'm a liar ?"

Jamie reached out a pair of supplicating arms.

"Storm Girl," he said, "I am firm in the conviction that you're most adorable. I have thought so all the time. I haven't been able to believe, ever, not for a minute, that you could possibly have needed me for yourself, and now that I know you didn't, now that I know your courage and your bravery, I haven't words for the cowardly thing I did yesterday. Can you ever forgive me ? Molly Girl, can you ever forgive me ?"

It did not seem quite possible that Mollie Cameron was standing in the doorway looking at him with an amused face, almost laughing.

"In consideration of what has happened," she said, "in consideration of how I used you to serve my own purposes—and I will have to admit that I intended to deceive you ; I meant you to believe that I wanted help for myself when, all the time, I wanted it for Lolly, and I wanted it so desperately, because of the debt Don and I owed her mother——

She stopped abruptly, and the laughter had vanished.

"I've been over talking to Aunt Margaret," she continued, "and I know now that you know all there is to be told about the situation save one thing. There is one other thing that you *must* know. Through some loss or delay in the mail, more than a month after Don lost his life, I had a letter from him that was the only comfort Lolly and I had during the bitter days when I had her hidden in my rooms in the city and was managing letters for her to her mother, supposed to be written in Sacramento. Of course you will guess that I made the arrangements at the hospital, and with our combined earnings we paid the bills. I never thought that she could not endure giving birth to her baby. I did not dream that she would have to go, but I think *she* did because she insisted on having arrangements made that provided for that contingency. We shaped her letters so that Aunt Margaret would not be too much surprised, and I thought we had everything fixed. And then Lolly would take that certificate to the hospital with her. She was so eaten up with shame, she just would have that where the doctors and the nurses could see it. She was forced to offer proof because her self-respect had been so endangered ; she was bitterly hurt ; and that's how it came that Aunt Margaret found it yesterday when she went to look over your things to see what needed mending."

"You will believe," said Jamie, "that I had not opened that packet. I did not know to whom you had turned over the certificate and the ring. I did not know in whose name you had taken out the licence. I only knew, when I reached the hospital, that if I opened my mouth to say that I never had seen the girl they led me to, I might put her openly to the shame she had lost her life in enduring alone, so I kept still even when the doctor rated me scorchingly."

Molly Cameron extended her hands and advanced to the middle of the room.

"Oh!" she cried. "Oh, that's a shame! But Lolly told her nurse—I *heard* her tell her—that you were wonderful, that you had been fine, that no other man would have done one thing so fine as you did! I heard that!"

"The nurse stood up for me," said Jamie. "She told the doctor things that made him apologize. Never mind that! It hasn't anything to do, or, rather, it has everything to do, with what I did yesterday."

Then Jamie advanced and opened his arms.

"Is there any hope at all, Storm Girl? Is there any hope at all, Molly Cameron, that you can forgive me? And will you believe that the wound that I carried that night on the rock, the wound that I thought, as surely as I think that God lives, would end me in a few months at the extreme limit, will you believe that we have healed it, your Aunt Margaret and I, with salt water and sunshine and a careful diet? Will you believe that I am a whole man again, even if my body is scarred? Will you?"

"Oh, Jamie!" said Molly, "I never knew any Scotsman that could talk so much! America has done something awful to you! You aren't a *real* Scotsman at all! A real Scotsman would close up the few steps between us and ask, 'Will ye?' and then take it for granted that I would and get down to business!"

Jamie drew up his shoulders. He took one breath that went to the depth of his lungs and acted accordingly.

By and by, when she could find breath for anything, Molly Cameron twisted her head free and turned her face to the ceiling and said: "I weel. Whenever ye want me, I weel!"

And Jamie said: "I want you right now, to-day if you say so, the very first minute we can get to the Licence Bureau and get the legal documents. I'm tired of adventuring. I want to settle down and spend the rest of my life loving you and keeping bees."

"What's that Licence Bureau going to think," inquired Molly Cameron, "if the same girl goes to it for another licence under another name in such a short time?"

With his arms tight around her Jamie laughed down into her eyes. "You leave that Bureau to me! It's got to be in charge of someone that's human. I'll go and interview them, and I'll guarantee that there won't anything unpleasant occur when you arrive. There have been times in my life when I have been able to do quite a canny job of persuading people."

"Yes," admitted Molly Cameron, "I'll have to vouch for that statement! I'll back you up as the greatest persuader I've ever known! If you hadn't been such a persuader it never would have occurred to me to let you in for all the annoyance that you have suffered at my hands ever since the great storm."

"Don't you mind about annoyance or about my suffering at your hands," said Jamie. "There's only one thing I want to know. Do you understand right down in the depths of your heart that I never could believe that you wanted that certificate and that ring and my name for yourself?"

Molly Cameron looked him straight in the eye.

"Sure you couldn't!" she said. "Of course you couldn't! You're enough of an outdoor man yourself to know the outdoor kind of a girl when you meet her. Sure you wouldn't think a thing like that about me!"

Then she put both arms around Jamie's neck, and she had only a short distance to draw his head before it was level with hers.

"What I think about you, Jamie MacFarlane," she said, "couldn't be written in many books, but there is this I want to know before you see that Licence Bureau. Are you going to let me go on, two or three days a week, teaching Americanism? I'm just crazy about my work! I think it's one of the most interesting jobs that any woman in this country has to-day!"

"Of course," said Jamie; "of course I'm going to let you. I'm going to let you do exactly what you please and I am going to go with you and see how much assistance I can give in teaching Americanism. I've had some fairly stiff training to fit me to teach Americanism. There are a few things I know about the war end of the game about as well as any man could know them. And there is one question I want to ask you before we go to the Licence Bureau. I want to know if we may have a Scotch Presbyterian minister to marry us right here in this house that belongs to us? I want to know if afterward you will go to church and to Sabbath school with me? I want to know if we may have God and the atmosphere of religion in our home? I want to know if our children may be born to an inheritance that is like that bequeathed to me and, no doubt, to you, by our own parents?"

"Of course," said Molly Cameron. "Of course. I wouldn't want things any other way, and I would dearly love to be married here in the little house that is a shining monument to a man who was a friend to both of us. I knew and loved the Bee Master too. I have read almost every book in his library. I've dusted his pictures and his precious furniture. If he hadn't been stricken you would have met me here long ago."

"It strikes me," said Jamie, "that there are times when you have been here, anyway."

"Very few," said Molly. "I just couldn't keep away all the time, Jamie lad. Ever since that night on the rock I've been unable to make my heart behave at all whenever I thought of you. To tell the plain truth, I love you! I love you, Jamie MacFarlane! I loved you in the storm, and I love you here in the garden, and I even loved you down on the beach yesterday when you had the nerve to let me know what you really thought of me. I was pretty mad when I ran after you, but just the same, when I got through speaking my piece, if I had found you I probably would have told you that I loved you, dear Keeper of the Bees."

"Well, how come?" said a voice behind them, and Jamie and Molly turned to see the little Scout standing in the doorway with wide eyes.

"Hello, Jean Meredith!" said Jamie suavely. "Come and see what's happened in this family now?"

Jean Meredith walked in and set her hands at her waistline and, with elbows akimbo and her head on one side, peered up at the pair.

"Well, if anybody asked me," she said, "I'd say you are a fast worker! I don't think it's a week yet since your wife died, and here you got Molly all cottoning up to you, just like dad and mother! Can you beat it!"

"Not very well," said Jamie. "You will have to take it for granted that there are some things in the world that such little people as you don't understand."

"Well, don't take too much for granted," said Jean. "Maybe I understand more than you think I do. Anyway, you needn't think I ever thought that little Jamie had a mother and she died and you took him and walked away and left her. That ain't the way men act when their wives die. That made a good story, but *you* can tell it to the world. *I* ain't a-going to! It's a good deal more sensible that you got Molly in your arms. I'll believe that all right! If I was you that's what I'd do. Say, is this stack of lumber out here for Chief's stable?"

"It is," said Jamie.

"Well, then, hadn't we better get busy?"

Jamie smiled.

"Can't you give a man a day off ?" he asked. "Don't you see that when I get my coat on I'm all dressed up in my Sunday clothes ?"

"Yes, I see," said Jean, "but Molly ain't all dressed up in *her* Sunday clothes, and *I* ain't all dressed up in *my* Sunday clothes. The sensiblest thing you can do is to go and take them things off and get into your working clothes and come on and get to work on my stable. And besides that, if your ears wasn't all gummed up you'd hear that there's about three swarms of bees on the rampage, and one of them's mine, and two of 'em's yours. I heard 'em way down the street."

Jamie hesitated, his mouth open, and looked at Molly Cameron. Molly was Scotch only one remove herself.

"You must save the bees, of course !" she said. "Change to your bee clothes and capture the swarms. If you want to celebrate, I will go where I can dress and we'll celebrate this evening."

"All right," said Jamie, and went to his room.

It was while he was making a lightning change that he heard a shrill whistle, and looked out of his window in the direction from which it came. He was in time to see the faces of Fat Ole Bill and the Nice Child and Angel Face peering over the fence from the vantage ground of the lumber pile, a row of faces forlorn past description. It seemed that Jean Meredith's ears had been awake to other sounds as well as the bees. Jamie watched her as she came down the side of the house and started in the direction of the call, looking precisely the same little Scout that he had known from the beginning.

He opened the door and called softly to Molly : "Come and see this. The Scouts mutinied the other day and beat up the Scoutmaster and almost broke her heart. Now they are calling her."

Together they stood at the window watching to see what would happen.

Within a few yards of the fence Jean paused, hooked her thumbs in her trousers' belt, and with an immobile face surveyed her Scouts.

"Well," she said tersely. "What do you want ?"

Fat Ole Bill evidently had been elected spokesman.

He stood up and said, "Aw, come on ! Let's go down on the beach and play ! We'll play Injuns or pirates or bandits, or whatever you say !"

"*Yes*, you will !" said the former Scoutmaster with fine sarcasm. "*Yes*, you will ! After the way you served me the other day! After the way you broke your sakerd oath! You're nice Scouts, you are, taking a sakerd oath, and then going back on it. *Yes*, I'll *ever* come with you again!"

Then the Nice Child brought the battery of black eyes into full play.

"Aw, come on!" he pleaded. "Ain't nothin' no fun without *you*! We didn't know you thought up everythin'. Honest we didn't! We didn't know we did what you told us to. We just stand around and look at one another like three fat-headed fools. We ain't had no fun since we acted so mean. Aw, come on! We won't do it any more! We're awful sorry. Ain't we, Ole Bill! Ain't we, Angel Face? Ain't we awful sorry?"

"Yes," said Angel Face, "we are awful sorry. We apologize. It's like both of 'em says. We ain't havin' any fun. Won't you please come on? You can be The Limit again. Won't none of us say a word."

Jamie's shoulders lifted; his chest drew in. He leaned forward and rested his hands on the window-sill and brought his face level with the child's head. He opened his lips and then waited a second to be sure. But there was no hesitation whatever on the part of Jean Meredith; she slowly shook her head.

"You might as well go on and think up something you can do. Do all the things that we used to do over, and do them better," she said. "I'm *through*. I ain't risking no more of what you gave me the other day! This morning when I was brushing my teeth I saw the calendar and it's the thirty-first. I ain't going back to risk a lickin' from three boys after this only on the thirty-second of the month! You get me? You can just go on! I'm not afraid of you. I can lick any of you yet, or I can lick all of you. I'm not afraid of you. I'm just *done* with you. Anyway, them boards you are standing on are to make Chief a stable and I'm going to do the stunts what Scout Camp Number Twenty-two is doing. I'm *through* with *make-believe*. I'm going to be a real Scout after this, and I'm going to ride a horse and I'm going to carry a crop and hit him a crack if he goes to back over too steep a place. But I ain't a-goin' to hit him any other time. And I ain't a-goin' to hit anything else *that ain't big and strong as I am*. Laugh *that* off! I'm through!"

Jean Meredith turned on her heel, hitched up her trousers and marched in the direction of the back porch. The Keeper of the Bees, leaning on the window-sill, tightened his arm around the Storm Girl and studied the face of Jean as she came toward him. The lines of it were unalterably set.

"She means it! She'll stick!" said Molly Cameron.

And Jamie hugged her tight and said, "Amen!"

THE END